1

BOHEMIAN
INTERLUDE

THOMAS J TURNER

3

DEDICATION

This Novel is dedicated to my long time best friend, Trudy. . Whenever I have needed help or assistance in any aspect of my life, she has been there for me, time after time. She has patiently listened to me read her my new and improved chapters, repeatedly. She has many times provided me with thoughtful comments or given me helpful ideas or suggestions. Thank you Trudy. May the rest of your days continue to be happy.

I would be remiss if I didn't thank Sarah, my editor, who did an awesome job helping me finally put this book together. She helped me move forward from a precarious writer's ledge where I had been stranded for over a decade.

A special thanks to Rich, co-founder of our Portland workshop, 'People's Ink', and a very cool visionary who believed in me when others doubted I could pull it off.

4

TABLE OF CONTENTS

LEAVING BERKELEY

CHAPTER ONE

Joe Bailey hovered in the kitchen doorway, waiting for his parent's acknowledgement. Bud and Alice Bailey sat at the walnut kitchen table, drinking percolated coffee and discussing the fall 'Monkey Wards' catalog. Bud dragged a piece of white bread toast across his plate, mopping up the last of his fried eggs. It was almost time for him to leave for his construction job.

Joe cleared his throat and rocked on the balls of his feet, "I'm leaving now."

His mother slowly turned her head. Alice was forty five. She had prematurely gray hair and the distressed look of one who suffers from chronic migraine headaches,

"That's nice, dear."

Bud glanced up from his reading and stuck out his gnarled right hand, the one he accidentally shot a nail through a year ago, "I need your house key."

Joe removed the key from his ring and dropped it into his dad's open palm, which snapped shut like a human Venus flytrap.

Alice rose from her seat and shuffled to the kitchen counter, "Joe. I have some canned food you can take with you."

"Thanks," he said. He had not even thought about food.

"You're going to miss my home cooking, son," she said, handing Joe a full paper sack.

Joe peered into the bag and saw cans of chili, tuna fish and Spam. There was also a can opener, the tiny two-fingered type that tears up your fingertips and only partially opens the can, necessitating a hammer and steak knife to complete the job.

Joe closed the bag. "Nothing but the best, I see."

"What did you just say, boy?" Bud pushed his chair back from the table and stood up to his full height, with his work boots on, of five foot seven. He was short but stout, with an oversized head. His dark eyes smoldered dangerously behind his heavy black framed glasses. He had his fists ready.

Joe attempted to stare his father down, but it was no use. Nineteen years of intimidation and bullying had left their mark. He looked up at the clock. It was nearly seven.

"I thought so," said Bud, standing down. "You're a chicken shit, son. The yellow streak doesn't run in my side of the family, Alice."

Joe felt his ears burning as he walked out the back door with his paper sack full of cans. He paused on the porch. His twelve year old brother, Marvin, was staring at him from his bedroom window. He smiled at Joe, revealing hunks of peanut butter hanging from his braces.

"See ya, Marvin. I'm taking off now."

Marvin rolled his eyes and disappeared behind his curtain.

"Fine," said Joe. He walked down the driveway to his 1964 Ford Galaxy convertible. It ran good for a six year old car. It was already packed, and he was more then ready to leave.

Joe drove a few miles to the University of California, Berkeley campus and parked in front of a five story wooden apartment building on Walnut Street. He was there to pick up his friend and new roommate, Lance Potter. Lance moved to the apartment a year ago, when he thought he would be accepted at Cal. He wanted to live close by so he wouldn't have to commute. Now he was joining Joe as they traveled 300 plus miles up into the Feather River Canyon to attend a brand new school.

Joe honked the horn twice and got out. That was their secret signal. He looked up to the third story and saw Lance appear in the window. Joe leaned against the rear of the Ford and lighted his first Marlboro of the day. He took a deep pull and coughed.

Lance emerged from the building, lugging an enormous green suitcase and a single wooden stereo speaker that he had made in wood shop. He had never gotten around to building a second one.

"Joe. Smoking cigarettes is such a disgusting, blue collar habit. Why don't you just quit?"

Lance was tall and gangly and wore his brown hair long. He had John Lennon type wire framed glasses and was wearing his dad's discarded Korean War vintage leather jacket that had patches of green mold growing on it.

Joe took another puff and blew the smoke in Lance's direction. He opened the trunk and managed to squeeze Lance's suitcase into the crowded space. There was a noticeable sag to the back of the convertible, with the rear bumper close to kissing the ground, "Let's go, man. We're late," said Joe.

They drove down University Avenue towards the freeway, "Did you bring any gas money, dude?"

"Don't need any," answered Lance, pulling a siphon hose from inside his jacket. It smelled like gasoline.

"Next time we stop, put that in the trunk, you jerk. What if I had lit a cigarette? I could have blown us both up."

"When it's my turn to buy, Joe, just find me another Ford. It doesn't matter what model."

"Why does it have to be a Ford?"

"Why, it's karma of course. If I siphon gas from any other make and put it back in your Ford, your car will not run well and might even stall out. We could possibly get stranded somewhere, like Purgatory or Oakland. Pretty much the same place. Quite simply, we could alter our destiny as well as our auras."

Joe shook his head. He was used to Lance's cosmic pontificating. What Joe once considered as deep, heavy, profound talk, was now mostly irritating.

"You need to stop at Kathy's apartment. I told her I would drop by to say goodbye.""Damn, Lance. Didn't you just spend the summer with her? Weren't you with her all day yesterday?"

"That's irrelevant. I made a commitment. A man is only as good as his word, Joe. You should know that and support me in my effort to achieve my goal of total psychic awareness and balance."

"Whatever," said Joe, making a right turn on San Pablo Avenue.

"I've been analyzing your problem, Joe, trying to figure out why you are so obtrusive. You are jealous of my sexual relation ships. You react by standing on the sidelines, criticizing me and putting everybody and everything else down. I'll wager you've never even had a girlfriend."

"I have so."

"Yeah?" When and who with and how come you never told me before?"

"I had a girlfriend when I was on active duty with the Coast Guard last year. I met her in Norfolk, Virginia."

"How come you never shared this exciting news with me before now?"

"A gentleman never tells." Joe wasn't sure where he'd heard that line, but he was pretty sure it was dialogue from a 1940's Cary Grant movie. He hoped he had used the line appropriately

"What was her name?"

"It was, uh, Dinah." Joe knew how asinine that sounded as soon as the name tumbled out of his mouth. Dinah? Like Dinah Shore? My God, he thought. He was creating a web of lies about dating a woman who would be older then his own mother. Was Dinah Shore even still alive? He thought so, but couldn't remember what she was famous for.

Lance shook his head. "Bullshit."

Joe switched topics, "You know, Lance. Stopping to see Kathy is really going to mess up our timetable."

"A self imposed schedule. We don't have a precise time that we are expected to arrive in Keddie. This is merely a clumsy attempt on your part to exert control over me."

Joe grunted. Things were not starting well. Of course, he and Lance had not been getting along for weeks. Unfortunately, they had made their commitment months ago. Deposits had been made, fees had been paid, jobs quit. The whole enchilada. They were going to attend Feather River college for at least one quarter. Then, if life with Lance didn't pan out, Joe would return home in January. That is, if Bud would let him back in.

"So," said Lance, Why don't you put the top down. This is a functioning convertible, is it not?"

"Of course it is. Everything on my car works. I must tell you though, that driving with the top down is overrated. The sun burns holes in the top of your head. You are also exposed to other vehicles exhaust fumes, which the last time I checked, are still considered toxic. That's why there are so many bald people with emphysema in California and Florida. Convertibles."

"I suppose some of your supposition is valid. However, I was under the impression that baseball catcher's masks contributed to male pattern baldness and cigarettes, cigars and pipes led to lung disease."

Joe knew he was treading on thin ice, as Lance was already starting to lose his hair, "Football helmets are worse. Forty guys wear them and slam their heads into each other, causing brain trauma. There are usually only two catchers on each baseball team."

Hair had always been an issue for Joe. From the time he was six years old and growing up in Berkeley, he had gone to Frank's Barber Shop for his haircuts. Frank was a swarthy, heavily bearded Italian who reeked of Vitalis and mostly communicated in grunts. Half the males in Berkeley got their hair cut by Frank, and they all received the same haircut : an inch remaining on top, whitewalls around the ears, sideburns hacked off.

In his senior year of high school, Joe rebelled. Long hair was in, and Joe was embarrassed by the way he looked. Some schoolmates thought he was a nark or a Republican. He let his hair grow until it covered his ears. He wore baseball caps to the dinner table and avoided Bud, managing to go three months without having to see Frank.

One day, his dad noticed what was happening. He came home from work and slammed his cement covered boots down, "Boy!. Get yer scrawny ass down to Frank's and get your hair cut. Ain't no goddamned son of mine gonna walk around town looking like some kind of pinko queer hippie!"

Joe reluctantly agreed to get his hair trimmed the next day. What choice did he have? However, he would be damned if he was going to let Frank brutalize his head even one more time. He visualized Frank, standing in his barbershop and holding up his electric sheers, a manic grin permanently etched on his face.

Instead, Joe drove to his school friend Steve Whisenor's house on Stannage Ave. Steve was an ex-football center who had turned onto drugs the year before and no longer sacrificed his body for the entertainment of his high school.

Steve's parents were gone to play Bingo, so he put on a Judy Collins record and he and Joe shared some Lebanese Hashish and practiced being mellow. When they were spellbound by the hash, Steve cut Joe's hair with his mother's sewing scissors. He did his best, but the results were hideous.

When Joe returned home, Alice was cooking dinner. Bud was still at work. Alice took one look at Joe' hair, put her hand to her mouth and retrieved her yardstick, "You've been doing drugs with that awful boy, Lance, haven't you? I know what to look for. Your father and I aren't stupid. We know all about *What's Up Pussycat* and all that."

"Yeah," replied Joe, "You and dad are really on

top of it all right. Isn't it about time for you to pop some tranquilizers and go watch *As The World Turns?"*

Alice opened her eyes wide and raised the yardstick over her head, but Joe wasn't being hit anymore. He snatched the stick away, broke it over his knee and handed his mother the two broken pieces, "Don't ever strike me again, mom. I won't be abused anymore."

"Wait until your dad gets home." she had warned.

Joe remembered leaving the kitchen and pausing at thirteen year old Marvin's room. His younger brother looked up at Joe, pointed at his head, and laughed in his nasty, sarcastic way, "Har, har, har."

Joe pulled up in front of Kathy's apartment. She lived in a second story walkup over Moore's TV Sales and Service. She shared the two bedroom apartment with half a dozen freaks. No one was sure who actually lived there, and who was just crashing for a few days.

"There she is," Lance pointed out in an excited voice. Kathy was slumped against the front window of the closed TV store, smoking a cigarette and looking bored. She was a plain looking girl who wore glasses and had an uncombed tangle of mouse colored hair.

She stood up and stretched. Lance leaped from the car ran up and embraced her. Then they started making out, right there on the street. Joe got out and lighted another Marlboro. He leaned on the car and gazed out towards the bay.

When he finished his smoke, he glanced at his watch and then yelled at Lance, who was still groping Kathy while they remained lip locked, "Come on, Lance."

Some guy they barely knew drove by and leaned out his window, "Screw her. I did!"

When this grave insult elicited no reaction from Lance, Joe yelled louder, "Hey, Romeo! We need to go!"

Still no response. Joe got into the Galaxy, started up the engine, and put it into reverse.

"Wait," sputtered Lance, finally breaking away.

Joe stopped long enough for Lance to jump in. He blew Kathy a kiss as Joe squealed out, leaving a patch of burnt rubber.

Lance sighed heavily and turned to his friend, "Must you continue to act like some sort of deranged beer freak?"

"Shut up. Put your seatbelt on." They were finally headed for the freeway that would lead them out of town and to their new home in the Sierra Nevada Mountains.

Lance had one more caustic blast for Joe, "I consider your profane, impertinent demeanor to be symptomatic of some sort of deformed inner child, incessantly seeking attention and approval from folks, who in the end, really don't give a shit about whether you live or die."

Joe and Lance headed northbound on Interstate 80 towards Sacramento. It was eight O'clock, and southbound traffic was bumper to bumper. There were thousands of daily commuters, many with grim, desperate looks stretched across their made up faces. Joe tried to imagine what it would be like to be tethered to a daily job that required a tedious, long distance commute. Both ways. He visualized being one of them, ballancing a hot cup of coffee between the knees of his shiny, polyester slacks. He might be stressed out be-

15

cause he was minute behind schedule. Oh no. A harrowing fate, he thought. He never wanted to surrender his freedom and become what others considered normal. All to get to some boring ass, soul killing, mindless job. He'd rather sign on as deck hand on a rusty freighter sailing for Singapore. He'd just as soon hop a freight train headed south, leap off in L.A., and hang out in dangerous hobo camps, soaking up material and characters for his next story.

Joe Edgar Bailey fancied himself a fiction Novelist in the Jack Kerouac mold. He knew he was nowhere as good as Kerouac was, but he also hadn't had the same adventures or exposure to colorful, creative, demented friends to draw inspiration from. In short, he knew that he needed more experience and road trips to write authentically.

As they drove across the old Carquinez Bridge towards the blue collar city of Vallejo, Joe glanced over and saw that Lance was asleep. His greasy hair rested against the window, leaving smears. Joe would make him clean it off later.

To his right and floating on dirty bay water, Joe could see the Mothball Fleet. There were dozens of World War Two era Liberty freighters and assorted warships. Most of them were obsolete Destroyers, with a couple of Heavy Cruisers, their deadly fourteen inch big guns silenced forever. One by one, the old ships with histories were disappearing, suffering the inglorious fate of being cut up by Union workers, recycled and being reborn as cheap Japanese rice burner cars. Many veterans refused to buy them.

Joe flipped on the A.M. radio and was energized when 'Born To Be Wild' by Steppenwolf came screaming out of his single dash mounted speaker. He cranked up the volume, snapped his right hand fingers

and sang along with John Kay. Just listening to this
song made your blood pressure rise and your pulse
quicken and encouraged you to jump on your Harley or
Hot Rod and go somewhere, anywhere. Yes, thirsting
for fresh adventures. Taking on whatever came your
way with fearless, loyal friends.

Unfortunately, the one cool song was over too
soon. Joe was soon separated from his upbeat mood by
a long series of banal commercials for tires and hair
transplants. He wished he had one of those new eight
track players. How awesome it must be, to play whatever music you wanted, without all the crappy comm.-
ercials. Your play list was only limited by how many of
the large square tapes you owned.

Right now though, all of his limited financial
resources were being funneled into his second college
experience. His first one away from home and Bud and
Alice and the endless tension and drama that existed
within the walls of 825 Santa Fe. Avenue.

He, Lance, and Steve Whisenor recently suffered through a lame educational quarter at Laney
College in the shitty part of Oakland. Joe wasn't sure if
his fruitless spring term was his fault or the school's,
and their hopelessly slanted liberal agenda.

The morning sun finally broke through the
overcast sky. As it spread across Lance's face, he opened his eyes, "Where are we, Joe?"

"Heading east on 80 towards Sacto, where we're
gonna hang a left turn and head for Oroville."

Lance took off his glasses, wiped his eyes and
then propped his gold framed specs back up on his
face, "Say, Joe. I'm wondering something."

"What?"

"You wanna drop some acid with me?"

Joe glanced at his friend to see if he was serious

or jiving him. Lance and he did share a similar, warped sense of humor. They had a Mad Magazine influenced skewed outlook on life.

"I don't think that's a very good idea, Lance, at least not for me. Not unless you want me to be peaking on LSD while I'm driving us over some treacherous mountain passes. If you feel the need, go ahead. I plan on driving the whole way straight."

"Okay, fine. Just so you are clued into the status of my current inventory, I'll tell you what I have in my green suitcase in the trunk. I've got over a hundred hits of strong Orange Sunshine acid. The real thing, my friend. I also have fifty doses of some very mellow organic mescaline, a pound of fresh Magic Mushrooms, a few hundred reds, and a bag full of speed. None of this is recommended in conjunction with the use of alcohol of course."

"That's real solid, Lance. I brought along half a pound of decent weed and a case of Jim Beam Bourbon. Tell you the truth, man, I'm a little burned out on psychedelics right now."

Joe floored the 390 and swerved into the fast lane and passed an eighteen wheeler with a full load of crushed Ford's that would come back as Pepsi cans.

"That proves my hypothesis," answered Lance in a triumphant voice. He took an orange pill when he thought Joe wasn't looking. Joe saw it and glanced at his watch. It was past nine. Lance would start to come on in an hour, and would probably be peaking when they arrived at their cabin in Keddie. *Great timing*, thought Joe.

Lance continued, "Now I can better quantify your cloudy aura. You have regressed from an enlightened personage into a mean spirited, alcohol fueled shadow of your previous incarnation. All because you don't drop acid anymore."

"Can the mean spirited alcoholic crap, Lance. I'm not saying I'll never trip again. If I ever get the right situation , where I don't have to go anywhere, or do anything or talk to any straights for say, twenty four hours, then I'll consider dropping again."

"You shouldn't drop by yourself all the time either."

"What choice do I have? Take some and then huddle outside in the bushes all night, watching out for Howdy Doody, the demented Tooth Fairy and Godzilla?"

"Don't forget my all time favorite Japanese movie, Godzilla versus the Smog Monster. Godzilla won you know."

"Lance, can you imagine what it's like to take acid when you're sleeping under the same roof as Bud and Alice?"

"No. Actually I can't," answered Lance, flipping the sun visor down and staring into the mirror and then launching into a story.

"I know what you mean though, Joe. You're peaking and maintaining fine until the phone rings and it startles you. It seems as though the phone is suddenly alive, with the cord being like a long black snake. The mouthpiece is the snake head of course, and now you have to bring it close to your mouth. You ponder your options as the phone continues to ring. You don't answer. It could be your boss wanting you to come into work because someone called in sick with diarrhea, and you can't possibly leave the house. It might be one of your parents, demanding that you do something right now. Alternatively, it could be an emergency warning from the operator, wanting to inform you of an out of control inferno heading your way. You need to evacuate but you can't. You burn to death because of the paralyzing fear of the unknown."

"That's all valid, buddy," said Joe, " But I'll take it one step further. Someone knocks on your front door while you're sitting there tripping with some music on. You stand up and drift towards the portal to the real world. You hesitate, with your hand gripping the doorknob, doubt creeping up your back like a clawed hand from hell. It might be someone you know, a sincere looking Jehovah's Witness, or maybe an unknown freak who came stumbling down the sidewalk. His arms are outstretched and he had the look and demeanor of Frankenstein blasted on acid. He veers up your driveway and then pounds on your front door, demanding to be let in so you can experience partying with a dead person. He has a three quarter inch molly bolt stuck through his neck."

Joe turned on his lame radio, hoping they might play another cool song. He got The Archies and shut it off in disgust.

"The absolute worst case scenario for me," added Lance, "Is some melting faced weirdo getting too close to me and he has shit breath and he's attempting to lay some religious going to hell trip on me."

Joe steered with his right hand while leaning his left out the open window, "The last few times I dropped, I took it at home after dinner and lay awake until dawn."

"With Bud and Alice sleeping in the next room? My God, what did you do all night, Joe?"

"I mostly listened to records on my headphones. The Rolling Stones, Cream, The Doors, Led Zeppelin. I'd lay back, sink into my pillow, close my eyes, and groove with the music. I'd connect with the swirling spider web visuals on the inside of my eyelids. Black and purple orbs, spinning in the darkness. I never left my room. I couldn't run the risk of stumbling into one of my folks or even Marvin. Not in the dark when my pupils were as large as fifty cent pieces."

"Didn't you recently blow it big time?"

"Yeah, and it was a bad one too. I had the brand new Stones album, *Beggars Banquet.* I started it on the turntable, put on my headphones and dropped the tone arm. However, I forgot to hit the headphone toggle switch, so there I was, rocking out on acid with the stereo on full blast at two in the morning."

"What happened?"

"Bud ripped open my sliding door, knocked the headphones off my head, grabbed me by my throat and bitch slapped me while screaming obscenities. His breath smelled like a wet ashtray."

"Where was your mom?"

"Right behind him in the hallway, telling Marvin to close his door and stay in bed."

"Then what?" asked Lance.

"I went limp like I was a Berkeley peace demonstrator resisting arrest. That made my dad even angrier. He threw me down on my bed and challenged me to a fistfight. Oh yeah, he also broke my new record in half and tossed the pieces at me. That pissed me off. I just paid three bucks for it."

"Did they leave you alone then?"

"Yeah. My mom went back to bed and I heard my dad talking to someone on the phone. I spent the rest of the night freaked out, wondering it he'd called the cops on me. I thought about jumping out my window to escape if they came for me."

"Man," said Lance, pondering Joe's revelations. He rolled down his greasy window, letting in a blast of hot valley air that mingled with the warm wind coming through Joe's open window.

Joe glanced at the fuel gauge and saw that it was slipping below a quarter. He took the next exit and used his parents Chevron credit card to fill up his car. He had no intention of asking Lance to siphon gas out of another Ford in broad daylight in an unfamiliar location.

Joe filled it up with premium fuel. It was up to forty five cents a gallon. He wondered if gas prices would ever reach a buck a gallon. The day was growing hotter, and gasoline vapors drifted up from the pump and lingered in the air.

Lance had been standing there the whole time, his hands thrust into his jeans, his body leaned forward, as though he were facing a strong wind that Joe couldn't feel.

"So," declared Lance, "Instead of LSD, you prefer rot gut bourbon and Coke."

"Yeah. I guess that about sums it up. At least with booze, you know what you're getting every time. It comes in measurable quantities, and there isn't a social stigma attached to drinking. It's a sure thing Lance. You know what I mean?"

GARY HESS

CHAPTER TWO

Gary Hess staggered out of the Keddie Club. He was in a grand mood. Six doubles of Old Crow Bourbon and Coke chased with an equal amount of Budweiser did it for him most every afternoon. He celebrated after every shift ended at the Quincy Sawmill. He touched the left shirtsleeve of his stained white T-shirt to make sure his pack of Camels was still safely rolled up.

It was time for him to go home and root around for something he could eat for dinner. Then, he would take a short nap. If he timed it right, he could awaken refreshed, and then get drunk again before finally passing out for good around ten.

Drinking hard booze was his reward to himself for surviving another shift at the sawmill. Gary considered it a good day when he didn't cut off any fingers or limbs. Many of the older, senior employees were missing body parts, mostly arms, some legs.

Gary pulled out his wrap around shades and propped them up on his round, red face. He waddled crab like to his green 1953 Willys station wagon with its oversized mud tires. It also had a camouflage rack running across the front of the roof with four, powerful spotlights used when deer hunting. He loved his Jeep almost as much as he loved drinking.

The simple but distinctive vehicle served Gary's

backwoods lifestyle well. In the winter, the former resort community of Keddie, and the close by town of Quincy, got several feet of snow at a time. Owning a four wheel drive vehicle was mandatory, unless you were so well supplied with food and firewood that you could wait it out for weeks at a time. There were no convertibles in this part of the mountains.

Gay Hess was only twenty-three, but he already carried 235 pounds on his five foot eight frame. He rationalized his increasing girth by revealing to friends that the men in his family were naturally big boned. The weight didn't bother him so much, but the-spreading bald spot on the back of his head troubled him greatly. Gary always wore a black cowboy hat decorated with a band of beer can pull tabs around the top. His roommates speculated that Gary liked it so much he might even sleep with it on.

He opened the driver's door of the Willys, and stuffed his body behind the large steering wheel and then pulled the door shut, squeezing it against his monstrous thighs. He rolled down his window and fired up a Camel.

One of the reasons Gary drove the Willys was that it was a different make of vehicle then most everyone else in town had. The white mill workers preferred Fords or Chevys, with an occasional Dodge added to the mix. The local Mexicans liked Internationals, while the American Indians loved rusty old Studebakers.

He observed the hustle and bustle in front of the three story Keddie dormitory building. Local tradesmen carried around hammers, saws and buckets of paint. Gary sneered when he saw long hairs carrying bedding, clothes, and backpacks into the new student living quarters.

Gary decided that they were all snotty, rich kids, invading Keddie with their venereal diseases and Marxist agendas. He pulled down the hunting rifle from the rack in his rear window and caressed it. Gary loved the rich scent of the wood stock, especially after it was freshly polished.

Gary questioned the sanity of the Plumas County Commissioners who had structured a deal with the Peralta School District in Oakland. They were to share the building expenses and cost of starting up a brand new junior college in Quincy. He had enrolled anyway.

He wasn't anxious to share classroom space with queer potheads. The only potential redeeming feature, he thought, would be the opportunity to meet and screw some of the braless hippie chicks that were strutting around Keddie in their torn jeans and tank tops. It was about time for him to cash in on some of that free love he kept hearing about down in San Francisco.

Three miles south of Keddie, Gary turned right onto an unmarked dirt road. He rocked back and forth inside the Willys as he slowly steered around holes the size of bomb craters. The surrounding woods were dense, with an occasional driveway poking through the brush.

Gary had met few of his neighbors, despite having rented his place for over three years. He heard that the further up the road one traveled, the more dangerous things became. It was rumored that a group of hardened Vietnam combat vets were holed up in a fortified compound at the end of the lane. They were allegedly growing fields of pot and had the perimeter booby trapped and didn't take kindly to strangers tres-passing. The former soldiers carried shotguns, serrated fishing knives, and smelled of rotgut and weed.

Gary knew a little about Vietnam combat vets. His older brother, Jimbo, had been a Marine grunt, slogging through rice paddies in 1966. Jimbo had returned home on leave at Christmas. Everyone had been shocked by his gaunt appearance and haunted demeanor. Gone was the roly poly, mischievous big brother who had taken Gary fishing and let him drink one of the precious Budweisers that he kept cold in the Feather River.

In his place was a nervous, jumpy, thin Jimbo with dead eyes, who got rip roaring drunk at the Keddie Club or VFW every night of his leave. Jimbo announced that he had signed up for another tour of combat. His hands shook as he downed still another Bud. No one knew what to say, so they slowly melted away, leaving Jimbo standing alone by the Christmas tree, staring at the blinking colored lights.

Two days later, Gary drove his big brother to the Greyhound station in Quincy. Jimbo exited the Willys, slung his duffel bag over his right shoulder and said goodbye, "I'm not coming back, Gary. Take care of mom and the other kids. You're the big brother now."

On April 8th, Linda Hess nearly fainted when two Marines in dress uniforms walked up their front steps and knocked lightly on the screen door. Carl Hess slid behind his wife and put his calloused hands on her bare shoulders. The Marines handed Linda a telegram. They regretted to inform Mr. and Mrs. Hess that their son, James Raymond Hess, was missing in action and presumed dead. They said something about a helicopter crash at night over the jungle. They extended their sincerest condolences from the President of The United States, Lyndon Baines Johnson. Gary remembered his mom wailing and his dad wandering off in search of a bottle of whiskey.

Gary turned left onto a short, narrow driveway that ended in a clearing. He parked in front on an A-Frame cabin. He shared the rent with two of his mill worker buddies and former classmates, Randy-Bob Casey and Dave Krebs. Randy's VW dune buggy was gone. He and Dave were probably cruising around in the woods, drinking beer and running over whatever wasn't fast enough to evade their off-road tires. They probably had their hunting rifles with them, just in case they should run across some game.

They didn't have hunting or fishing licenses, but so what, they thought. Who was gonna call Fish and Game on them? The Vietnam vets? Not likely.

As soon as Gary dislodged himself from the Willys, the dogs started barking. That was good, he thought. The six of them were earning their keep. The large beasts circled around the fenced off dog run, growling, snarling and pawing at the red dirt.

Spit, who was part Doberman and part junkyard beast, slammed into the chain link cage, whipping his massive dog head back and forth. White froth flew off his black dog lips and a bit of it landed on Gary's face and arms, "Screw you, Spit," yelled Gary.

He wondered why Randy-Bob and Dave hadn't taken the dogs with them. He lifted up a half sack of dry dog food, "What's the matter, you mutts? You boys hungry or something? " He dumped the bag out on the ground in front of him, "Well then, have some. Oh. I forgot. You're dogs. You need a human to open the gate. Huh. Well, don't lose hope. Randy-and Dave should be home sometime before midnight. One of them is supposed to be feeding you this week."

Gary laughed and walked up the stairs to the second story front door. A small deck encircled the A-Frame. He wondered, just for the briefest of mom-ents, if it might be his week to feed the mongrels. Naw, couldn't be. Had to be Randy-Bob or Dave's turn.

He cringed when he opened the unlocked door. A disagreeable odor assaulted his senses. It was a mix of cigarette butts, remnants of moldy food, plus garbage overflowing out of the kitchen.

"Slobs," proclaimed Gary Hess. He walked through the living room, kicking debris out of his way. He made his way to the kitchen and foraged through the refrigerator until he found a complete six-pack of Coors. He pulled one out, ripped off the pull tab, dropped it to the floor, growled, and then tipped his head back and drained the can. "AArrggghhh, that tastes GREAT !"

He tossed the empty can over his shoulder in the general direction of the sink. It clanged off the wall and landed on the floor. Gary made a quick snack of salami, sharp cheese, peanut butter and Wheat Thins. He grabb-ed a fresh beer, and headed back into the living room with his snacks and Coors. Life doesn't get much better then this, he thought.

Gary used his free arm to clear the yellow vinyl couch of piled up trash, chicken bones and empty booze bottles. Once he had a place to sit, he popped the top on his new brew and again wished that they had a woman to keep the place clean, cook something besides Mac and Cheese, and do their laundry. None of them curr-ently had girl friends. For some reason that he didn't understand, no woman stayed around any of them for long, even though they were all employed and had money, food and alcohol.

No drugs, though. Gary wouldn't put up with it.

He suspected that his roomies might be smoking a little bit of pot. .He told them that he wouldn't tolerate it around him or inside their cabin. He hated drugs. Plus, his stepfather, Big Dan McGrew, was the Quincy Sheriff, so any sort of illegal drug use just wasn't acceptable.

He sifted through a weeks worth of mail. He threw the bills in one pile and the junk mail in another. Gary's heart jumped when he discovered the monthly newsletter from the Fascist leaning, 'White Is Right.' It was published monthly somewhere in Missouri by a group of righteous Caucasian brothers. The cover sho-wed Adolph Hitler doing a Seig Heil salute towards a Confederate flag.

His favorite feature in the newspaper was 'Where Are They Now?' This months story focused on the strong rumors that Hitler had survived the bunker in Berlin in April of 1945, and was currently living a quiet life of luxury in rural Argentina. A long range picture showed an old man with white hair and no mustache being pushed around in a wheelchair, a dark blanket covering his legs.

Gary's stomach rumbled. Inspired to barbecue a can of Spam,. he waddled back into the kitchen, looking somewhat like a swine on barbiturates. He used the twisty opener from the side of the blue can to roll back the top. He held the can upside down and shook it and quivering pork by-products with attached gelatin slid nicely into his cast iron frying pan. He then mixed up a bowl of glaze, using mustard, vinegar, water and brown sugar. He completed his culinary masterpiece by stab-ing twenty black cloves into the side of the Spam.

Once outside with his meat, another beer and a package of pork rinds, Gary poured some briquettes into the barbecue, soaked them with gasoline, and ignited the mass with a full book of lit matches that he tossed in from two feet away. Gary chuckled at the eruption of flames and admired his instant barbecue. He knew he was a redneck, and he was okay with that label as long as it came from another redneck. Anyone else calling him that was likely to get slugged in the face or kicked in the nuts.

Once the coals were glowing red, Gary placed his greased frying pan onto the grill. Sitting in the middle were four thick slices of marinated Spam, He returned to the kitchen to retrieve his loaf of Wonder Bread and some green Mexican hot sauce. Then, he would flip the meat and brush on more glaze.

Gary woke up, sprawled out on his bed where he had passed out after eating all four slices of Spam along with the whole bag of Pork Rinds. He had been awakened from his drunken slumber by the braying of his roommates, apparently playing cards in the front room. He also heard the distinctive jackass laugh of Reno Converse, a half-wit friend who was also employed at the sawmill.

It was one in the morning. Gary's head throbbed, as though a relentless blacksmith was pounding on his brain like it was an anvil. It must have been those multiple shots of tequila that he had tossed down the hatch before finally collapsing. Damn, he thought. He was supposed to be at work by six in the morning.

More annoying than his cretin buddies, though, was the frantic barking of the dogs. Gary once again wondered if it was, in fact, his week to feed the beasts.

"Damn it!" He sat up in bed, maneuvered his stomach to where he could step to the floor and put on his slippers and bathrobe. He knew he'd likely freeze his ass off while outside, but he intended to be quick about his mission.

Gary moved past his buddies. He put on his heavy jacket over his robe and zipped it up.

"Hey, there he is," slurred Randy-Bob. "Got any cash you'd care to lose?"

Randy-Bob already looked far older than twenty four. His teeth were going bad and deep creases lined his forehead.

"No thanks," replied Gary. I'm going out to feed the damned dogs. Between you dickheads and Spit and his gang of six, I can't get any sleep. Tomorrow is a work day for all of us you know."

Reno threw down two cards. "Hit me," Gary paused at the front door. "Hey Dave. When was the last time you fed the mutts?"

"Last week, asshole. It's your turn, or did you forget again?"

As Gary stepped onto the deck, a blast of frigid air ripped through his clothes. He pulled his coat tight around his throat and looked up at the stars. It was going to start snowing soon.

The dogs saw him and increased their howling. "Shut up! I'll feed you in a minute!"

Gary gazed into the clear sky, watching in wonder as a shooting star streaked across the velvety canvas and disappeared at the bottom of the far horizon.

He remembered another starry night, when he was fourteen. His mother, Linda, had made a serious blunder and served Carl chicken instead of beef for dinner. His father, drunk as usual, was enraged.

He knocked the plate to the floor, scattering chicken, potatoes, and vegetables across the carpet. Carl stood up and backhanded his wife. "I told you before, woman. You can only serve me chicken on Sunday. That's tradition in my house!"

Jimbo hustled Gary and the other kids together and fled out the back door. They went into the woods behind their house to Jimbo's favorite hiding spot, a small grassy meadow on top of a knoll. It was surrou- ded by mature Pine trees, with a majestic view of the Quincy Valley floor.

Jimbo started a campfire. Gary remembered them huddling together and his big brother telling them stories. There was a full moon, and the stars twinkled magically, as though he could just reach out and grab one or hitch a ride on a falling star. Back then, Gary still believed in his dreams.

The four of them, Jimbo, Gary, their sister Maureen and little brother Roger, sat like that for hours. They clasped their hands around their knees, listening to Jimbo's scary campfire stories and adventures. Jimbo had a vivid imagination, and liked to talk about Terry, the Pirate. He mesmerized his siblings with Terry's exploration of far off, dangerous lands. They forgot for awhile that they were hungry.

Once they figured their dad had passed out on the couch, they returned to the house and filed back into the kitchen and raided the refrigerator, looking for leftovers. That night, their mother sat at the full kitchen table, her head laying on one arm, crying.

Gary cautiously descended the slippery stairs down to ground level. The dogs barked louder then ever, led by the rabid seeming Spit. His relentless slamming against the chain link fence had started to bend it outward.

Gary lifted up a new, fifty pound bag of dog food. He opened the gate and stepped inside. The mutts approached him, growling menacingly. He flicked his free hand at them disdainfully.

"Back off," he demanded. Gary took two more steps before he realized that Blackie and Brutus were now behind him.

"Here, you bastards, "he shouted, dumping the sack upside down and emptying it onto the dirt. Some of the hungrier hounds shoved their dog mouths into the food.

Blackie and Brutus advanced on Gary, their black lips curled back in fierce snarls. White froth dripped from Spit's long dog mouth.

Gary stumbled and fell, and they were on him in a flash, nipping at his ears, hands and throat. He curled into a fetal position and cried out for help. He tucked his chin into his chest the best he could, trying to protect his soft, vulnerable flesh. He knew they would try to rip his throat out.

He felt sour breath on his face. Spit straddled Gary. The big dog gulped in air in rapid ragged gasps, fresh globs of spittle and froth dripping onto Gary's face.

A dog bit him in the ass, and another in the back of his legs. They were going to maul him!

'Blam! Blam ! Blam!' The noise of the gunshots ripped through the night. The dogs recognized authority and death when they heard it. All of them retreated to the far corner of the cage, whined, and milled around.

Randy-Bob, Dave and Reno, strode into the compound, all carrying pistols, daring the dogs to move.

Reno bent down and helped Gary to his feet.

"That was stupid, Gary," said Randy-Bob, "You know the dogs don't like you."

Gary put his hand on his butt, and it came back wet. He could also feel pain in his calves.

"You okay?" asked Reno, firing up a smoke.

"Yeah, I think so. They probably just broke the skin. Thanks, guys. You saved me."

"No problem," drawled Randy-Bob, emptying the three spent cartridges into his hand, "Been wanting to try out my new .357 Magnum anyway."

Gary emerged from the bathroom with gauze taped to his ass and his calves. They were still oozing blood and they hurt. He wondered if he should get a shot, or something.

"Hey," he said to himself, being that he was his own favorite audience, "With as much alcohol as I drink every day, I don't think an infection would stand any chance of surviving in my blood stream."

REMEMBERING OROVILLE

CHAPTER THREE

It got progressively warmer as Joe and Lance approached Chico. They drove with their windows down, mostly silent, lost in their own heads.

"How about we stop in Oroville for some lunch?" suggested Joe. It was the next town coming up after Chico.

"I guess so. Make it someplace cheap, though. I'm a little short on funds right now. I put almost all my cash into increasing my inventory. As soon as we get set up in Keddie, I'll start looking for customers. That shouldn't be hard, to find local heads or students like us from the Bay Area. Everyone wants to change their consciousness, or just get high. Speaking of high, I'm starting to come on, man."

Great, thought Joe. Three hours into their adventure and Lance was already low on money while coming onto some strong LSD. Oroville was just twenty miles ahead.

:Lance bristled when Joe suggested that he actually get a real job to augment the decent allowance he received from his parents. He probably had less then five bucks on him. He might have earned that yesterday when he and Kathy had hitchhiked to the local Christian Kitchen Blood Bank in Oakland and sold some of their blood.

"I'll see if I can find a Taco Tango or someplace similar where they sell ten cent mystery meat tacos."

"Righteous. Isn't Oroville where you blew the engine on your car a few months ago?"

"Yeah. We actually broke down about ten miles north of town. We eventually got towed back into Oroville."

"How did it happen?"

"It was the Fourth of July, and hotter than hell. I had Steve Whisenor and Jimmy Joyce with me. We were driving to Keddie on a scouting mission, I wanted to see where you and I were going to be living. You were yellow and back east, recovering from Hepatitis.

"Anyway, they came along for the ride because they didn't have anything better to do. We'd already blown the water pump in Sacramento, which put us four hours behind. So, I was pushing the old Ford here, trying to make up some lost time.

"I had it going 110 when we started losing power and the red overheat light came on. There was a big cloud of steam escaping from under the hood. I remember starting to pull over to the side of the highway and thinking, 'Oh no. This is not good.'

"Finally, the engine conked out altogether, and I had to steer really hard to get us off the roadway and into the emergency lane. It was early afternoon and getting hotter, and there was no shade where we were. We were stranded. Jimmy took off his T-shirt and wrapped it around his hand and lifted up the hood. A whole lot more steam and smoke came out. The engine smelled like my dad's cooking. Burnt."

"And then?" inquired Lance, propping his Army boots against the glove box.

"We waited around for awhile and let it cool down to the point where Jimmy was finally able to get the radiator cap off. The radiator looked empty. We filled it up with some creek water that we discovered on the other side of some rancher's barbed wire fence. The engine would crank, but it wouldn't fire. Pretty soon, we ran the battery down and gave up.

"Jimmy hitched a ride into Oroville and came back a half hour later riding shotgun in a Shell tow truck. Some old guy wearing greasy coveralls hooked us up and towed us back to his station, which was stupid on my part. All I had was my folks Chevron card, which I found out that they didn't accept at Shell stations.

"The same old guy opened the hood, checked it out, and told me that I'd at least blown the head gaskets and maybe more. He wouldn't know for sure until they pulled the intake manifold and cylinder heads off. He told me at least three days, and it would cost a minimum of $350."

"So, what did you do?"

"I called my dad and he got pissed and flipped me a lot of shit, like I'd blown up my car on purpose or something. He finally agreed to wire up enough money for the repair through Western Union. I was too embarrassed to ask him for more money for a motel room or food, so there we were, stuck in scorching hot Oroville with very little money, for at least three days. Steve and Jimmy starting throwing barbs my way. They had come along for a joy ride, and now because my car broke down, they were stuck too.

"At first, things weren't too bad. There was a Sambo's next door and we ate a meal there and then tried walking around town a bit. We didn't last long though, as the heat was way too intense. They started flipping more crap in my direction and I began throwing it back at em, telling them to piss off. I knew it was my fault. I got it already. Things went downhill fast from there, and we really started getting on each other's nerves.

"That night, as the sun started sinking and they were closing up the station, we asked the manager if we could crash inside the Ford that was torn apart in their shop. He said no way, boys, sorry. Insurance regulations and all that. He did tell us about a nearby park where we could throw down our sleeping bags for free.

"So, we grabbed a couple of six-packs and our bags and some cans of chili and hiked to the park, which was about a half mile away and not too far from a small creek. We pretended we were hobos. We made a fire in one of the metal barbecue grills and cooked the chili right in the cans. We also had a loaf of Wonder Bread, and we washed it all down with beer.

"After awhile, we got tired and spread our slee-ping bags out on top of some picnic tables. We slept up high because we were paranoid about snakes slithering into our bags seeking warmth. I recall our sleeping arrangements as being most uncomfortable."

"What did you expect, "asked Lance, "Sleeping on wood."

"I was afraid of rolling off."

"Did you?"

"Naw. I stayed on top okay and actually got a little bit of sleep. I woke up the next morning and looked around for Steve and Jimmy, but they were both gone. I hiked back to Sambo's with my bag and check-ed inside, but they weren't there. I asked the station manager if he'd seen them, and he said yeah, it was earlier that morning. They had been hitchhiking at the northbound on ramp with a homemade sign reading 'LAKE TAHOE."

"They didn't tell you what they were doing? They just split and left you in Oroville by yourself with no money?"

"Yep."

"So what did you do then?"

"I mostly hung around the station, bored shitless. I even asked the manager if he could hire me for a couple of days to pump gas, because I was experienced, but he said no, they didn't need any help. Therefore, broke and hungry, I walked into Oroville in hundred degree weather and shared lunch with some smelly bums at the local homeless shelter. It was a humbling, humiliating experience."

"I'll bet. Didn't you sleep in the park again, and have some kind of problem?"

"Yeah. That was the night from hell. It started out all innocent. I was told the car wouldn't be ready until noon on the following day, so it was another night in the park for me.

"Things started out okay. Some bum named Keith shared some cold hot dogs and a gallon jug of warm Chablis. Keith was gross. He was covered with dirt and open sores, and he was all ratty and missing hair in odd chunks, like someone had ripped some of it out by the roots. It was hard to tell how old he was. My best guess was somewhere between 40 and 70. I'm not kidding.

"After eating and drinking, Keith told me weird stories about how he lived in a cult back in Ohio. It seems their primary goal was to contact Satan and offer to exchange their souls for everlasting life. Around nine, Keith said he had to hang a log and he crashed right into the bushes and disappeared. I didn't think much of it. Just another bum stumbling around in the dark. Strangers in the night and all that."

"Yeah," said Lance as though he was getting tired of Joe's long winded story that never seemed to end.

"I spent an hour on my back," droned on Joe, "I tried to get to sleep, but it was no use. My stomach literally ached from the crap food and cheap alcohol I had been downing.

"Then, after about an hour, I heard rustling noises in the same bushes Keith had stumbled into hours previously. It was pitch black. I tried to find my flashlight but it was gone. I think Jimmy Joyce stole it. The noise got louder, like something big and nasty was headed my way."

"What was it? By the way, we just passed a sign saying downtown Oroville next exit."

"Thanks, Lance. Anyway, buddy, I wish I could tell you what it was, but I never found out. As it got closer, things started smelling real bad. It was such a repulsive stench that I cannot adequately describe it. The closest comparison I can think of is what a human corpse might smell like after a week in this freaking sun.

I heard it emerging from the underbrush, breathing heavy with short wheezy gasps. It sounded like a monster dragging chains."

"Were you scared?"

"Hell yeah! I tried to climb out of my sleeping bag in a hurry, and had one leg out, and then it was there, right in front of me! It had huge red eyes. I honestly thought I was going to die."

Joe took the off-ramp and they stopped at a red light. Joe pointed to his right, and there it was, the Shell Station with Sambo's right next to it. Joe made a left turn and they headed into what Joe said was the Mexican side of town, where they were most likely to

find gut filling food at a cheap price. Joe wondered how
anyone could possibly make a profit selling tacos for a dime.

"Did the monster say anything?"

"No. It just gurgled. I got this huge rush of adrenaline and rolled off the table and took off running as fast as I could. When I reached the street, I looked back, but couldn't see if anything was following me because there were no streetlights. Just the moon, and it was a sliver that evening.

"I spent the rest of the night hunkered down in a booth at Sambo's, drinking coffee.

"The worst thing, Lance, was that it was easily the scariest experience of my life, and I had no one to talk to about it."

"Couldn't you have chatted with the waitress?"

"Here we go," said Joe, pointing to a small Mexican restaurant that advertised tacos for a ten cents.

He pulled into an empty parking lot and kept the engine running for a moment while he answered Lance's question.

"That wasn't an option. When she came over to refill my coffee for the tenth time, what was I supposed to say? 'Uh, maam, are you a local? Were you aware that there is a rotting flesh sub-human haunting your local park? Maybe you've seen it come in here and order a Belgian Waffle to go?"

Joe shut down the 390 and he and Lance left the car. Joe made sure to lock the doors since they were in the middle of what passed for a ghetto in Oroville.

After a quick, greasy meal at the Typhoid Mary café with ptomaine special tacos featuring some still moving meat, Joe and Lance returned to the car with both of their stomachs rumbling dangerously. Joe informed Lance that they needed to fill up the gas tank again, and it was his turn to pay.

Lance again flipped down the sun visor and stared into the mirror as he spoke, "You've got your parent's Chevron card, right?"

"Yeah."

"Tell you what, my good friend. You use your card again, and I'll reward your generosity handsomely with product."

"I'm listening," answered Joe. He started up the motor and gunned the engine. He loved the throaty sound of the rumbling big block and dual exhaust with loud glass pack mufflers. He also dug the '390' emblems that were mounted on the bottom of both front fenders, advertising to other drivers what he was running under the hood.

"I'll pay you back with ten reds and 20 bennies. How's that sound, pal?"

"Cool," said Joe, happy with the deal.

Ten miles north of Oroville, they made a right and drove east up into the mountains. The bare brush scenery of the brown foothills gave way to red dirt, green ferns and mature, sweet smelling Ponderosa Pines. As they worked their way up the two lane road into the Sierra Nevada Mountains, they could see the Feather River far below them. It followed a picturesque route through the steep canyons, heading back towards Oroville and Chico. On the opposite side of the river, train tracks ran along the ridge, sometimes disappearing for miles inside long tunnels.

The boys from the big city became instantly enamored with the fragrant scent of Pine Trees. They were accustomed to asphalt, telephone poles and bus stops filled with miscreants and inscrutable midgets. The little people were considered 'cute' by some, but Joe knew many had a chip on their shoulder. It came from being callously exploited in 'midget bowling contests' down at Big Al's Lanes. Scowling tiny people were to be feared and avoided.

Lance stared out his window, the acid apparently silencing his tongue while plowing up fresh electrified furrows that led directly to his brain.

It was two O'clock when Joe and Lance neared the turnoff towards Keddie. By this time, Lance had revived, sat up straight in his seat and began talking loudly about his theories regarding nuclear fission waste winding up in their fluoridated drinking water. He also briefly touched on robots, computers, space aliens and how much his stomach hurt ever since they ate that crappy Mexican food in Oroville. He needed to use a restroom bad.

Joe saw that they were rapidly approaching a vintage log cabin Flying A gas station on the right side of the highway. Joe pulled up next to some old style gas pumps with glass bowls on top. The place somehow appeared to still be open for business. It looked as though it might still be 1940 in this neck of the woods called Keddie.

"I saw a bathroom along the side, Lance."

"Cool," he said, dashing from the car after Joe applied the brakes.

Joe shut off his engine. The car didn't need fuel yet. He looked up at a sign board that announced that premium gas was forty-eight cents a gallon. Another sign promised that large amounts of S&H Green stamps would be given to the purchaser.

An old Dodge pickup rested on a lift high up in

the air in the garage, but there was no sign of anyone working on it.

Lance came walking back stiffly. He gingerly opened the door and sat down carefully, as though he had just completed some task that had drained him of all vestiges of life.

"Problem?" asked Joe.

"Yeah, man. That bathroom didn't have any toilet paper."

Just then, an older man came out of the office and stopped at Lance's open window.

"You didn't just use that bathroom, did you son?"

"Well, yeah. I had to go bad, man. How come you don't put some toilet paper in there, mister?"

"Kid, those bathrooms have been out of order for two years."

"Thanks sir,' said Joe, peeling out. He pulled out onto the highway and then immediately moved into the left turn lane. He patiently waited while a speeding logging truck rushed by, creating a strong wall of turbulent air. It seemed to lift the heavy car completely off the ground for a few seconds.

"Wow!" exclaimed Lance, grabbing Joe's right arm, "What was that? A rocket ship hauling dead trees?"

Joe shook Lance's arm loose. He was beginning to feel a bit strange himself, "Sit back and chill, Lance. We're nearly at Keddie, and we gotta check in, so at least attempt to appear normal." He noticed that his voice was beginning to echo in his own ears.

'Normal," slurred Lance, rolling the objectionable word over on his tongue, "What's that, Joe? I mean really, man. Who the hell are these total strangers to tell me to be *normal,* like I gotta take a dammed test or something, to see if I'm *normal* enough to even be here?"

Lance pretended he was the Mexican Bandito confronting Humphrey Bogart in *The Treasure of the Sierra Madre.* "Hey, gringo. I don't got to show you no freaking badges, eh?" Lance laughed long and loud at his own cleverness.

After crossing the highway, Joe drove them up a narrow paved road that dipped up and down like an asphalt roller coaster. Joe wondered if somehow Lance had dosed him. He felt that familiar queasy feeling in his stomach that he had attributed to their lunch, but now he also had that scratchy sensation in the back of his throat.

As they passed a grove of Evergreens, Joe looked at Lance, who was still laughing, and suddenly had three heads. Green and orange tracers and orbs radiated off of Lance's neck.

Joe stared. He had never before realized what a stoned purple aura Lance had.

Joe stopped the car in the middle of a one lane suspension bridge. Below them, the Feather River roared like thunder. Steep canyon walls were on both sides of the crossing..

Joe turned and grabbed Lance by his collar "Did you dose me, you fuck?"

Lance stopped laughing, "Yes."

"When did you do it, and why?" Joe released his friend from his grip.

"I just put one hit of acid in your coke when you used the bathroom in Oroville. I wanted to get you away from booze for at least a day."

"Thanks, you fucking moron," said Joe, settling back in the driver's seat and gripping the steering wheel with two hands. It felt alive, and Joe was overwhelmed with the sense that he no longer knew how to control it.

A horn honked. A large, red faced young man driving an early fifties green Willys station wagon was hanging out of his driver's window, waving his fist at them. They were blocking the only way in and out of Keddie.

"Okay, okay, okay," said Joe. He struggled with the gear shifter, suddenly uncoordinated and not sure of how to drive anymore. He managed to get the Galaxy moving off the bridge. The other driver screamed obscenities at them as they passed. Lance lifted his hand and gave the pissed off crimson colored maniac the peace sign, as though somehow this universal hand signal would dissipate this fellows rage.

Joe felt dizzy and woozy and didn't know how much longer he could fake that he knew what he was doing, guiding this two ton sheet metal monster down the narrow road that was twisting like a snake. Oh my God, he wondered. What was he doing driving upside down, and who was the joker next to him who continued jabbering, making no sense whatsoever?

The road began a sharp incline. Joe proceeded at ten miles an hour, cautiously cresting the hill, making sure that the road continued on the other side. He wanted to make sure that they weren't driving up some cliff only to plunge off, dropping in a slow motion tumbling, twisting death dive to the boulders that lay below.

It soon became a non-issue for Joe as they gradually descended the other side and pulled safely into the tiny former resort community of Keddie, California.

To their right, Joe could see a cluster of small brown cabins, some of them clearly occupied, with gray smoke curling out of tall chimneys. Joe peered out and scanned for gun toting locals with red spray painted necks, or forest dwarves who liked to hide behind stumps and become one with the trees.

They drove slowly past a rustic Post Office and small General Store. Directly past that was a three story dormitory looking building with dozens of windows. Painters worked from scaffolds two stories above the ground. A moving van sat out front. Workers carried furniture and desks inside.

"Over there," pointed Lance. Directly across the road was the Keddie Resort Lodge. It was a long, two story building with a rustic, old west look about it. Stone steps lead up to massive twelve foot doors. A restaurant operated on the bottom floor. The second story had windows with shutters, apparently rooms for rent, or perhaps students would be living here too.

"I think this is where we should start," reasoned Joe. He hung a sharp left turn and parked on a sloping lot in front of the lodge. When they emerged from the car, they were once again struck with the pungent, pleasant smell of the day and end of summer in the mountains. Up above them, on a hidden bluff, there were the sounds of a railroad switching yard. Joe and Lance paused for a moment and listened while a loco-motive gunned it's engines and crashed into a freight car, apparently hooking up.

"Look," said Joe, pointing to a row of six cabins on the far edge of the large, paved parking lot. "We should be over there. One of those babies is ours. I wonder if our roommates are here yet?"

They climbed the steps, confused looks on their faces as they glided upwards, both clinging to mere shreds of their conscious, logical minds. Lance was peaking, while Joe was still coming on, getting higher by the minute. Joe hoped they could just get their cabin

keys and go crash on their beds for awhile. The hell
with food or even unloading the car. He hoped Lance
wouldn't start laughing, because then he would laugh
too, sometimes for hours, not knowing why.

Blackberry vines curled through overhead
sheets of lattice, fashioning a roof of berries and prickly
leaves. The sweet smell of the day was acc- entuated by
the ripe fruit. The wrap-around front porch felt damp
and was clearly old. Gray wooden planks buckled under
their feet.

On the left side of the front doors was a hand
carved wooden bench occupied by two girls they knew
from high school, Carlene Romo and Debbie Glenn.
They greeted each other with smiles. Lance and Joe
mumbled something unintelligible and plunged through
the massive doors and spilled into the entryway. They
were clearly in no condition to trade banal small talk
with anyone, especially loose chicks from their old high
school that they barely knew.

The boys stopped, astounded by the panorama.
Two story high walls covered in knotty pine paneling
ended at the peaked ceiling. The surfaces were decorated with animal hides, Indian artifacts and framed
black and white pictures showing Keddie scenes and
people from around the turn of the century. An Elk
head hung over an eight foot grandfather clock. It's
plastic eyes surveyed the scene, keeping track of the
comings and goings of visitors, guests and ghosts.

To their right, a glass door led to a bustling
restaurant. Wonderful smells of hot coffee and sizzling
burgers and crisp French fries drifted their way. Inside,
the room was crowded with railroad workers and cowboys. Four crusty looking older men, all wearing bright
white cowboys' hats sat at a table by the window. They
drank coffee and smoked. One of the men observed Joe

and Lance staring at them. He said something and they turned as a group and glared back.

"Local color," observed Joe.

"Mutant inbreeding," concluded Lance.

They turned back and continued scanning the entryway to the Keddie Resort Lodge. There was a huge rock fireplace in the center of the wall. In front of the hearth was a worn brown leather couch and several over-stuffed chairs.

Dominating the room was a ten-foot Grizzly Bear perched on a stand. It was stuffed in an upright position with massive claws unfurled from mammoth paws. The bear's mouth was wide open with yellow fangs pushing out against taut black gums in one last, fierce snarl.

"May I help you boys?" The words were spoken softly by a pint sized man with a friendly, cherubic grin. He stood in front of an open door and was wearing Monkey Wards tan work clothes. An old canvas hat was pulled down over his forehead, his tiny pink ears sticking out like an elf.

"Yes," answered Joe, his voice echoing off the walls, not sure if he should pretend to be an adult and offer to shake hands, "We're new students from Berkeley, and we rented one of the cabins. Is this the right place to get our keys?"

"Yes, yes, of course." The diminutive man of unknown age rubbed his miniature hands together, "My name is Guy. I am the maintenance man for the Singh family. Follow me into the office here fellas, and we'll get you checked in."

Guy turned on his heels and he limped into the office as though he had an artificial leg.

Joe leaned over to Lance and put his hand in front of his mouth as he spoke, "I thought Peter Lorre was dead."

"Who's that, Joe?" Lance wasn't much for movie star trivia. He was too spaced out most of the time to remember much beyond his most immediate friend's names, and where he lived. Yet, in the next breath he could launch an hour long discourse on ancient Greek Gods and what each of them represented in real life. Alternatively, he could spell out the Latin alphabet backwards.

He was simultaneously maddening and brilliant. Joe wondered sometimes if Lance's non-stop use of strong, mind bending drugs was scrambling his brain. He wasn't sure how well his weird friend was going to do in the upcoming college classes.

They followed Guy into a large office that had minimal furnishings and smelled like curry, which Joe despised and Lance would only eat if he were turning yellow again. Several young women were standing on one side of a card table, talking to a middle-aged Indian woman dressed in a bright orange sari. Her naturally dark hair was streaked with iron colored gray, and she had the traditional red Tikala in the middle of her forehead.

An angry looking Indian man wearing a turban, stood at a wooden desk and shouted into the phone, "I don't give a damn about your union problems. I have problems too. I ordered fifty mattresses and box springs with all the appropriate bedding, and I need these items today. I have dozens of students arriving who have already paid their money and now they are sleeping on hard, cold floors."

He listened for half a minute, uttered an obscenity and then a threat before slamming the phone down. He looked up and glared at Joe and Lance who were weaving around in front of his desk, their eyes half open, silly grins on their faces.

"Please see Mrs. Singh at the next table. She will check you in."

"Groovy," answered Lance. He and Joe maneuvered over to a spot behind three girls who were receiving keys and bedding and boxes of pots and pans and dishes and most everything one needed to set up housekeeping in a cabin. The boys didn't want to intrude on their space, yet they also wanted to make it clear that they were next in line.

They could sense and hear new arrivals lining up behind them Neither of them wanted to turn around and look, in case they should see someone else they knew from Berkeley, which was a strong possibility. They didn't want to engage with anyone.

Finally, it was their turn.

"Yes?" said Mrs. Singh, holding a clipboard in her hand, "What are your names, please?"

Fifteen minutes later, after scribbling their names in sloppy cursive more then a dozen times, Joe and Lance were officially checked in at Keddie. They staggered blindly out of the office with boxes of vital supplies and most importantly, the keys to their cabin.

They headed across the scorching hot parking lot, dropping items as they went, fully intending to re- and pick up the random utensils and pots they had dropped.

There was a loud metallic crushing noise. Some leering cowboy in a monster 4x4 Dodge had just deliberately run over one of their pots, crushing it.

"Huh huh, huh huh," slurred the driver.

"Shit," muttered Joe, staggering on. He knew that he would also have to retrieve his car.

"I gotta get out of the freaking sun and lay down," gasped Joe.

"I hear you, man. Just put one foot in front of the other."

They reached the half sized white picket fence and kicked open the tiny gate.

"Guy must live here," remarked Joe, his mind fully blown but somehow still able to make one of his frequent, sarcastic observations.

"Don't laugh, Joe. He might live in the back room with a female circus midget. Remember, we signed up for this blindly. All we know about our roommates is that they will be males and are most likely from the Bay Area."

They walked past a gigantic Sequoia tree that stood nearly as tall as a Redwood, but much wider around. The cabin was a simple box with a small front porch. Two partially rusty metal seashell chairs sat empty in the shade of the overhanging roof. Joe tried his key but the front door was unlocked and he and Lance entered, gratefully putting down their boxes on a small round dining room table.

There was a small kitchen behind the table. A round edged humming refrigerator, sink, stove and tall dark green painted cupboards.

They took in the tiny front room furnished with a worn two person cloth couch with a couple of weird looking pillows. There was a scarred coffee table and a standing lamp with a tasseled shade. One overstuffed chair with long wooden armrests. No TV.

They started down a hallway and came upon the first bedroom containing two single beds with no box spring or mattress, just a mesh of steel. Two small dressers stood against one wall.

"Charming," said Joe.

"Delightful," added Lance.

Through the bathroom, another door led to the

back bedroom. It was larger, and both beds had matt- resses and were fully made up.

On the nearest bed laid a piece of binder paper with large words written in black crayon : THIS IS MY BED. SCOTT. The other bed also had a similar paper. Joe picked it up and read it to Lance, "THIS IS MY BED. CHRIS."

"I don't like the sound of those names, Joe. Scott and Chris? Come on."

"I told you we should have left earlier," accused Joe.

"It wouldn't have made any difference, man. They've probably been here since yesterday."

Lance cleaned his glasses with the edge of his blue chambray shirt and they returned to the dining room. The table had four mismatched wooden chairs.

"Ozzie and Harriet revisited," declared Joe.

"Deranged Leave It To Beaver," added Lance, stroking his chin like he did when he was slipping into a period of deep pontification.

Joe brought the convertible over and backed it up into their dirt driveway with a heavily leaning garage in the rear. He and Lance hauled in thick clothes to put down on the bare springs of their beds so they could lie down, knowing that they probably wouldn't be getting their mattresses before tomorrow.

Joe laid down with the room spinning and the walls feeling like they were moving in and out to his every inhale and exhale. He was really stoned. He tried closing his eyes and practicing deep, focused breathing. He willed himself to relax, while his mind galloped across the frontier of his brain, with a million scenes a minute flashing by. It was like an impossibly fast paced distorted series of random, scary images and irrational thoughts.

Lance was quickly asleep. Joe never could understand how his friend could snooze while tripping on LSD. Joe envied him. It sometimes kept him up for days. But, then again, Lance had already destroyed so many brain cells that maybe it didn't matter what he was on anymore. He just went right to sleep, whenever he wanted.

Joe wondered if someday Lance wouldn't wake up. Joe would get up as usual, and probably wouldn't think something was wrong until two days later, when he realized that Lance had been sleeping for a very long time.

Then again, he could enjoy fine health and love past 100. Fat chance, smiled Joe.

FAMILY DINNER

CHAPTER FOUR

Maureen Hess moved nervously around the rental house that she shared with her boyfriend, Sam. It was getting close to the time they should be leaving.

She lighted a menthol cigarette, took three puffs, and then stubbed it out next to a dozen other barely smoked cigarettes. She was trying to quit. Maureen could hear Sam in the bathroom, whistling while he shaved.

She didn't know how he managed to be happy most of the time. Occasionally, she resented his steady, good mood. She always loved the way he looked, though. Sexy in clothes and even better without.

It was her mother, Linda's, forty-fifth birthday party. The whole family would be there, eating together, pretending for at least one night to tolerate each other. However, if her step-dad, Big Dan McGrew was drinking, anything could happen.

Big Dan was well known as a mean drunk. Since he was the Sheriff of Quincy, he could get away with virtually anything. Maureen's older brother, Gary, was a stone cold alcoholic. Sam drank beer in moderation. She liked that about him.

Linda quit drinking altogether after Jimbo was lost in Vietnam. It just made her sadder and once even made her consider suicide. She couldn't do it course, because it is considered a mortal sin by the Catholic church. Plus, little Roger still needed a mother.

Maureen's fourteen-year old brother, Roger Hess, was by all reports, quite a strange kid. He was quiet, odd and secretive. He pursued grotesque hobbies like torturing cats and birds. He spent most of his time locked in his bedroom, conducting bizarre experiments.

When Sam came out of the bathroom, Maureen whistled, "Damn, Sam, you sure clean up good. I can't wait to show you off."

Sam smiled. He was a well built six-footer with a handsome Scandinavian face. His long blonde hair was pulled back into a long ponytail. He was dressed in a dark cowboy shirt, clean bell bottomed dress jeans, and his rarely worn rattlesnake boots.

"All you need now is a white cowboy hat, Sam."

"I'd wear a paper sack over my head if I thought it would make your folks like me better."

"They don't dislike you, Sam." Maureen reached over and adjusted Sam's collar. She reveled in his manliness, and pulled him into her for a warm hug.

"They're old fashioned that way," she continued, "They think that if we're living together, we should be married." She kept her head pressed to his chest, listening to the reassuring beat of his heart.

Sam hugged her back, and then retrieved Maureen's coat from the hall closet. He helped her put it on. "I really don't care what they think, Maureen. Big Dan is homophobic alcoholic. I'm sorry, but your mom reminds me of a zombie. I don't recall her ever saying more then a handful of words to me."

"She's like that with everyone. Ever since….."

"I know. Ever since Jimbo was lost in Vietnam. Quite frankly, I'm sick of hearing about it constantly, Maureen."

She buttoned her coat, "One thing I've learned out of this Sam, is that you can't put a timetable on someone else's grief. Remember, I lost my big brother. I'm never going to stop missing him."

"Sorry, babe. I don't mean to be insensitive to your family's loss. It just seems to come up in every conversation when we're with them." Sam opened the front door, "Shall we go my dearest, and enter the lion's den?"

Maureen drove her brightly painted VW Bug onto the gravel driveway that led to her childhood home, a 1950's ranch, with peeling white paint and a blue tarp covering the far corner of the roof. Broken and discarded major appliances sat in the front yard.

She parked next to Gary's Willys. Big Dan's black and white Sheriff's Cruiser was parked in front of the house, backed in, poised for a hot pursuit. Linda's old Plymouth station wagon sat in the garage, unmoved since 1967. The garage door was broken and hung down crooked on top of the car's hood.

Sam and Maureen's feet crunched on pea gravel as they walked up the driveway, holding hands and swinging them back and forth as lovers do. Frogs and crickets sounded off in the nearby woods.

An overhead floodlight clicked on, illuminating their path. Inside the house they could hear Frank Sinatra belting out *My Way*.

The weathered front door swung open and Big Dan McGrew filled up the doorway.

"Welcome!" he bellowed, his face glowing red. He was still dressed in his Sheriff's uniform and held a drink in his hand. He had his duty belt on, complete with pistol.

He tried to give his stepdaughter a hug, but

Maureen gave him an air kiss and danced by him. She had no intention of giving Dan the opportunity to grope her, especially right in front of Sam.

Dan grabbed Sam's right hand and crushed it with his grip, "How ya doing, buddy?"

"My name is Sam, remember? I'm doing fine." Big Dan squeezed his hand harder and grimaced, pouring it on. Sam gripped back as hard as he could.

"When you gonna make an honest woman out of Maureen, huh boy?"

"When we're ready, Dan, you'll be among the first to know, okay? Can I have my hand back now?"

"You getting smart with me, son?"

"No sir."

"Good," said Dan, a smile reappearing on his cloudy face, "Just wanted to make sure." He released Sam's hand.

Big Dan punched Sam sharply in his left shoulder and walked away, chuckling. Sam rubbed his shoulder. His arm had hurt him for a week after Dan's last hard punch. A large purple and black mark took two weeks to disappear, and now he had done it again, the bastard.

Sam turned towards the couch. Gary sat there, a can of Budweiser in his hand.

"Hi, Gary. How's it going?"

"Well hello, lover boy. Welcome to Hell House."

Big Dan reappeared with a cold beer. He handed it to Sam, "Here. No hard feelings, okay?"

Sam, grateful for the beer, popped the top and took a sip all the while staring at Dan. "There might be the beginnings of some hard feelings if you keep slugging me."

Dan laughed, "What you gonna do about it,

boy? Punch a Sheriff? Huh?"

Sam sat on the opposite end of the couch from
Gary, who was overflowing from his corner spot halfway over into the middle.

Maureen stood in the kitchen doorway and
talked to her mother, who was putting the final touches
on a Prime Rib dinner with all the fixins. She had pre-
prepared a massive bowl of mashed potatoes, au jus
sauce as well as lumpy brown country gravy. Also,
freshly picked corn on the cob from her garden, a green
salad and a heaping plate of fluffy, homemade buttermilk biscuits.

"Mom. How come you're cooking your own
birthday dinner?"

"Well, Maureen, I don't see you volunteering.
What options do I have. Should I have Roger cook?"

"What about Dan? Why couldn't he have taken
you out? We could have all met here afterwards for
dessert and you could have opened your birthday presents. He sure doesn't spend any of his big fancy salary
maintaining this house. At least our real dad, Carl, with
all his faults, kept things up. When he wasn't drunk."

Linda pulled the succulent roast out of the oven,
"That wasn't very often dear."

"As far as your stepfather, he works hard keeping all of us safe. How he spends his salary is his business. As long as Roger and I have a roof over our heads
and food to eat, then we're satisfied."

Maureen was stunned. It was the longest string
of words from Linda to her since Jimbo had been
declared dead by The Marines.

Linda stirred the gravy, "What you need to do,
dear, is concentrate on pleasing your man. When are
you and Sam going to make it legal and get hitched and

provide me with a grandchild before I die of old age?"

Maureen ignored the bitterness, "Well, mom. Let me at least set the table."

"I'll manage. I always have. Go on. Visit with the men. Tell them to expect dinner in ten minutes."

A Merle Haggard drinking song was playing on the console stereo. Big Dan McGrew sat backwards on a wooden chair, telling Gary and Sam about a recent car crash involving a car load of Indians who had been partying at the Keddie Club on their payday.

"Yeah, it was quite a mess, I tell ya. They hit a tree head on at better then 60 we figure. It was down at that hairpin turn at Dollars Corners. When we got there, the car was still smoking and steaming, The driver was impaled on the steering column, dead.

"The Indian riding shotgun had gone face first through the windshield and we found him fifty feet away, lying in some bushes with a broken back and not much of a face left. The two riding in the rear had seat-belts on, and they weren't hurt too bad."

Gary spoke up, "Have you ever noticed, Dan, that most of the car accidents around here involve drunk Indians, or Mexicans who have been smoking pot?"

"Not really," he answered, looking at his stepson with distaste. Big Dan McGrew was many things, but he was not a racist. During his days of combat as a Marine Sergeant during the Korean War, he had fought for his life at the Chosin Reservoir. Men of many shades had fought together, and Dan didn't care what color his fellow soldiers were as long as they could fight like they weren't afraid to die.

Sam spoke up, "I haven't noticed anything like

that either, Gary."

"How would you know? Are you like on the police force now or something? You don't know shit."

"I hear things," answered back Sam. He never had cared much for Gary. He couldn't believe he and Maureen had come from the same lineage.

"I hear things too," said Gary, draining his beer.

Maureen entered the room treading lightly. Dan was busy putting on some more Sinatra and Gary and Sam were looking everywhere but at each other.

"Where's Roger?" she asked. "Mom said dinner will be served in ten minutes."

"He's probably in his room, Maureen," said Gary in a caustic tone of voice, "That's all he does, right? He lives in his room."

"Yeah," said Dan, sitting down again and listening to his favorite song, *Send In The Clowns.*

Maureen despised the song. She never told anyone, not even Sam, of her irrational fear of clowns. Circus clowns were the worst she thought. Filthy, disgusting, tramps made up in hideous different colors. An orange Afro wig, large red shiny lips, and those gawd awful two foot clown shoes often completed their evil ensemble.

"I'll get him," she said, speaking to no one. She halted at the beginning of the long, dark, hallway. She tried both light switches but neither of them worked. Geez, she thought, Dan was so lazy he wouldn't even replace a burnt out bulb or two.

As much as she feared and disliked her real dad, Carl, he would never have let things go the way Dan had. Maureen didn't care what her mother said about his drinking. Carl got his chores done. She was fully aware that Big Dan was a lecherous, dangerous, drunk. Maureen made sure she was never alone with him.

Several 'KEEP OUT' signs decorated Roger's door. Maureen knocked anyway. Not getting a response, she opened the door, It would only go halfway, as it was bumping up against something that was big, furry, and not moving.

Maureen took two steps back, stunned by the toxic smells emanating from his room. The stench of formaldehyde overwhelmed her. She hoped her brother wasn't drinking it.

"What?" came Roger's adolescent voice from the shadows. There were no lights on in his room either. She couldn't even tell where he was.

"It's almost time for dinner. You need to wash up."

"Why?" His response came from the other side of the room.

"Because it's what you do, Roger. You wash off germs so you don't get sick. This is especially important for you, what with all your, uh, experiments."

"Get out, evil woman. I'll come out when I'm good and ready, and you can't make me. You're not my mom."

Now it sounded as though he were suspended from the ceiling.

" Come out now you little twerp. Did you get mom anything for her birthday?"

"No. Why should I?"

Maureen gave up and rejoined the men in the living room. Dan was demonstrating a Police chokehold on Sam, pretending to crush his windpipe with his nightstick. Sam was kicking his arms and legs out and turning blue.

Gary sat back on the couch and chortled, "Better you then me, buddy," he said.

"Let him go!" shouted Maureen.

"Okay," said Dan, shoving Sam back onto the couch.

Linda meandered into the dining room carrying a platter of Prime Rib and her carving knife. The table was fully set.

"Dinner," she announced in a weak voice.

Big Dan wobbled over to his seat at the head of the table with a nearly full glass of vodka and ice.

"Sam," he slurred, "You sit down there next to Gary who gets the other end spot. Maureen, you're here. Where's Roger?"

"He's still in his room," answered Maureen, "I tried to get him to come out, but he refused."

Gary!" Yelled Dan. "Go get your brother!"

Gary got up and sauntered down the hallway and kicked the bottom of Roger's door, "Hey punk! Dinner. Now! Don't make me come in there and get you. I'll mess you up bad."

Roger emerged from the gloom. "Okay, okay, you didn't have to yell at me."

Gary slugged him in the back of his head and propelled him towards the table, "Sure I did."

"No running in the house, Roger," yelled Big Dan, used to keeping order.

"Good job, bro," said Maureen sarcastically. She wondered it she was the only one who noticed that Roger did not physically resemble anyone in their family. Plus, even Linda admitted that he acted like a kid that been dropped on his head a few too many times.

Dan finished his drink, "Quiet everyone," he said, raising his hands, "Time for a blessing on our food."

Everyone shifted in their chairs, avoiding eye contact with Dan.

"Sam," said Dan, "Since you're going to be our future son-in-law, I designate you to say a prayer for this food that God provided."

"And Linda cooked." whispered Maureen, pretty sure that she was the only one who appreciated the irony of what Dan had just said.

Sam gulped, closed his eyes and joined his hands together. He was desperately trying to remember a simple food prayer from his days as a kid in Denmark. Then he realized that it didn't matter, because he could only repeat it in Danish.

"Dear Lord…..we are gathered here today…..to thank thee, oh mighty one, the God of pestilence and despair…..for this righteous food. Uh, thank you for this nice day, and uh, creating women….amen."

"Dig in!" yelled Dan, nearly tipping his chair over as he and Gary went for the Prime Rib at the same time. Dan crammed a full piece of meat into his mouth along with a mouthful of ketchup. Bits of Prime Rib dropped from his mouth as he chewed like a cow with his mouth open.

Everyone else went slower, politely passing platters of food clockwise, filling their plates.

Linda moved back and forth like a waitress, bringing condiments, more hot rolls and some milk.

They ate in silence.

Finally, Big Dan spoke up, "How are things in school?"

"Are you talking to me?" asked Gary, who was moving his mouth back and forth across an ear of corn, ripping off bites saturated in melting butter.

"No," replied Dan, "I'm talking to the frigging wall, dip-shit!"

"Sorry. I wasn't sure. Maureen is signed up for classes too, you know. Most of us locals got first chance to set up our schedules today. The foul smelling freaks from Oakland and Berkeley get to choose from what's left on Thursday. Classes start next week."

"Hey," objected Maureen, "I've met some of them when I've been working at the Keddie Restaurant, and most of them are really nice. They don't tip too well, but many of them are broke."

"Broke?" snorted Gary, "How can rich kids be busted already? Most of them just got here."

"What makes you say they're rich kids?"asked Maureen

Gary was just warming up, "Can you afford to move to Oakland to attend college?"

"No."

"Yeah," added Dan, "Just remember Maureen, that a lot of these big city kids are bringing drugs and diseases with them. I'd caution you to not get too friendly too quick, not unless you're okay with getting the clap, crabs or hepatitis. I've seen some young women come down with all three."

Maureen scowled at her stepfather.

Gary slammed a heavily buttered roll into his mouth. "I'll tell you what, sis. I was in Keddie when a lot of them were arriving. Lots of longhaired, pinko, fag, potheads. I didn't hardly see anyone who looked even halfway normal. Plus," he sputtered, 'Two of them were parked on the one lane bridge yesterday when I was trying to leave Keddie. How stupid or stoned do you have to be to park in the middle of the bridge?"

Maureen had heard enough, "You are so ignorant and prejudiced that it is disgusting. You automatically hate anyone who doesn't look or act just like you."

"You're right on the money miss liberal smarty

pants. I'll tell you what, Maureen. You can take all your Grateful Dead albums and pot and shove it where the sun don't shine, and I'm trying to be polite here, mind you. I'll be damned if I'm going to stand by and watch those queers and addicts take over our town."

Dan slammed his fist down on the table, "It's a sign of the times, I tell you. The end of days is what it is. All of this was predicted back when Nostril Damius was writing the Bible, way before they even had printing presses."

Sam leaned back in his chair and picked at his teeth with a toothpick. "I believe, Dan, that the name is pronounced 'Nostradamus' and he had nothing to do with writing the Bible."

"Who cares how you pronounce a dead persons name, you smart ass. The facts of the situation is that we are literally being invaded by Jewish hippie scum who smoke pot and shoot up LSD. It's the beginning of the final breakdown of our society, and it's been predicted since the Dark Ages of 1959 for sure."

"Uh, Dan," continued Sam cautiously, aware that he was in dangerous territory,

"I believe people go on LSD trips by eating a sugar cube dosed with it or dropping a colored pill. They don't actually inject acid."

"Oh," said Dan, whose face was now bright red, "So now you're an expert on how to take LSD, huh?"

Maureen spoke up, trying to rescue her boyfriend, "So, mom. How does it feel to turn forty-five?"

"About the same as forty-four. Just another year closer to death."

Roger, who hadn't said a word throughout the entire dinner, raised his right hand which had purple blotches on it, "May I be excused? I'm at a critical point with one of my experiments."

"Hell no, boy," roared Dan, once again the life of the party. "Everyone into the front room. We'll have Linda open her presents as soon as she's done clearing the table. Babe, do the dishes later."

There were three presents on the coffee table. Dan went over and put his favorite Tom Jones record on the stereo. *What's New Pussycat* blared from the speakers.

Linda sat expressionless on the couch in-between Maureen and Sam. She finally put her carving knife down on the table.

"All for me?" she asked in a flat voice.

"Yeah babe. All for you!"

Linda picked up her first present and it seemed to be heavy. She read the tag, "To my main squeeze. Love, Dan."

Linda had trouble with the ribbon, so Gary sprang forward and slit it open with his sheath knife.

She slowly unwrapped a gigantic black frying pan.

"That's so you won't burn my eggs anymore, sweetie."

Big Dan leaned over and lightly backhanded Sam, "Boy. You like my present to my woman or what?"

"Yeah. Great choice."

Next, Linda unwrapped the present from Maureen and Sam. She held up a tie dyed T-shirt.

"Time to update your wardrobe, mom," said Maureen.

Dan snatched it out of his wife's hands. "You ain't wearing that, woman. Not unless you're fixin to take up pot smoking and shooting LSD"

The final gift, an envelope from Gary, was a

year's subscription to the racist newspaper. "They only print the truth, mom. You'll learn all about the creeping menace of hippies, Negroes and queers."

"Hey, Roger," said Maureen, "What did you get mom for her birthday?"

"That's hilarious, sis," he answered, sulking while occasionally smelling his stained hands.

"Many thanks, everyone," said Linda.

Big Dan McGrew stood up, "Let's all sing Happy Birthday, and then you can get the cake and ice cream for everyone, Linda."

After a half hearted rendition of the traditional birthday song, Linda picked up her knife and rose like smoke from a campfire.

"Do you need any help, mom?" asked Maureen. "No."

A few minutes later, Linda returned with a sheet cake covered with dozens of candles, all lit. Tears welled up in her eyes as she stared at the flickering flames. She blew out the candles and then carved up the cake by slashing her knife downwards seven times.

"Who's the last piece for?" asked Roger.

"Why, my eldest son, James, of course." Linda focused her eyes towards heaven, "I had a dream last night that my Jimbo came home for my special day."

"Mom," said Maureen, holding her mother's hand, "Jimbo's not coming back. Not in this life, anyway."

Linda started bawling.

Maureen led her to the bedroom, trying to share her burden and pain.

ACID HEADS

CHAPTER FIVE

Wednesday started out as a promising day. Two box springs, mattresses, comforters, pillows and sheets were dropped off at ten in the morning by two young guys. They were working out of the back of a semi that had somehow managed to negotiate the narrow road and bridge leading into Keddie.

After making their beds, the boys unloaded the Ford. The first thing they hooked up was Joe's half-assed cheapo plastic stereo from Monkey Wards. It sounded marginally better when Lance plugged in his solitary wooden speaker.

"I still don't understand why you didn't build another speaker, Lance. You had all year to do it."

"How many times are you going to ask me that same question, Joe? I refuse to discuss it any more."

Joe put on the new Rolling Stones live record, *Get Yer Ya's Out.* They listened to the lively first song, featuring Keith Richards ripping lead guitar, *Jumping Jack Flash,* over and over.

When all their clothes and miscellaneous possessions were stored away in the flimsy dressers, Joe asked Lance where he was keeping his huge stash.

"It's still in your trunk in the green suitcase. It'll have to stay there for awhile until I can figure out a better spot. I certainly can't bring it in here, not until we know who our mysteriously missing roommates are, and how they feel about such matters. I wonder what the deal with them is? Maybe they don't even exist."

"Hold on a second, Lance. Stay on the subject I started with. You mean to tell me that wherever I travel around here, I have to haul around your illegal drug inventory? So now, buddy, I'm taking most of the risk. If I get busted for what you have, along with my half a pound of dope, I'll go to jail for sure. Maybe even State Prison. I'm not comfortable with this set up at all."

"Gimme your car keys," said Lance, reaching out his long, bony hand. Joe complied.

"I'll be right back. Don't go anywhere." Joe couldn't recall Lance ever acting this assertive before.

Joe sat and waited on the far right end of the cloth couch. He had already decided that this was the spot where he would sit and write stories and poems in his journal. He certainly had plenty to chronicle already, with acid inspired thoughts, ideas, and fragments of poems and sardonic prose bouncing around inside his head. He just needed a stiff whiskey, a joint, his notebook, and a pen.

Lance came back shortly as promised and handed Joe his keys. He offered him a small brown paper lunch sack, "Go ahead. Look inside. We're now partners in the drug trade, whether you know it or not. You committed a felony by hauling me and my mobile drug store up here to Keddie." He laughed and Joe stared at his friend, wondering exactly what he was finding so amusing at the present moment. Joe wondered if Lance was stoned already.

Joe peered inside and saw four individual baggies. Three of them held different sized and colored pills. The final baggie was full of Magic Mushrooms.

"So, what's all this?"

"Easy, man, I put up the cash for the stash, so I am by reason of commercial default, the CEO of what is now our little venture. It's like I hold fifty one percent of our stock, if we had any. Here's the deal. I make all the contacts and all the sales. All you have to do is supply me with a trunk key so I can access my supplies any time you're home, or even if we're in school and I need inventory. For just that simple little thing, a key, I'll cut you in on the profits.

"Don't worry, Joe. My plan is foolproof. You know I never get caught, and neither will you, because you're working with me. Like I said, simple. The stash is what I owed you for gas plus a bonus to hold you over for awhile."

"So what are these?" asked Joe, holding the bags up.

"Well, the bag of Magic Mushrooms are obvious. I would highly recommend that we take these together for the time being, you having had some bad trips recently. It's a much different, more profound high then you're currently used to.

"The red pills are downers, which I know you prefer to uppers. However, if you're feeling a bit slug-gish when you get up, then you take two of the whites ones, which are crosstops, or beens as some prefer to call them. It's what long haul truck drivers use."

"Speed?"

"Yeah, but be careful, Joe. Don't get hung up on them. They're highly addictive, and cause your teeth to rot in six months and eventually, you'll feel like killing yourself. The final bag has a few hits of Orange Sun-shine acid. Like I told you in the car, this batch is the best I've ever had, and you know I've sampled a few in my time."

Yeah, like maybe a thousand times already,

thought Joe.

"Now, since I've been so generous with you, partner, how about giving me a lid of that Mexican weed, so I don't have to keep bumming joints off you, which has become tedious."

"Okay, sure. I'll get you an ounce now. By the way, partner, does our enterprise have a name, just between you and me of course."

"Snatch Enterprises."

"Yeah. That makes sense. We used that name when we were making our Super 8 films. Say," asked Joe, suddenly inspired, "You wanna eat some Magic Mushrooms?"

This time Lance was the cautious one, "Aren't we supposed to drive into Quincy today and sign up for our classes at The Plumas County Fairgrounds?"

"Yeah. So what? Look at what we pulled off yesterday while we were blasted on acid. The mushrooms should just make us, well, mellower then we already are."

"Maybe. They also make you barf for a while. That's when your trip rapidly escalates. Don't underestimate the 'shrooms, Joe. They can kick your ass."

"What the hell, buddy. We'll drive to town with the convertible top down. Just don't puke down the inside of my window channel. It's impossible to get that vomit smell out."

Two hours later they were sprawled out in the front room, listening to a Ten Years After album. They loved Alvin Lee's soaring guitar solos and singing.

Lance had sunk so deep into the overstuffed chair that he was barely visible to Joe, who was so high that he was seeing double, "How long do you recon that they'll be open for class sign ups today?" inquired

Lance.

Joe spoke slowly, enunciating every word as his new, weird sounding voice ricocheted off the cabin walls and bounced back at him, "How should I know? I don't work there. Right now, I'm in a cabin with you, and dude, I am incredibly high."

"Yeah, well that's groovy, but not very helpful."

"Well, man. We got plenty of time. Really, it shouldn't take more then an hour or so to set up our schedules. How hard can it be?"

"I feel like we should go soon, so we still have a choice of classes and times."

"Maybe so, Lance, but I'm not even going to try and drive while I'm this blasted. Don't you remember yesterday when we almost were stuck after we left that gas station? I don't plan to go there for gas for a while. Not until they forget about you and whatever you did in their bathroom."

"Yeah, well, if it was closed, why wasn't the door locked?"

Lance pulled himself up and out of the chair and glided towards the table, a silly, distorted smile on his face. He hadn't shaved in a few days, and his thick red-dish beard was growing out, giving him an even more authentic John Lennon appearance.

Joe knew that Lance loved to explore the outer regions of his consciousness. He was always attempting to actually break on through to the other side that Jim Morrison and The Doors sang about. Lance knew that it would only be good if he could also return, to not be stuck in some weird parallel reality forever. As he continually tested the boundary of his sanity, he recognized that he was in a Holy Grail hunt for the legendary but elusive ultimate high. He just had to get there without dying.

Lance tried communicating with Joe without speaking. He would use mental telepathy, *"So...Joe. Can you hear me okay?"*

Joe looked up at Lance from the far corner of the couch. He realized their latest record had stopped. Now, he could actually hear Lance talking to him without moving his mouth.

'Yes...I can. This is, quite amazing, friend. How are you doing this?"

"I've been practicing."

"Great. I don't know, Lance...I had no idea that we would...

"Get this high? Just on Magic Mushrooms.? I tried to warn you..."

"Yeah, this is...uh...fun no doubt. Maybe it, wasn't such a hot idea...How are we ever going to get to Quincy, now? I...can't possibly drive...right now."

Lance launched himself from the kitchen chair, moved over, and stood in front of Joe, a concerned look broadcast across his face, "Don't ever say that, man. Don't doubt your sober decisions when you're stoned. If you do, your life will no longer make any sense if you start reacting to everyday situations backwards. I say what better way to explore our new environment then by tripping on mushrooms. I truly believe you were inspired, Joe."

Joe was now too stoned to respond . He instinctively knew that he and Lance needed to get out of the cabin for a while. He also realized that they hadn't eaten since their horrid, cheap taco lunch the day before in Oroville. His stomach grumbled, empty, but he was incapable of figuring out what he could eat. Maybe they needed to go to the General Store and buy some fruit or chili or something.

"All right then, brother," said Lance, clearly the

more lucid and functional of the two old friends.

Lance flung open the front door, and Joe cringed at the sight of the real world just outside. He felt fear and trepidation. It was as though there were hidden, evil forces, lurking behind the Sequoia Tree, waiting to swallow them both up.

"Come on Joe," urged Lance, "Get up and join me. I intend to explore our immediate neighborhood. If everything is cool, maybe we should hike up to the bluff and check out the trains. Sounds like they have a large operation up there. Maybe it reaches the clouds. Don't worry. If we run into straight people who want to engage with us, I can maintain and talk with the fools."

Lance hopped down the cabin steps and Joe stumbled after him, his upper body bent forward, his head sideways as he tried to get his single vision back. He waved his hands back and forth in front of his face, trying to clear a path through his overgrown and frightening mental jungle. He joined Lance by the tree. Joe could feel his heart thumping in his chest, and he struggled for breath, reaching up to massage his throat while he attempted to remember how to swallow and breathe.

Lance ignored Joe's obvious discomfort and growing panic. "Follow me," he said, walking rapidly out the tiny white gate and heading up the steeply inclined path past three similar cabins and stopping at the edge of the road and looking around.

Joe could barely walk, his whole world bouncing around with every jarring step. He stopped to try and steady himself. He removed his hand from his throat and was now breathing okay, although his chest ached and felt constricted. It was no use, he thought.

It felt to him like he was on a gray U.S. Destroyer, plowing through stormy seas, bouncing from

place to place when he was on deck. He was trying
to avoid tumbling overboard and disappearing in the
ship's wake, one hand outstretched, willing them to
come back but knowing he was about to drown. He
would then swallow a gallon of seawater and drift down
to Davey Jones crowded locker on the ocean floor. Joe
would become one with the fishes.

Lance disappeared from his sight. Joe was on
his own, weaving through strange, uncharted territory.
He decided his best bet was to stare at the ground that
was directly in front of him. He was attempting to min-
imize his chances of human contact of any kind. He
knew that as soon as he figured out how to talk again,
whoever was near him would immediately know he was
tripping.

His legs felt unusually heavy, like he was wa-
ding through nearly cured cement with his combat
boots on. He stopped thinking when he reached the
scary edge of his own perilous mental cliff. He peered
over the edge, resisting the urge to jump and end it all.
It was at this critical point that Joe realized he was
without shoes.

The red dirt swirled before him, splintering into
a million different directions. Purple cracks spread
everywhere as the soil began shifting faster. Slight gaps
became ever widening craters and they got larger still
with his every subsequent breath. He realized that he
was in danger, about to be swallowed up. Soon, he
would disappear down a deep fissure and fall thousands
of feet, landing in a never land where he would be competing for air and rancid Twinkies with millions of
blind moles. It would be just like living in the rank
sewers of L.A.

He suddenly desired a map of Hollywood,
showing where all the big and famous movie stars

supposedly lived. Joe chuckled at the idea he had of him selling phony Hollywood maps. Hell, he could just put an X next to any house he wished, and print that so and so lived here, and another so and so star lived there, and so on. Who would ever know the difference, since the tour busses in Hollywood rarely stopped in front of a stars house? No one would know if it was just a schmuck like Scott Scheinblum living there, or Dinah Shore for Christ's sake.

Joe came back to reality and reeled sideways and smashed into the half sized picket fence. He had only managed to travel ten feet, and was now sprawled in the red dirt with no shoes, hugging chipped white stakes. He glanced straight up and got dizzy and was temporarily blinded by the sun. It's multiple rays were split into a kaleidoscope of spinning, merging colors, many of which he never even knew existed.

He was sliding towards total panic. What if their roommates decided to finally show up and they found him like this. What would he do then? What could he do?

Joe slowly became aware of multiple loud noises. Birds chirping for no reason, random cricket sounds, lonesome frogs pleading for a mate, relentless blue woodpeckers eating a nearby cabin.

He was also acutely aware of the cars and trucks that pulled in and out of the parking lot. Fortunately, no one seemed to notice him. Above, on the bluff, the locomotives continued to gun their engines and make screeching metallic noises leading to loud crashes. Joe put his hands up to his ears in a futile attempt to block out the unpleasant, jarring sound track to his latest, veering out of control, internal adventure.

Lance reappeared. He was standing there, studying Joe's contorted position.

"You sure didn't make it very far, bud. Hey, give me the car keys. I just made our first sale. There's a group of heads from Oakland living in the cabin at the top. A cool guy named Greg gave me quite a large order. I'm telling you right now, we've stumbled into a potential gold mine here. Greg tells me that there's plenty more people like us, serious freaks, living in this compound."

Joe dug out his keys and handed them to Lance, who didn't seem to be affected at all by the large amount of mushrooms they had both consumed a couple of hours previously.

Joe felt deathly ill. This was not fun at all. He leaned on the fence and heaved repeatedly until he was empty and he thought there was nothing left to come up.

When Lance returned fifteen minutes later after delivering his order, Joe felt as though he had figured it all out.. He was experiencing a moment of stunning clarity, where he felt he had finally grasped the truth of his situation.

"I know what you're trying to do to me, Lance."

Lance handed him his keys back, "What am I trying to do to you, Joe?"

"You're attempting to take control of my brain."

"Oh yeah? How did you deduce that, and what is my motive, to take control of your brain? Why would I want to, even if I could, which I can't. Not today at least. I'm all booked up. There's a guy named Chad who lives in the bushes. I promised him my brain snatching services first."

"Huh?" responded Joe, unable to follow Lance's twisting chain of random thoughts that were thrown together, constantly spilling out of his mouth.

Joe scooted on his ass away from the mess he

had just made. He was still dry heaving every few minutes. He felt as though maybe he should be wearing a sandwich sign board warning sign, plus maybe some yellow Police incident tape to keep innocents away.

He forgot about Lance, who was now bending over him again, trying to see eye to eye, to somehow engage with him on some sort of level where he could ascertain the truth about his friend's current mental state.

Lance chuckled, "Okay, Joe. You busted me, man. I was planning on excavating your brain with a can opener and shovel. I'm actually a cannibal." He grinned, and his pupils were huge. His glasses magnified his eyes, making them look larger still.

Joe climbed up and stood on his bare feet, which were now covered with red dust. He needed a glass of water bad and to brush his teeth to get the nasty puke taste out of his mouth.

He shoved Lance in his chest, pushing him back a few feet, "Out of my way, you traitor! I recognize your dirty deed for what it is. I'm fully aware of your sinister plot, and will not easily concede to you what is left of my brain."

Lance beamed, "This is so cool, Joe. You're actually freaking out on 'shrooms. Oh man, I wish you could show me how to get where you're at."

Joe stared wide eyed at Lance, not believing what he was hearing, "Listen my friend. You do not want to be me right now. I'm in serious physic trouble here, dude. Get me some freaking orange juice to try and bring me down. I need some real food, too, something filling, but not greasy or still moving."

"Okay, man. Now that I have some cash, I'll go buy us some grub over at the General Store."

A minute later, Joe straightened up and swiveled

his head towards the restaurant. He was somehow able to zero in on a conversation taking place inside at the round corner table. Muffled voices rose above the blue haze of burning cigarettes and the dark mist that emanated from the coffee cups, many of them labeled with the regulars name or initials. They were discussing himself and Lance.

"Lance," said Joe, straining to hear the conversation, "Listen."

Joe had a vision, and could see them clearly. There were four, old, creased cowboys, all wearing bright white cowboy hats that seemed florescent. Joe decided to nick-name them the 'Marlboro Men.' They were hoisting tankards of thick black coffee to their barbwire lips.

The largest of the men strode to the lobby phone and inserted a dime. He got a dial tone and then put in the special number he had been given. While he waited for someone to answer, he turned his back on the others and squinted through smoke colored eyes that had seen it all and then some.

"Hello?" came a neutral male voice.

"Yeah, this is Clint Mapes, checking in."

"Yes, Clint. You have news for me?"

"They're here you know, blasted on something for the second day in a row."

"Okay, Clint. Good work. I'll notify The Retrievers and tell them to stand by."

"So, that's all you need from me?"

"Yes, Clint. Keep your eyes on them and call back if anything changes."

Clint hung up the phone and returned to his spot at the table, closest to the window so he could keep an eye on his black Ford 4X4.

He filled his buddies in on the current state of

their observation and what he had just reported in the quick phone call. He grabbed a Marlboro from the open hard pack that lay in the center of the table, right next to the chrome napkin holder.

Charlene, the long time, middle aged waitress came over to refill their mugs for the fifth time that morning.

One of the Marlboro Men slapped her on her lumpy ass.

She pushed his hand away, "Don't, Charley."

All the men at the table laughed. Charlene returned to the back with a load of dirty dishes.

The new fry cook, Jesse, looked up from the grill where he had four different breakfasts going, "Hey, Charlene. Those cowboys giving you a hard time?" His voice was raspy. His dirty blonde hair was pulled back into a ponytail, while his face was pock-marked from teenage acne. He had tattoos on his arms. He couldn't have been more than in his late thirties, and he had a hardened look about him that made most men back down from him, even though Jesse wasn't that big.

Charlene paused at the swinging doorway, "Naw, not really. Charley is just showing off because I've been dating Earl. He's the oldest guy of the four. He smells a whole lot better than Charley. Has more teeth, too."

Jesse grunted, apparently not completely satisfied with Charlene's answer. He dished up two orders, which Charlene took away.

Jesse picked up an egg, expertly cracked it with one hand, slid it onto the grill and underhanded the shell into a nearby garbage can. It was obvious that Jesse Ray Barnes had cooked a few breakfasts in his time. He was listening to a Top 30 radio station from

Sacramento, where they played all the hits. Since they were so far away, the reception was poor with static.

He used a bent coat hanger for an antenna.

When Charlene returned for the other two orders, Jesse finished his thoughts. "Well babe, I try to mind my own business, but if those assholes keep giving you grief, let me know. I'll be glad to go over and have a little talk with them."

Charlene felt a sudden cold shiver as she watched Jesse in action, starting another Omelet. There was something powerful and a little bit scary about this smaller man. She wasn't sure she wanted to unleash him on the old men who sat at the table and had a large influence on what happened in Keddie.

Lance helped Joe to his bare feet again, "Come on, man. Pull it together. You stay here and try to chill while I run over to the store."

Lance helped Joe onto the porch, where he chose to sit on one of the sea shell chairs, "Maybe you need to throw up some more, bro," advised Lance.

Lance departed with his long spider like strides. It occurred to Joe, as he sat on the porch clutching his aching gut, that he was quite simply too stoned to know what to do.

Thank goodness, Lance was apparently fully functional. Usually, it was the other way around, with his buddy being out of it. Joe wondered if he was hungry, or if it was the Magic Mushrooms tearing up his stomach and making him feel like he still needed to puke some more.

Had he been poisoned and was actually dying? Maybe they weren't safe mushrooms to eat, although Lance had never supplied him with any sort of bogus product before. What if he had a ruptured appendix, and by the time anyone diagnosed it, he would kick the can from an exploded gut? Joe wondered if that were the case, how bad it would hurt, and how long would it take him to die?

Lance came back shortly with a sack of groceries and a gallon of milk, "Come on inside, and I'll fix you up with some pancakes. Drink some milk now, and maybe it will coat your stomach. You should feel better."

While Lance bustled around in the kitchen, Joe slumped in a chair at the table and sipped a cold glass of milk. He held one hand to his stomach, which rumbled. He swore to himself that he would never again eat Magic Mushrooms. He was tired of praying to the great toilet God in the sky. He couldn't see himself doing any more acid or mescaline either, but he wasn't quite ready to say never again on those two just quite yet.

Joe heard laughter outside, getting closer. There was the heavy thud of multiple people on the porch. The door opened and Joe put his hands across his eyes and peered at the new arrivals between his fingers.

He saw two young couples, dressed like weekhippies with new blue jeans, fresh tie-dyed shirts, and styled hair on the two males. Their bodies seemed to be of normal shape and size, but when Joe dropped his hands and looked at their faces, he recoiled in horror.

Their facial features melted, their eyes, noses and mouths sliding down like wax baking in a hot oven. The cabin walls behind them moved back and forth, pulsing as though alive, rushing towards Joe's terror stricken face and then retreating back to the limits of his vision.

A tall male with a hooked nose, dark features and long frizzy hair slid forward like a human slinky.

He stopped too close to Joe, peering down at him. He offered his hand in slow motion, "Hi…you must…be…our new roommates…cool…my name is …..Scott….. Scheinblum."

His voice sounded as though he were talking through a reverb, his words deflecting off Joe's skewed vision. Joe offered up his right hand and Scott shook it aggressively.

The texture of Scott's skin was rough, like sandpaper. Joe abruptly pulled his hand back and stared at it. He let out a shrill cry and dashed for the kitchen sink, turned on the cold water full blast, rotating his hand. He glared back at Scott, who had a perplexed look on his face, wondering what in the world Joe's problem was.

Scott slunk over to the kitchen doorway and spoke to Lance, who was at the stove with a large plastic spatula. He was staring at an empty frying pan with the burner on high, a goofy, dreamy smile on his face. He turned to face Scott, "My name is Lance."

He didn't offer his hand. Joe was still at the sink, running water over his right palm..

"What's wrong with your buddy here. Lance? By the way, what's his name? He doesn't seem capable of communicating right now."

"His name is Joe, man."

"Joe Man?"

"No, dude, just Joe. You're bothering me, Scott. I'm trying to cook Joe a pancake."

"Where's your pancake batter?" asked Scott.

"Batter?" replied Lance, looking around and not finding any.

Joe shut off the water, took a long appraising look at Scott, walked past him, sat down and then burst out laughing, a little vomit escaping from his mouth and dribbling onto his empty plate. He picked up his utensils, "Fork you, snot. Oh, I'm so sorry, *Scott.*"

Lance emerged from the kitchen, waving his spatula around, pretending for a minute to be Lawrence Welk, leading his mostly dead orchestra. Lance looked at Scott too, and also began laughing.

Scott retreated to the front room, where another male and two girls waited.

"Scott," said one of the melting face girls, "You're wasting your time. They're obviously stoned out of their gourds. You might as well be talking to the wall."

"Yeah, man, " said the other, taller girl who was also a brunette," Good luck guys. These are your cabin mates for the next three months. Ha."

Lance climbed up one of the chairs and aimed his spatula right at Scott, and then brought it back up to his mouth, acting as if it was open mike night at Denny's. "Hey, hey, looked here boys and girls, women and men, children, dogs, stoners and straights. We're all related, you know, back from the original Adam and Eve, which I also believe is what you might politely currently refer to as a skin magazine. Can you still remember dreams from before you were born? I can." Lance dipped his front shoulder and moved his lowered arm back and forth like a robot. "Follow the ball now. Watch it. I'm going to try to fool you. Got any spare change you'd care to wager on the eventual outcome? Huh, *Scott?*

"By the way, my full name is Lance Granger Potter. You can call me Lance for short. The handsome half Irishman over here is Joe Edgar Bailey. He's not feeling very well this morning, a touch of the flu perhaps. How should I know? I never finished medical school. I intend to make him a pancake as soon as I find the damned batter.

"Sorry, but I can't visit anymore right now. Maybe later, over tea and crumpets, we can exchange motorized birth certificates and sexual preferences. Rest assured, though, despite what you might be thinking right now, we all really do exist in a parallel universe."

"Are you quite done?" asked the first girl.

"Yes. Now I must find my batter."

The second woman spoke next, "My name is Susan, Lance. I want to thank you for that marvelously informative little speech. You've now cleared up all the mysteries of our universe and wrapped them up in a neat little box. Haven't you?"

"You're right. Groove on, Susan."

"Charmed, I'm sure," managed Joe, who wiped his mouth with the sleeve of his red flannel lumberjack shirt.

A half hour later, Joe stood in the center of their room, turning in slow, deliberate circles, staring at the ceiling tiles and trying in vain to count the hundreds of holes. The total came out different every time.

Lance spoke, "Try laying down and relaxing, Joe. You're bumming my trip because you got so ripped you've forgotten who you are and where we are."

"Like I can somehow control how high I get? I told you, that's why I prefer booze now. It's much safer."

Joe finally sat down on the edge of his bed. The bathroom door was closed, and he listened as someone took a long shower. He was also hearing voices. He knew that the rest of them were gathered in the back bedroom and murmuring about him and Lance.

Finally, someone left the bathroom, the door

being shut from the other side. A few minutes later, they heard people moving down the hallway. The front door opened and closed. Joe froze in position, listening for any noise that would indicate that any of them had stayed behind.

Satisfied that they were alone again, Joe opened their bedroom door and walked around the cabin and found no one.

"They're gone," he announced. "The freaking bastards are finally gone. Come on, Lance, let's listen to some music."

Lance jumped up, a joint dangling from the edge of his mouth, "Put on *Jumping Jack Flash.* We haven't heard that one for awhile."

As soon as Keith Richards guitar came blasting out of the speakers, and Mick Jagger started singing, the boys could finally relax and enjoy their high. A shared number successfully smoothed out the rough edges of the 'schrooms.

Feeling organic, Lance made a pot of green tea and added some of Joe's weed to create a potent thirst quencher. He poured them each a cup, and they held their glasses just so, with their pinkies extended into the air. They practiced their phony English accents, which made them sound more like retarded hillbillies than limeys.

Each succeeding record they played sounded better than the previous one. They moved into a comfortable groove and were transported to another dimension, where all concepts of time and reality hung suspended within the vortex of their current psychedelic experience.

There were no problems, no past, and no future. The only thing that mattered was right now.

"Everything is nothing, and nothing is everything," repeated Lance, smiling in his contented, cosmic way. He had said it at least six times thought Joe.

"Where are we right now, then?"

"Good question, considering it is doubtful that we even exist. "

The boys partied on for another two hours, and were maintaining fine until they both took two reds, and within a half hour, they were snoring in their beds.

They were awakened by a sharp rap on their bedroom door. Lance reluctantly got up, grumbling to himself. Scott stood there, leaning over, his long arms folded across his chest. He weaved around like the human slinky that he obviously was.

"Hey, Lance. Fellas. We need to talk."

Joe propped himself up on one elbow, "Hey, beam me up, *snotty*. I'm sorry. That should be, beam me up, *Scotty.* "

Scott moved past Lance and stood at the edge of Joe's bed, his hands resting on his hips, looking like a six-gun shooter from Tombstone.

"Look, *Joe,* that's twice today that you've deliberately mangled my name, and I don't appreciate it. How would you feel if I referred to you as, I don't know, *Joe Schmo.* There, how do you like that, having your shoe on someone else's foot?"

"What you just said about my shoe made no sense," said Joe, sitting up and flexing his fingers, ready to form a flat palm, "First off, I gotta tell you that you have no imagination, Scott. Is that the best insult you can come up with? Joe Schmo? Secondly, if you do keep calling me that, I'll punch you in your long nose. Then, depending on what sort of mood I'm in, mellow or violent, I might kick your whole face in. *Scott.*"

Scott stepped back and bumped into Lance, who shoved him towards the door.

"Well, okay then. Now that we've got that settled, I think, come on into the front room and meet with us.

"What day is it?" asked Lance, looking concerned.

"It's Wednesday. All day."

"Did you guys register for classes already?"

"No. All the Bay Area transfers register tomorrow, starting at nine. Tomorrow is Thursday by the way."

"Huh?" said Joe, confused as to what they were jabbering about, wondering why this hook nosed dweeb was still in their room, bothering them, making demands.

"Come on and join us, guys. We need to establish some house rules that we can all live with. Chris and I don't like the condition you two were in this morning, Let's go. We've got organic chicory coffee, and Susan made a loaf of her famous brown bread."

Joe and Lance followed Scott into the front room. Chris sat on the couch in Joe's favorite spot, sipping a cup of coffee.

Joe realized he was still barefoot. His feet were covered with red dirt. He had thrown on his filthy jeans and vomit stained lumber jack shirt over his bare chest and he was already itching, so he started scratching his armpits while he was moving.

Joe and Lance were directed to two dining room chairs that were set up across from the couch.

"My name is Chris Jewell," said an earnest looking fellow who had blonde dreadlocks that appeared perfect.

Chris used both hands to lift up a plate, "Here. Have a piece of organic wheat brown bread that Susan just made."

Joe reached out, his stomach still rumbling like a volcano getting ready to erupt; only it wouldn't be molten lava coming out.

The thick piece of brown bread felt unusually heavy. He looked up with his head again twisted sideways. He saw Susan and the other girl staring at him from the table.

"What's your name?" he asked the first girl.

"Claire."

"Claire," he repeated, "I like that name. It sounds like a name from *The Great Gatsby.*"

"Who is that?" she asked. "A new rock group?"

Joe shook his head feebly and tried to take a bite. The crust was like petrified wood. He about broke his front teeth off, trying to break off a piece. He finally succeeded,. He chewed, but it never got smaller. He struggled with it, chewing until his jaw got tired, gagging as the piece expanded in his throat, choking him. He ran into the kitchen and retched into the sink.

A moment later, Lance put his right hand on Joe's back, "Hey, man. You all right?"

"Yeah. Great. Never been better." Joe washed the remnants of the brown bread down the sink.

"Have some chicory coffee," suggested Scott.

Joe and Lance poured themselves cups and returned to their chairs. They sipped at it and both put their cups down on the coffee table. Joe thought that the foul smelling and nasty tasting dark liquid tasted like burnt transmission fluid.

Scott began speaking, "We couldn't help but notice that you two were on drugs this morning. You're probably still on them now. You people seem really out of it. Especially you, Joe."

"My," answered Joe, "You're very perceptive. You must be a college student."

Scott ignored the latest insult, "Chris and I don't do drugs, nor do we wish to be around people who are using."

"Did you two ever get high?" asked Lance, "I mean, you guys are sort of dressed like stoners, but then again, you're a little too neat, a bit too clean."

"Well, yes," answered Scott, "I've been clean for two years now. I took some bad LSD and wound up in a psych ward at the hospital for a week. I thought Chris here was trying to infiltrate my brain. Since then, I've never even been tempted. I get high on life."

"What about you, *Swish?*" asked Joe, managing to slur his name too.

"My name is Chris. I used to smoke pot, but I got bored with it. I think for me it was a matter of growing up and learning to deal with my problems and not running away from everything."

"That's the key," chipped in Claire. She was wearing what looked like expensive clothes and also had on a lot of flashy jewelry, "Learn to embrace reality. You have to get your attitude straight before you can experience any measurable growth. It's okay to be normal."

Lance glared at Claire, repeating that dreaded word, *normal,* to himself, over and over.

"He didn't like my brown bread," sniffed Susan, "It won an award at a county fair."

"What county?" asked Joe, "Bangladesh?"

"What is this," asked an obviously agitated Lance, "True confessions from Ken and Barbie?"

"Hardly," answered Scott. "Bottom line is this, you wasteoids. We came up here to attend school and earn our two year degrees. Then, we all have plans to transfer to universities on the east coast, like Harvard and Yale. We knew it was a crap shoot renting a cabin in the woods with strangers. Sharing our living space with a couple of druggies is not going to work for us."

"So," laughed Joe, "When are you moving out?"

'Ha Ha," said Chris.

"Okay then. Here's something we can all live with," said Scott, "We don't care what you two do outside of the cabin. If you use any more drugs here, we'll report you to the Singh's."

"Oooohhh, we're like totally scared, Scotty." said Lance.

Joe stood up, "Listen *fellas*. Stay out of our way and you might not get hurt, and we might allow your continued, inconsequential, shallow existence. Keep screwing with us, and you're gonna be very sorry. We're crazy and don't care about you or anything else. Got that?'

Scott and Chris sat in silence, their mouths hanging half open.

ORGANIC FEAST

CHAPTER SIX

Thursday morning. Registration day for Joe and Lance and the rest of the invading horde of unwashed acid heads and unrepentant weirdoes from the gritty East Bay. At the time, Oakland was proudly declared to be 'Bump City,' by the popular local soul group 'Tower of Power.' Next door was Berkeley, a human Petri dish of radicals, naïve liberals and committed people who rallied and marched against the insane Vietnam War. In addition, they joined any other cause they deemed viable. Their primary objective appeared to be to create random chaos, and hopefully bring down the U.S. Government.

Joe and Lance stood in their small backyard. Leaves were beginning to fall from scrub trees. The sun peaked through the branches and created a collage of moving shadows. The boys were sharing their first marijuana cigarette of the day.

Joe pulled a small paper sack out of his coat pocket and poured a dollop of Old Crow into his crappy tasting, bitter coffee. He wondered if Susan or Scott had brewed the swill.

"Want a little belt?" inquired Joe, holding his bottle aloft. He loved the way a bottle of booze felt in his hand. He also craved the comforting warmness of whiskey to start his day. No thoughts of food.

"Thanks, but no thanks. I don't want to show up for our registration smelling like a booze hound. You do know the smell lingers for hours, don't you? Matter of fact, in your case, I don't think it ever completely goes away anymore."

"Oh, but going there smelling like a Rasta from Jamaica is okay?"

"Big difference, bro. When you smoke weed like we're doing, the wind blows away the bulk of the fumes."

"Nice try, Einstein, but no cigar. Lick your index finger and put it in the air like this." Joe did, and turned around in a complete circle, "Just like I thought. There is no wind this morning."

"What exactly, does that prove?"

"Hell if I know. I used to watch Mr. Greenjeans do it on Captain Kangeroo."

"Well, I basically want a clear head with a base line of mellowness. I was talking to that local chick, Maureen, who hangs out at Greg's cabin and works part time at the lodge restaurant as a waitress. She said most of the good classes are nearly full because the locals got to register already."

"So," said Joe, finishing his coffee with a frown, "We get the remains."

They jumped into the convertible and Joe went through his familiar ritual of lowering the top. They liked riding like that, cool wind in their faces, grooving on the day. He fired up the reliable 390, and the big block came alive, with an uneven, light cam upgrade, which resulted in a loping, rumbling exhaust. Joe dropped the Ford into gear and peeled out of Keddie for the first time since they'd arrived a couple of days previously.

They quickly reached the intersection to the highway, with the old gas station just across the way.

"Over there," shouted Lance, pointing at two girls, standing on the opposite side of the road, looking good with their thumbs out..

"That's Carlene and Debbie. They must not have a car. Let's give them a ride. We can talk to them today like *normal* people."

Joe cautiously looked both ways, twice, before crossing the highway and pulling up in front of the girls. Bud had given him many safe driving tips.

"Morning, ladies," said Lance in an enthusiastic circus barkers voice, "Are you desiring a ride into Quincy for class registration?

"We sure are," said Debbie, a sincere looking smile on her open, friendly face. Carlene stood there, not looking at anyone, but monitoring the ride situation.

Lance leaped out, swung the car door open wide, pulled the front seat back forward, and gestured for the girls to enter.

Debbie and Carlene clambered in. Lance slammed the door extra hard, smiled with a crooked grin, and spoke sharply to Joe, "Carry on, Jeeves."

Joe grimaced at Lance's lame attempt at humor, undoubtedly trying to impress the girls with his worldly ways. Ordering him to drive. My gawd, thought Joe, sometimes he thought Lance would sell him out for a joint.

He stole a glance at Carlene's beauty from the rear view mirror. She was dressed in tight white shorts and a loose green blouse. Her simple but smart look accentuated her tanned arms and legs. She had long, luxurious black hair that cascaded down her back.. When she caught his eyes in the mirror, Joe felt embarrassed and turned red and tried to focus on

95

driving. The heavily traveled two lane road had many twists and turns.

Halfway through a hairpin corner, Joe cranked the wheel hard to the right, floored it and the car kicked into passing gear. He went into a controlled skid, straightened the wheel, backed off until the tires gripped and the nose was headed in the correct direction and then blasted towards the next curve. He was having fun, showing off, hoping to impress Carlene. Lance could have Debbie. She was nice, but a little bit too preppy for Joe's likes. He preferred brown skinned women like Italians, Mexicans and American Indians.

Joe slowed down a bit as he dreamily piloted his car towards Quincy. His thoughts fluttered back to 1968. Carlene Romo was a junior in high school while Joe was a senior.

She was popular, with a reputation among the guys in the locker room as a chick that was willing 'to go all the way.' Carlene was a near perfect mix of French and American Indian. Joe had been secretly in love with her from a distance for two years.

Joe knew that Carlene had no idea of his infatuation with her, nor the long distance longing, and the physical pain he suffered whenever he saw her walking hand in hand with another guy. There seemed to be a different suitor every week. None of them ever lasted for long. Maybe she got bored easily and dismissed them without a second thought, knowing that the following day, a parade of hopeful guys would ring her doorbell, inquiring if she was available for a date.

Carlene's brother, nicknamed Squirt for his diminutive size, was in Joe's class and they occasionally played sandlot baseball on the high school diamond, which was close to Squirt's home on Key Route Boulevard. To get to school, all he had to do was walk out his front door. After their game, they would sometimes duck under the empty green bleachers and sneak a smoke. Squirt was short, so Joe used to kid him about how cigarettes had stunted his growth, but his semi friend did not find such speculation amusing.

One warm spring Saturday, after a long pick up game at the field, Joe returned with Squirt to his house to get a cool drink. Carlene was at the door, and Joe remembered his heart leaping into his throat. She was wearing skimpy cut-offs and a white halter top with no bra. Joe greeted Carlene, and she said hello back but didn't use his name.

He wallowed in her sweet as an Easter Lilly essence. Her aura was like an intoxicating perfume that nearly made him mad with teenage angst and unfulfilled desire.

He and Squirt sat in the kitchen drinking red Kool Aid and eating cookies, when Bobby Carbo showed up. He was four years older then Joe and Squirt, and was a no nonsense hard guy who dropped out of school in the 10th grade to take a half-assed job on a factory assembly line.

The sight of Bobby striding through the front room brought back terrifying memories for Joe, from being in the same P.E. class. Whenever they went swimming in the nearby school pool, Carbo swam around, looking for someone he could try to drown.

The coaches thought it was amusing when Bobby leaped out of the water and pounced on top of some 85 pound kid, holding the 13 year old's head underwater. Sometimes the coaches had to use a long painted pole to rescue the eighth grader, yelling at Bobby to go play with kids his own size.

Joe heard Carlene's door close. Shortly after, there was nasty sounding laughter, and then the sound of bouncing bedsprings. Then the bed springs began a slow, rhythmic squeaking, gradually building up to a furious pace. Bobby grunted and Carlene moaned.

"Is it like this often?" asked Joe, trying to avoid using the name Squirt too much, but his real name, Randolph, was almost as bad.

Squirt shrugged his shoulders, "What can I do? She's who she is, and I have to live here too. It really gets bad when multiple guys climb through her window at midnight."

There was another volley of ribald laughter, and then the sound of a door opening and heavy footsteps coming their way. Bobby Carbo burst into the kitchen. his groin covered with a bath towel. Sweat was glistening on his muscular body. and ran in droplets over the large Devil tattoo on his right shoulder.

"Hi, Bobby" squeaked Squirt.

Kiss ass, thought Joe

Bobby ripped open the refrigerator door and scanned the contents, "Hey! Pip Squeak! Don't your old man drink beer?"

"No. Even if he did, don't you think he'd notice if you took one?"

"Probably not. I'd shoplift a replacement. Soon as I was done with your sister that is." Bobby Carbo finished with his trademark, sinister laugh.

"Big deal," replied Kenny, "Everyone sleeps with Carlene. Everybody except Joe."

Joe hadn't seen that rip coming. He wondered if Squirt was preparing to heave him even further under the bus. *Nice friend*, he thought.

Light footsteps sounded in the hall, and Carlene joined them. She wore a bathrobe loosely about her body, revealing a copious amount of cleavage. Joe appreciated the whiteness of her large breasts contrasting nicely with her tanned skin.

"Bobby," she whined, reaching for him, "You said you'd be right back. I'm tired of waiting."

"Hold on, Carlene. I gotta finish a little business with these two punks, first."

Holy crap, thought Joe. *Why would Carbo be mad at him?*

Carlene dropped a bomb, "Squirt is not my real brother by blood. We're both adopted. Do what you want with him."

Bobby turned on Joe, "What are you looking at, punk?"

"Nothin."

"Bullshit! You was checking out my woman's boobs. I remember you now. We was in the swimming pool together in P.E. I thought I drowned you."

Penny grabbed Bobby by his arms causing her bathrobe to fly open, and Joe got a quick eyeful as she pulled Bobby from the kitchen.

Just before disappearing from sight, he pointed at Squirt and Joe, "You turd eater's best be gone when I come out again!"

Joe and Squirt stared at the table top, then Joe stood up and silently slipped out the back door. He never went to Squirt's house again.

Joe was startled when Lance shouted at him to slow down. They had just entered the Quincy city limits, and Joe was clocking 75 in a 35. The tires screeched when he slammed on the brakes.

He glanced in the rear view mirror again, and saw Carlene and Debbie laughing.

They cruised through all three blocks of the

Quincy main drag, passing a grocery store, a couple of cafes, a hardware business and ten bars. Joe slowed slightly as the granite façade of the County Courthouse loomed into view, its flags whipping in the breeze.

Nearing the far city limits, Joe turned left into the Plumas County Fairgrounds and parked in front of the 4H building. The barn doors were open, and Joe observed the corrals and stalls that held prized animals during the annual summer fair.

The girls hopped out, yelled thanks and disappeared into the administration building

"Guess that's where we should go too," said Joe

There were only a dozen other assorted cars and trucks parked around them.

Inside the building was an auditorium with a dozen folding tables set up in a semi circle. Men in shirtsleeves and no ties and women in plain dresses sat behind the tables with clipboards, schedules and class rosters.

Small clusters of students milled around, talking amongst themselves, discussing classes that still had room for a few more. Voices and scraping chair sounds echoed around the large room that was other-wise mostly empty.

Lance picked up a brochure from an unmanned table and Joe squeezed closer for a look.

"What are you doing, Joe? Don't take the same classes as me. Geez, we already live in the same place and are business partners too. Let's not spend all our days together also."

"Sorry, man. I thought you might want to ride to school with me, seeing as how you don't have a car of your own. Then again, you're always burning me on gas money, so screw it. Walk or hitchhike you jerk."

"I'll manage," answered Lance, turning his back

on Joe.

Joe grabbed another brochure and stepped away from Lance, peering at it, not knowing where to start. He had naively assumed there would be counselors available, but he didn't see any. All of the tables were clearly marked as to what class they represented.

While Joe pretended to look at the brochure, Debbie walked by and laughed at him, "It might be easier to read if you turned it right side up."

Joe mumbled thanks, turned it around and continued to be distracted. He observed his best friend joining a group of six who were all dressed like freaks. The guys had long hair with colored headbands. The girls were wearing brightly colored clothes, and one of them had on a men's Stetson Hat. They greeted Lance warmly, and Joe felt himself feeling jealous of the ease at which Lance made new friends.

Joe gravitated to the English table. It was his favorite subject. He saved everything he wrote; even the stuff he immediately knew was crap. He assumed that all writers sometimes wrote junk, mainly to get it out of their system, where its disastrous influence could no longer contaminate the quality writing that they knew was somewhere in their head. It was just waiting to be tapped into, like an undiscovered rich vein of gold.

A hatchet face older woman greeted Joe. Her coarse gray hair was pulled back into a severe bun. She smelled like mothballs, and her garish red lipstick emphasized her oversized mouth. Joe speculated that she probably stuffed deep fried Pygmies into it, bit them in half, and then spit out the crunchy heads. Her nametag read 'MS. GERTZ.'

"Yes?" she asked in a challenging voice.

"Uh, yeah. I'd like to sign up for creative

writing 110, with Mr.Bellamy."

"Fine. I need to see your college transcripts."

"Transcripts? No one told me to bring those to registration."

"I have to see them, young man," demanded Ms. Gertz, "I can't just take your word for it. Hurry up. You're holding up the line."

"I had Laney College mail them up here a month ago. Don't you have them on file?"

Ms. Gertz pointed to a huge stack of dozens of bank file boxes, "It's probably in there somewhere. We will be moving all the records into the new campus this spring. There is no sense in pawing through them now. Where would we store them? Out where they keep the 4H pigs and cows?"

"Well then, dammit it lady. What the hell can I take then? Do I have to start all over again with bone-head English 101 because you people don't have your shit together?"

Ms. Gertz stood up. Crap, thought Joe, she was taller than Lance. He looked to see if she might have an adam's apple that might reveal a reason for the fact she was the size of a pro football lineman and looked just as fierce.

She poked a sausage sized finger in the center of his chest, "How dare you use profanity with me, young man. Get out of my line right now. You won't be taking *ANY* English classes as long as I'm department head."

Joe glared back at her. *Bitch!*

As he turned to leave, he heard, "Hey Bailey."

It was Elliott Rosen, a member of his high school graduation class of 1969. Elliott was the pro-totype Jewish carpenter hippie, with his long frizzy hair, slight build and scraggly beard. Joe would never have tried to grow it out if he knew that it was going to look like he had glued random pieces of Brillo Pads on his face. Maybe he would suggest to Rosen that next time he was back in Berkeley for some Bar Mitzvah, that he see this great local Italian Barber by the name of Frank.

"How ya doin, Elliott?" asked Joe. They exchanged soul shakes.

"Fine, man. I didn't think I'd see you and Lance here. Where are you guys crashing?"

"In a cabin in Keddie with a couple of real assholes. What about you?"

"I got stuck in a cheap apartment in town. I live right over a Chinese Restaurant where I eat so often that they felt sorry for me and let me be a part time dish-washer, even though I'm not Chinese."

"No," said Joe, "You're not."

"Too bad for now. Maybe we can work some-thing out to share a house for next quarter. What about Lance?"

"What about him?"

Joe worked the rest of the tables, managing to avoid any more out of control profanity laced tirades. Within two hours, he had signed up for 15 units that included Archery, Volleyball, Music Appreciation, Sociology, and one tough one, Biology. He had taken it twice in high school and despised cutting up frogs and flinging dissected guts at chicks who he knew were squeamish. He hated the stench of formaldehyde, and he now associated it with death.

Finished, Joe drifted outside and sat on the grass near the flagpole. He could hear the flags whipping around, sounding like someone pounding on taut canvas with a nightstick. He wondered if he should bother waiting for Lance. Screw him, he thought. If he didn't need his rides anymore, he'd just split and hopefully leave him stranded. *Ingrate.*

He enjoyed a Marlboro and watched as more students filed out of the building. Some of them drove away, others walked to the main drag and dis- appeared in seconds. He mostly saw kids he decided were 'heads.' He saw very few 'straights, which is what everyone thought he was. He still had almost five years left in The Coast Guard Reserves, so he had to get his hair cut short every month, right before his weekend drills.

Lance finally sauntered out of the administration building and joined him on the grass, "How did it go? Did you get all the classes you wanted? I did."

"No. I got them all except for creative writing. I ran into a road block there."

"Was the road block named 'Ms. Gertz'?"

"Yeah. How did you know?"

"I overheard her talking to a colleague and I think they were discussing you. Something about reporting the incident to the dean and getting you suspended."

"Great," said Joe, tossing his butt to the ground and letting it smolder, "I go through all the bullshit to get here, and then get kicked out on my first day because they're too lame to have the transcripts in correct order. I just can't catch a break, Lance."

Lance didn't respond. Instead, he pulled out a joint and smoked it by himself, eating the short roach. He didn't offer any to Joe,. *Dickhead.*

"So," said Joe, "I saw you're friendly with that hippie looking group that left in the VW. How do you know them?"

"Actually, none of your damned business. We're not married, you know."

"Man, why are you so touchy lately?"

"Sorry. That was the local chick, Maureen Hess, the waitress I told you about. She came to be with her new friends, all transfers from Laney. They just ordered twenty more hits of acid. I'm going to run out fast at this pace."

"Cool."

Lance dug into his pants and pulled out a wad of cash. He peeled off a ten dollar bill and handed it over, "Here's your cut for the week."

"Double cool. That'll buy me two fifths."

"By the way, try to stay sober this afternoon. We're invited to an organic dinner tonight at Nature's Health Foods. It's just down another block. Maureen said it would probably be black beans and dirty rice. It's only a buck."

"All right. As long as they don't serve brown bread by Susan."

Once back at Keddie, Lance walked over to Carlene and Debbie's cabin and invited them to go to the organic dinner. Joe didn't care about the meal. He was just excited about the prospect of spending more time with Carlene.

With nothing pressing that they had to do or accomplish, Joe and Lance, sat on the front porch in the seashell chairs and openly smoked a joint. It was another gorgeous afternoon in the mountains, although it felt a bit colder than the day before.

"You know what your core problem is Joe, besides being severely out of balance?

"What?"

"You view reality as essentially evil."

"First define reality."

"Right here, right now. This is all that matters,

all that counts."

"If a bear takes a dump in the woods and there's no one else around, will it smell?"

"Boy did you mangle that one. It's supposed to be about a tree falling. Does it make any sound if no one is there to listen?"

"Who gives a shit? You wanna know what my problem is, huh Lance? I am terribly disappointed to find out that nearly everything I thought was true is a lie. Usually, a big fat lie."

"And I thought I was cynical," answered Lance.

"I hate it when people label me as a cynic. I'm a realist. Next, they point out that I'm sarcastic and negative too. I'm just trying to explain reality to them, that there is a disnctive possibility that they don't even exist. I understand that the concept is some times hard to grasp, but does anything in life besides death ultimately make any sense?"

Lance changed the subject, "I miss our old buddy, Alex Chance. I wonder how he's doing in Army Helicopter Flight School. I wish he was here right now, so we could get high with him and laugh about old times."

"Yeah, I do too. I'd still like to know what made him want to volunteer for hazardous duty. I think the casualty rate for Helicopter Pilots in Vietnam is over 50%."

"Well, Alex is an adrenalin junkie. I learned the hard way not to dare him to do something dangerous and stupid, because he would do it. The only catch was, you had to do the same stunt with him."

"What's the scariest thing you and he did?"

"The dumbest and most frightening thing we did was to race down a steep hill while we were inside separate Safeway shopping carts with no way to steer or stop. We wound up shooting through a red light at the intersection at the bottom of the hill. We missed all the cars, but we slammed into the curb at high speed and it threw us into some bushes at least 20 feet away.

"We easily could have been killed or seriously injured. Alex dared me to do it again, but I said no, we might not be so lucky the next time. I think he was disappointed."

Joe pondered something, "I wonder if Alex will try and fly a combat mission while on LSD?"

"Well, if anyone could pull it off, Alex could."

Carlene rode up front with Joe while he drove them back to Quincy for the organic dinner. They hadn't said even ten words to each other, while Lance and Debbie were in his back seat, gabbing like a couple of girls. Joe turned on the radio and only got static. He wondered what the hicks around here listened to for entertainment. The daily farm report? Scratchy recordings of roosters crowing?

Joe shut if off, mad at himself for not being able to start a conversation.

"Carlene," he finally blurted out, "What's your major?"

"Same as yours and everyone else too. Basic courses until I finish my second year, and then I'll select a major and probably finish my B.A. at Hayward State."

"Uh, are you taking Biology this quarter?"

Carlene nodded her head.

"How about that. We have at least one class together. I can give you a ride if you want."

"We'll see."

Nature's Health Foods was located in a run

down building with chipping orange and yellow paint that was previously a ten cent Taco joint. Some lazy ass painted the bright orange sign 'NATURES,' right over the flakes

Joe parked next to Maureen's psychedelic painted VW. There was also a 1961 Dodge Dart, a red torpedo back mid sixties Volvo, a black Hearse that had been seen around Keddie, and a converted school bus that was hand painted with crazy swirls and random designs in bright, day-glo colors.

Nature's was crowded, with twenty or so young people sitting cross legged on the floor, surrounding low tables made of plywood sheets.

Joe smelled Patchouli Oil and unwashed organic bodies. He observed one long hair reading *'Bury My Heart At Wounded Knee.'* A lame Bob Dylan record was being played with his twangy voice coming out of shitty speakers.

Joe felt uncomfortable, as though he didn't fit in at all. Maybe Lance did. At least he looked the part. The four of them squeezed into a small spot that was at the far end of the table. They folded their legs into the lotus position, something that Joe found unnatural and painful. If God wanted people to sit like that, he would have given them bent legs to start with, and chairs would never have been invented.

A bald, middle aged man in a white robe appeared. He tugged at a chain around his neck. and produced a tiny bell from behind his long white beard. When he shook it, everyone fell silent.

"Welcome, brothers and sisters. My name is Malcom, and the young people working in the kitchen and serving you are members of our collective. We are The People's Commune. We love you. Many of us live in the school bus outside. We have opened 'Natures' to provide residents with an alternative to the meat eater restaurants in this town. We serve healthy, tasty vege- tarian meals. If you still eat meat, I would strongly urge you to stop. You are eating something that was once alive and had a soul.

"Our members will serve you now. We will have Sunshine walking around your table with our donation jar. We are suggesting that each of you offer a dollar to help cover our costs. If you are broke and hungry, then please, break bread with us for free and then donate when you are able. No one, in this wealthy, bourgeois country of ours of haves and have nots, should ever go hungry.

"Afterwards, you are all invited to join us in group meditation and some chanting. Now, please eat, and be happy. Cast your worries to the wind. You are among friends now."

There was a smattering of applause as Malcom moved down the table, shaking hands, hugging, putting his hand on shoulders. He greeted familiar faces and introduced himself to strangers. Joe thought his de-meanor to be similar to a politician working a room, seeking donations and votes.

Anemic looking young people with shaved heads served dinner. They all wore long white robes with colorful sashes of deep purple, green, blue and some darker brown ones. Joe wondered if the sashes were an indicator of some sort of level achieved, or if they held any particular significance.

Large bowls of a goopy brown concoction were passed from hand to hand. No one talked much. Joe wa-tched in disgust as his fellow diners dug into the glop with a wooden serving spoon and dropped it onto their paper plate with a thud.

When it was passed to Joe, he only took a tiny

serving, "I'm not very hungry."

It smelled and looked burnt. He looked around and observed others eating it.

Joe addressed a longhaired pimple faced kid who was sitting near him, chewing earnestly, "What's this called?"

"Organic wheat germ porridge."

Joe took a tentative bite, chewing the porridge for a while and then spit it back on his plate. It left a disgusting taste in his mouth. He reached for one of the communal water jugs, removed the cork and drank deeply and placed the jug back on the plywood. Bits of debris and brown chunks were floating in the water.

A smiling, waif of a girl stopped next to Joe and held her donation jug out. Joe looked up, smiled back, and then wondered if he should pay for Carlene too. It wasn't as if they were on a date, plus she had ignored him all evening, but maybe if he did, she might like him better.

Joe handed the girl two dollars, "What's your name?" he asked.

"My name is Sunshine. What is yours?"

"Joe."

"Well, Joe. How do you like your dinner?"

"You want the truth?"

"Of course. Our master, Malcom, teaches us that speaking the truth moves us closer to our vulnerable inner child."

"Well, no offense intended, Sunshine, but I can see why all you members are so thin. I wouldn't feed this to a dog. I'm going to leave here hungry, and go find myself a giant cheeseburger with fries and a large coke. What do you think of that?"

Sunshine set the jar down, picked up Joe's right hand, and held it between her own small hands. She closed her eyes and contemplated for a moment, "I sense a great deal of anger in your aura."

She released his hand, picked up her jar, and smiled.

"You sense aura pretty good," remarked Joe.

"Anger is fear. It is negative energy disguised as pain. When I gave up sugar, salt and meat, I was able to move beyond basic enlightenment. Our master is a prophet of God, sent to us from the heavens to show us the way to a higher level of awareness and under-standing. Our goal is to be able to interpret true reality through the activation of our third eye."

Joe could only stare. He was enamored with her beauty and tranquility.

"Goodbye Joe. Come back. We offer classes on these concepts that are available to nonmembers. The donation is only five dollars for an hours lecture from Malcom."

Sunshine lingered for a moment longer and then moved down the line, collecting more dollars.

"Third eye?" muttered Joe, raising his eyebrows and looking around.

Carlene turned to him, "Did you pay for mine too?"

"Yes."

She resumed her conversation with Debbie.

Joe went outside to catch a smoke. He walked over to the bus and checked out the psychedelic paint job. It had been done with brushes, and some panels looked like real art. Others appeared as though some drunks had thrown a can of paint against the side and watched it splatter and drip down the sides, and then they just left it like that. Hippies, he thought.

A few minutes later, Lance joined him, "We're gonna stay for the meditation and chanting. It's free tonight. How about you, Joe? It might do you some good, shake off some of that cynicism that you are shackled down with. Plus, I saw you talking with that cute little chick. I tried to imagine her with hair, and I think she'd be perfect for you."

Joe tossed his cigarette to the dirt and ground it out, "I can't believe you want to spend time with these commune fools. They think Malcom is a prophet sent by God, and they call him master. If you don't watch out old buddy, they're gonna hook you by promising you the world, and as they're reeling you in like a fish, they're gonna be taking your wallet. If you don't watch out, they could steal your life too."

Lance started back, and then paused, "You're right, Joe. Maybe mellowness isn't for you. There's no alcohol here, is there? Go ahead and split. Malcom already said he would see to it that we got a ride back with Greg, who is driving the Hearse. They live in Keddie too."

Joe headed for his car and watched as his old friend disappeared inside.

ROAD SIDE HAIRCUT

CHAPTER SEVEN

It was Tuesday, the inaugural day for the brand new Feather River College. Classes took place at the County Fairgrounds. The new campus, halfway between Keddie and Quincy, would open in the spring of 1971.

Gary Hess walked across the fairground parking lot towards his first class in temporary Module D at nine A.M.. He occasionally paused to pull up his pants that sagged because he refused to buy a larger size, and now they wouldn't fit over his ass. That is why he was also wearing his long, winter raincoat even though the sun was out.

His new fancy cowboy boots from Roy's Outfitters in Quincy made an impressive clomping sound on the asphalt. He practiced strutting a little bit, kind of like those Black Panther Negroes did down in Oakland. He'd seen them on TV, and it looked like they were attracting a lot of chicks, maybe because of the cocky, fluid way they moved. Unfortunately, with his current girth, it made him look like a 250 pound spastic struggling to walk with a large stick up his ass. In addition, he didn't know what to do with his arms and hands, so he wound up thrusting them in and out in herky jerky motions.

He felt a nervous flutter in his stomach. It was

the same feeling he used to get on the first day of high school, when he had new clothes to change into for at least the first three days. Back then, he would agonize over what he could wear, and he was already self conscious about his increasing mass.

It was common for him to get into a fistfight during the first week. It was usually some new kid in school, who wanted to make an instant name for himself by beating up the local, acknowledged tough guy, Gary Hess. Gary would win of course, usually with just one or two of his heavy punches that he deliberately aimed for his opponent's throat, nose, mouth, or perhaps he would give them a sharp kick into their gonads, just for variety.

Gary could also take vast amounts of punishment if needed. He actually liked the taste of his own blood, and just that first drop would turn his vision red and then he would go berserk, putting more then one kid in the hospital. He was never charged with assault, because he had at least fifty witnesses that would testify that he was defending himself, and it also helped that the Sheriff was his step dad.

The older and larger he got, the less he had to fight. He had earned his reputation as a cruel and vicious thug, evolving into the quintessential bully. He was able to get his weight under control for awhile when he played football and wrestled as a heavyweight at Quincy High School. He earned two varsity letters, but didn't bother to get a purple and yellow Quincy High School varsity athlete jacket. What for, he thought?

His long career as a bully started in grammar school. He and his buddies, Randy-Bob, Dave and sometimes Reno, would steal other, weaker kid's lunch money. In high school, he rolled with the fast crowd, drank beer for lunch with the others, and walked around cocky with a pack of Tareyton's rolled up in his T shirt. He wanted to look like that cool biker dude, Marlon Brando, in *The Wild Ones.*

By the time they were seniors, Gary Hess and his buddies were scaring many of the adults in Quincy and Keddie. All of their fathers still worked at The Quincy Mill. They drove badly dented pickups, bowled on teams on Wednesday night at Big Al's Lanes, and flirted with the cute waitress from the snack bar, Trudy.

The grown men had one other thing in common. They had lost control of their sons. As a group, Gary, Randy Bob, Dave and Reno had allegedly beaten up a carload of Indians, robbed them, and then launched their car off a steep cliff into the Feather River. There were other, even more disturbing rumors too, but no one had identified them so far as the assailants.

Gary walked into the light blue temporary classroom. He passed an unoccupied teachers desk on the right, stopped, and looked down an aisle with two desks with chairs on both sides. It went back around forty feet he figured. He observed his sister, Maureen, halfway back, laughing with some of her stoner friends. She saw him and then looked away and kept talking to a guy with a long blonde ponytail.

Fine, sis. Go ahead. Act like you don't know me. Maybe I won't know you so well anymore either.

He took the first aisle seat next to a small, nervous fellow. Gary sort of recognized him from Quincy High. He wondered if he had beaten the guy up in high school, or maybe stole his lunch money when they were 12. Hell, he couldn't remember all his victims. In addition, they changed the way they looked over the years. *Assholes.*

Gary scanned the interior walls. They were replaceable gray panels, with clear evidence of recent water leaks and erosion damage. The ceiling was small white squares with infinite amounts of holes and six, long, humming, overhead fluorescent lights.

Behind the wooden desk that had an empty surface, were a blank chalkboard and an American Flag.

A younger looking woman hurried into the mobile and dropped her briefcase and a full brown lunch sack on the middle of the desk. She wore thin framed glasses with round lenses on her short nose, and had a soft featured, kind face. She pulled off a heavy winter coat and hung it on the rack.

"Good morning. class," she said in a cheery voice, "I hear it gets cold around here in the winter, so I've come prepared. My name is Amy Hanson, and I'm sorry if I'm a bit late."

Gary focused on a large chrome peace symbol on a silver chain that hung from Amy Hanson's neck. *'So, it's gonna be like that, huh? A hippie instructor?'*

Gary heard a couple of guys behind him, snickering. He wondered if they were laughing at him, and if so, why? They did it again, louder and Gary turned quickly, accidently hitting his seatmate in his face with his elbow, "Sorry," he said, not even looking to see if he had caused any damage.

Ms. Hansen cleared her throat, and Gary returned his attention to her. He thought she was attractive in a sexy librarian sort of way. Not really his type though, as he doubted she knew how to kill, gut, and cook a squirrel in less than two hours. That's the kind of woman he was looking for, not one of these educated, stuck up bitches.

"I will be your instructor this quarter. We are

going to dissect society as a whole, and learn how it impacts us as individuals and groups. I know for a lot of you, this is your first college experience. It is my goal to not only teach you, but to also challenge you. I want you to realign your core belief system relating to our society and how your perceptions may or may not be valid. Why do different groups of people behave the way they do? A lot of the benefit of a college education is learning how to expand your horizons and experimenting with fresh ideas, and then applying these newly discovered concepts to your own lives."

Gary shifted in his chair. He glowered at the guy next to him, who was holding a Kleenex up to his bloody nose. The fella scooted closer to the wall, apparently to maximize the amount of space between him-himself and Gary.

Gary Hess sighed. Five minutes into his college education, and he was already bored. Who cared how other people lived? As long as he had Spam to eat and booze to drink and fish to catch at the lake, and of course his Jeep, then he was fine with the way things were. Why were the liberals always trying to change everything into communism?

Amy continued. "There will be mandatory reading assignments on a weekly basis in one of four textbooks. You will be required to purchase them, or at least have weekly access, maybe double up with a friend from this class. I will pass out a mimeographed list indicating the texts, and the assigned reading for this week. "

A girl directly behind Gary raised her hand, "Ms Hanson?"

"Yes. Please call me Amy."

"Okay, Amy. Where is the campus bookstore?"

A weird duck voice came from the back,

"Where the pigs are. Oink, oink."

Amy ignored the comedian. It was her theory that if you recognize him right away, it would give him validation. She passed a stack of book lists down each row. Gary grabbed two, wadded one up and tossed it towards the fellow that he had mistakenly belted in the nose with his elbow. He laughed when the dork cringed and instinctively raised his hands to protect his face. His nose was already swelling up. Gary looked at it and chuckled.

Gary pondered the list of four different textbooks. He wondered how much each of them would cost. He'd never had to buy schoolbooks in high school.

Amy returned to the front of the room and continued her lecture, "In this class, we will study current American society and compare it to others, such as ancient Rome and Greece. We will list and consider stereotypes, prejudices, and alleged truisms. The first topic we're going to tackle is a hot one. Vietnam. We will discuss the root cause of this absurd, illegal war, and the incalculable damage it has inflicted on Vietnam and the Vietnamese people."

Gary raised his hand, and heard the snickering again. Now he was sure they were mocking him.

"Amy, you just mentioned all the damage to Vietnam, but what about the sacrifice and loss and injuries to thousands of our serviceman? What about the incalculable damage they've absorbed, trying to save freedom for people like you."

"People like me, huh? Just what exactly is that supposed to mean?"

"You're a liberal hippie, right? Look what you're wearing around your neck."

"What is your name, young man?"

"Gary Hess, maam."

"What my political views are is my business. In addition, as far as the way I look, I dress myself. The question is, who dresses you? Your mother? I'm sorry, she must be blind to send you out the door looking like a picnic table."

Gary couldn't think of a good comeback. Why was this professor insulting his mother as well as him?

"Well, *Gary Hess,* let's suppose I am a liberal. That doesn't make me any less patriotic then you. Have you ever served in the military?"

"No, maam. I'm not able to qualify physically."

The comic in the back was at it again, "Oink, oink."

Amy took in a deep breath," I'm afraid I don't have any sympathy for baby killers. Our misguided, programmed soldiers are sacrificed like Chessboard pawns. They damage their bodies and lives for what? The benefit of a few cynical and rich? Our troops invade a sovereign country and then bomb the hell out of civilians, mothers, children, and helpless old men. All slaughtered or splashed with napalm. Our men rape, pillage, and annihilate, all under the ruse of this absurd concept that we are making a stand in the sand, preventing the creeping cancer of communism. Oh no, if our arms manufacturers don't make their obscene profits, life as we know it is gone."

Joe whispered to Lance, "She talks just like you. Never shuts up."

When Lance didn't respond, Joe poked him in his ribs until Lance let out an audible "Ug!"

Amy paused, "I'm sorry, Gary, but when our soldiers get wounded or killed, I feel they're getting exactly what they deserve."

Gary responded hotly, "My older brother, Jimbo, is missing in action. Four years now. He wasn't a murderer or rapist. He was a mill worker and fisherman like me, and yeah, Amy, he was fighting for the rights of confused people like you. You've no right to spout off propaganda when you don't know what you're talking about. You're not patriotic. You're a traitor in disguise. Jimbo was just following orders."

"Hitler's henchmen claimed the same defense in the Nuremberg trials after World War Two. They hung most of the Nazis pigs. Swine. I'm almost sorry your brother is missing, Gary, but if he'd had the moral courage to become a contentious objector or seek political asylum in Canada, then he'd most likely still be alive."

"Yeah," came the now familiar, sardonic voice from the back of the classroom, "He'd be living in a tarpaper shack with no electricity or water, driving a wrecked pickup, drinking beer and working at the dumb mill. That's a life?"

Gary swiveled around and stared, but he was looking at twenty other students, and couldn't tell who had said it for sure. He was suspicious of the straight looking guy sitting next to the smelly hippie. The shorthaired dude looked like a smartass, even when he wasn't talking and was just sitting there.

He wondered if they were one of those queer couples that were now called gay.

Gary returned his attention to Amy who avoided his hostile glare. He felt himself getting madder, losing control. Damn, if she were only a man. He'd invite him outside and then he would pummel him, teaching him a lesson he'd never forget.

Amy returned to her lecture, as though nothing of significance had just transpired. She was a veteran of Civil Rights marches in the south, and more recently, had helped lead a sit in and radical revolt at Cal

Berkeley. She had teamed up with fellow activists to organize mass protests that tied up the cops and nearly paralyzed at entire city. Martial law was declared at one point, and the National Guard had been called up and large amounts of troops were sent to Berkeley.

Amy jumped at the opportunity to teach at Feather River. Retired from rabble rousing, she could now focus on snow skiing in the winter and rafting in the summer.

Dealing with local half-wits like Gary Hess was child's play for Amy. She cut her radical teeth by hanging out with and supporting the Oakland Black Panthers and isolated pockets of secretive Weather Underground members.

"There will not be any tests in this class. It is simply pass or fail. If you do not show up for five classes, without a doctor's excuse, you'll be booted out. This class is full, and your spot will be taken by the next person waiting in line. Ideally, I'd like all of you to finish the semester, but sometimes situations change. People change. Any questions?"

"Sort of like a Soccer game that ends at nothing to nothing."

This time Gary was able to positively I.D. the speaker. It was that straight looking smartass sitting with John Lennon.

"What was that?" asked Amy. She knew she had to confront him and embarrass him in front of the class. She'd seen his kind before. Their cynicism and sarcasm and negative vibes were like having a blooming poison oak plant hanging from the doorway. If he kept it up after being warned, she'd drop his ass.

"If there are no tests," he said, "How will be judged?"

"What is your name?"

"Joe Bailey."

"Cho Mama," said Lance in a low voice that sounded similar to a duck.

Amy knew she had no choice. She had to do battle with both of them now.

"Excuse me. What did you just say? I was asking your classmate what his name is, and for some reason, you responded with a joke name delivered in a weird voice. What gives with you two? This isn't grade school you know."

"Cho Mama, Amy," responded Lance in a slowed down voice, "Is inner city slang, most comm.-only used by hip Negroes with an East Oakland killing zone address."

"Are you mocking me, mister…..?

"Lance Potter, and I'm glad you got to meet me. I'm from Berkeley, and in that city, as well as parts of Richmond and the flatlands of Oakland, 'Cho Mama' is a commonly used descriptive adjective."

"That's very interesting, Mr. Potter. I earned my Masters Degree in Education from Cal Berkeley two years ago. In all my time in the Bay Area, six years, I can't recall ever hearing that phrase used even once. I intend to honor my contract and teach this class. If I have to remove you two clowns, right now, to protect the rights of the other students to learn, I won't hesitate to do so."

"Sorry," muttered Joe.

"Yeah Amy, sorry. It won't happen again."

"It better not, because one more smart ass remark or animal noise from either of you, and you both get kicked to the curb. Is that clear to you?"

They nodded their heads and folded their hands on top of their desks.

Lance, having eaten three bowls of Joe's

homemade chili passed a major silent gas bomb. Students near him began gagging. Fortunately for Joe and Lance, Amy was outside for a minute, talking to some older guy in a suit who had requested her presence a few moments previously.

Gary was offended by the odor. He turned around and started to get up, but changed his mind, figuring this wasn't a good place or time to rearrange their faces. He'd get them eventually. He always did.

Amy returned and offered up another apology and then launched into a lecture about Vietnam since World War Two. She gave the class a history lesson when she described how the French had committed combat troops to the area and suffered so many causalities that they had completely withdrawn. For color, she added that this included a company of crack, highly trained, French Foreign Legion mercenaries.

Gary sighed as Amy droned on. He didn't understand. If this was a Sociology class, why was she spending the hour talking about Vietnam? He doodled in his notebook, drawing pictures of planes, ships and swastikas. The whole scene was making him sleepy. He'd had to move to the afternoon shift at work, so he could take classes in the morning. He wouldn't get home from the mill until after nine.

He realized that his schedule was going to put a serious crimp in his drinking time.. Oh well, he thought. It would save him some cash, and he might even start losing some weight to the point where his jeans would fit again.

Gary Hess reported to work at the Quincy sawmill at noon, slamming his time card in and listening as the hammer clicked. He pulled it out and inspected the fresh black ink mark. Right on time.

He carried a metal lunch pain filled with baloney sandwiches, two bananas, and a large thermos of coffee. He also carried a bottle of Tums, just in case his sometimes sensitive stomach acted up at work. Only sissies and dudes with pony tails went home sick because they had stomach cramps or the trots.

Gary made five dollars an hour. A lead man could make up to $7.50 hourly, plus overtime. It was a coveted position, with openings only occurring when someone retired or died. The work certainly decreased ones hearing ability, and despite wearing required goggles, eye injuries were common, as were severed limbs. Gary had been fortunate so far, and still had all his digits, arms and legs.

Gary went to the locker room to change into his grungy work clothes. He smelled the sawdust, sweat and machine oil on them. He only washed them once a month, or more often if his co-bitched him out for stinking up the lunch room.

As soon as Gary entered the main sawmill, he was hit with the horrendous screech of massive saws that made boards out of trees. The harsh metallic cutting sound never ceased. Sawdust was everywhere.

Gary joined Reno Converse at the quality control station that was at the end of the line. They had an easy job, checking 2x4's, larger boards and plywood. They both had over five years on the job, so they had some seniority. They were still inside the dammed mill, but at least they didn't do the dangerous cutting jobs anymore.

Reno gave Gary a head nod. They had known each other for ten years, and considered each other to not only be good friends, but stand up guys who could be counted on in a pinch.

Gary recalled the time he and Reno as well as

Randy-Bob and Dave had stumbled into an outlaw cantina in Tijuana. They were quickly surrounded by armed thieves who demanded their watches and wallets. They had to fight their way out of that one, dismantling the smaller men before they were able to use their knives. The owner called in a complaint, wanting them to pay for the damage to his cantina. The local Federales chased them to the U.S. border, where they got through barely in time. They never returned to Mexico after that frightening but bonding experience.

Outside at break time, Gary and Reno puffed on cigarettes, "How's school going, Gary?"

Gary spit on the ground, "I had my first class today, and it did not go well."

"How so?"

"The instructor, Amy, is a traitor to this country and a major hormonal bitch. There's also a couple of real jerks from the Gay Bay that I intend to straighten out one of these days. The tall goofy one with long greasy hair has already been hanging out with Maureen and her friends, probably selling them LSD. I don't like it, Reno, and I'm not gonna just stand by and let these punks ruin our town."

"What's happening after work?"

"One beer at the Keddie Club. Maybe more. I don't have to get up until nine tomorrow, so I have a little time. You know buddy, I'm feeling kind of pissed off right now, like I want to hurt someone. Bad. You ever get like that?"

"Yeah, sure Gary. I have my moments. I think everyone does. It's just that we go a little further than everyone else."

Gary laughed for the first time that day, "Yeah. We do get a little carried away sometimes. I can still remember the look on the faces of those stinking

Indians when Randy-Bob rigged up the accelerator with a rock and sent their piece of shit Buick flying into the river."

"Yeah. That was cool. Too bad we didn't leave them inside before Randy did it. That would have been boss."

"Yeah, well maybe we can arrange for that Lance Potter drug dealer and his jerk friend Joe Bailey to take the same plunge, and we'll see if their car floats or sinks right away like the Buick."

Gary entered the Keddie Club with a mighty thirst. His ears rang from eight hours inside the saw-mill, and his throat was parched. He wondered if he should buy a pair of fifty nine cent earplugs. He had seen some at Appling's Pharmacy. He'd noticed that the older workers all seemed hard of hearing, and a lot of them had died of lung or skin cancer. He lighted a Camel and wondered if it might be something in the water.

Jake, the bartender, set a cold can of Bud and a shot of Jack Daniels in front of Gary. Jake was a retired Marine lifer who had served a tour of combat in the Korean war.

"How ya doin today, Gary?"

"Not so good, Jake. Those queer hippies from out of town are really starting to annoy me."

"Don't worry, Gary. Most of the kids will only be here a few months. They'll blow their minds on Marijuana and flunk out and soon and as we get our first big snow, they'll be running back home to rich mommy and daddy. Most situations resolve them selves. You gotta learn a little patience."

"I don't gotta learn nothin. Fix me up with another shot of Jack. I feel like getting drunk."

Jake poured him another shot of Jack Daniels and moved to the other end of the bar to serve a hard looking guy named Jesse, who was new in town. He was wearing a waist length black leather jacket, mostly sipped draft beer and was working as a cook at the restaurant. He too seemed out of place in Keddie, and Gary eyed him suspiciously.

Gary's friends joined him and they moved to an upholstered booth and drank, smoked and took turns playing pool.

Gary suddenly found himself being challenged by the new guy, who took off his leather jacket and carefully hung it from the coat rack before he grabbed a pool cue. Jesse racked the balls. Gary broke and sank nothing. He wondered if Jesse set him up with a loose rack. Jesse ran the table on him in five minutes, slamming shot after shot screaming into the leather pockets. When he was done he laughed, retrieved his jacket and left the bar.

Gary sat back down at the table.

"What the hell was that? He ran the table like a pro," observed Randy Bob.

Gary stared through the smoke from four cigarettes and said, "There's something fishy about that guy. He just shows up out of nowhere and starts strutting around Keddie wearing a freaking leather jacket like he's in the big city or something."

Reno was pretty good at sizing people up, "I wouldn't underestimate the dude, Gary. Just the way he carries himself is a tip off. Did you notice the way he was balancing himself on the balls of his feet and how he kept rotating his neck and his shoulders. The guy was a pro fighter I bet ya."

"Yeah," observed Dave, "I know some of his face crevices is zit scars, but it looks to me like he's been carved up a bit too."

"Humph," grunted Gary, "He doesn't look like such a bad ass to me. I'm going to add him to my shit list, which is starting to get long."

Gary left the bar at eleven with Reno and wobbled to his jeep. Randy-Bob and Dave piled into Randy's dune buggy. They were headed back to the A--Frame to play a few hands of Poker for quarters. Reno would probably stay over, sleeping on the couch.

As they cruised down the highway, Gary spotted a lone, long haired hitchhiker with a thumb out, headed in their direction. Thinking it might be a hippie chick, Gary pulled over.

His headlights illuminated the person, "Aw geez, Gary. It's one of those damn queer hippie guys."

"Roll down your window, Reno."

The stranger approached them, bent over and peered inside. "Hey. Thanks for stopping, guys. I'd just about given up on getting a ride. I'm trying to get back to Quincy where I have a room over the Chinese restaurant. It's getting damned cold out here."

Randy-Bob pulled up behind Gary and Reno. His headlights lit up the interior of Gary's Willys.

Gary spoke to the hippie in folksy, friendly voice, "Guess you're new in town, and don't know how dangerous it is out here at night. These here woods are full of all matter of wild things. I think there's a tribe of Big Foots too. I saw one once when I was hunting."

"Yeah, I've seen one too," added Reno, taking a slug out of a can of Bud that he had left the bar with, "They smell real bad, and they love meat. Human meat."

The stranger gulped and looked behind him, scanning the woods.

"Plus," said Gary, "There's wolves, mountain lions, cougars and some twelve foot tall Grizzly Bears. Hell, it was just last year, right about this time, when a hiker disappeared from this very spot. There wasn't much left of him. Just a pile of bones that were picked clean."

Terror now spread across the kid's face.

"Wow," exclaimed the hitchhiker, "I had no idea, guys. I'm from the Bay Area, and the scariest thing we had were Black Panthers."

"Black Panthers?" exclaimed Reno "Where did you seem them? They're somewhat rare I would think. Aren't they supposed to be in Africa?"

"No, there were a whole bunch of them, living in the Oakland slums, and openly carrying around rifles."

"Animals carrying guns?" repeated Reno, his eyes getting wider.

Gary chuckled and slugged Reno in his shoulder, "He's talking about those uppity darkies, the ones who wear black berets and joined together to fight whitey, except they're gonna lose."

"Oh," said Reno,

"Say fellas," said the kid who was shivering, "I don't mean to be pushy, but I think I'm on the verge of hypothermia, and I can't feel my feet anymore. Can you give me a lift into town, and then we can talk about it more during the ride?"

"That depends, friend," said Gary, his tone changing to serious.

"Depends on what?"

"What your name is boy, and what you are. That's critical information that I must have before letting you ride on my back seat."

The stranger backed away, "Its okay. Forget I

asked. You guys go on now. I'll wait for someone else."

"Too late," muttered Reno. Exiting the Willys, he nailed the stranger on the jaw with his best straight right, which immediately dropped the kid to the ground.

Gary joined Reno and they laughed, lifted Elliott up and threw him across the hood of the Jeep. Randy-Bob and Dave jumped in, one with a tire iron and the other with a bloody golf club.

Gary slammed the young man's head into the hood, clutching his collar and then bringing his face close to his own, "Last time, punk. What's your name?"

"Elliott Rosen," he stuttered, "I don't want any trouble, guys. You can have my wallet. There's eight dollars in it…..just don't hurt me any more."

Gary pulled Elliott off the hood and shoved him towards Dave, who pushed him roughly into Randy-Bob, who then heaved him at Reno, who stepped back and delivered a kick into Rosen's right kidney. Elliott dropped to his hands and knees, spittle drooling from his bloody mouth.

"Elliott Rosen, huh?" sneered Randy-Bob, who slammed the tire iron across the small of his back, "Sounds like a Jew bait name to me."

"Kike asshole," yelled Gary, who stomped his boot down on Elliot's neck, "How about we fire up the ovens, huh punk?

"Dave," said Gary, "Get my bolt cutters. This shithead needs a haircut, real bad."

"Wait," shrieked Elliott, "What are you going to do to me?"

"Shut up!" roared Reno. He pulled Elliott's head back by his hair and then pressed his buck knife up to his throat, "Maybe I should do the world a favor and slit your throat right here. Then we'll dump your scrawny body in the woods, and the animals will eat you."

"No!"

"Hold him down, boys." said Gary, who was brandishing his heavy bolt cutters with long, vicious looking jaws, "I'm doing you a favor, boy. Your long hair makes you look like a sissy."

Randy-Bob held Elliott in a Full Nelson hold, while Reno held down his legs and Dave tried to control his thrashing arms.

Gary laughed and hacked away, cutting out huge hunks of hair from random spots. Elliott screamed and tried to break away. When he cried out in pain, his tormentors laughed even harder.

A car headed their way, driving south towards Quincy. Gary took a final violent cut and then pushed Rosen's face onto the dirt, "That's all we got time for tonight, *Elliott!* If we ever see you again, we'll finish the job and pour Draino down your fat Jew mouth. You shouldn't have killed Jesus. You got off lucky tonight, punk."

Gary and the boys piled into their vehicles, whooping and hollering. Gary peeled out, spraying gravel and dirt over Elliott, who lay on the ground, rolled up in a fetal position. trying to protect his head.

As Randy-Bob drove he approached Rosen. Dave heaved a full bottle of Budweiser. It smashed into his leg, "Here, fag. Just in case you get thirsty."

He and Randy-Bob roared with laughter.

As Gary sped off, Randy-Bob drove close to Rosen, who was crawling towards the road with one hand upraised and pleading for help as another car roared by.

Randy-Bob miscalculated and they felt a 'thump thump.'

"Shit, Randy-Bob, I think you just ran over the

sum bitch."

"So?"

"Shouldn't we go back and check on him?"

"Why? Being run over by a Dune Buggy is no big deal. We hardly weigh any thing. He might have some broken ribs or something. Let's go play some poker.

Dave glanced back into the darkness, but couldn't see a thing.

KEDDIE CLUB

CHAPTER EIGHT

After two weeks of living in Keddie and attending school in Quincy, Lance and Joe settled into a comfortable routine. They went to some of their classes, took a few indecipherable notes and even studied a couple of times.

They rarely saw their roommates, as Scott and Chris had purchased the Keddie premium package, which included breakfast and dinner at the lodge student dining area.

Lance now spent much of his spare time with Maureen Hess and her local acid head gang,. as well as the Bay Area partiers who occupied Greg's cabin at the top of the parking lot. Lance's classes, except for Archery and Sociology, were different from Joes.

The result was that Joe frequently had the place to himself, which was fine by him. He smoked grass and cigarettes, drank whiskey and beer, and sometimes ate speed to enhance his creative moods. Once he was feeling properly inspired, he would start writing in his journal. He penned caustic short stories, weird, non-rhyming poems, or occasionally an essay on how screwed up virtually everyone and everything in life was. He angrily wrote about how irritating and phony he found society in general.

Instead of using psychedelics, he drank reg-regularly, rationalizing his daily alcohol use by reading that many of his favorite authors were heavy drinkers. Kerouac obviously, plus Hemingway, Fitzgerald, and many others too. Joe figured there was a direct correlation between regular inebriation and his best lines and stories.

When Joe felt the need to alter his simple routine, he would treat himself to a decent, filling meal at the Keddie Restaurant. Sometimes he played pool in the student lounge, located in half of the lodge basement, across from the Keddie Club.

Joe played a passable game of pool, in that he won more then he lost. He never felt comfortable betting on the outcome. He didn't have money to lose. In addition, he was aware that some sneaky guys played poorly deliberately when there were no stakes. When the green stuff was brought out, they suddenly became sharp shooters, revealing themselves to be a hustler on the prowl for suckers, slithering up to the table and sinking all his balls with ease.

Then they would they would lay out their scaled, snakeskin palm in demand of immediate payment of the chump's gambling loss. The hustler's pupils were frequently tiny pin pricks that were capable of keen focus when playing a higher level of opponent.

Joe's primary motive in hanging out in the dank basement was financial. It gave him a venue to meet fellow students that were under age but craved alcohol. Joe let them know that he had a Military I.D. that said he was twenty two, allowing him to buy booze for his new friends, for a modest fee of course. Joe had cleverly put clear tape over his Coast Guard I.D, and with the steady hand of a semi experienced forger, he altered his birth year from 1951 to 1949. He didn't see the need change his California Drivers License.

Joe felt his rates were reasonable. When purchasing a six-pack for instance, he only took a single can as his payment for services rendered. For hard booze, he charged fifty cents for a pint and a dollar for a fifth or quart. He rarely drank wine himself. However, he would gladly purchase it for someone else for just a dollar. Screw top fortified wines such as Ripple, Night Train and Mad Dog 20-20 were quite popular.

The Keddie General Store was old fashioned, as they carried a little bit of everything, from food, ice and beer to clothes, brooms and hammers. It was a small building that had merchandise hanging from every possible location, with overflow stacked haphazardly on the floor.

An older couple, Jim and Sue, owned and ran the business, one of them on duty at all times, six days a week. They were closed on Sunday so they could attend church together. They re-checked Joe's I.D. every single time he purchased more alcohol. One day, as Jim was ringing up another six pack and a fifth of Old Crow, Joe finally asked a question concerning Jim's daily behavior that had been bothering him.

"Sir, Jim. I was wondering why you require me to show my I.D. every single time I purchase alcohol. I must be your steadiest customer. Do you think I'm going to come in here someday and somehow be younger then I was the day before? Do you think I'll suddenly become illegal?"

Jim took off his glasses, "Listen good, you smart ass. I don't believe that you're twenty-two. I check your I.D. every time because it's the law. I'm not going to have my fifty thousand dollar liquor license suspended because of you. Really, though kid, you need to cut back on your drinking. You need help. Do you even realize how much booze you're consuming each day? You're a full blown alcoholic son, at whatever age you really are, and I'd guess eighteen, nineteen tops. I don't see how you could possibly attend any college classes, not when you're drinking all day and night."

"Thank you, sir. You've been a big help. Oh yeah, I almost forgot. Gimme a hard pack of Marlboros, two beef sticks and a bag of cashews. Do you want to see my I.D. for the smokes?"

"Smart ass," said Jim, ringing up Joe's purchases.

Joe's biggest problem was food. He was a novice, limited cook with a budget of fifteen dollars a week to cover all of his needs. He wound up planning all of his meals around a pound of hamburger. It would last him three days before turning brown and eventually green, at which point even Lance wouldn't eat it. He started with a cheese burger the first night, a big pot of spaghetti on the second, and then finished up with some homemade chili. He quickly tired of his own cooking. Occasionally, he would resort to eating an entire box of sugary cereal with a quart of milk.

Back in May, when they were planning their great adventure to Feather River, Lance had assured Joe that he could eat quite well on just fifteen dollars a week. What Joe didn't take into consideration, was that Lance rarely ate.

One crisp fall morning as Joe walked past the lodge, the San Francisco Chronicle caught his eye. 'JIMI HENDRIX DEAD.' Joe dug out a dime and pulled a newspaper from the rack. He felt sick to his stomach. Hendrix had been found dead in a London flat from a suspected drug overdose.

Jimi Hendrix was one of his favorite musicians, and Joe had partied and sang along many times to

'Foxy Lady' and 'Purple Haze.' He wondered if any of his friends had heard the news yet. He felt the need to talk to somebody about the tragedy.

He folded the newspaper and entered the restaurant. It was nearly empty, with just the usual four crusty cowboys sitting at their round corner table, all smoking Marlboro's and drinking endless cups of coffee. He figured they probably didn't even know who Jimi Hendrix was. Joe wondered again what the deal was with the constant presence of various different Marlboro Men. What did they do, live at the freaking table?

As soon as Joe entered and sat at the counter, the biggest of the cowboys got up and passed close to him, sniffing at the air, stopping at the phone in the entryway.

Joe picked up a stained menu, even though he knew what was on it. He looked it over anyway, hoping perhaps he had overlooked something that was different. He glanced over as a thin Marlboro Man was pointing at him, saying something with the other two laughing heartedly.

Charlene set a glass of water in front of Joe, "Know what you want, kiddo?"

Joe detested being called 'kiddo.' He found it demeaning, like she literally thought he was just some punk kid. He made a point of pulling his dog tags out and toying with them. Kids don't earn dog tags he thought. Men do, and they don't come easy. It was especially irritating though, because 'kiddo' came from this loser server.

"I'll have the hot Roast Beef Sandwich, with just water to drink."

"Coming right up, kid," said Charlene, popping a pink bubble from her ever present thick wad of gum.

Joe noticed a new guy, sitting behind the corner on a stool, peeling a sack of potatoes. He had a pock-marked face and a sallow complexion, as though he hadn't been in the sun for a long time. He had dirty blonde hair pulled back into a short ponytail, a white muscle man T-shirt, with a tattoo of a big heart with a red arrow on his right shoulder. There was also an orange and brown roaring lion on his left shoulder. Joe figured the man had to be at least forty. An old dude.

"Hey brother, "said the man, looking up, revealing yellow and green eyes, "You gotta an extra nail? I ran out and don't get paid until tomorrow and I'm like 'jonesing' for a smoke."

"Sure," answered Joe, pulling his pack of 'boros out of his coat pocket and handing Jesse four cigarettes, "There you go, man. One for now, three for later."

Jesse lit a wooden match off the knee of his new blue jeans and blew out perfect smoke rings, which Joe wished he could do. The man extended his calloused hand, "Jesse."

"Joe Bailey. Terrible news, huh?"

Huh? What's that, brother?"

"Hendrix, man. Jimi Hendrix is dead."

"That a fact? Didn't he do some purple song or something?"

"Yeah. Purple Haze."

"Sorry, Joe. I've been away for awhile, and haven't really kept up with what's going on in the real world."

Charlene brought Joe his lunch. As she took the coffee pot over to the Marlboro Men, Jesse poured Joe a large glass of milk. "Here, kid. On the house. A hot roast beef sandwich always tastes better with milk."

Joe used his last piece of white bread to sop up

the gravy. He finished the milk, savoring every cool drop. His stomach was full. Life was good for another few hours, until it was time to figure out what to eat again. He hated to admit it, but he did miss his Mom's cooking and regular meals. He even sort of missed Bud too, and yeah, Marvin. He was becoming a copy of himself, but still in his own way, establishing his own identity.

Joe stood in front of the old fashioned cash register with his last five dollar bill.

Jesse rang up the meal as zeroes, took Joe's five and handed him back five ones.

"Hope you enjoyed your lunch, young man, Please come back and bring your friends next time."

Later that evening, Joe sat in his spot on the far end of the couch. He had his journal, a purple pen and a tall glass of bourbon and Coke on the rocks. He also had two fat joints, a nearly full box of Wheat Thins and some salami and sharp cheese. He was set.

Joe put on Steppenwolf and rocked out, letting his mind travel to that special place that he could only access on occasion. He called it his 'creative zone'. When he was feeling it, he knew he had to write, to get his words down on paper as rapidly as possible. He could always edit it later. That's how Kerouac worked. Capitalize on a creative burst and ride it until it ran out. Sometimes, for his idol, it lasted all night and occasionally into the next week.

Lance made an appearance at ten. He was wearing his deteriorating leather jacket and was holding a pillowcase that Joe assumed was full of dirty clothes.

"What ya been up to?" inquired Lance.

"I've been on a creative frenzy. I just wrote a good poem, or at least I think it's good. You wanna hear it?"

"Sure. Just let me get in the door, change my clothes and get a drink. You got any smoke?"

"Of course. What happened to that lid I just gave you?"

"Oh, that only lasted a few days. When you're partying with a bunch of freaks, it doesn't last long. I'm going to need to get back to the Bay Area to pick up some fresh inventory soon. More acid" he grinned, "Lots more acid. When is your next reserve meeting?"

"Not for another week."

"Well, figure on me going down with you.."

Lance joined Joe and fired up the number Joe handed him. He too had a large tumbler of whiskey and Coke. The ice cubes rattled because Lance's right hand was shaking, like he was having tremors or an epileptic fit. His face was twitching, his facial muscles changing every five seconds.
"You okay, man?"

"No, not really. I didn't listen to my own advice and I've been frying for three days on cross tops, and now I'm out, so I figure I got withdrawals or something. Maybe the booze will knock me out. I'm jonesing for some speed, and it sucks. The come down off this crap is dangerous. It puts you into a black mood and you feel like killing yourself."

"Okay fine. Let me know if I can help you."

"Help me what? Kill myself?"

"Naw, you know what I mean."

"All right, I'm ready now," said Lance, propping his smelly feet on the coffee table. His big toes were sticking out of ragged holes in both toes.

Joe stood up and held his journal out, pretending that he was an inspired author, doing a reading in a

crowded coffee house in San Francisco in the
1950's. Kerouac, Ginsberg and Corso were in the
crowd, passing around a jug of red wine with all the rest
of the beat poets and their Bohemian audiences. Some
folks, feeling moved by the inspiring poetry and electric
vibes, stood and bent forward with their heads parallel
to the floor and snapped their fingers to the rhyming
spoken words.

Others swayed their shoulders and hips and
danced in place to a new and exciting collective vibe.
Live readings by heavy poets and writers, a few who
were destined to become famous.

Joe cleared his voice,

"Trees, tall and strong
soon to be cement
while concerned citizens
worry about football score,
and when the President dies
from eating a polluted
Mexican TV dinner,
his mourners will
trek to Disneyland,
and search for God
on the Matterhorn."

Joe looked at Lance expectantly,
"Is that it?"

"Yeah, that's it," said Joe, his smile beginning
to melt. He visualized the coffee house audience booing
him off the tiny platform, grumbling and demanding
that Ginsberg get up and re read Howl, his epic, break-
through poem. Kerouac threw Joe a disappointed glare,
which hurt the most. Joe hadn't realized that he sucked.

"That's good, man," said Lance, heading for

another full glass of Joe's booze, "Profound even."

Joe couldn't tell if Lance was mocking him or not. He read his poem over again, and then threw his journal down on the table and started sorting through the orange crate, looking for an album he hadn't heard for awhile.

Lance opened the refrigerator, "Hey, Joe. Is there anything to eat? Maureen and Sam ran out of food stamps, so I was hoping you had something."

"There's some of my homemade chili in there."

"How old is it?" asked Lance, lifting the cover off the pot and taking a close look and a sniff.

"How should I know?"

"Well, you made it, right?"

"Yeah. What's your point?"

"I don't see any mold. I don't know man. The last time I ate your homemade chili, I had the runs for three days."

"Well then, don't eat it asshole."

They heard a timid knock at the front door. Joe opened it, and there stood Bruce, a friend of Scott's, which was hardly a positive recommendation.

"Hiya mates," said Bruce in his phony British accent. "I left my math book here, and Scott said I could drop by and retrieve it." Joe nodded and Bruce made his way into the cabin. Joe could care less if Bruce stole everything of value out of Scott and Chris's room. Heck, if Bruce needed a pillowcase for his loot, Joe would suggest that Bruce use Scotts. Just a few days ago, Joe had transplanted an anthill and put it under Scott's bed.

A minute later, they could hear the crisp chords of an electric guitar coming from the back bedroom. Joe and Lance entered just in time to listen as Bruce easily ripped off an authentic sounding Chuck Berry riff.

Bruce paused, adjusted two strings, played a sample chord, and this time did *Mona,* which was a commonly covered tune.

Joe observed the fine looking black guitar that was connected to a nice sized Marshal amp sitting on the floor.

Bruce tried to sing it, but he sounded like a hungry cow trapped in the bedroom. His guitar playing was excellent. After warbling *Mona* a dozen times, he stopped, not able to remember any other lyrics.

"Wow Bruce," exclaimed Lance, "I didn't know you could play."

"Yeah. I can do a few chords."

"Can you do Honky Tonk Woman?" asked Joe.

"Sure." Bruce dipped his shoulder and launched into the signature Rolling Stones song, playing the familiar intro. He used the end of his guitar to point at a silver microphone that was facing Joe on a chrome stand.

Joe put his mouth close up to the mike, did a little jig, and pretended he was Mick Jagger, on stage in front of fifty thousand screaming fans. He gripped the mike just as Jagger would and started singing along to Bruce's authentic Keith Richards guitar lead. Joe sang tentatively at first, but then finished louder with more confidence. He thought he sounded okay, especially since he had never sang in front of anyone before, fearing he would be laughed at. As he stood there, enjoying the positive endorphin rush, he thought back to last fall.

Joe had desired to become a musician as well as a writer. Why not, he thought. He already had lyrics, and could easily pen more. First though, he needed to learn how to play the guitar. He requested one from his folks, and a week later Bud came home and wordlessly handed Joe a cheesy $19.95 piece of shit Chinese built guitar. It came from the only store he ever seemed to shop at, the local shithole in Richmond, Monkey Wards.

Joe sat in his bedroom with his sliding door closed and repeatedly practiced the only three chords he knew. He could read music because he had been a Coronet player in the high school band. He had also been a member of the U.S. Coast Guard Marching Band while still in boot camp. However, he wasn't yet to the point where he could read and play simple guitar music. Joe was somewhat dismayed because after a couple weeks of daily, hour long practices, he pretty much sounded the same as the first day he had tried.

One Friday night, his family crowded into his room and had a musical intervention. They complained as one that his playing sucked, always had, and would most likely continue to be like a cat scratching a chalkboard.. They told him that he could only practice when no one else was home. They said even their cat Augie, hid underneath Marvin's bed whenever Joe insisted on continuing his horrid racket. A week later, Joe sold his crappy guitar at the Saturday Berkeley flea market for a five dollar bill.

He and Marvin got their own bedrooms when their sister, Claudette, turned eighteen in 1964. In her desperation to escape the tyranny of the Bailey household, she married some nice guy named Vern who she had only dated for two months.

Augie mostly slept at the end of Joe's bed at night, going to sleep along with the whole Bailey family. Marvin got jealous and demanded a turn with her sleeping on the end of his bed. He suggested to Joe that they should take turns, maybe flipping the cat back every week.

The very first night Marvin got his wish, he woke up to a horrid smell and mess. The cat was gone, but left a message by not only throwing up on Marvin's prized Roy Rogers bead spread, but also leaving behind a huge hairball the size of a tennis ball. Then for her grand finale, Augie turned around and shit on his pillow. It reeked of feline diarrhea, with some of it splattered on his face. Marvin never asked for Augie again.

Bruce played a medley of popular rock tunes and then set the guitar carefully back in its black case with a dark green felt interior.

"Man, he said, "I love playing that ax. It's a mid-1950's Fender Stratocaster. I think you'd have to agree that it sounds damned good. It has a unique, rich, distinctive howl. I'm jealous that Chris owns it and not me. I told him just yesterday that he should loan it to me. With that guitar, I could get into a cool band and maybe we'd take off and get rich. I told him when I could afford the damned thing, I'd pay some ridiculous price for it. He said he'd think about it, which usually means no."

"Yeah, don't give up. It fits you well. Say, Bruce, you wanna get high with us?", asked Joe.

"Uh, okay, but just as long as Scott isn't around. You know how he and Chris feel about drugs."

"Yes," said Joe, "We do. Join us in the front room."

An hour, two joints and a few hard drinks later, Bruce agreed to join the boys for an evening stroll around Keddie. When they reached the outside of the raucous Keddie Club, they paused and glazed longingly inside.

It was Friday night and payday for many. Cars and trucks were parked everywhere. Jacked up 4x4's that arrived late and couldn't find a parking spot drove up onto logs and over bushes. No one cared.

The leather padded front door of the bar was propped open. Loud country western drinking songs blared out of a jukebox. Glasses tinkled, the cue ball was driven into pool balls and they landed in leather pockets with an audible thud. Men yelled louder and louder, trying to be heard over each other as they lied, bragged, and threatened each other. They banged empty glasses on the counter and demanded more booze from Jake, and his partner, Bob, who helped on Friday and Saturday nights.

A thick cloud of blue smoke hung in the air. The boys could see outlines of men, many wearing cowboy hats.

"Man," said Bruce, "I'd give my left nut to be able to have just one drink in there. It looks and sounds like so much damned fun. It's a bitch only being nineteen."

"Yeah," agreed Joe, "Sure is, Bruce."

There was sudden, angry shouting from the bar. then the sound of glass breaking, and someone big came flying out the door backwards. He fell to the ground, holding his head in his hands and yelling in pain. A large cowboy followed him out with a pool cue in his hands.

The Keddie Club quickly emptied, the men forming a circle around the combatants.

The cowboy lifted the pool cue up high and then smashed it down on the downed man's upraised right knee, and the man screamed out again.

"This is barbaric," said Lance, "How can you

guys enjoy watching this mindless violence?"

This is cool," said Joe, "Hold on a minute. I
want to see if someone dies."

"No one is going to die," remarked Bruce, who
turned to continue their stroll. "Everyone got paid today, The cowboys, ranchers, train crews and Indians are
just letting off a little steam."

"By beating on each other with pool cues?"
asked Lance.

"Better then getting smacked over the head with
a full beer bottle," said Bruce.

The cowboy had a sick look of enjoyment as he
hit the man again, "Don't get up Pete, otherwise I'm
going to keep beating on you. You never should have
insulted my truck."

Pete laughed, "Okay Jackson, you win. I take it
back. Your Chevy is a nice truck. Come on man, let me
buy you a drink."

Jackson laughed too, reached out his hand, and
helped Pete up. They put their arms around each other
and staggered back into the bar. All the other drinkers
filed in behind them, returning to their spots and downing more straight shots with beer chasers.

"Man," said Bruce, watching as the last man
returned, "Just one beer in the Keddie Club. That's all I
want. Then I could die a happy man. That's not too
much to ask for, is it?"

"Maybe Lance and I could arrange for you to
realize your dream. Tonight."

"How?" asked Bruce, moonlight reflecting off
his eyes, making them glitter.

There was more bedlam inside the club. It was a
chair breaking, and more angry, inebriated shouts.

"Temporary white hair," answered Joe as the
three of them hunkered into their coats and started back

towards the cabin.

"Come on, Joe. Don't even suggest that we do it again."

"Again?" asked Bruce, "You've done this before? Successfully?"

They were now walking on the paved section of the vast parking lot, "Well, yes. It was back in the Bay Area just about a year ago," revealed Lance. "It was a blue's concert with, I can't remember, somebody like 'Blind Lemon Chiltin', or 'BB Queen', someone famous. A mutual friend of ours, Alex, wanted to attend very much. He was heading off to a four year enlistment in the Army the next week. Only problem was, Alex was 18 and looked it. The concert was 21 and over."

"Yeah, yeah, spare me all the details. How did you do it, and you say it worked?"

"Well, we started by dressing him in square clothes with old brogines for shoes. His dad was a Mormon Bishop."

It was becoming apparent to Joe that Lance was increasingly unable to just utter a single word or a simple sentence. Everything that came out now was at least a paragraph.

Lance continued, "We turned Alex's hair white for a day. It worked fine, and Joe also made one of his awesome phony I.D.'s, but you're not going to need that. Bruce, by the time we're done with you, you'll look old enough to be collecting Social Security. Alex got in fine, and had an awesome time listening to the Blues Legends who were so old that they could keel over and die at any time. Alex said he drank a lot, and even got to dance with some foxy chicks. I guess if you want it bad enough. Bruce, Joe and me could fix you up. It's not easy, and requires supplies, so we'd need, say, ten bucks for our troubles."

"You bastards," said Bruce, "Fix me up. I'll pay you in the cabin once I can see inside my wallet."

Bruce sat in a straight backed chair in the dining room of the cabin. His clothes were completely covered by one of Scott's sheets that Joe had ripped off his bed, leaving the rest of Scott's bedding in a heap in the middle of the bedroom floor. Newspaper was spread out underneath Bruce's chair.

"Close your eyes, dude," said Lance.

He dumped a nearly full sack of flour over Bruce's head. An enormous cloud of white flour dust billowed into the air and spread as far as the kitchen and front room.

Bruce's blue eyes were the only things on him that weren't white. He blinked and then opened his mouth, gasping for a clean breath and then sneezed. Flour flew off him and onto the newspapers.

"Don't wanna make that mistake again, " said Joe.

"What?" asked Bruce.

"Nothing," said Joe, "Stand up old man."

Bruce rose to his feet. Lance pulled the sheet away, and more flour dropped to the floor and also covered the top of Bruce's tennis shoes.

"Perfect job, as always," said Lance, brushing off a little flour from the tip of Bruce's nose and then carefully cleaning his face with Scott's washcloth "Hell, man. You even look better than Alex did. A lot more of the flour is still on your head, as well as your eyebrows. That's a common mistake among amateurs, forgetting the eyebrows. Now, Bruce, you gotta walk slow and stiff, because every time you move you're gonna lose more of the flour."

"Okay," muttered Bruce. Joe opened the front door and Bruce walked out like a robot, slowly lifting his right hand into the air as he departed.

"Good luck," yelled Joe before slamming the door.

He turned around and he and Lance burst into laughter and gave each other high fives. They were both five dollars richer, and they'd had fun doing it.

Joe began sweeping up the mess.

"I wasn't sure we had any flour, Joe. What would we do with it? All we know how to cook is hamburgers."

"Susan left it here a few days ago when she was doing some baking with Chris, who is such a wuss that he was wearing a chick's apron and helping her and acting like he was fine with the scenario. I wanted to ask him if his balls got cut off or something."

Lance laughed as he watched Joe dump his dustpan full of flour, dust, insects and crumbs back into the sack, which he then folded up neatly and placed back in the cupboard where he had found it.

"What you gonna do with your money, Lance?"

"Buy me a steak dinner over at the restaurant. How about you, Joe?"

"I'm a gonna go over to the General Store and buy me a fifth of Old Butthole."

"Old Butthole? What is that?" asked Lance.

"It's this ass kicking ninety proof rot gut bourbon that's made in rural Ohio."

"My God, Joe. You might as well be drinking gasoline."

"No, its good stuff I tell you. You know, maybe we should turn off the lights. We don't want to look like we're still up after Bruce gets tossed out of the Keddie Club on his ass."

"Yeah, man. We don't give refunds. No guarantees either. Everything is as is. "

They both laughed and Joe shut off the lights and they partied in the dark, once in awhile speculating on Bruce's fate and laughing some more.

NARCOLEPSY

CHAPTER NINE

The following week, Joe ratched up his courage and knocked on the front door of Carlene and Debbie's cabin. He felt his stomach flutter when Carlene answered the door, a questioning look on her face. Joe had a brief flashback of the summer day when he had gone to Squirt's house for refreshments and wound up being threatened by Bobby Carbo.

"Hi Carlene," said Joe enthusiastically.

Carlene looked directly at Joe, appraising him. Joe's legs became rubbery. She was wearing her green shorts and a thin white top with her lacy bra visible underneath.

"Yes?"

Joe hesitated and fought the urge to bolt to the safety of his own cabin and hung in, "So, How ya doing, Carlene?"

"Fine. Is this a social call, or do you have an agenda?"

Joe nervously wiped at his mouth, "Uh, I just wanted to know, uh, if you'd like to study Biology together. There's a lot I struggle with. Maybe we can help each other."

"No."

"Okay then. Moving on, I'd like to invite you out to dinner with me tomorrow evening."

"Where to? Not that crappy organic place we went to last week I hope."

"No, no. When you first drive into Quincy, there's a steak house called 'The Iron Horse' on the left of the highway. It's supposed to be pretty good."

"Yeah, I guess that would be okay. But I'm not going to just hop in bed with you afterwards because you buy me a meal. Let's make that clear from the start, Larry."

Joe immediately felt sick to his stomach, "The name is Joe. What time can I pick you up? I prefer going a little earlier, before they get crowded and we might have to wait for a table."

"Between four and seven. I'll come over to your cabin when I'm ready."

"Great. I know….."

Carlene shut the door while he was still talking. Joe looked at it for a moment, wondering why she continued to treat him like a piece of dog shit she found clinging to the bottom of her shoe. He wondered if he smelled bad, or did he have a hunk of spinach stuck to his teeth?

Joe made a booze run, picking up a half gallon of Vodka and a quart of Grapefruit Juice. Jim said nothing, taking his currency, returning change and giving him the fish eye, squinting at him until he departed.

Back at the cabin, Lance was sprawled out on the couch, staring at the ceiling.

"What's up?" asked Joe, excited that he had succeeded in getting a date, "You don't seem to be shaking anymore."

"Yeah, I kicked the habit. I need to take a shower and get a fresh shirt. What ya got there, drink supplies?"

"Yeah. Got stuff for Greyhounds. This is for me and Carlene."

"What?" said Lance, sitting up, "You and Carlene?"

"Guess what we're doing tomorrow night?"

"Getting drunk and playing doctor?"

"No, dumb ass. I'm taking Carlene out to dinner."

"Where? The Keddie Restaurant? I was just by there and they're having a special on Rocky Mountain Oysters and Carp dip."

Joe paused, acutely aware that his friend was mocking him. He spoke slowly.

"No, Lance. Carlene is special to me. I'm taking her to the best joint in town, 'The Iron Horse.' We're gonna get New York Steaks, or maybe Prawns. I like those too. Whatever she wants."

"You suddenly got that kind of money, Joe?". Lance automatically pulled out his own wallet. He flipped through a few bills. Seemingly satisfied, he put it back in his rear pocket only to find Joe glowering at him.

"What? You think I stole my dinner money from you? How insulting. How the hell would I get into your wallet? You fuck. I'm gonna use my parents credit card. I'll just owe them the money. The Master Card is bound to impress Carlene."

"Sorry, Joe. I've gotten very paranoid lately. I think I'm being watched. You too."

"Yeah? By who?"

"Wish I knew, but I think it might have something to do with the Marlboro Men."

"Humph. I don't know about anything like that. You wanna hear my date strategy?"

"Sure. But I gotta warn you. Give me the Classic Illustrated condensed version. I gotta use the toilet pretty soon."

"Have you ever thought about talking to a doctor about your bowel situation?"

"Piss off. What's your great strategy? I'll tell you if it's realistic or point out any potential pittfalls. Remember to focus on her feelings and emotions, and pretend like you have some too, even though we both know you don't."

"Thanks for the pep talk. Okay, cutting to the chase. I'm gonna buy her an awesome dinner, bring her back here, get drunk and see if I can score."

"You will. Everyone else has."

Joe paused. "Waddya mean 'everyone else has?' Does that include you?"

"Well, uh, sure, yeah, a couple of times. I think. Uh no, actually, I believe it was three, no, four times. Less than ten, I can assure you of that, Joe. That doesn't count mutual oral sex, does it?"

Joe was speechless. He felt his legs give way and he fell back into the chair, holding his head in his hands.

" It wasn't a big thing. Just casual fuck buddies, you know? "

"No. Actually Lance, I don't"

"It didn't mean anything. Besides, that was over two years ago. What does that have to do with now? It was almost kind of like shaking hands, plus Carlene always had a drawer full of rubbers. I mean, that's not really sex if you're wearing a condom, is it? It's act-ually quite similar to watching TV. Just something to do. Our parents didn't have the entertainment options we enjoy nowadays, thanks to their personal sacrifice in the last great war.

"Imagine, manning a machine gun nest on Wake Island with John Wayne who has turd breath and insists on continually goosing you with his bayonet and laughing to keep you loose as thousands of fanatical Japanese are massing, about to overrun you. "Switching gears here, did you know the Nazis, including Hitler, believed in the occult, and openly worshiped Satan?

"You know, this whole situation causes me to consider the great depression, when hungry men without hope or a chance, rode the rails, not realizing that the trains never moved anymore. It was kind of pathetic, really, men starving and shrinking daily, struggling to slide open the freight car door every morning and seeing the same dammed scenery again. They never moved. To save money, the Pygmies in charge at the 205 Club intended to drop an atom bomb on Dayton, Ohio."

"Why do you persist on changing the subject every time I ask you a question you are uncomfortable with?" demanded Joe.

"Geezuz, Joe. I'm just trying to make you feel better. It's not like I sneaked over there and did Carlene. No, I just did Debbie instead, for a single hit of acid. She was easy."

Joe abruptly returned to the kitchen. He ripped the top off the vodka bottle and took a long gulp. He wiped his mouth, "Damn."

Lance leaned against the door frame, "Hey look, Joe. I told you I was sorry. She's not your private stock, you know. "

Joe looked Lance in the eye for a moment and then burst into laughter. Lance joined in, and for a little while, Joe felt everything between them was all right.

An hour later, the boys were going at it hard,

well into the Greyhounds. Joe agreed that he would just buy a replacement bottle tomorrow. Lance surprised him by handing him a ten, "Your share," he said.

They were listening to Santana and digging the hot Latin beat of the drummers and the scorching guitar work of Carlos Santana. Joe and Lance were both standing on the carpet near the front window, singing along and dancing to the lively music.

Lance had his fluid Grateful Dead moves down, while Joe felt stiff and awkward despite the copious amount of liquid courage he had downed. Joe felt more comfortable shadow boxing, throwing imaginary punches at Gary Hess's face. He didn't even know the shithead, but sensed their paths were about to cross.

Someone was at the door. It seemed to Joe that someone was always at the door, knocking, wanting to come in. Why didn't they go next door once in a while, just for variety?

While Lance went for the front door, Joe reached over and lifted the tone arm off the fairly new record, but then dropped it and watched helplessly as the needle bounced and then cut a deep groove across the entire surface, "I hope it's not Bruce," he managed.

"Naw, no chance. If he was gonna hassle us about the flour deal, he would have done it before now."

Lance partially opened up, revealing a medium sized hard looking dude wearing a waist length leather jacket and cupping a smoke in his hands, "Hi. Is Joe here?" he rasped.

"Who are you?" demanded Lance, weaving around, unsteady on his feet.

"Jesse Barnes. I'm the new cook over at the restaurant. Who are you?"

"Lance Potter. What the hell do you want?"

"I just told you, retard," said Jesse, roughly pushing past Lance and greeting Joe like they were old buddies. Jesse removed a fifth of Tequila from inside his jacket. He took a slug and then offered it to Joe who shook his head, "No man. Thanks, but I'd better not add anything different to what I already have on board. Let's see, so far bourbon, vodka and beer. I don't want to make it worse. I already know I'm going to regret this tomorrow."

"What the hell, kid. You only live once. You ain't hurting nobody but yourself, and you got plenty of miles left on your odometer. Look, guys. Don't let me cramp your style. I was just walking by, see, looking for something to do, someone to hang out with.

"I can't handle that freaking Keddie Club very often. Too many inbred assholes spoiling for a fight. Besides, I don't exactly fit in there. You think they'd like me better if I got me a mountain man shirt, some suspenders, a cowboy hat and smelled like horse shit?"

"Only if you dribbled tobacco juice down your chin while you're talking, "added Joe.

"Oh. So anyway, who was that you was just playing? That dead purple guy, Hendrix?"

"No. Carlos Santana."

"Is he a Mexican?"

"Why would it matter what he is?" asked Lance, sounding hostile.

"Nothin, man. I got lots of friends who are beanerds. Oh, I'm sorry," said Jesse, pretending to throw a punch and stopping just short of Lance's nose, "Am I being insensitive? Geez, guys, can I party with you or not? Or do you wanna fight me. Huh?"

Lance stepped back, seeking to get out of Jesse's range, "We don't even know you."

"I already told you. Do you have some kind of mental issues, Lurch? For the last time. I'm Jesse Ray Barnes. What better way to get to know me then by partying a little bit. Well, go on then, Joe. Put that last record on, or that purple song by the stiff. It sounded great from outside. it should sound even better in here." He took another slug out of his Tequila and then put it away, not offering any to Lance.

"I guess that's ok," said Joe. He went back over and put on the Stones live. As soon as the familiar song started up, Jesse snapped his fingers, "Yeah! Now that's what I'm talking about."

Jesse peeled off his jacket and draped it over the back of a kitchen chair. He closed his eyes, puffed on a cigarette and grooved to the beat.

Lance yelled at Joe, "After this song, why don't you put on Ten Years After."

"Ten Years?" yelled Jesse," I just did ten years in the joint, and it wasn't much fun."

Joe approached Jesse and talked loud as the Stones continued to blare out at top volume, "Where you from, anyway, Jessie?"

"Sacramento."

Lance pulled the record off .

"Why'd you do that, man?" asked Jesse, "It was just starting to sound good."

"It's too loud to visit. Plus, you're giving me a headache."

Joe spoke again,"You were starting to tell me about Sacramento."

"Not much to tell. Truth is fellas, I just got out of San Quentin a few weeks ago."

"What for?" asked Lance.

"Can't tell you. My counselor in the big house told me to keep that to myself. Otherwise, I'll be judged and have to constantly explain myself. So, I did a crime. I did my time, and now I'm up here, looking for a fresh start. Believe me when I tell you, don't ever do anything bad enough to lose your freedom. Thank you Lord," Jesse traced the sign of the cross on his chest, kissed his fingers and threw his hand towards the ceiling.

"Was it bad in there?" inquired Lance.

Jesse took another drink. "You probably want to know a couple of things. Like I already told Lurch, it isn't in my best interest to tell you why I was incarcerated. I'll leave it up to your imagination. Am I a murderer, rapist, an armed robber, what? Your next greatest interest is in wondering if I bent over for the soap in the shower, right? Was I someone's bitch? Well, I ain't gonna talk about that neither."

"Sorry, said Joe, "I can't imagine being locked up for ten years."

"It could have been longer. I got out for good behavior, which ain't easy being as how you're locked up with a bunch of animals. The worst convicts are the lifers who have rage. Some of them accept the fact that they're never getting out and they shrink before your eyes. Every day they're a tiny bit smaller. They give up and got nothing to live for and would just as soon die.

"Then there are the other lifers, the ones who don't mind killing one more guard or fellow convict. What does it matter? They can only fry you once, and if you're not getting out, then why bother playing by the stupid ass prison rules and the individual gangs codes of honor."

"Who are you, really?" asked Lance.

Jesse ignored him, "You boys smoke pot?"

"On occasion," said Lance, quickly.

Jesse pulled out a baggie with a little green,

160

leafy material in the bottom. He proceeded to roll a one paper joint, expertly moving it back and forth between two fingers and rolling it closed, licking the glued edge shut.

He handed it to Joe, "You first, my friend. Hey, stilts, what happened to the tunes? Put on some- thing good or I'm gonna kick your ass."

"What?" asked Lance, "Are you being serious, and why do you keep calling me weird names?"

Jesse laughed, "You're funny, *Lance.* One thing both of you need to learn, right now. If you plan on taking someone out, you don't tell them what you're going to do first. You just go ahead and do it, and then if your victim wants to talk while he's bleeding to death, you can be a good Christian and listen. Or, if he's boring or he slept with your woman, you can shoot him again right in his pie hole. It all hinges on respect. You either earn it, or you die."

Jesse saw that Joe was still examining the joint, "You gonna light the dammed thing or you gonna stare at it all night?"

"This isn't spiked with anything, is it?"

"Gimme that," said Jesse, firing it up. It smelled nasty to Joe. Jesse held it in, blew the smoke in Lance's face and handed it to Joe.

"What do you mean, spiked? Like with Angel Dust or insecticides? Naw, I'm just a simple, mellow guy, fellas. I don't do any other drugs. You never know where the shit is really from, and they can cut it with rat turds or battery acid and you'd never know until you suddenly can't think clearly or form a simple sentence.

"Hard drugs make you do crazy ass shit, be- cause you're too screwed up to hold down a job, like who wants to work anyway. Trouble is, you always need more money everyday, because your habit keeps expanding from occasional play time into a full blown thing.

"Next thing you know, you wake up in jail and they're telling you that you did this terrible crime and how do you want to plead and you don't know, because you have no memory of the entire last month. For me, personally, I once lost an entire year. I think it was 1959.

"I just remember the constant noise at the 'Big Q.' The only place where it was sort of quiet and you could think a little bit without getting a shank stuck in your ribs was the chapel. Yeah, man. Finding God got me out of there five years quicker. Ha."

Joe had to light the joint again, took a tentative hit and launched into a spastic coughing fit, "Taste's like dog shit," he said, offering it to Lance who shook his head.

How odd, thought Joe. Never in his life with Lance had he ever seen him turn down anything, even snorting model glue or huffing oven cleaner. There was clearly something wrong, but what?

Jesse let it burn down and dropped the long roach into his baggie, "You guys got anything better?"

"No," said Lance quickly, "All we got is booze and cigarettes."

"Lance," said Joe, "Come out to the car with me for a moment. I forgot to give you something. Jesse, make yourself at home. We'll be right back."

"Okay. Whatever, man. You guys are hard to party with."

It was cold outside. It smelled like Pine Trees, with needles starting to accumulate on the hard packed earth. Winter was just around the corner.

Lance and Joe stood next to the Sequoia,

hugging themselves, wishing they had put their coats on.

"What's the problem, Lance? I've never seen you act this hostile before."

Lance glanced back at the cabin and hissed at Joe, "Don't party with him. Your new friend is a narc."

"Why do you say that?"

"That crap he's carrying around in that bag and calling weed, isn't. I suspect it's oregano. See, they don't let narcs carry around real dope, turning people on. I'm surprised he hasn't tried to buy some drugs from me yet."

Just as they turned to go back inside, Jesse came out, buttoning his coat, a smoke dangling from the corner of his mouth. Lance tried to give him a wide berth but Jesse pretended to stumble and wound up plowing into Lance with his left shoulder and knocking him into a flower bed.

"Sorry," muttered Jesse, leaving Lance laying there and next veering towards Joe.

Joe braced himself in case Jesse decided to have another pedestrian accident. Instead, he stopped, "Your buddy there is a dick. Good thing he's not in San Quentin. He wouldn't last two days before he'd be some black Bubba's bitch."

Joe observed Lance pick himself up and run into the cabin.

"Hey, Jesse. Sorry about Lance tonight. He had a bad trip yesterday, and he's not acting like himself."

Jesse brought the Camel up to his lips and locked his green and yellow eyes in on Joe's, who could only handle the intensity for a few moments before looking away.

Jesse blew perfect smoke rings towards the twinkling stars.

"He's a dork and and a spaz. Why the hell do you live with him?"

"We've been best friends since eight grade. We have our ups and downs, but we've also got a lot of good history behind us. I guess I'm just loyal."

"Loyalty and a bullet can get you killed. Look, Joe. Sorry to crash your scene. I just get lonely. I sleep on the couch at my sister's house, but she's got five young kids and an old man who's kind of a roid, so I can't hang out there much.

"Don't get me wrong. I appreciate them giving me an address and lining me up with a job. I had to have those two things to get parole, which is difficult to pull off when you're behind the walls. My bitch old lady Stella sold my bike and divorced me, so I had no other place to go.

"Let's go do something soon, huh Joe? You'll find I make a good friend. You back me up, I back you up. No man stands alone, at least not for long."

"That sounds familiar, a classic line. Who said it first?"

"Dick Nixon or Yul Bryner. How the hell would I know, kid? I got an 8th grade education, and I don't even know how I got that far."

"Well, anyway, thanks for the free meals and multiple milks. I'm low on money."

"Forget about it, Joe. See ya around soon, huh?"

Joe watched as Jesse walked confidently up the sidewalk and kept going towards the bluff and the railroad, which was oddly quiet tonight.. A shiver ran down Joe's spine. The thought of hanging with a real life criminal was simultaneously exciting and dangerous.

Joe realized that maybe he didn't necessarily have to travel down Route 66 with Buzz Murdock or

Todd Styles from the famous television show to have adventures. It was also possible to have them close to home You just had to know the right people, and Jesse Ray Barnes might be just the guy to help him cross over from boring conformity to a life of danger and adventure. That's what he really wanted, not some straight job with a salary, pension and even some of those new ones that came with health benefits. What good was that?

Joe went back inside, closed and locked the door.

Lance sprung up from the couch like a life sized jack-in-the-box." What the hell bro! We gotta get all of our stash out of your dresser and bury it."

"What do you mean, 'my' dresser? I thought your inventory was in my trunk. Why is it in my dresser and not yours?"

Lance looked away, "Mine is full of sex toys and condoms."

The back yard was pitch black. Lance focused a flashlight on the hole Joe was attempting to dig in the rock hard dirt with his pint sized folding Army issue shovel that he had pulled out of his trunk. While he bent over and thrust the dull edge into the ground, Joe thought of Squirt. He would have been perfect for this dumb ass job. Hard as he was trying, Joe was having trouble getting deeper then a few inches.

"Hurry," urged Lance, who was clutching his precious stash that was inside of a shoebox, wrapped up tight with cut up paper sacks and tape. Lance had explained to Joe that keeping moisture out was their most important task. Even a little wetness could potentially ruin everything. Lance had mentioned that if that happened, he would be forced to sell sips from a

Dixie cup for a few bucks. The thick liquid would be a potent mixture of psychedelics, uppers, downers, and mescaline. No one would know how much was too much or too little, not until they had some, and by then, it would be too late.

Joe stopped, holding the shovel out," You wanna dig?"

"No, no, Joe. you're making progress." Lance shined the light on a pathetic little pile of dirt. Perspiration beaded up on Joe's brow.

"Then shut up!" said Joe, slamming the shovel as hard as he could into the dirt.

Lance acted excited, "Go Joe! I know you can do it."

"I thought I told you to shut up. Maybe Jessie's right."

"Right about what?"

"You being a spaz."

"Aw come on, Joe. That's not nice. You don't even know the guy, he's obviously a narc, and you're taking his side against me."

Fifteen minutes later Lance gently placed his stash into the hole after kissing the box.

Joe laughed, "You gonna say a prayer now? I've got one. Ashes to ashes, stash to jail."

"That sucks and doesn't come close to rhyming. I've got my whole life savings invested in that box."

The rear bedroom light clicked on. The curtains parted and the window opened. Scott stuck his head out, "What are two idiots doing back there?"

Lance responded in his phony English accent that was improving, "I say old chap, we're looking for your mother's chastity belt. Obviously she wasn't wearing it when you were created out of some infected

166

sperm."

"Sarcastic bastard!" Scott slammed the window shut.

"I do say," said Lance towards the closed window and the shadow of the hated dweeb Scott, with his huge hooked nose clearly visible in the sha- dows, "Why don't you just piss off, SNOT!"

Joe was astounded. He had never seen such rage exploding from his previously mellow friend. Perhaps the quicksand of his lifestyle was dragging him down to depths he never knew existed. Joe was truly concerned for Lance's mental health, as he continued to drop LSD, Mescaline or do Magic Mushrooms every single day. Add the booze, weed, reds and speed, and it only seemed logical to assume that he would eventually crash.

Joe and Lance drove into Quincy the next day, feeling a bit sheepish, knowing they had surrendered to their paranoia. Jesse hadn't come back with the Sheriff. Even the Marlboro Men now seemed benign. Why would they have it in for two kids from Berkeley they didn't even know? Still, Jesse wasn't clear of their mistrust. He could just be laying the groundwork for a bigger bust later on, where they could not only arrest Joe and Lance, they could possibly get to 'Mr. Big,' their supplier.

Just to be cautious, Joe and Lance agreed to keep their stash for sale buried for another couple of days. They still had their personal supplies that they had carefully counted out, plotting their highs, and lows for the next three days. Then, if the coast was clear, they would retrieve Lance's box, and he could fill his orders. They had firm plans to drive back to the Bay Area that next weekend.

In Sociology, Amy announced that the class would discuss the programming of boot camp recruits by the various different branches of the service, which in time of war was four. The Army, Marines, Air Force and then the Coast Guard, coming under control of the Navy, temporarily transferred from The Treasury Department.

She claimed that young soldiers and sailors were brain washed and often physically abused by sadistic D.I.'s with low I.Q.'s. The recruits were brutally broken down within a week, usually in mere days. Then, they were slowly built back up, and eventually converted into men who would follow any order, no matter how insane, immoral or just plain crazy, all without question.

Gary sat by himself. A few students had already dropped out, while there were always a few more that were sick or just didn't show up, like those two Berkeley jackasses that he still owed a beating to. No one had the nerve or desire to sit next to Gary.

When occasionally at class, Lance sat with Maureen and her friends, while Joe would mostly sit by himself, staring at the ceiling, still hopelessly attempting to count the holes, always coming up with a different count every time.

When Joe and Lance were missing, Maureen would wait until class was over and Amy would walk over to the nearby river to smoke and read, as her next class didn't start for an hour. Maureen would sneak back in and mark Joe and Lance as present. So far, a month into classes, they showed a perfect attendance record.

Joe returned to the cabin by himself and took a

shower. Even though his hot date with Carlene was hours away, he was nervous and wanted to start getting ready. He dressed with care. Joe put on his seldom worn dorky white levis and a blue cotton shirt. He completed his admittedly preppy ensemble with clean white socks and brown hush puppies. Joe then poured a handful of refreshing Aqua Velva on his hands and slapped it everywhere there was open skin, even putting some on his crotch. That ought to be the clin- cher he thought. By the time he was through screwing around, it was after three O'clock.

He was hungry and hoped he wouldn't have to wait until seven for Carlene to come over. Being inex- perienced, he had allowed her to name the time. He should have just told her he was picking her up at five, and that would be that. *'No backtalk, woman, get in the car.'*

Joe sat on the couch and wrung his sweaty hands together. He reviewed some of the lines he had planned, 'My, you have pretty brown eyes, Carlene,' 'Yeah baby, when they made you, they threw away the mold,' and finally, before payoff time, 'Carlene baby, I fell in love with you the first time I saw you.'

He picked up his Biology textbook, and tired to read, but couldn't concentrate. His stomach fluttered and turned. He looked at his watch every few minutes, willing time to go faster. He got up and paced the floor, listening for any sign of Carlene.

Shortly after seven, Lance entered the cabin and let in a blast of frigid air.

"Hey Joe. What's with the geek outfit.? You going to an American Legion social or something?"

Joe looked forlorn.

"Oh yeah, that's right. You're taking Carlene to

dinner. I forgot. Say, isn't it kind of late? Seems like you should be there by now."

"Shit Lance!" exploded Joe, "It's way after seven. I've been freaking sitting here for hours, going crazy. Now she doesn't even show up? I am righteously pissed."

"Sorry, man. I can find you an easy piece of ass if you want. I'm telling you, one hit of acid usually buys me an hour of fun.

"Thanks, Lance, but I'd like to have a real relationship."

"Yeah, man. I used to think that way too. Now, it's just easier doing a different chick every night. That way, nobody gets jealous or spoiled."

Joe walked angrily into his room and ripped off his square clothes and shoes. He put on his flannel jeans and lumberjack shirt. He moved into the kitchen to scrounge up something to eat.

As he sat back on the couch, preparing to bite into a baloney sandwich on white bread, there came another knock at the dammed door.

"I'll get it," said Joe, anger rising like bile in his throat.

"Hi," said Carlene who was dressed in casual clothes, "I was just wondering if I could borrow a pan. I need to cook some liver for my puppy."

"I didn't know you had a dog," said Lance from the chair.

"I just got him. I named him Joe. He's so adorable. I just love him."

"No," on the pan said Joe in a caustic voice, "What the hell happened to our dinner date tonight?"

"Oh, wow. Was that tonight? I thought it was next week."

"How could you think that, Carlene? I was very

specific about it being tonight. You said you'd come over between four and seven."

"Well, you don't have to get sarcastic with me," she said.

"Yes I do."

Carlene turned and walked down the stairs and headed back to her cabin.

Joe slammed the door and slumped against it, "Okay, that's it with her. I'm done. Time to idolize someone else."

"I totally agree, Joe. You deserve better."

BACK TO BERKELEY

CHAPTER TEN

It was the last week of September 1970. Crisp
brown and yellows leaves fluttered to the ground,
creating deep piles. Guy would do the best he could to
clean them up. The miniature elf man, limping along
with a lame leg, tried valiantly to keep up with the
additional daily volume of leaves, pine needles and
road kills. Joe viewed him with pity, but also grudging
respect. The man was doing the best he could with what
he had, and who should ever expect more then that
from anyone?

Faded scarecrows made of straw and dead
people's clothes wilted, no longer charged with the
protection of the vast cornfields that were dying too.
Football was being played at Quincy High, and it was
popular among citizens who led otherwise boring,
predictable lives. They liked screaming and yelling for
two hours on Friday night. They felt fully alive at least
once a week. In addition, they wanted to support their
team, kids that many of them had watched grow from
toddlers into young adults.

Joe and Lance were loading up. It was Friday
morning, and they were heading back to the Bay Area
for the weekend. Chris and Susan were joining them,
and promised Joe they would chip in some gas money.
Joe had made them agree to not hassle him and Lance
about finding Jesus or giving them snarky looks if they
should decide to smoke a joint. The acid was allegedly

all gone, so that option was off the table.

Before leaving, they stood in a loose circle and drank MJB coffee. Joe had laced his and Lance's, adding 4 ounces of whiskey to each for their breakfast. Chris and Susan tried to chew some of her brown bread with great difficultly. Chris in particular, who finally resorted to an old Three Stooges move. He put one hand on top of his head, the other on his chin, to add extra force to his chewing. Joe also observed his eyes bulging out of his head. Susan acted as though every-thing was just fine, matter of fact, excellent. Joe and Lance laughed aloud when they observed a queer look on Susans's face. She stopped chewing, reached into her mouth and removed a twig that had been swept into the flour bag a few nights before by Joe.

Once in the car, they took a right turn onto the lightly traveled two lane highway that paralleled the Feather River and would lead them past Oroville and Chico. Oakland was a six hour drive. Joe would drop off Chris and Susan somewhere an hour out of his way in the Oakland Hills. Next, Lance at Kathy's, and then he would return home for the first time in a month. Joe felt dread whenever he thought about seeing his family again. He was leery as to how it might go.

Joe put on his Military issue shades, fired up a smoke and proclaimed, "This is gonna be a great week-end." No one answered him. Joe didn't even believe it himself.

Lance stared out his window and Chris and Susan cuddled in the back seat, enamored with each other's company. They spoke in lover's whispers into each other's ears, laughed at something said, and held hands. Joe supposed they were in love, something he had never experienced and wondered if he ever would. Was he doomed to a loveless, childless, sad life, destined to always be alone?

A early 1950's Ford pickup truck tailed them.
Joe made out two forms in the front seat, both wearing
cowboy hats. He grinned, floored it and quickly left
them behind in a cloud of dust and exhaust smoke. He
watched them disappear in the rear view mirror as their
presence was reduced to the size of a fly in mere
seconds.

He briefly considered the meaning of their
following them. Were they a couple of hicks heading
into the larger town of Chico for a yard of fresh ma-
nure? Or were they part of the same contingent of the
Marlboro Men that Joe now suspected was much larger
than the same four cowboys who seemingly lived at the
restaurant. Or, was their presence on the road this morning merely a coincidence?

He slowed down to negotiate some of the sweeping curves that gradually turned them from north to
west, and then eventually south towards Sacramento.
The sameness of the scenery made him a bit drowsy
and his thoughts drifted. He and Lance had also smoked
a huge bomber in the backyard before leaving, and Joe
had a pleasant buzz going.

He was attending classes even less. He was
drinking more and noticed his hands trembling at times.
His love life was hopeless. In addition, his once rock
solid relationship with old friend Lance was drifting
more out of control. Lance's moods were unpredictable,
as he veered from the comfortable harbor of long term
friendship to recent incidents of outright hostility. Joe
wasn't sure if it was him causing the riff or if Lance's
brain was finally imploding, leaving behind random,
isolated, pockets of his former self. They were not
linked together, instead, leaving large gaps of blank
spots

Joe hadn't bothered calling his parents to remind them of his weekend drill. Why should he? What were they going to do, deny him the use of his own room? He wondered how events would go down when he walked in the back door, unannounced. It never occurred to him that his seemingly simple plan might not work if, say, no one were home. Maybe his family had gone on vacation, perhaps a long boring road trip to Cleveland.

Joe required a place to crash and desired some home cooked meals. His surprise visit and interaction might go okay, or it could be a disaster, and there might be some carryover from his last, caustic breakfast visit with Bud. Still, a weekend with access to a fully stocked refrigerator was quite appealing, so he was willing to compromise and even be sociable, if the vibes allowed it.

Then again, what was he supposed to talk to his mother about? How her migraine headaches were slowly killing her, and how well her new tranquilizers were working?

What about the feisty, perennially pissed off Bud? 'How deep was the mud on the job sight today, pops?' 'Run any hippie queers off the road with your big truck lately?'

He at least had a slight chance with Marvin. Kids his age frequently matured rapidly, and he was nearing thirteen, and the dubious status of a teenager.

Joe returned from his musings and found they were already out of the mountains and rapidly approaching Oroville. He glanced over and saw that Lance's head was lying on the open window frame, half in and half out, with a few apparently unnoticed bugs splattered on his face. He had on tiny purple biker shades, was counting highway markers and muttering to himself in a consistent rhythm, "Mile three hundred and seventy and counting, rat-a-tat is that, man, rat-a-tat is that, man, rat-a-tat is that," and on and on.

Joe observed Chris and Susan in the rear view mirror, locked in a tight embrace. Susan met his eyes and gave him a saucy smile. Joe felt heaviness in his stomach. No way, he thought. He wasn't about to fall for that one random brief invitation. Besides, should they somehow hook up, it would quite naturally lead to his daily exposure to her allegedly award winning brown bread. It would likely cause him to choke to death or eventually starve from lack of adequate nutrition.

That wasn't how he visualized his demise. He knew he was supposed to drown. He just didn't know when or where. He supposed it was going to be a big surprise.

"Hey Joe!" said Susan in an excited voice. *Oh no, he thought, please don't reveal your love for me now, especially in front of Chris and Lance.*

"'Yeah?'"

"There's an awesome swimming hole coming up soon. How about we take a quick dip? We have plenty of time."

"Yeah," Joe agreed, "We do have a little slack time I built into our schedule. Does anyone have a bathing suit with them? I don't"

"No one does," said Susan. "It'll be more fun that way. If we all swim together naked, we will be pure and free. It's like when you're first born,swimming out of your mother's birth canal, being slapped on your tiny ass and taking in your first breath. Back then, we all started equal, in the same place. Born without sin."

Lance didn't say a thing, continuing to count off

highway markers as they zoomed by. A large bug splattered on his glasses, and he was forced to pull his head back inside and furiously try to clean the squished bug off his lens using spit and his shirt, which merely spread bug guts all across the lens.

"Turn left here!" shouted Susan.

Joe complied and whipped the steering wheel, roaring through an empty dirt turnout and skidding to a halt in a gigantic cloud of dust just a foot from a steep drop off. They all exited the car in a hurry, eager to be outside in what was shaping up to be a mighty fine California day.

"Up here," shouted Susan, having run up a berm that was crowded with ferns and small bushes. They joined her at her vantage point, and were struck with the roar and sparkling beauty of the Feather River that lay right below them.

"Far out," said Lance.

Joe had a sudden flashback of Henry Fonda tooling along in a dust bowl era Model A truck. Scruffy, dirty relatives stood on the running boards and clung to any part of the huge load that they perceived to be secure. Kids of all ages and sizes sat on the back edge of a stained mattress that hung over the road by a foot. The cargo area of the truck was impossibly loaded with beds, dressers, food, tools, a couch, camping gear and most importantly for their survival, as many full water jugs as they could carry. They had been forced to leave behind a large, perfectly good pile of possessions. A lifetime of work and scrimping and saving, all for nothing. The Oklahoma dust had probably covered most all of it up by now anyway.

A contemplative John Steinbeck, dressed in fine, expensive clothes, would follow behind the 'Jobe' family. He was a back seat passenger in a regal yellow

Stutz Bearcat driven by a stern looking chauffer, allowing Steinbeck time to write his epic, American tale of struggle and survival, *The Grapes of Wrath.*

Susan sprung to life and ran down the rocky bank towards the raging river with clean clear water, ripped off her clothes while she ran and shouted out in glee. Chris and Lance were right behind her. Joe paused, smoking, assessing the situation. Who were the crazy ones now? The water had to be freezing ass cold, plus they had no suits or towels.

"Come on in, Joe," yelled Susan. She stood in the middle of the river, naked. Her breasts hung heavy, and she waved at him. Lance and Chris plunged into the fast moving water. They too were nude. Chris was wide and hairy while Lance was tall and gangly and bright white with little body hair.

Joe shrugged his shoulders, approached the river, looked around, and hid his car keys and wallet under a nearby flat rock. He removed his clothes and carefully folded them and left them on top of the same rock.

Not being one of those hardy souls who can dive into icy water and be just fine, Joe gradually waded in. Damn, he thought, it was colder then he'd imagined. He gradually crouched down and immersed his entire body, except his head, and he swam towards the others.

"Over here, Joe!" yelled Lance. Joe swam in the direction of his friend's voice, unable to see much because of the swift current and choppy water. He finally joined his friends on the far side in a quiet, tranquil cove. It was almost like sitting in a clear lake with calm water, while the river raged right next to them.

Chris and Susan embraced under a small waterfall that originated from far above them on a rocky cliff.

Lance treaded water, spreading his arms out with a hypnotized expression. Joe wondered if he'd dropped acid again, despite his statement about being out. Lance was rarely out. It made sense. He had counted highway markers for a good hour, and was acting stoned, spacey and withdrawn.

Susan stood up, water dripping off her. Joe couldn't help but look. Chris caught him in the act and stared back at him and slowly wagged his index finger back and forth.

Joe started back while he still could. The coldness of the river water was clearly affecting him, making his limbs feel heavy and he felt the beginnings of mental confusion. As he struggled, he wondered if he was still capable of getting back. It should be an easy task. Just swim back. It's only fifty feet or so. Joe had the reoccurring vision, the one right before he drowns. This time he pictured himself going down, one hand still in the air, and his friends losing sight of him and not knowing where he was and being unaware of his watery fate.

He heard Susan giggling as she knifed past him with powerful, easy strokes. Next came Chris and Lance, clearly oblivious to his struggle. He summoned his last bit of energy and gratefully stumbled up on the rocks, feeling the instant euphoria of one who has just dodged a bullet. He dressed, retrieved his wallet and keys and walked silently back to the car. He wouldn't waste his breath attempting to explain his frequent drowning premonition to his friends. They wouldn't understand.

Instead, he would internalize the incident, and store it away for future contemplation, when circumstances were more cathartic.

Two hours later, they stopped in Sacramento for fuel. Lance and Chris headed into the station while Susan stood near him in the sunshine and stretched out her arms.

Lance returned,. "I'll get us some gas in Berkeley, Joe. My siphon hose is still in your trunk."

Chris came back with two ice cold cokes. Joe watched the price on the pump stop at twelve dollars for a fill up.

Chris handed two crumpled dollars to Joe, "Here's our share. Should be good enough for the round trip. I mean, you two were coming down here anyway, so it's almost like we're hitchhikers."

He and Susan laughed, climbed into the back seat and enjoyed their cokes.

Joe didn't say anything, but now he was thirsty too. He charged the gas as usual and added the two dollars to his nearly empty wallet. He got some tepid water from the station's drinking fountain.

Joe delivered Chris and Susan to a posh mansion in upscale Piedmont, which was the wealthy part of Oakland, castle like houses nestled in the hills.

"I'll pick you up around five on Sunday. I'll drive here directly from the base."

"Where's your base?" asked Chris.

"In the Alameda Estuary. They call it Government Island, but when I was in boot camp there, we called it 'Devils Island.' Whatever you call it, the fact is the place is an obsolete shithole from World War Two."

Chris gave Joe a mock salute and grabbed Susan's hand and skipped up the red walkway of a large, three story house. A black lady in a maid's uniform answered the door.

Two bucks, thought Joe angrily. At least one of the spoiled brats lived in a palace like this, and they give him two lousy, stinking dollars after taking him a good hour out of his way? He felt like wadding up the currency, knocking on the front door and politely requesting the pleasure of the presence of Chris, and then lunging forward, forcing his mouth open and shoving the two dollars down his throat. If he choked to death, all the better.

Upon returning to Keddie, Joe would arrange for his asshole friend Scott to commit suicide by pouring a jug of Draino down his nose after forcing him sign his own suicide note.

Joe dropped off an unusually quiet Lance in front of Moore's TV store. He warned Lance to be packed to leave by six on Sunday evening, and if he wasn't ready, Joe was prepared to strand him in Berkeley. As it was, even if everything went smoothly, they would be returning after midnight.

Lance nodded his head in apparent agreement. Joe laughed aloud when his obviously stoned buddy took one step, tripped and fell face first onto the sidewalk. Lance got up, brushed himself off and limped towards the stairway that led to Kathy's apartment.

Joe parked in front of the family home on nearby Santa Fe. Ave, which in his town, meant he lived on the correct side of the railroad tracks. His grandfather, R.C., had built the modest single story stucco house in the early 1920's. Over the years, the home had been enlarged by Bud, adding two bedrooms, with an elderly R.C. sitting on a chair and telling Bud how to do things when his son was a skilled journeyman carpenter.

Joe walked up the long steep driveway to a

white, two car detached garage. R.C. constructed this building too, and used it as an auto shop in the 1930's, specializing in Model T's and Model A's. R.C. was capable of working on anything from a lawnmower to a gigantic farm threshing machine.

Joe could see remnants of masking tape on the left garage door that he had put up years ago, to simulate a baseball strike zone. He smiled as memories of his years as a baseball pitcher in the mid and late 1960's came flooding back to him. He recalled practicing pitching nearly every day for years, throwing a tennis ball from exactly sixty feet six inches back, which is the official Major League Pitching distance.

He would fire up exactly 100 pitches, and was capable of being inside the strike zone consistently, 85 per cent of the time, and the others didn't miss by much. He tossed up a potent mixture of fastballs, a sharp dropping curve, screwballs and a devastating, off speed change up, which he used as his out pitch.

He built up his arm this way, and when he pitched for real on organized teams, including his high school, he was known for his poise and composure on the mound, and also his virtually pinpoint control.

He rarely walked anyone, and enjoyed drilling an occasional batter in the ribs, just to show them he was the boss, at least while standing on the pitching mound. He had adopted the fierce demeanor of pro pitchers like Bob Gibson and Don Drysdale, who were so mean that they would brush back their own mother if she were batting and crowding the plate .The only issue for Joe was that these men were tall and muscular, and he was averaged sized. Didn't matter, he thought. If he didn't like a kid, and the score wasn't close, yeah he'd drill em, and then laugh. Even then he knew to never apologize. For anything. Ever.

Often, when Joe was practicing, he would bring out his cheesy transistor radio and listen to KSFO, the AM station that broadcast the Giants games. His favorite moment was when a S.F. batter would hit a home run, and the announcer's voice would get excited as they followed the progress of the bomb and yelled out their own, distinctive homerun calls.

For veteran announcer Russ Hodges, who dated back to the clubs existence in NewYork in the 1950's, it was an emphatic "And you can tell it BY BY BABY!"

Lon Simmons, part Indian and former pro pitcher had his own call, "And you can TELL IT GOOD-BYE!"

In 1967, Joe visualized himself someday proudly posing in his crisp clean San Francisco Giants uniform. He fantasized about reading newspaper stories about himself, *'Local boy makes good!'*

There would be other boys like him, with dreams of stardom. He vowed to be one of those nice stars, who despite their recognized greatness,.would remain humble. He would devote an hour after each game to signing baseball cards of himself. He imagined the kids going home and demanding three Mickey Mantle's for just one Joe Bailey.

He strode back to the start of the driveway, turned and squared up to the tape. He bent over, hands on his knees, getting the sign from Edgar Lonus Bailey, no relative but a legendary Giants slugging catcher. Joe nodded his head, stood up straight, rocked back and forth, launched into his full windmill windup and threw an imaginary pitch at a make believe batter.

"Strike!" he yelled out.

Joe dropped his hands. He could hear his past calling to him.

He watched in amazement as a twelve year old

version of himself emerged from inside the garage, walking right through the wood. He was dressed as a 'Pirate,' and clutched his worn glove that needed to be replaced but there wasn't any money. Other kids wore baseball cleats. Joe was forced to wear his everyday black Converse high top tennis shoes. There was a wide smile on his youthful face as his ghost passed right through him, leaving behind a fleeting moment of icy coldness, profound sadness, and a morbid sense of futile finality.

Whoa, he thought, snapping back. That was way too real.

Joe climbed the back door stairs and entered the house. All of the Bailey's used the back door. The front door was reserved for spiritual scouts such as the re-lentless Jehovah's Witnesses. Or, the pathetic, broken down Fuller Brush Man, practically begging you to buy something, anything. 'A toothbrush for Christ's sake' he would cry out. It didn't matter what it was. He had to make a sale.

Joe walked through the claustrophobic laundry room that smelled like Tide. Alice was in the tiny kitchen, standing at the stove, stirring a pot. It smelled good, with a rich mixture of spices, and meat cooking, mixed with the sweet fresh fruit smell that emanated from a basket of bananas and apples that hung in the sunny kitchen window.

'Hi, mom."

She turned around, a wooden cooking spoon in her hand, "Joe. What are you doing here?"

"It's my duty weekend, ma. I hope it's okay if I sleep in my old room for a couple of nights. You won't see me much, as I'll be gone all day Saturday and Sun-day. I'm leaving directly from Alameda to head back to the mountains after Sunday's drill."

Alice gave Joe one of her tranked out, lopsided grins, "Well, I can invite you to dinner. As far as sleeping here, I don't know. You'll have to clear it with your dad first. He's at the hardware store picking out some grout. He's going to re-do our bathroom tomorrow."

Dinner smelled good, "What ya cooking, mom?"

"Cow liver with onions, bacon and brown gravy. You always liked it when you were growing up."

In other words, thought Joe, '*Look at you now. A drunk and a drug addict.*'

His mom returned her attention back to the dishes she was preparing. Joe realized that she had nothing else to say to him, even though they hadn't seen each other for a month.

Joe felt a surge of sarcasm overwhelm his common sense, "Yeah, mom, things are going really well for me at school. I've got straight A's so far. I've been voted the Class President and I've become a nationally recruited Football Quarterback."

"That's nice, Joe," she said, reaching into a cupboard, drinking something out of a bottle and then returning it.

Joe snickered. In reality, if they knew of his 1.0 grade average so far, there would be hell to pay. His parents would be outraged. For this clear failure, these kinds of results, they were paying out all this money?

Joe opened the refrigerator door. He blinked when he saw shelves full of bacon, eggs, salami, cheese, French bread, milk, real butter and so much more. He salivated, but settled for pulling out a jug of apple juice and taking a big slug.

"Use a glass, Joey. How many times do I have to tell you?"

"Sorry. What else are we having?" No one else could get away with calling him 'Joey.'

"Fried onions with potatoes, onions and peppers, and asparagus."

"It all sounds great except for the asparagus. Leave that slimy crap off of my plate."

No reponse.

"Nice visiting with you, mother. I'm going to go say hi to Marvin."

"Joe."

"Yeah, ma?"

"It's okay to greet your little brother, but your dad and I don't want you to spend anytime alone with him."

"Why? Geez, he's still my little brother, isn't he?"

"Yes, of course." Alice swiveled back to face him, "He's at a very impressionable age, and we can't afford to have you warp him with your bad habits and caustic attitude. Your dad will want to go over it in more depth with you, probably tonight, if he allows you to stay."

Joe was insulted, "Gee mom, I wasn't planning on shooting up Marvin with heroin until at least Christmas."

"Save the sarcasm for your dad. He deals with it better then I do."

"Meaning he can still punch me out if he's in one of his pissed off moods. He comes home, sees me, becomes enraged and starts chucking 2x4's at me, all the while blowing sawdust out his nose and ass."

"I said that's enough!"

Alice flipped the dark liver over in the frying pan. Hot grease sizzled and popped and Joe was always amazed that his mom didn't have a face full of grease burns, "If you have issues with him, don't talk to me about it. Talk to him."

Joe shook his head and entered the short green hallway. It was carpeted with cheap gray industrial carpet that Bud and his crew had ripped out of an office building they were re-modeling.

"There's nothing wrong with this carpet, Alice," he had said. "It's got plenty of years left in it. I just need to get my friend Fresco over here to lay it down." Yeah, thought Joe, Fresco had put it down all right. Three months later. It always had a prominent, printing press ink odor that never went away. Bud and Alice tried everything to get the offending stench out. They shampooed it several times themselves, once even paying cousin Bernie, who was a professional carpet cleaner with his own company, to try it. No dice. Years later, it still smelled like a mixture of clown vomit and spilled ink.

Marvin was locked in the bathroom, making exaggerated grunting and groaning noises. He spent an unusual amount of time every day doing his 'big job'. He stopped up the plumbing for their only toilet at least once a month. Bud was the only father on the block that walked around his house with a plunger tied to his belt.

One time it was backed up so bad that Bud had to hire his black laborer buddy, 'Spoony, to help him dig up the plumbing all the way to the street. Bud had been angry about that one for months.

Joe walked into his old room at the end of the hallway. He opened the sliding door and it made a familiar rubbing noise. The air in his childhood room was stale, as though the door hadn't been opened since he had left. He sat down on his bedspread, which was dusty.

His room seemed smaller, claustrophobic. The

wallpaper was peeling and the ceiling needed painting. He glanced at the floor and the same ugly and brown vinyl squares that he used to push his toy trucks and cars around on, complete with sound effects. For the first seven years of Marvin's life, he and Joe had shared the room, sleeping on a rickety wooden bunk bed that Bud had salvaged from the local dumps.

Joe had the top bunk, which he preferred. He didn't want to be sleeping on the bottom and potentially get crushed if there should be an earthquake and the top bunk with box spring mattress and body came crashing down. Better that Marvin should get it.

At age eight, Marvin moved into the vacant front bedroom.

Joe opened both windows to get some fresh air flowing. He gazed around his room, half empty and stared at his possessions that he had deemed non-essential for Keddie, or were clearly too large to bring along. It seemed as though he were staring at someone else's things. Everything that remained was a link to his past, but none of it seemed important anymore. Joe's core values and mantras were evolving. His personal beliefs and morals were becoming more defined. After reading Kerouac's *On The Road,* he had decided to become a minimalist, collecting experiences, not things.

He also longed for more adventure. He had gotten quite a bit when on active duty in the Coast Guard, but that was hardly enough. He craved more. Joe knew that the best approach would be to hitchhike across the Untied States. Maybe he would live some-where else for a while, or maybe he would hitchhike right back. Who knew how long it would take. That was irrelevant. He wanted to travel light, with a rucksack and a book, just like Jack used to do. That is if he wasn't riding along in a stolen car at a hundred miles an hour. He would be blind stinking drunk, with the driver, Dean Moriarity, lit up and babbling away, casually steering with one hand and wildly gesticulating with the other.

There was only one thing standing in his way. That was the fact that he was committed to the Coast Guard Reserves until July of 1975. That might as well be fifty years from now, he thought. He was going to lose some of the prime traveling and adventuresome years of his life. On the other hand, he had a cakewalk compared to the poor souls around his age who were in combat. in Vietnam.

The Rolling Stones sang about this dichotomy of opposing forces in their popular song, *'You Can't Always Get What You Want.'*

Now, he was starting to understand what that meant. He realized that it would probably be the first of many comprises he might have to make as an adult. He decided right then and there to not worry about it. Joe vowed not to live a life of regrets, and to not live his life in fear of the unknown, of what might happened.

He focused his attention on the old fashioned, large black metal closet doorknob. He smiled wryly, remembering many a night where he had stared at the doorknob in the dark gloom of his room, dreading what might be on the other side. He wondered when the scary boogeyman would emerge from his hiding spot in the middle of his hanging clothes.

Joe expected the boogeyman would burst out some night, display the craziness of his un-human essence, and finally reveal his murderous intentions regarding Joe.

Joe's childish paranoia became ten times worse when he started eating LSD and spending the entire night in his room, afraid to move, always listening for the sound of something big moving around in his closet. Perhaps a wheezy breath, or heavy footsteps.

Occasionally, he tired of the nightly games, got a shot of courage along with a blast of boldness, and would rip open the damned door. He was in the mood to confront whatever it was that hid in there, taunting him. The closet was always empty.

The closet was of normal length, but it was unusually long, traveling the entire backside of his next door parent's room. Joe had plenty of space to store his clothes, shoes, and board games with lots of room left over. At the very end was a tiny dresser so small that it looked as though it belonged to an elf.. It was mostly filled with his old schoolwork. He saved everything back then, even his baby teeth

He recalled discovering a quarter under his pillow. He was told that some obscure fantasy figure called 'The Tooth Fairy' had visited him in the middle of the night. Joe pictured a sissy man in pink tights and a fluorescent blue dress flying from home to home all across town He would raise and enter kids windows, spitting quarters out of his mouth under pillows of sleeping children. He never ran out of change, and also repelled flying female wood vamps with his corrosive, metallic breath.

As soon as Joe walked inside, he felt a cascade of emotions nearly overwhelm him. He fought the urge to run, and instead turned to his left and parted the stiff yellow curtains. He used to spy on their neighbors mid-twenties daughter, Sandy, who liked to sun bathe in a skimpy bikini on their back lawn. Sometimes, to get a closer look, he would use the scope from his rifle. There was something decadent and dangerous feeling about focusing the cross hairs on a prone, relaxed person.

Sandy was totally oblivious as to what he could do if he was like those sick cowardly bastards who took over a tarpaper rooftop and picked off total strangers with a high powered hunting rifle. That wasn't him. Joe was a bit baffled that Sandy's small breasts appeared to be round, not pointed like all the other women he had so far observed in his life..

When he was twelve, Joe ordered a 'spy hole drill' from an ad on the back of his Sgt. Rock comic book.. He intended to drill into his closet wall, to see into his parent's room and observe exactly what they did in there every night. He vividly recalled the metallic click when his folk's retired for the evening .and locked themselves in.

Alice intercepted his order in their mail while Joe was at school. She gave it to Bud, who walked in on Joe who was reclined on his bed, reading 'The Carpet-baggers' by Harold Robbins. Without saying a word, Bud got a sick crazy leer on his stubbled face and slowly crushed Joe's new spy-pen drill in his powerful, gnarled right hand. The broken pieces fell to the floor. Bud didn't say a thing. He simply turned and walked away, his heavy footsteps shaking the house.

Joe left the closet, closed the door and rubbed his eyes, willing himself to return to the present. Bud would be home soon. He needed to gear up, mentally, but instead, impulsively crawled under the covers of his bed and soon felt at peace. It was as though he was a kid again, with no worries, no problems, and no past.

Joe's eyes popped open, and he was momen-tarily confused as to what he was doing in his old bed in his former room. Then he heard his dad's loud, angry voice coming from what sounded like the front room. Joe got up, straightened out his rumpled clothes and began the familiar, uneasy trip down the green hallway, past the dining room, and into the front room, to greet Bud.

He found his father sitting in his brown Naugahyde recliner from good old Monkey Wards in nearby Richmond, just two blocks from what many considered the far edges of a dangerous ghetto, where white people sometimes disappeared. Bud had a burning cigarette in one hand and an open can of Regal Select in the other.

He was still wearing his cement splattered work clothes. His boots were lying sideways on the carpet in front of his chair that was reclined all the way back. He rested his smelly feet on the upraised footstool. His ripped yellow socks that started out white a month ago reeked.

His father was watching fake wrestling on channel two. Platinum blonde bad guy Ray Stevens was using dirty, illegal holds on his perennial opponent, the good guy, Pepper Gomez, who had flat ears and a phony smile.

"Hi, dad," said Joe, passing quickly in front of Bud, whose eyes never left the mayhem on the screen. He raised his cigarette hand as a greeting, the cancerous smoke drifting around the room, seeping into the drapes, through the paint and into the walls of the house his father, R.C. had built.

After taking a severe looking beating from the movie star handsome Stevens, Pepper suddenly rallied, jumping off the ropes and slamming down on top of Ray, who appeared stunned as Gomez pinned him and he won. The sparse crowd stood and gave him a standing ovation. They were aware that next week, Ray would probably win.

The only other regular wrestlers included 'The

Sheik,' supposedly from Persia. He was constantly throwing small explosives at the fans and liked to chase the car salesman from Val Strough Chevrolet up a ladder during a commercial break. The viewers were told that if 'They Came Down Today, To Buy A New Chevrolet,' that they would throw in a full can of fresh, MJB coffee. Big deal, Joe remembered thinking.

Then there was 'The Sloth', a big wreck of a man who was still dangerous but always lost. He wasn't real popular, and fans usually streamed for the bathrooms or snack bar whenever 'The Sloth' was wrestling.

Bud drained his beer, crushed the can and tossed it at Joe's face, who caught it before it hit, "That soldier is dead. Go get me another one," he demanded.

Joe complied, although he resented his dad's insulting, rude demeanor. After handing his father another cold Regal Select, Joe sat back down on their sponge like coach that was a weird, band aid color.

"How's college going?"

"Okay."

Bud glared at him, and Joe was sure that he saw wisps of dark smoke come out of his dad's large ears, "That's it? Everything is going, *okay?"*

"Yeah, you got it, dad. That's it. School is going fine. What do you want me to say?"

Bid fired up another smoke, "After a freaking month at school, with us spending big money on your education, plus giving you food money and a credit card for gas, that's all you have for me*? Okay? Fine!"*

Joe sat up straight, ready to engage the beast, "Okay dad, if you really want to know, I could use more food money. Fifteen bucks a week doesn't begin to cut it. I sometimes go hungry."

"Hell, son. Going hungry once in a while is

character building. Did I ever tell you about living through The Great Depression, and watching my old man about killing himself for his family. He dug freaking holes all day for a sack of rice, Joe. A qualified mechanic, builder, farmer, painter, R.C. could do anything. His reward? Digging freaking holes all day, and then his job the next day was to fill them back up again."

"'Yeah, you've told me those hard time stories before, I don't know, maybe ten, twenty times."

Alice shuffled into the front room wearing her night clothes, fuzzy slippers and pink bathrobe. She was holding a cup of hot tea.

"You slept right though dinner, Joe."

"Why didn't you wake me ma? I'm starving."

Alice sat in her green cloth swivel chair, "Tell you the truth, son, I forgot you were even here."

Bud spoke angrily, "Don't bitch your mom out, Joe. If you're hungry, go make yourself a baloney sandwich on Wonder Bread. We got plenty of that."

"Bud," said Alice, "Remember what Doctor Masters said about you not getting so upset all the time. You've go an ulcer, and here you are drinking beer and yelling at Joe. Remember, your brother, Cliff, died when his stomach exploded after eating a bowl of Cream Of Wheat for Christ's sake. I could understand it if he was competing in a hot pepper eating contest with three Mexicans and a deaf kid from Honduras. I think you should take one of my 'happy pills' dear. I'll be glad to get you one."

NO ALICE!," roared Bud, "I DO NOT WANT ONE OF YOUR HAPPY PILLS!"

Joe stood, "Are we done, dad?"

"No. Stay away from Marvin. You're a bad influence on an innocent kid .Other then that, truthfully, it was nice of you to drop by and see us, but I don't want you sleeping here anymore."

After eating a cheeseburger with fries with a large, Vanilla coke at nearby Foster's Freeze, Joe sat in his car and smoked. He needed a place to crash, but where? He supposed he could go to Claudette's house, but she and Vern lived way out in the Livermore area. Too far to drive tonight and too far to come tomorrow. He just wanted to sleep alone, and could use the back seat he supposed if he had no other options.

He fired up the 390, roared up Solano Avenue and drove like a maniac up into the Berkeley Hills. He skidded around corners on two wheels, barely maintaining traction, a maniacal look broadcast on his face, going even faster, defying death on every curve.

Joe smelled something familiar, like a rancid, stale fart odor.

Marvin's head popped up from the back seat, "Surprise! Slow down Joe, you're scaring me. Do you always drive like you wanna die?"

Joe slammed on the brakes, and the big Ford convertible skidded to a stop in front of a posh Grizzly Peak house.

Joe turned around, his right arm resting on top of his seat, "What the hell are you doing in my back seat?"

"Trying to get out of the house, just like you. I don't have a car though, so I'm stuck there most of the time. I can't keep going down to Melvin Hanks house and playing G.I. Joes He's beginning to bore me."

"Damn, Marvin. How did you get inside my car?"

"Same as you, The doors were unlocked"

Joe glanced to his right. The Bay Area spread

out before him. A million different lights, all turned on at the same time, illuminating The Bay Bridge and The Golden Gate. It didn't seem real to him, this panorama of beauty, a vast nighttime playground where all kinds of crazy stuff was happening. Meanwhile, here he was, parked in the hills with his much younger brother, Marvin.

"Sorry, kid, but I gotta take you back. They don't want me around you, because I might corrupt you."

"Too late. Come on Joe, just let me ride around with you, at a much safer speed I hope. Try to imagine being the only kid left at home, without you to yell at. So now, I get all of their rage while you're driving around like you think you're Parnelli Jones, defying death ever chance you get.'

Joe turned the car around, "Wait, Joe. There's a whole lot more. They're now telling everyone they only have two living children. Me and Claudette."

"What?"

"Yeah, it's true. They're convinced you're a heroin addict, and that Lance is a queer, and they're not sure about you. They paid for your schooling to get you out of the house. They don't want you back."

Joe drove slowly back, his mind reeling with Marvin' s stunning revelations.

LANCE'S DILEMMA

CHAPTER ELEVEN

Lance and Kathy walked hand in hand down the northern section of Telegraph Avenue. It was where it was all going down, all happening, the East Bay's version of the Haight Ashbury. Hippies, junkies, and hustlers mixed with real students, cops, normal merchants and straight citizens.

At Cal Berkeley's Sather Gate, radicals with long hair and colored headbands sat behind flimsy card tables and urged passer bys to sign their petitions. Some of them were polite, but others were aggressive and relentless, hassling anyone who got within ten feet of them, "Hey! You! Are you a registered voter? Your future depends on signing this. Do you even care?" Lance and Kathy strolled past hip retail stores, selling books, incense, donuts, hippie clothing, palm readings, magazines, homemade jewelry and much more. In addition, if you knew where to look, who to ask, and who to trust, nearly any sort of drug imiag-inable was available. Weed, hashish, LSD, mescaline, reds, cocaine, speed, heroin. More recently, a new recreational drug appeared on the street., a white powder called 'crank.' This crank stuff was so powerful, that after snorting just two lines, the user sometimes turned into a person who believed they had super powers, like Superman. They would quickly become more delusional, thinking they could now perform superhuman feats of strength, like lifting up the front end of a full sized Buick, or even being able to fly safely from a fifth story window down to Monkey Wards.

Unfortunately, when the effects quickly wore off, the user craved more, feeling suicidal if additional magical white powder was not forthcoming. He would be in such despair that he might hitchhike to the Golden Gate Bridge, seeking a free ride to his own demise. He was also in a hurry because he wanted to arrive before his newly rotted teeth fell out when walking sideways down the street, scaring others with his grim, demonic, spastic facial expressions. Now there were hundreds of freaky Frankenstein's, lurching around the Bay Area with their arms outstretched, willing to kill faceless people for a few lines of crank.

Finally, at the southern end of the Golden Gate, he would take the eastside walkway. Never the left. Leaping to death from the west side meant facing the Pacific Ocean, impulsively jumping and spiraling down to their painful demise when they smacked into water hard as cement. Their broken body would eventually sink down past large curious fish with bug eyes and open mouths, also landing at Davey Jones locker.

The decision of plunging from the east side meant a long last, final look at the glittering lights from tall, downtown buildings. They reflected off of the choppy bay waters. The end result was the same, with only a one percent chance of surviving the fall.

Lance nodded his head whenever he passed someone he knew, or had gotten high with or possibly slept with, not that he could begin to remember them all. He also attracted the attention of a few who had ripped him off. with bogus, worthless merchandise. Or, worse yet, robbed him of his cash, pushing a huge hunting knife up against the center of his gut, threatening to shove it in if he didn't immediately comply with their demand of all his money.

He observed spade drug dealers, trying to conceal their thin bodies behind stop signs but never fully succeeding. He saw one who was all right, an older dude who called himself 'Otis,' and they traded power salutes. Lance always felt slightly absurd whenever he did it. It seemed to him as though its use should be restricted to black revolutionaries, not whites such as himself. Or, worse yet, blacks who were radicals on the weekend and then drove an A.C. Transit bus for a good living during the work week.

Lance and Kathy entered 'Kips,' a popular college hangout that included an outdoor beer garden, party lights, live music on the weekends, and indoor pool tables. It was populated with cheerleader types with wide, manic Colgate grins and assorted Cal fans. They knew it was the place to be seen if you were a preppie, which was most definitely a shrinking sub culture, at least at the radical Berkeley campus. Kips was clearly a throw back to the problem free days of the early 1960's.

Inside, where the bathrooms, bar and pinball machines were located, dozens of conversations mixed together to form one large mass of voices. A college football game from Ohio was on TV. The Buckeyes were playing an exhibition game against crippled residents of a local retirement home for clowns. The volume was turned up to maximum, adding to the din.

The whole place, inside and out, smelled like pepperoni pizza vomit and spilled beer. Pictures of famous Cal football players hung crookedly from the walls, and a locked glass display case contained a collage of blue and gold Cal Pennants, expired schedules and a uniform top.

Without breaking stride, Lance and Kathy bounded down a flight of cement steps that led to the basement. They walked through a dark and dank storage room. Kathy shivered and Lance put his arm across her shoulder and pulled Kathy into the warmth of his moldy jacket.

Above them, they heard the muffled noises of Kips. People laughing, the TV blaring , music playing and the nonstop scraping sound of tables and chairs being dragged across the floor.

"This place gives me the creeps, Lance."

"Don't worry, babe. I've been here many times, and it's gonna be okay. I promise."

They reached the far wall and a metal door with no visible handle. Lance knocked three times, paused and tapped once more, "Secret door code," he said, "Not too many have it." A metal slider at the top of the door slid opened. Two eyes glared at them from the dark..

"Password?"

"Screw Nixon."

The slider closed. Three locks clattered, and the door was partially opened.

"Lance," came a deep voice from the shadows, "Good to see ya man."

"Hi, Brad."

The door closed behind them. The room smelled of Frito's and whiskey. Someone had been smoking dope, and a strong odor lingered. Multiple black lights bathed the room in a purple hue. Framed, psychedelic posters hung from every wall. Scattered day glo clouds floated on a fluorescent blue ceiling. The floor was cement, covered with glowing purple circular stepping stones that led the way to a large, wooden desk. The

Youngblood's signature song, '*Come Together*', played softly in the background.

A short haired young man sat behind the desk, his hands casually wrapped around the back of his head. He was wearing a Cal Letterman jacket with the year '1966' prominently sewn on next to a large letter 'A', indicating the wearers participation in a varsity sport at Cal. The man rested his fluorescent orange tennis shoes on top of his desk.

"Hi, Chaz," said Lance, "Brad, I know you're still in the room somewhere."

Lance addressed Chaz, "There aren't any other doors out of here, are there?

"Only the doors that open up your own perception. I distinctly recall your last visit, Lance. You never did pick up the Huxley book, 'The Doors Of Perception,' did you?"

"No, man. I've been really busy with school,"

"Where are your manners? Who is the young lady that you have chosen to bring into my den of inequity?"

"Chaz. This is my old lady, Kathy."

"Nice to meet you, Kathy." Chaz pointed to a pair of plush armchairs in front of his desk, "Have a seat."

"How long has Kathy been your old lady, Lance?"

"Four months."

"Five," she corrected, raising her hand to her mouth and biting her knuckles.

Chaz continued his good natured banter, "Now, Lance. Are you really a college student?"

"Yes, I am. At least I haven't been attending the same school for eight years."

Chaz laughed, "It takes time to get a BA in

Business Administration from Cal. Enough of the verbal foreplay. His voice turned serious, "Time to do business. I assume that's why you dropped by."

Chaz pulled the chain on a green desk lamp and it clicked on. The partial light framed his small featured face in shadows.

"I need two hundred hits of acid. Good stuff, Chaz."

Chaz sounded hurt, "Don't I always get you good product?"

"Yeah. Sorry, man."

"Forget about it. Just don't do it again, or I might let Brad have a go at you."

Lance cringed when he heard Brad crack his knuckles from right behind them.

"I got 200 hits. You want it or not?"

"How much, Chaz?"

"Same as always, pal. Fifty cents a hit up to five hundred doses. Then you get to buy wholesale, as many hits as you want for just forty cents a pill. Best deal in town, I tell you."

"How strong is it?"

"Bad ass strong," Brad rumbled.

Brad appeared directly behind a grinning Chaz. He was holding a large black pistol with his right hand. Damn, thought Joe, the dude was gigantic, and looked like he could just throw on some pads and a helmet and go play a Cal football game today.

"Deal," said Lance.

Chaz stood up and met his grip.

Lance dug into his wallet and dropped 10 twenty dollar bills on the desk. Chaz picked them up, counted them again and stacked them neatly on his right.

Chaz pulled a metal box from underneath his

desk, popped two clasps and swung the lid open. He selected four folded white bundles wrapped with string. He returned the box to its hiding spot. The money disappeared.

Lance knew better then to unwrap the bundles in the dark. Chaz was a bit odd, but had always been a straight shooter when it came to business. Joe watched as Brad tucked his gun down the back of his pants.

"What's this shit called?"

"Why, it's Purple Haze. It was named in honor of our recently departed guitar God, Jimmy Hendrix. By the way, Brad doesn't make jokes. He doesn't understand sarcasm or half truths. When he tells you it's strong, he means it. As for me, I would urge you to be cautious, and start out with half a hit."

"Half a hit?" replied Lance, laughing as he and Kathy stood up, "I've never taken less then a full hit, even first time out. I can handle anything."

Chaz remained seated, "Where did you say you're going to school, buddy."

"I didn't say. It's Quincy."

"Where the hell is Quincy?"

"It's in the lower part of the northern edge of The Sierra Nevada Mountain Range. It's basically a logging town full of hunters and fishermen, Indians and quite a few drunks. There's also a lot of freaks there too, You got anything else right now, Chaz? Maybe some mescaline?"

"Yeah, matter of fact I can let you have fifty hits of very organic, very mellow brown mescaline for say, twenty bucks. Such a deal I give you.."

"You should be a used car salesman, Chaz."

"Fuck you. Twenty bucks. Every word you say now costs you another five bucks."

Lance nodded, dropped another twenty and

Chaz pulled a small bundle out of somewhere and put it on the table.

Lance knew that Chaz had this weird thing about not taking money directly or handing over product. Everything was laid on the table and retrieved by the new owner. Chaz had once given Joe a vague description of some weird drug dealer entrapment law.

Lance knew it was time to leave. Business completed, small talk dealt out, money exchanged for drugs. They had more stops to make. Brad opened the door and they left in silence.

"Come on," said Lance, breaking into a trot, dragging Kathy along, "There's people trailing us. I could feel them in there with us. We need to get over to Tim's place and see what he has for sale."

Once they reached the busy sidewalk in front of Kip's, Lance dragged Kathy into a narrow alleyway, "SShhh, I want to make sure we've lost them."

Lance flattened against the brick wall with his long arms outstretched.

"Lost who?" asked Kathy, adjusting her glasses.

" I've never seen them yet."

"Then how do you expect to recognize them?"

"Quiet. I gotta concentrate, Kathy."

Lance and Kathy held hands again as they sauntered south on The Ave.until they reached Channing Way and turned right and walked down the pleasant, tree lined streets. It was a nice day in the Bay Area. Lance had his purchase safely tucked into a money belt that he wore disguised as a pants belt, holding up his worn jeans. He wasn't about to get robbed again. He occasionally glanced over his shoulder, making sure they weren't being tailed.

Lance spoke to Kathy, "Why didn't you send

me a postcard and tell me you got kicked out of your apartment? That was a real bummer last night, sleeping in your parent's house in different rooms. I'm hoping that Tim not only has some speed for sale, but maybe he can put us up for a night."

"I didn't have a stamp."

"What?"

Kathy snuggled up the mold, "You're the man. I'm expecting you to figure this shit out for us, or I'll find an old man who can. Maybe Joe."

"Joe?" exploded Lance. "You haven't screwed him, have you?"

"Not yet."

They stopped in front of a seedy looking three story apartment building.

"I hope Tim is still here," said Lance.

"Why wouldn't he be?"

"Because he's a strung out junkie who risks his life daily committing crimes to get money for multiple fixes for him and his old lady, Tina. He could be dead from an overdose or a crime gone wrong. He could be in jail. He might have been evicted. Lots of things could have gone down in a month. In a junkie's life span, that's like a year or two. Hell, I don't know. Lots of weird things used to happen in just a single day. Wouldn't it seem plausible that something bad has happened to Tim Blodgett."

"Why would I care? He's not my friend. I don't like having drug addicts in my life. Apparently you do. Don't they have a kid, too?"

"Yeah, they had a little girl two years ago. They named her Brandy, of all things. If we ever have children, I'm not naming them after booze, drugs, or a sex act. Can you imagine our first son being named

'Bourbon Blowjob Potter?' The last time I saw Tim, he had just hocked their baby stroller for a fix. I think Childhood Protective Services took the kid away before he could sell his daughter on the black market."

"Good. Junkies shouldn't have children."

"Most people shouldn't have kids."

Lance and Kathy turned into the entryway of the apartments. It smelled like urine and garbage.

"I think trying to stay with Tim Blodgett, even for one night, is a big mistake, Lance. If he's still here, I bet his place is filthy and full of contagious diseases, not to mention the brain dead weirdo's that are always hanging around him."

Lance couldn't help himself, "In other words, like the pad you just got evicted from for some of the same issues."

"Real funny, Lance. It wasn't that. We never paid our rent."

The elevator door slid open, and a scraggly young man with a dirty comforter wrapped around him stepped out. He managed to get eye contact with Lance, who was following Kathy into the elevator.

"Got any spare change, man?" asked the kid, thrusting out a dirty hand.

"No," said Lance, hitting the third story button twice. Their senses were further assaulted by the stench of human waste. Used condoms, discarded needles and yellow newspapers littered the floor.

"Don't say anything. Try and breathe shallow," advised Lance.

They got out on the third floor and entered a hallway that seemed to stretch all the way to Oakland. It was dim because only a couple of hall lights were working

They walked down the worn, carpeted hallway,

one cautious step at a time. As they passed rooms, they listened in on the noises of people living. Loud TV's, angry arguing and shouting, the raspy cough of a sick child, toilets flushing, random laughter and crying. Doors being opened and slammed shut, over and over

"I could never stay here," said Kathy, "I can't believe you actually lived here with Tim Blodgett and Tina."

"I had nowhere else to go except the street."

Lance knocked on apartment number 330. He could hear someone inside swearing. Somebody else groaned, and the toilet kept getting flushed.

Lance pounded on the door with both of his fists, "Tim never did like opening doors."

"Really?"

The door opened, and there stood what was left of Tim Blodgett. He was shirtless, bright white and painfully thin. His long red hair was piled up on top of his head, making him appear taller than his five foot six. His eyes were bloodshot, "Yeah," he slurred, "What the hell you want, huh? You gotta lot of nerve, waking up me and my old lady before noon. Waddya want? I ain't got no money. Nothing." He pulled his empty pants pockets all the way out, "See, man. I'm innocent you heartless fucks! Get out of here!"

"Tim. It's me, Lance Potter."

Tim rubbed his hand across his eyes and appeared confused, "Do I know you, man?"

"Of course you know me. I lived here for two months last year, remember?"

"Oh yeah, sure."

Inside the murky darkness of the apartment, several shadowy figures lined the couch, their heads nodding, burning cigarettes dangling from their hands.

"Shut the damned door, Tim!" shouted a guy.

"Do I owe you money or something?" asked Tim, scratching at the multiple open red sores and purple lesions on his arms.

"No. I came here for two reasons. Do we really have to have this conversation out in the hallway, for everyone to hear?"

"Fug em," slurred Tim, reeling around on his feet, "No good greedy bastards. The whole lot of them I tell ya. Okay, come on in if you insist. Who's the bitch?"

Kathy snarled, "I am not a bitch, you brainless pile of shit. I'm Kathy. Don't you remember us slee-ping together recently, Tim?"

Lance stared at the top of Kathy's head. He didn't know Tim Blodgett had screwed Kathy. How long ago, he wondered?.

Had they done it more then once? He and Kathy would have to have a long frank talk about this. He needed answers.

Once inside, Tim moved uncomfortably close to Kathy and leered at her, "I remember you now, *Kathy.* You gave me the clap, you bitch!"

Kathy tried to hide behind Lance, who was now holding Tim back at arms length. Kathy shrieked out, "I didn't give you the clap. You gave it to me, you bastard!"

A partially dressed wreck of a skuzzy chick came staggering out of the bathroom, holding a burnt spoon and a cotton ball. She shuffled forward and her head dropped. She was passing out on her feet.

Tim swiveled and stopped the young woman in her tracks, "Tina, you bitch! You were supposed to save me the cotton, remember? Now we're completely out. I gotta go hustle us up a couple of fixes so we don't get sick, you frigging whore!"

Tim turned back To Lance and Kathy, acting surprised that they were still there. "Did you need something?"

"Yeah, Tim. You know where I can score some beens or reds?"

Life flashed into Tim's eyes for a moment. The rusty and corroded gears and wheels began turning inside his head. He still recognized opportunity when it saw it.

"Sure, buddy, I can get whatever you want. Give me your cash and I'll be back, in say, uh, two hours."

"No way, Tim. You get a finders fee when you deliver me safely to the proper person, I don't get ripped off or robbed, and we get back safely. Then, you get paid."

"What's it worth to you?"

"Twenty bucks, and that's being generous. Take it or leave it."

"I'll take it. Let me get dressed.'

"We'll wait for you out in the hallway."

Once they were outside the apartment door, Lance turned on Kathy, "When did you do that parasite, and how many times?"

"None of your damned business, Lance. Who I screw is up to me. Right now, you're at the top of my list, but that could change if you keep pissing me off. I'm telling you, I can't take much more of your weird behavior. People following you. Why would anyone follow you?"

Lance hugged her, "I'm sorry, babe. I just love you so much. I don't want to share you."

A dour old lady wearing an unraveling gray sweater hurried past them, "Get a room!"

Tim came out a moment later. A suede fringe

jacket hung loosely on him. He was small skeletal junkie wearing a large coat.

"Hey, Tim," asked Lance, "Why are you wearing my jacket?"

"Huh?" asked Tim, wiping his nose on the right sleeve, "Your jacket?"

"Yeah. It was stolen last year, right out of this damn apartment. Don't tell me you don't remember. What the hell are you doing with it?'

"I swear to God I found it in a dumpster." He held his sleeve out. "Here, Holmes, smell it. Tell me it don't smell like a dumpster. Huh?"

Lance sniffed at it and then quickly pulled away. The jacket smelled like death.

"See. I told you. Now come on then. Time's a wasting. We've got business to conduct. I thought you two were in a hurry."

Late that afternoon, Lance and Kathy stood at a bus stop on San Pablo Avenue, thumbs out, trying to get a ride to Garfield Avenue at the base of Albany Hill. They were forced to spend another night at Kathy's parent's home. Lance was loaded down with inventory, having made several more large purchases, all now crammed into his money belt that was out of room. Having so much illegal merchandise on him with no car and a girlfriend who was becoming increasingly sarcastic and hostile was getting to him.

"I think I've figured it out, Lance."

"What? A place to live?" A job?"

"No, not that. Why are you so assertive when Joe isn't around? It's like you're a completely different person."

"Very perceptive, my dear. I let Joe take charge because he's got a really big ego that requires him to be the leader, or at least get the majority of the attention. Yes, it's deliberate on my part."

Just then, a newer Oldsmobile station wagon stopped in front of them. A large, older man wearing a white cowboy hat got out. The driver was wearing a similar hat.

"Come on and get in, kids. Where you wanna go?"

Both of the men smiled widely.

DUTY CALLS

CHAPTER TWELVE

Joe returned a protesting Marvin back to the house. He went inside and collected his Coast Guards dress blues uniform, white hat and shiny black shoes. A fellow coastie told him that instead of wasting time or money polishing his dress shoes, that a monthly application of Johnson's Floor Wax would maintain a mirror like gloss. He wouldn't have to hassle with shoe shining anymore. *Perfect,* he thought.

Without saying a word to anyone, Joe left the house. He laid his uniform on the back seat and took off in search of a place to crash. Sleeping in his dusty bed under the same roof as Bud and Alice wasn't going to work anymore. He might be able to grab a spare cot on the base for Saturday night, but for tonight, he was on his own.

Joe drove half a mile to Stannage Avenue and the two story wooden house that Steve Whisenor shared with his girlfriend, Brie.

Steve answered the door, "Whoa, Joe. You're back in town. What's up?"

Joe could hear a Moody Blues record playing in another room.

"I'm kind of desperate, Steve. I'm wondering if I could sleep on your couch just for tonight. I'll be gone by seven tomorrow morning, and I think I can stay on the base tomorrow night."

Steve hesitated, not inviting him in, "I don't know, Joe. Brie doesn't like you much."

'"Who does she like? You?"

"Wait here. I'll go ask her. Don't try to come in. She'll sic her Pit Bull on you."

"Great. Yeah man, go get permission for me to stay in your house that you pay the rent on. Grow some hair on your balls, Steve."

Steve rolled his eyes and looked behind him, where Brie, a hefty brunette with black triangular 1950's style glasses, stood in the kitchen doorway with her arms folded, scowling.

After a brief conversation, Steve returned, "I don't know, Joe. Me and Brie are, uh, having some issues right now." Steve leaned forward and whispered to Joe, "Hormones, man. You know how women get."

Joe put one foot up on the doorsill, "Hey, Brie. What's your problem with me? "

Brie strode forward, her arms still folded, a sour look on her face, "Well, if you really want to know, Joe Bailey. I'll tell you. The last time you were over here with Steve you got drunk and loud and told some offensive blonde jokes. If you think you're so funny, why don't you try the open mike night at the local comedy club?"

Joe smiled, "Come on, Brie. Why would you care about blonde jokes? You're a brunette for Christ's sake."

"That's another offensive issue for me. Your frequent, profane language."

"Please Brie. If you don't okay it, I'm going to have to sleep on my back seat again, and it sucks."

She paused, and then whispered something to Steve, who nodded his head.

"Okay, Joe," said Brie, "You can spend one night on our couch as long as you behave yourself. You cause any noise problems or even pass gas, you're out of here. And, stay out of my kitchen. I don't want you breaking anything."

"Thank you, Brie."

She headed back to wherever she hung upside down in the dark.

"Steve, I gotta be in Alameda for inspection by eight. You got an alarm clock?"

"Don't need one. I go to bed early and get up by six. I'll make some coffee and wake you up. We also have some organic brown bread."

Joe arrived early for his reserve meeting at the Yrbea Buena base. Marines patrolled the steep, windy road that led down from the top. They loved to lock up sailors in their brig on nearby Treasure Island. Joe had been involved in more then one run-in with them, and was somewhat insulted that they viewed him as a common 'swabbie.' He was considered a lower life form in the eyes of the heavily armed Marines.

Joe respected U.S. Marines as tough guys, but never sought out any as potential friends or drinking buddies. Besides, they would refuse to be seen sitting with him in a bar if everyone were in uniform. You were quickly taught to stay with your own kind. There were fewer fights that way.

Joe Edgar Bailey was an E5 Petty Officer, a Port Security Specialist. Just last year, after a hellish boot camp, he spent four months in Virginia, where he was cross trained as an aquatic cop and emergency fireman. He too carried a sidearm, a clumsy but man stopping .45 caliber in a white holster with one extra clip. He only wore it, along with a white web belt with a white night stick when on certain, occasionally more dangerous assignments. The local Customs Department also used Port Security personnel as backups on large maritime drug busts.

Joe parked in the back of a large, paved parking lot bordered by thick groves of the damned Eucalyptus trees. They were all over the Bay Area. It was like fifty insane Johnny Appleseed clones had criss crossed the entire area in the 1850's, heaving out millions of seeds. Then laughing and shucking off their hayseed clothes, they revealed the clown gear that they customarily wore every day. They then noisily boarded a train headed for Dayton Ohio.

It kind of freaked out the other train passengers at first, riding with fifty manic clowns, all beeping bike horns and tripping each other with their gigantic shoes and one of them even dumping 10 plastic flies in his Clam Chowder. He called the waiter over and went off on him, his huge clown lips flapping like a white Louie Armstrong.

Things worked out okay when the clowns organized a Bingo game for everyone in their car. When the train stopped in Ohio, most folks were feeling good, and some were no longer frightened by clowns. Still, others panicked and ran, foolishly looking back over their shoulder, as though killer clowns with floppy shoes and baggy orange pants with red suspenders could somehow chase them down.

Joe rolled down his window and listened to the steady roar of traffic overhead, vehicles making clunking noises as they drove over the metal plates that connected the Bay Bridge to the short tunnel. Bump bump, bump bump. Over and over forever.

. Once through the tunnel, traffic emerged into the sun and the final bridge span that led to the fabled, golden city of San Francisco.

Joe carefully ate the second of his gooey, dripping jelly donuts. He also sipped from a large coffee. No booze. They would smell it on him and they would make a little phone call to the Marine officer on duty.

He considered the irony of his double life. He lived with a medium level drug dealer, and then every fourth weekend he reported for duty, never knowing what his job might be. It could range from oil pollution investigation, search and rescue, or doing safety inspections on speed boats full of bikini clad beauties. Occasionally, a heart thumping, adrenalin rush, a real drug bust. It made him feel badly when he watched guys just like himself in civilian life being led away in handcuffs, their lives about to be ruined.

He was on the base emergency call list as a backup firefighter if a blaze should be raging out of control on a ship or in a warehouse. He was also on The Custom Departments short list of qualified, trained bodies available for quick deployment. Joe hadn't bothered contacting either agency about his moving six hours away. He had instructed his family that if someone official called for him, they were to reply that he was sick in bed with an acute case of Leprosy, Bari Bari or Syphilis. Joe did not have a phone in his Keddie cabin, so there was no way to contact him to report for duty, even seven hours late.

Bud and Alice didn't think much of his plan, and openly stated that it was his moral and legal obligation to be available. Otherwise, what was the point of all his training? What about his solemn commitment when he stood with forty others and swore allegiance? Shouldn't he feel grateful that he wasn't slogging through a rice paddy in Vietnam?

His folks didn't know that Joe was frequently threatened with Vietnam by his CO, Captain Harvey, who didn't seem to like him much. "If you miss any more meetings, Bailey, I'll have them active your ass and send you over to the Mekong Delta, where you can play your little games while wearing a flak vest. You'll be wondering if it's a real family in the sampan you just stopped, or if its full of Viet Cong who could suddenly stand up and fire AK47's at you and yell "Die, Yankee Die! How's that sound, Bailey, huh?"

At home, it was up to Marvin to get to the phone first. Joe was royally screwed if a call came in when his little brother was in school. At night, Marvin was moving fast after the first ring, charging out of his room and diving for the call. That was fine with Bud and Alice. They didn't really want to talk to anyone anyway, not when Lawrence Welk, Jackie Gleason or Dean Martin were on television.

In addition to the forgery work Joe had pulled off with his Coast Guard I.D, and moving away without telling anyone, he had sarcastically listed his civilian occupation as a Mortician. In reality, he had a part time job at Slick Pippins Union 76 station near the corner of Gilman Street and Santa Fe Avenue. He pumped gas, cleaned bathrooms, and did oil changes.

If he didn't like the customer, he might slice his fan-belt halfway through with a razor blade, so the prick would get a few miles away before the belt broke and left him stranded. He also carried an ice pick, both as a potential deadly weapon, and he could also use it to poke a hole in some assholes top radiator hose. Same result. The shithead would get to the other side of town before his car overheated. *Served the bastards right, he thought, treating him like some sort of punk kid.*

He laughed at the absurdity of him supp-osedly

being a Funeral Director at age nineteen. He was pretty sure you needed a college degree, and then a few more years of training after that. He had zero interest in pursuing death as an occupation.

He wasn't quite sure what he wanted to do with his life yet,. but he damned well knew he didn't want to be some hourly, powerless, pathetic creature that allowed a time clock to run his life. He knew that security and a regular paycheck came with a heavy price. The prime years of his life, mostly wasted, leaving him one stinking week of annual vacation. No freaking way, he thought.

Joe walked slowly to the Duty building. Once inside, he went directly to the bulletin board to see what his assignment was for the weekend. He searched for his name on a mimeographed list. Damn, he thought. Another weekend of oil pollution duty. Oh well, he would be able to spend the night on base because now he was on call.

Usually, not much of consequence happened. The worst culprit was the U.S. Navy dumping old fuel oil. If he reported them, his officer in charge would tell him to forget about it. Captain Harvey knew it was a waste of time and resources if he pursued a complaint with the Navy. A higher ranking Coast Guard officer would in turn tell him to forget about it and stand down.

Someone heavy bumped into Joe, sending him reeling into the wall. Joe spun around, irritated, his hands flattened out, ready to deliver a karate chop to some choades neck or nose.

A short, portly coastie put up his hands in a defensive pose," Geeez, Joe. You sure are jumpy."

"Victor Molina," said Joe. Molina was a Puerto Rican with a protruding stomach, rosy cheeks, and red framed glasses.

Joe dropped his hands and relaxed, "You could get hurt sometime, doing that."

Victor made an odd grunting noise and pushed Joe away from the bulletin board. He was surprisingly strong.. "Let me see too. Aw shit, oil pollution duty again. That makes three months in a row, the bastards. I don't think Captain Harvey likes me much. Probably because I'm a minority."

Joe looked unhappy, "That means I'm stuck with you all weekend, jack-off. Do you remember how much damage you caused to that pursuit boat last month?"

"Sure I do. Like I told everyone then, it was an accident. The tide changed or there was a rogue wave or something, and all of a sudden, the dock was there. I didn't try to hit it on purpose. They were able to salvage the boat, weren't they?"

"Yeah, fortunately it sunk in shallow water. I'm surprised that you're even allowed on the base after all the damage you've caused lately."

"None of those six other accidents were my fault either. I think they harass me because I'm a minority, man."

"Victor, let me explain something to you, because I'm sick and tired of you always blaming your personal harassment bullshit on being a supposed minority."

"Supposed?" questioned Victor

"You're not black, or a Mexican. You're Puerto Rican for Christ sake. You just look like a Mexican. The truth is this. Either you suck or you don't. It doesn't matter where you're from or what color your skin is. Guess what. You suck."

Molina got a twisted look on his face and backed up a couple of feet. He held his arms out, and

Joe saw his black, fingerless gloves. Wide leather straps with chrome studs and spikes adorned Molina's wrists. Around his neck, holding his dog tags, was a chain metal dog collar.

Victor looked at his wrist watch, "Ah, mon, we got fifteen minutes left. Come on out to the parking lot with me so I can take off my accessories. I want to show you the custom work I'm doing on my mom's Pontiac."

"You have a car that actually runs? Oh, I'm sorry, it's your mom's car. That's why it runs. You probably haven't started customizing the engine yet."

"Real funny, asshole. I've got lots of cars that run. I just don't bring them out in public much, because the local cholos get jealous and try to steal my ride while I'm still in it. Can you believe that?"

When Joe and Victor returned to the lot, they found a small group of Coast Guard men in dress blues gathered around the long pink and black four door Pontiac. One joker from their unit, a horse headed jerk nick named 'Skully,' stood up front, pointed at the 59 and brayed like a donkey. He kicked the right front fender and everyone laughed, "What a piece of shit, Molina. I'm surprised they let you on the base with this, I don't know, this weirdo monstrosity."

"Hey!" yelled Victor, running towards Skully, his arms flailing around like a human eggbeater, "Don't be kicking my mom's car!"

Skully brayed again and then merged into the crowd. Molina carefully inspected the fender. There was no dent. Not even a scratch.

Joe checked out Victor's customizing as the group from their unit turned around and headed into the Duty building.

Orange and red painted flames started from

behind the front wheel wells and decorated both doors. The rear fender wheel wells had been torched out to make room for 60 series racing slicks. Molina had jacked up the rear end two feet by adding some white air shocks.

Dingle balls, probably cut from his mother's bed spread, hung around the headliner. Victor had also painted the rear differential cover silver, just like all the other local hot rodders liked to do.

Molina's crowning touch was the hood. A chrome high rise Edelbrock manifold with a gas sucking Holley double pumper carburetor with a chrome air cleaner. It now stuck up a foot through a ragged hole that Victor had cut out in the center of the hood.

"Nice car," remarked Joe sarcastically.

"Thanks," said Molina, apparently assuming Joe was serious, "Wait until I replace the engine with a high performance 389. I got it being built right now at Banjo Little's speed shop. When I'm finished, my mom will get to the grocery store faster then anyone else in our neighborhood."

"Did your mom ask you to do this to her car?"

"No, mon. It's her birthday present. Next, I customize my dad's new Cadillac. When I'm done with it, there won't be another one like it on the planet."

"I can believe that, Molina. Come on, it's time for inspection."

Forty squared away Coast Guardsmen stood at attention on the small plaza near the water. Joe could hear flags whipping around in the wind. It was cold near the bay. He stood in rigid formation with the others, arms at their sides, hands flat, head held upright and eyes pointed straight ahead. The officer of the day walked slowly down the lines of men, inspecting them from top to bottom. If they paused in front of you, there was usually a problem.

Joe had learned early on in boot camp to never make eye contact with the Officer. Instead, you continued staring straight ahead, trying to not even blink. Occasionally, an Officer would inform a man of a deficiency in his uniform, usually scuffed shoes that didn't gleam. If he couldn't see a reflection from the top front of your shoe, it was unacceptable. In boot camp, you could count on being harshly punished, often in unusual, demeaning fashion.

Joe still had bad memories of failing a inspection because of a single 'Irish pennant,' which was merely a loose thread On that day, he was forced to stand at attention for three hours in the hot sun. First, the officer screamed at him, his angry face mere inches from Joe. He, along with two others, were forced to 'high port' an M1 carbine and run around a display anchor for three more hours, yelling out in unison, "I am a cockroach," (To high port is to move your weapon up and down, and in and out while running)

If one should fail a reserve inspection, you got a 'gig'. Too many of those and they would arrange 'special duty' for you, such as cleaning toilets all day with someone's toothbrush. Didn't matter whose. You just grabbed one, scrubbed a few toilets or urinals and then put it back where you found it. Also, it was common to be told that you were an embarrassment to the Coast Guard, God, your country as well as yourself. "Don't you have any pride, son?" they would say.

After changing into work clothes, the oddball crew of Joe Bailey and Victor Molina were aboard a 41 foot pursuit boat, supposedly prepping it for an upcoming patrol. They were both E5 Port Security Specialists, having attended both boot camp and advanced training in Virginia together. Molina had somehow lied and got his records altered to show he was also a qualified marine engineer, capable of performing maintenance and even engine repairs if needed.

Joe recalled the first time he questioned Molina about his new rating, "How hard can it be, mon?" defended Victor, "I tune up everything at home, from my old mans lawnmower to my mom's toaster. I install engines in my Hot Rods too, so why shouldn't I be able to handle a boat?."

The fairly new patrol craft had dual turbo charged motors, twin screws, overhead police type flashing lights as well as a siren. Semi automatic weapons and .45 caliber pistols were locked up below, and only the coxswain of the boat had a key.

It was a multipurpose work horse of a boat, used for search and rescue, ship boardings, and many other jobs.

It was also used to retrieve dead jumpers from underneath The Golden Gate Bridge. Joe had already been involved in this unsavory mission. The body he had seen had no bone structure left, The corpse lay on the deck of the small boat, jelly like limbs spread out in all directions. Joe was glad when one of the regulars finally threw a tarp over the corpse.

Last winter, he was on a training patrol in Virginia, when a call came in about a body floating near the shore. The stiff floated upside down, his legs and arms outstretched, the unmistakable stench of death lingering in the air. The Coxswain, Mr. Daniels, used a grappling hook to snare a leg. When he pulled on it, the leg came off.

"Shit," he said, "Sam. Get a line." Joe watched as Mr. Daniels lassoed the torso. He then started up the boat and dragged the corpse along until he veered the boat towards the bank and then swiftly cut it to the port side and the body landed up on shore

He cut the line loose and instructed Sam to call 911, and let them know that the fire department had a body recovery to handle.

"I ain't bringing that stinking, rotting corpse on board my boat. I bet you he's been underwater for a month or more. I can tell you that he doesn't have any eyeballs left. Did you know that, Bailey?"

"Know what, sir?"

"That crabs eat the eyeballs first thing."

"No sir."

Mr. Daniels moved closer to Joe, "By the way, Bailey, you didn't see anything."

"Yes sir. We got the call, patrolled the coordinates, and were unable to locate a body."

Mr. Daniels slapped him on his back, "Good job, son. We'll make a good coastie out of you yet."

It was a gorgeous blue skied day, and Joe was feeling good. Even though he was leery and appre-hensive of water, he also enjoyed being around it. He continued to hear the heavy traffic on the bridge far above them. Outside their little man made harbor, beautiful sailboats with tanned gorgeous people cruised by them, weekend sailors leaning back and adjusting the jib. Power boats roared by in the middle of the bay, some heavy on the throttle.

Joe knew that he and Victor could go after them, but why hassle with it? He was perfectly content to walk around and flip toggle switches and check gauges and pretend to make pencil marks on a clipboard with no paper. He would stand back when Molina occasionally fired up the twin turbo charged engines, laughed like a rabid chipmunk, and then shut them down.

"See," Molina would say, "I told you I know what I'm doing!"

"Yeah. Right."

"Oh man, Bailey. I wish I could get a hold of one of these bad boys and transplant it into my '56 Chevy, mon." Molina knew Joe worked in a gas station, "You think it would fit?"

"Of course not, you frigging moron. These are marine engines. Made for boats. Not cars. Get it?"

"Shut up, Joe."

Joe went inside the small cabin to use the tiny head that was stuffed into the far corner with a flimsy red curtain around it. The toilet was clearly intended for midgets, as Joe, who was only average sized, could barely fit into the area. He urinated, flushed it using a long handle that stuck out the side, and he then pumped sea water back into the bowl, using the same handle. He wondered how a fat ass like Victor could ever use it. Joe didn't bother washing his hands since he hadn't urinated on them.

When Joe returned topside he took one look at Molina and jumped back. Victor had replaced his regulation white USCG hard hat and now had on a black pork pie hat. He wore a jean jacket over his regulation blue chambray shirt. The front of the jacket had patches advertising car parts, like Hooker Headers, STP, Moon hubcaps and many more.

Most disturbing though, was the giant red Nazi Swastika that was sewn onto the back of his jacket.

"Molina. Are you nuts?"

"As a matter of fact, I just may be. I've gone out on patrol like this before. Of course, I never actually pulled anyone over. In one case, I had no choice, and the old guy was Jewish, so he said he was offended, and demanded my name. I told him I was Skully."

Victor did his standard laugh and then continued, "What this is called, is freedom of expression. I'm expressing myself. This is who I really am, Joe. I have rights guaranteed by the United States Constitution, even if I am from Puerto Rico."

Joe placed both of his hands on top of Molina's shoulders, "Listen to me. If you get caught in that get up, you'll get a Court Martial for sure. You'll probably get prison time in a Marine Brig in Death Valley, and then you'll get booted out of the service. Dishonorable Discharge. Besides that, did you even think about the position you're putting me in, '*Spiktor.*'

"Huh? What'd you just call me, *Joe Schmo.*?"

Joe kept his eyes on Victors black gloved hands. He was outweighed by a hundred pounds, but he was also quicker and in better shape. Plus, he knew how to properly throw a punch.

"You heard me, *Spicktor.* I'm a petty officer too, and you're way out of uniform. If I don't report you, I'm not doing my duty. If I do report you, I'll be known as a snitch. Some choice you're leaving me, chump."

Victor laughed and pulled a gigantic crescent wrench out of his back pocket, "You know, if I clocked you with this, you might die. If I really wanted to, I could kill you. Right here, right now. So, go ahead, try and be a hero.'

Joe faked a right and when Molina fell for it, Joe drilled him hard in his left kidney, the heavy blow making a fleshy 'thunk' noise.

"Ow," said Victor, dropping to his knees, "Why did you have to do that, Joe?" Molina rubbed his kidney area, "Damn, dude, I think you broke something."

"Screw you, fat boy." Joe hopped down on the dock and pretended to be making more notes on his clipboard. He found an upside down bucket to sit on. His expert assessment was the boat was ready to go, but the crew wasn't doing so hot. Joe looked up just in time to see Molina heave a nearly full bucket of used crank-case oil into the bay.

"What are you doing?" screamed Joe, running back aboard.

"That's dirty, used oil. We're not putting that in my baby's engines, no sirree Bob. It's used up oil with no further use and besides, I need the bucket for drinking water."

Their two way radio crackled to life, and Victor picked up the black mike on a stretch chord, "Petty Officer Bailey speaking. I'm on break right now. Call back later."

Victor hung up and laughed. "You shouldn't have slugged me like that. It still hurts. I know you had a few amateur fights. You ain't fooling me none."

"You asshole. Now they think that was me."

"It was you."

The radio came to life again, and this time Joe dived for the mike and got there first, "Petty Officer Spiktor Molina speaking,. Why do keep hassling us, dude?"

Joe watched as Victor stepped backwards, tripped on another bucket and flew backwards into the harbor, causing a gigantic splash.

"Man overboard!" he shouted

Joe ignored him.

A angry voice crackled from the other end. Joe got a sick look and hung up. He walked over to where Molina was floundering around. Joe knew he didn't swim too well.

"Help me you prick!" yelled Victor.

Joe threw Molina a life preserver.

"That was the Officer On Duty. He wants to see us in his office in fifteen minutes. You fucking jerk. You really did it this time!"

Joe and Victor entered the ground floor of the command center. Victor wore his proper uniform, having stashed all his non regulation items in the trunk of his mom's car.

Joe's feet hurt. He had switched over to his official U.S. Coast Guard steel toed safety boots when they put on their work clothes. The soles had plenty of tread left, but the steel in the toes was exposed.

Joe wore his duty boots on his job at Slick Pippin's Union 76 station and repair facility. Joe's boss, Slick Pippin, was too cheap to supply Joe with a rubber hammer to reinstall hubcaps after he checked brakes or rotated tires. With the small easy ones, like the famous Chevrolet 'Dog Dish' caps, he used the palm of his hand to slap them back on. For the bigger, full cover types, he was forced to drop kick them back on with the toes of his boots. It worked all right, and he pretended he was kicking someone in the face, but now the front toe leather was gone, and he had barely started the second year of his six-year enlistment.

Joe followed Molina as he climbed the stairs to the second floor where he entered the closed, Officer's mess hall. Victor flicked on one small light over the stove and flung open the refrigerator door.

He leaned over and started pulling out lunch

228

meat, cheese, lettuce, bread, condiments and a couple of Orange sodas.

"Hey. We don't have time for this. We were supposed to be over there to see the O.D. five minutes ago. Now, he's really gonna be pissed. at us," complained Joe.

"So, we had a little delay. Cool your jets, Hondo. I'm hungry and I require nourishment, now."

Victor built himself a gigantic deli sandwich that he could barely fit into his mouth. He took a monstrous, greedy bite and looked up at Joe and chewed and half of it tumbled out of his mouth onto the floor.

"Nice going," said Joe. He was hungry too, but wasn't insane enough to rob the Officers private stash.

Molina burst into laughter.

"What's so damned funny?"

Victor pointed with his free hand, "Look behind you, Joe. Mon, what a slob. Brand new carpet, too."

"Oh shit," mumbled Joe. He had left large, greasy gas station foot prints on the beige carpet.

"Hey," said Molina, "We better get out of here."

Captain Harvey glared at Joe and Molina. They were sitting in arm chairs in his third story office that had a marvelous view of the bay. Joe had taken his boots off in the hallway.

"I can't believe you two are under my command. Playing games on the radio when you're on duty. What if it had an emergency? I should court martial you bozos, but I don't want to waste the time or the paper. Bailey! Where's your boots?"

"Sir, I left them in the hallway because I didn't want to soil your new carpets, sir."

"Well thank you for that one,. small favor.

That's new carpet you know."

"Yes sir," said Joe, "We know."

Joe looked down at Molina and saw half of a sub sandwich sticking out of his jacket pocket.

"Listen, plans have changed for you two. We just got a report on a fresh oil spill just outside our harbor. Do you two think you two can handle the investigation by yourselves without sinking our boat or shooting someone? You don't have a key to the gun locker, do you?"

"Yes sir, and no sir. We do not have a key."

"Carry on," said Captain Harvey, picking up a report off of his desk.

As soon as Joe and Victor departed, Lt. Staley, Captain Harvey's adjutant remarked, "I can't believe those two actually made it through boot camp."

"And Port Security School," added the Captain, "There's something wrong with this pair."

"Yes sir."

Joe had Chris and Susan in the back seat the next afternoon when Joe pulled up in front of Moore's TV shop. Lance sat with Kathy, slumped up against the front window. A suitcase sat next to Kathy. She was smoking and blowing smoke out of both her mouth and nose at the same time.

"What's going on?" he asked Lance as he got out.

"Kathy got kicked out of her apartment because of you, so she's coming with us. She doesn't have anywhere else to go."

"Because of me?"

"Yeah. The landlord was here when you peeled out last time, so they booted her out."

"Whatever," said Joe, heaving Kathy's dumb

ass suitcase into the trunk on top of some spilled engine oil. He slammed the trunk lid, "Fine," he mumbled.

He climbed behind the driver's seat, with Kathy sitting in the middle next to Lance. As he backed out, she subtly scooted over until her hip was resting against his.

When he glanced in the rear view mirror, Susan winked at him.

Joe glowered back. He thought things were really going to get interesting now. Where was Kathy supposed to sleep, and why was she coming on to him? With Susan he figured it was just a big running joke, and it was always on him.

PURPLE HAZE

CHAPTER THIRTEEN

Gary Hess sat in front of a crackling fire of pine logs in the rock fireplace of the A-Frame. Randy-Bob and Dave had gone deer hunting, so he was enjoying a rare night of sober solitude. He stared into the blaze and willed himself to not have a drink. He couldn't remember the last time he hadn't had a drink for a whole day and night and that alarmed him. Was he becoming an alcoholic? Well, he decided, he would see how many days he could go without any alcohol. Not even one beer. He needed to lose some weight, and figured laying off the brewskis and pork rinds might help some.

Gary scooped some trash off the floor and tossed it on top of the burning logs. Sick of his job, weary of his roommates, and avoiding the dogs, he had to admit he was just plain lonely.

He knew his lonesomeness was somewhat his own choice. The holiday season approached, and Gary always made sure he was single at Christmas. That way he didn't have to buy a disposable girlfriend an expensive present, and he avoided a lot of the nauseating sentimental holiday crap. like roving bands of Christmas carolers downtown.

Gary had tried starting conversations with some of those cute hippie chicks by asking what their astrological sign was, but they would look him up and down, point and laugh, and generally seemed repelled by his very existence.

Instead, they were drawn to the sissy boys with ponytails and marijuana, who acted like they were part female too. There was one particular Keddie chick that had really caught his eye though. He asked around and found out her name was Carlene Romo. Man was she a fox.

Gary was also increasingly concerned about the flood of illegal drugs that were saturating his hometown. He had watched as some of those hippie punks openly smoked marijuana. Others staggered around with glazed eyes and a stupid look on their face, dancing to that gawd awful Grateful Dead crap they called music. Hell, even a Mexican or Indian could tell it was tuneless garbage. Now Waylon Jennings, Merle Haggard, Johnny Paycheck, that was real music. Those guys really knew how to sing too, instead of just shouting into a mike. They had harmonies and melodies. They weren't drug addled pantywaists either. They were real men.

Gary tried to talk to Big Dan about illegal drugs in Quincy and Keddie one night when he stopped to visit with his mom for ten minutes. Dan was there, and sober. He listened politely to Gary's concerns and then replied with a stock answer, explaining that he was unable to comment on an ongoing investigation.

Big Dan abruptly changed the subject, "Did you hear about that hippie kid who got beat up and then run over just outside of Keddie?"

Gary feigned surprise, and then interest, "No. I didn't. What happened to him?"

"He's still in the Quincy Hospital. He was lucky to be wearing a backpack that absorbed some of the weight. He'll live, but he may be permanently crippled because of a spinal injury. It's too early to tell."

"Well, gosh Dan. That's terrible. What kind of a lowlife runs over someone and then just drives off?"

Dan stared at Gary, waiting for him to blink. He did. Twice.

Big Dan finally lifted up his coffee cup, "That's what I'd like to know."

"If I hear anything, I'll be sure to clue you in. If I were you, I'd check out them Indians. They do shit like that to each other all the time."

"Thanks for your information, Gary. You've been a big help."

"Bye mom," waved Gary, in such a hurry to leave that he didn't even hug or kiss her. Linda waved at Gary's wide backside.

Once in his Jeep, he headed for one of the nearby cliffs. He found a choice spot, grabbed his bolt cutters and heaved them as far out into the Feather River as he could. Gary snorted. Since when did it become a crime to run over a Jew or a queer?

Then he had come home, started a fire and sat in front of it and thought. Mostly bad things. He spent quite a lot of time compiling a list of enemies, people who he owed a beating. He wanted to handle them in correct order.

The front door of the A-Frame burst open, and two stoners walked in, holding Maureen up between them. Her head was rolled to the left, her eyes were closed and she moaned.

Gary jumped up, "What the hell did you do to my sister? There, lay her on the couch. Careful. She don't look so good."

The doper guys laid her down, and she groaned. She rolled up into a fetal position, "Make it stop."

Gary kneeled at her side and held her hand. "Make what stop, Maureen?"

"The faces, the colors, the echoing voices. Make it all stop. Don't you see them too?"

Gary looked up at the local freaks. He had seen them around. One of them was Ross, and the other one was Lonnie. He wasn't sure who was who though.

"Okay, what's wrong with her? Is she having a marijuana overdose, or something worse?"

The shorter guy shifted around like he needed to pee, but was too stoned to ask. Gary didn't want him urinating in a closet, "What's your name?"

"Ross."

"Well, Ross, if you gotta use the bathroom, it's right down the hallway. Turn right when it starts to smell real bad."

"Thanks, Gary."

"Purple Haze," said the older, taller guy. This must be Lonnie, thought Gary.

"It's really strong LSD, man. We all handled it fine, but Maureen flipped out. First time ever, man. She's always been able to maintain before."

Gary checked Maureen's pulse. He earned his first aid certification at the mill, so he knew a little bit. He looked at his watch. Her pulse was slow, "How long has she been like this?"

"Uh, like six hours, man," answered Lonnie. His attention had been drawn to the large clock on the wall, He was mesmerized by the circular movement of the second hand and leaned towards it, like he was being sucked towards the wall piece, "Huh?" he said.

Gary checked Maureen's forehead while she continued to moan. She felt hot. Crap, this could be serious. He went to the phone to call an ambulance. Since their place was nearly impossible to find, he instructed Lonnie to go down to the highway and wave the ambulance in.

"Okay, man," agreed Lonnie, happy to be out of the stuffy room with this scary, humongous Neanderthal type who kept shouting at him for no reason.

Ross returned, "You got any orange juice, Gary?"

"No, I don't. What the hell! You think I'm running a restaurant here while my sister could be dying?"

"No, man. You got it all wrong, dude. The orange juice might help bring Maureen down."

Gary reacted angrily, "She needs a doctor, not OJ. By the way, Ross old buddy, where did you guys get this purple poison?"

Ross looked terror stricken, "I can't tell you that, man. That's bad karma, and not cool either."

Gary reached behind the couch and pulled out a wooden baseball bat that had a heavily taped handle, "Now Ross. Imagine me swinging this hard at your nose, and then connecting. Visualize the pain, the hospital, the numerous reconstructive surgeries. Think Ross, think. Give me the name, or I'll bust you up real bad, and I ain't a kidding partner."

"Yeah yeah, I know you're not kidding. Aw geez, what choice do I have? We got it from that tall Lance Potter guy in Keddie. Man, now I feel like such a snake."

"Okay. Get out of my house or I'll sic my dogs on you. Don't ever come back here. Stay away from Maureen too. Forever."

"Okay man," said Ross, "Like take a chill pill or something, buddy."

"GET OUT!" roared Gary. He could hear a siren approaching.

Joe sat on the front porch in one of the sea shell chairs. It was cold enough for him to see his breath in front of him. Still, it was better then being inside, listening to Lance and Kathy having sex.

She had only been sharing Lance's single bed for a week, but Joe was already tired of the games they were playing with him. Joe would get up in the morning and leave the room and the door would close behind him. The noise would start slowly, just the bed springs randomly squeaking and hilarious laughter. Then the springs would squeak in a gentle rhythm, quickly increasing in pace, and Kathy would begin that damned moaning and Lance his grunting. Within two minutes, the headboard would begin slamming against the wall.

The first night Kathy was there, they had done it while Joe was in the room. They apparently thought he was asleep, or more likely, they didn't give a shit. Joe had wanted to crawl into a hole somewhere.

Joe sipped a cup of coffee with no booze. He knew it was time to cut back. He was getting the shakes when he was sober, and he knew his once even tempered personality was just a memory. Now, he was irritable and volatile. He'd had the same headache since they were down in Berkeley a week before. He knew people went out of their way to avoid him, so now it was time to be sober for awhile. He needed to be straight while he contemplated his living situation and pondered his options and next, best move. He no longer considered returning home in January an option.

Joe tuned into the familiar morning sounds. Radioactive crickets, black frogs that were up early, and blue woodpeckers who could drive cabin owners mad with their coordinated assaults on the siding and trim.

There were also the steady engine sounds of trucks moving in and out of the restaurant parking lot, drunk in the morning cowboys leering out of their broken driver's window, going 'heh-heh-heh.'

Up on the bluff, locomotives gunned their massive engines and slammed into freight cars, all day. For supposedly living out in the country, Keddie was actually quite a noisy place.

Joe wondered if the Marlboro Men were still in the restaurant. He was half tempted to drift over there and order a short stack of pancakes with extra butter and Maple syrup. He would also drink real coffee, which always tasted better then the bitter swill he and Lance drank. The acidy metallic taste was getting worse. Joe wondered if they were supposed to wash out their coffee pot once on a while or something.

Then again, maybe he'd go to the restaurant a little later, when the place wasn't so crowded, and hopefully, the Marlboro Men would be gone. They would return to their ranches, cabins or caves. Joe could picture some of them living in the town of Quincy in a powder blue house with a white metallic snow roof and plastic flowers and trees that they pretended to water.

Others would probably live somewhere deep out in the woods, holed up in a fortified compound that looked like a fort in Indian territory in the 1880's. They would limp around inside, cradling a shotgun or re-peating rifle, always on the lookout for intruders who might be abnormal. Marlboro Men had no problem defining abnormal. All of the answers were available in The Bible, but you had to study it to know where to look. One also had to have faith, and daily prayer was essential. They knew God was on their side.

Instead, Joe decided to visit the student lounge,

maybe play a game or two of pool. Perhaps he could drum up some alcohol purchasing business. If he got lucky, he could earn enough to order an open faced turkey sandwich with brown gravy poured over the meat and white bread. Joe's mouth watered. It almost sounded better than his pancake idea.

If he could stay away for a few hours, everyone else in the cabin would probably be gone. There wasn't much to do there except eat and sleep. Joe speculated that one of these mornings, Lance was going to slam Kathy into the headboard one too many times and break on through into the bushes just outside.

The Keddie student lounge was a joke. It consisted of a sagging ping pong table with paddles but no balls, a lumpy, broken down couch, and a few chairs with stuffing coming out of them. One thing actually functioned. A regulation pool table with all the balls and two pool cues. It cost twenty five cents to play.

When Joe entered, there were a couple of jokers playing pool. One of them was a short, fat guy dressed in gray sweats and a black cowboy hat. The other player was a short, geeky kid with glasses and acne. Most of the balls were still scattered on the green felt. Joe watched with amusement as both of them struggled to make even simple shots.

Joe put a quarter underneath the felt ledge near the coin slot, indicating he was challenging the winner of this sluggish game. He sat down in a chair, patiently waiting for someone to lose. On the next shot, the geek lost when he sank the eight ball in a corner pocket by mistake.

"Oops," he said in a blasé tone, as though he were used to losing. He left and the fat guy, who looked familiar to Joe, told him, "Rack em up, boy. You're my next victim."

"Sure thing, pal," answered Joe. He decided he didn't like his adversary, who was being cocky when he sucked. Joe would have to teach him a lesson in humility.

Joe racked the balls loosely, an old pool hustler trick he had learned about when watching Paul Newman in 'The Hustler.' A loose rack usually meant the balls wouldn't travel far on the break.

That was it, thought Joe as he chalked his tip and his opponent prepared to break. The big slob, who he decided looked like a 'Bluto,' probably thought he was the reincarnation of the legendary pool player, Minnesota Fats. The only trouble was, Fats was still alive and winning tournaments, and Bluto sucked and didn't know it.

Bluto swaggered to the end of the table, folded his gut over the edge and eyeballed the pack. He slid his cue back and forth with his right hand and slammed the end of his stick into the cue ball. The loose pack broke apart slightly, but not much. Bluto seemed pleased with himself because he had sunk a single colored ball. He missed his next shot, a simple cut into the corner.

Joe observed that Bluto obviously knew nothing about hitting the cue ball low, to keep it close to the pack, where a skilled player could pick off his balls, one by one. He didn't even know how to put 'English' on the ball. Minnesota Fats he was not. Hell, thought Joe, smirking, Bluto wasn't even good enough to be 'Keddie Fats.'

Joe surveyed the table, formulating a plan. He sank several stripes, while Bluto waited on the couch, further crushing the cushions with his excessive weight.

Bluto got one more missed shot before Joe ran the table, sinking all his balls and then calling the eight ball in the side pocket and slamming it home. Joe tried not to smile too widely, but he was getting better. Maybe it was time to start playing for a little money, perhaps a dollar or two. Bluto, with his inflated ego, would make a prime first victim.

Instead, Bluto muttered an obscenity, dropped his cue on the table and stormed outside. Joe was left to practice alone, sinking the rest of the balls with ease.

Jesse Ray Barnes came sauntering through the connecting door to the Keddie Club with what appeared to be a mixed drink in his hand. Jake was right behind him, "Hey! You can't take liquor in there. It's illegal."

"That so?" answered Jesse, pausing to down his drink. He handed the empty glass back to the bartender, "Sorry," he muttered.

Joe thought that Jesse acted somewhat like the famous hard guy, actor, Steve McQueen. They didn't look alike, but Jesse carried that same, dangerous aura. The doomed "James Dean' persona some called it.

Jake returned, slamming and locking the side door behind him.

"Asshole," muttered Jesse. He focused his glittering snake eyes on Joe.

"What's going on?" he asked, pulling his pack of Camels out of the side pocket of his long leather coat. His voice was raspy. Joe wondered if Jesse had undiagnosed throat cancer, or maybe it was diagnosed and he just didn't give a shit.

"Just shooting around."

"Wanna play an old guy like me?"

"Sure."

Jesse allowed a quick sneer to cross his face before he shoved a quarter into the slide. The pool balls thudded into the return and rolled to the end of the table where Jesse scooped them up and carefully arranged them in the triangular rack, making sure the deadly eight ball was in the center. Joe watched Jesse move the rack back and forth until it was tight, and then he lifted the rack straight up and hung it below the table.

Joe rubbed the end of his cue with blue chalk, making it squeak. Bluto slunk back into the room and put a quarter down. His face was red and he smelled of alcohol.

That was who he was, thought Joe. It was that asshole from his Sociology class, Gary Hess. Why wasn't he over playing in the bar? Probably because he sucked even worse over there.

Jesse lighted his smoke and let it dangle out of the right corner of his mouth, "Come on kid, break already. I ain't getting any younger standing here."

Jesse swiveled and directed his voice to Bluto, "What the fuck you looking at, you fat pile?" Bluto quickly glanced away from Jesse's glare.

"Nothing."

'CRACK.' Joe sank two solids and scattered the rest of the balls all over the table. The better to pick them off, he thought . He put down another ball before missing his next shot. It was Jesse's turn now.

He hit the cue ball softly and a stripe dropped into an end pocket. Jesse walked around the table, squatted down and assessed his potential shots. He stood up, bent down low and powered another ball into the corner, this one landing with an audible 'thud.'

Jesse continued to knock them down, some of the shots easy, others seemingly impossible. Joe never got another turn.

Jesse winked at Joe, "You've got potential, kid. If you don't mind a little coaching, I could make you a lot better."

Joe caught a quick flash of a skull behind

Jesse's façade. Then, his normal, scarred face returned.

The surly Gary Hess walked up and without a word he slammed the quarter in and began racking the balls. When finished, he removed his cowboy hat and picked up the other cue and began chalking it.

Jesse laughed, "Hey lard ass. Put your hat back on. The glare of the lights off your bald spot is blinding me."

Gary glowered at Jesse, apparently considering his options.

"Hey, pal. Just kidding," laughed Jesse, sitting down on the couch and throwing his arm across the top.

"You're not funny,' answered Gary.

"That's what everyone tells me. I'd starve if I tried to do stand up comedy."

Joe broke the pack with a hard hit and sank a solid. Before hurrying onto his next shot, Jesse spoke up, "Slow down, Joe. There's no time clock for pool. Survey the whole table first. Concentrate on your next target, but also set yourself up for the following one too. I want you to get down low like I did, and take a picture in your mind and visualize the ball going in. You already know how to put English on the cue ball, now lets see what you can really do."

This time Gary got three shots, missing them all before Joe put him down. Gary threw the pool cue down on the table before he stomped out again.

"*Asshole,*" declared Jesse, "He won't be back, at least not today."

"Why did you insult him? How did you know he was an asshole, which he is by the way."

"First of all, I don't like lard asses. Secondly, I wanted him out of here so I could give you private lessons. I don't want to teach him anything. What's the dickheads name anyway? I see him in the Keddie Club all the time with his retarded friends."

"Gary Hess."

"Gary Hess." repeated Jesse. His eyes widened, and a wicked smile spread across his pock marked face, "Me and him are gonna get to know each other, and I don't think *Gary* is going to like that much."

Joe set his cue on the table and sat in a worn out chair across from Jesse.

"So, Joe. What's new in your life?"

Joe paused, "You really wanna know?"

"Yeah, sure. I wouldn't have asked if I didn't."

"Things could be better. I'm not gonna ask you what you were in prison for."

"Good," said Jesse.

Joe observed tattoos on his knuckles, "What does that spell out?"

"Can you read?"

"Of course."

Jesse held both his hands out, folding his fingers into fists.
The ink was a little faded, but Joe quickly figured it out.

"F...U...C..K...Y...O...U. Clever. Must go over real big on job interviews."

"I don't do job interviews. They either they want me or they don't. Why go through all the bullshit of filling out forms, only to be told to go piss off. Yeah, I shouldn't have done it. It's kind of embarrassing now. That's why you usually see me wearing gloves."

"Okay, now that we've clarified that issue, I've just got one more question to ask."

"Shoot."

"How come you want to hang out with a college kid like me? I don't know how old you are, but I'm guessing you're maybe forty."

Jesse peered at his fingernails that were bitten down to the quick, "What you really wanna know, Joe, is if I'm a nark or a queer. Right?"

Joe felt his ears burning.

"Well. Yeah."

"Kid, I'm as far from a nark as you can get. I'm a frigging paroled, convicted felon. You think the Sheriff's office would hire me? Ha. Here's what I know. Your spaced out buddy, Lance, is the major drug dealer in town. I knew it the second day I was here. The cops know about him and are just waiting for their undercover punk to make a few buys. I'm also straight. I do women, not boys."

"Great. Glad to get that issue clarified."

"Another thing, Joe. Watch out for that group of old farts who sit at the round table by the window for hours. They've got something cooking regarding both you and Lance. I'll find out eventually, but it may take time. In the meantime, be careful of those old fools. They might look feeble and harmless, but they've got some sort of nasty agenda., so don't say nothin in front of them.

"Thanks."

Jesse raised his right hand out, palm facing inward. His voice got hoarser, "Forget about it."

"Okay."

"I'm not a cop, nark or snitch. I'm just a regular guy who rides a Harley when I have one. I got no friends around here, just my sister and her family and I can already tell they want me gone. I'm from the big city like you guys. I'm not some cow turd kicker. Why do you guys think I'm the fuzz, anyway?"

"Because your weed is so shitty."

Jesse laughed at that one, "I know it's shitty. I bought it from some rip off for ten bucks. That's partially why I came to you boys. I heard your music blasting, so I thought, Jesse, go check these dudes out. Maybe they can get me some decent shit, you know what I mean? I got bad vibes from your buddy, so I didn't even ask."

"We figured you were setting us up for later."

"Nope. I'm a straight shooter, what they call a stand up guy. You can trust me with your life if I like you."

"What happens if you don't like someone."

Jesse smiled, his pinpoint pupils boring in on Joe, "There are various solutions. Drop the subject, I don't like talking about shit like that. It can be dangerous."

"For who."

"I said fucking drop it, Joe!"

"Sorry. You wanna shoot another game of stick?"

"Yeah, but not here. You got wheels, right?"

"The maroon Ford convertible."

"How about I.D.? Can you get into a bar?"

"I don't know. I've never tried. I've been buying liquor at the General Store every day without any problem. I forged my Military identification."

"Nice, kid. Don't be stupid. That's a Federal rap."

"Oh. I never thought about that."

"Well, you better start thinking. Otherwise, you're liable to mess up big time like me and be put away to do a dime."

"A what?" Said Joe, putting his hand up to his cheek.

204

"I did a dime. Ten years. Let me see your I.D. I'll tell you whether it'll work or if it's a useless piece of crap. I'm always honest, man."

Joe pulled out his red Coast Guard identity card. Regulars got green ones, and he'd had one for his six months active duty. They exchanged it so he longer had PX privileges, although he could still drink in the EM clubs.

Jesse studied it, turned it over and back, and then held it up to the light and squinted, "Yeah. Not a bad job."

He handed Joe his card back, "I can see where you added the tape, but you can't feel any edges, so it should work fine where we're going."

"Where? The Keddie Club?"

"Screw the Keddie Club and all the dumb shit hicks that hang out there, spoiling for a fight. I'd give em a beating, but then I go back to the joint for assault and do five more years. The hell with that."

"That's called doing a nickel then, right?"

Jesse draped his leather covered arm over Joe's shoulders and led him towards the door and out into the real world, "I'm gonna take you to a Hanky Tank Bar just down the road a spell. I hear they got live music sometimes, but we're not going there for the tunes. We're going to play pool with strangers."

"I don't know, Jesse."

Jesse punched him in the shoulder. Joe never saw it coming. He was fast, "Come on, kid. Stop leading such a safe, sheltered life. Get out and live a little. You might even see Carlene there."

Joe stared back at Jesse. How did he even know Carlene? Had Jesse already done her too? Was there some sort of clipboard signup list somewhere that he needed to get on to get his turn? Then Joe remembered that he had given up her, so why was he still jealous of her boyfriends?

Joe drove them north on the highway on the blustery day. Hard hitting rain pelted the windshield.

"Does it snow up here much, Jesse?"

"You gotta be kidding, right?"

"No, I'm serious." Joe was glad to be relatively straight as he negotiated the many curves. He flicked on the high beams, but they didn't help much.

"Kid, we're gonna get like ten feet of snow soon. I've spent winters up here be fore. You need a four wheel drive, or at least tire chains."

"What are those?"

Joe noticed that if Jesse didn't feel like answering a question, he just acted as though nothing had been asked of him.

Jesse insisted on keeping his window down as he chain smoked Camels. Rain ran down the right side of his face, but he didn't mind. He liked it, "It feels good, Joe, being free and outside. I feel alive again."

"What was it really like in there?"

"San Quentin Prison? Worse then anything you can imagine. Unless you've been locked up with a bunch of animals, you couldn't possibly understand."

The rain came down in sheets. Water stained the door panel on Jesse's side and water pooled on the carpet, "Shit," said Jesse, rolling up his window almost all the way, leaving a one inch gap at the top.

"Thanks," said Joe, "You got much family?"

"Tell you what pal. You ask too many damned questions."

Joe nodded his head as they slowed for a hairpin corner. All that Joe knew about prison was what he had seen in movies and read in books. The most descriptive was Eldridge Cleavers thin book, 'Soul On Ice,' which had somehow wound up on his required reading list when he took English 101 at Laney College.

"There it is, Joe," said Jesse, pointing to a bar set deep on the right side of the road. A blinking sign on the roof advertised it as 'J.D.'s ROADHOUSE.'

Joe wheeled his convertible into the muddy parking lot. and stopped near a raised up Chevy truck. The back window had the standard two rifles hanging from a rack. There was also an NRA sticker. As he and Jesse circled around the pickup, a German Sheppard in the bed rose up and barked at them loudly, pulling on his chain.

"Come on Joe, let's go have some fun." Jesse took off running, splattering muddy water on his jeans. Joe was right behind him.

J.D.'s Roadhouse had a long covered porch decorated with colored plastic party lights that swung in the wind. A wave of rowdy noise and a cloud of smoke greeted them as they entered the front door. A horse-shoe shaped bar sat in the middle of a fairly large room.

The bartender, a middle aged man with a mustache waved them over.

"Should we go see him?" asked Joe, who had never been in a real bar before, just the EM clubs on military bases. Those bars were full of sailors and sometimes Marines, all getting plastered and listening to the same six good songs on the jukebox. before the inevitable fighting started.

"We have to," said Jesse, putting a hand on Joe's shoulder, "Relax kid. Let me do the talking." Jesse strode confidently through a crowd of cowboys and ranchers. Many of them were hard looking, unfriendly appearing men, some with even harder looking women.

Joe followed in Jesse's footsteps, head down, trying not to step on anyone's feet.

The bartender sized them up, "You're okay," he said to Jesse, "You. Kid. Let me see some I,D."

Joe dug out his wallet and handed over his Military identification. He plunged his shaking hands into his front pants pockets and grasped his keys.

The barkeep held Joe's card underneath a strong lamp and examined it.

"Hey Ed," yelled a bearded man, bellied up to the bar, "How about a little service here."

"Hold your horses, Jack. I'll be with you in a moment."

Ed handed Joe his I.D. back, "I don't know. You sure don't look twenty two to me, junior."

"Good genes," interjected Jesse, maintaining a friendly open smile on his face, "His whole family looks young. You'd probably even card his dad, he looks so damned youthful. All of them. I'm not kidding."

"Save the bullshit for someone that cares. What do you guys want to drink?"

"Two Buds," said Jesse, laying a five on the scarred wooden counter. Ed reached into a massive cooler with a clear door. Joe could see dozens of bottles of ice cold beer, mostly Bud and Coors, along with a local favorite, Brew 52. Joe thought it tasted like donkey piss. Ed pulled out two long necked Bud's, popped the caps and set them down on the counter. He glanced derisively at Joe and slid three dollars towards Jesse, who picked up two and handed one back, "Thanks," said Ed.

Jesse led Joe through the swaying crowd to a small empty table in the back.

"You passed your first test just fine," said Jesse, taking a slug out of his Bud, "Just remember that many bartenders are retired bullies, and don't take crap off of anybody. Otherwise, they wouldn't be working the counter. It's best if you can stay on their good side, especially if you're ordering food or mixed drinks. Remember to tip the barkeep. That way he'll pour you heavy drinks, and he won't tell the goober manning the kitchen to spit in your food."

"Got it," replied Joe, sipping on his beer and lighting a smoke. He could feel himself relaxing as he surveyed his surroundings. The country western music was too loud, and men yelled, brayed and shouted in the typical style of Road Houses. A thick blue haze of cigarette smoke floated above the swirling mass of drinkers.

Jesse turned to Joe and struggled with his hoarse raspy voice to be heard above the din of the crowd, "What we're going to do now is watch the pool players, and see who's good, and who isn't. Most of these guys probably know each other, so none of them are likely to be hustlers or ringers. It's the strangers they watch out for."

Their view of the action was constantly obscured by a non stop procession of drinkers running to the head, desperate smiles on their faces. Toilets and urinals constantly flushing distracted Joe from the game. More people continued to pour into the bar, wet and thirsty.

Any shelter in a storm, thought Joe.

Two large men dressed like loggers finished their game. Another, even more brawny man in a green Pendleton rose to challenge the winner. Massive veins stuck out on the mans neck as he bent down and shoved a quarter home, releasing the balls from inside the pool table.

Jesse slid up and put his quarter in the ready position. He was back before the balls were racked.

"Number one rule for shooting stick in a strange bar with no brothers to back you up is to never play for money. Act humble and say you're not very good and offer to play for beers. Most guys are cool with that, and if they're not, they're either a hustler or an asshole. So, go ahead and play and lose your first game and walk away like you're pissed at yourself.."

Joe was enthralled, "What do you mean by brothers? Do you come from a large family?"

Jesse chuckled and lighted another smoke, "Back in Sacramento, kid, I used to ride with The Skull Diggers. You ever heard of them?"

"Yeah, of course." Joe was now really impressed with his drinking partner and volunteer teacher.

"Don't ever party with them, Joe. If they come into a bar you're at, leave. Not unless you got some kind of secret death wish. Even the other clubs were afraid of us."

"Is that one of the rules?"

"For you. Not me. I can't be active while I'm on parole. Plus, my old lady Stella sold my bike for dope money. You can't ride with the Digger's if you don't have a chopper. That really pissed me off, Joe. I know where it is though. Some weekend tough guy who sells real estate has it in his garage."

"How you gonna get it back?"

"I thought I told you to stop asking so many questions."

"Sorry. Just curious."

"Well, sorry and too many nosy questions can get you a bullet in the back of your head in my world."

Men near the pool table cheered as a man spun the eight ball into a side pocket and instantly lost,

"Crap."

Jesse stood up, "Rule number two. Keep your mouth shut, and you might have a problem with this one. Say hi and be friendly, but don't start bragging about yourself and shit you own or try to be a funny guy and tell jokes. Never volunteer information about yourself, and this is real important. Never admit anything, even if you get caught with your hand in the cookie jar. Always plead innocent."

Jesse sauntered off to the table.

Plead innocent, thought Joe. *Innocent of what?* Did Jesse have criminal plans for himself and him? Was that why he was grooming him? Was he planning some major crime and needed an accomplice?

Jesse quickly set up the rack, made a few easy shots and then missed a harder one on purpose. He stood back and watched the man in the green shirt run the table.

"Good game," said Jesse, putting his cue back in the rack on the wall.

Jesse returned to their table carrying two fresh Buds, ice running off the sides of the brown glass. He sat down and cracked a few peanuts into his palm, dropping the shells on the floor. It was that kind of place, where they only swept up once a week on Sunday afternoons.

"Rule number three, and then that's it for class today. Always know where the back door is, and don't tell anyone what you're driving. They might go out when you're not looking and disable your car so they can roll you in the parking lot later. This is especially relevant if you're stupid enough to flash a big roll. This one should be obvious. Take a twenty out and put it in your front pocket and use that for drinking money. Don't wear diamond rings or flashy jewelry either.

Leave that glittery shit at home, unless you can't
trust your old lady, and if you can't, then why are you
living with her anyway?"

Both of them took long pulls off their fresh
beers.

Kathy sat at the dining table and whined,
"Lance. I told you I'm hungry."

Lance peered into the refrigerator, "I know,
babe. That's why I'm still looking, making sure I'm not
missing something."

"I looked fifteen minutes ago, and it was empty.
You think that somehow food just magically appeared
in there since then?"

Lance slammed the refrigerator door, "I just
thought of something. I haven't checked all the
cupboards."

"Go for it."

One by one, Lance opened all the cupboards,
and found nothing. He reached into the one at the top
and rooted around, "Hey. I found something, Kathy."

"What is it?" asked Kathy, a little life in her
voice.

Lance pulled out half a loaf of Wonder Bread. It
had green mold all over the wrapper. He flung it into
the garbage sack, "Ew," he said, washing his hands, "I
remember putting that up there when we first moved
in."

"Great," remarked Kathy, "The mold was the
same shade as your jacket."

"Knock off the sarcasm, will you. I'm doing the
best I can here."

Kathy sniffed, "Why can't we just go over to the
restaurant like we always do?"

"Because we can't afford to eat all our meals

out. It might help if you learned how to cook. I realize to you that's an unknown concept, actually cooking a meal, but trust me. Folks do it all the time. Some people never eat out, and we've been doing it three times a day. "

"I can too cook. I know to fry burgers, hot dogs, spaghetti and chili. How am I supposed to prepare anything if the refrigerator is always empty? What about food money?"

"Everyone has a God give right to eat, whether they have money or not. It's not like we're living during the Dark Ages."

"When was that, 1959?"

Lance stared at his old lady, "I've always managed to find food before."

"Like when you were living on Walnut Street last year and got Hepatitis and turned yellow and screwed up your liver?"

"That's not funny, Kathy. Maybe I should have just left you in Berkeley."

Scott and Claire entered the cabin and headed directly into the back bedroom. There was a murmuring of angry voices, and then Scott stuck his head out from the hallway, "Hey roomie. It's time for you guys to buy some toilet paper. We're out in case you hadn't noticed. Lord you guys use enough. Plus, we now have another resident also using supplies."

"It's okay Scott," answered Lance, "I've been using your bath towel to wipe my ass."

"I've been using Chris's," volunteered Kathy, "Lance said it was okay. Plus, I earn my keep. I used your toothbrush to scrub the edges of the toilet. It was really gross down there I'll have you know. Joe gave me that suggestion, saying that's how they did it in the Coast Guard."

Scott moved into full view. Claire appeared next to him and clutched his shoulder as Scott breathed heavily, his face turning crimson. "You assholes!"

"Scott old buddy," said Lance,"Tell us how you really feel."

Scott yelled, "And, if you don't mind, you fuck bunnies, when you guys are doing it, like every hour, could you hold down the noise?"

"Yeah," added Claire, "Maybe move your bed away from the wall. It gets really annoying. It's one of the reasons I hardly come over here anymore."

Lance and Kathy hitched a ride to Quincy with a local rancher who was driving a rusty red early 1960's Dodge pickup. He hadn't said a word when he pulled over, just pointed at the bed of his truck. Once moving, he spit a glob of chaw out his window every two minutes. Tobacco juice stains coated the drivers side door and bed.

Lance and Kathy moved over to the right side and huddled together. It was frigid weather, and they were sharing the bed with a couple of hay bales and an overly friendly German Shepherd. The dog smelled bad, and had large patches of hair missing from his head and back. He kept jumping up on them, trying to lick their faces.

"Get away from us!" shouted Lance, finally shoving the dog away.

The dog growled and bared his teeth and white froth dripped from his mouth.

When Lance tried to switch positions, the German Shepard pounced and leaped on his back and wrapped his dog legs around him and started dry humping him.

"Do something!" shouted Lance, unable to

shake the hundred pound rabid dog off his back.

"Ew gross," shouted Kathy. She pounded on the rear glass, caught the rancher's attention and frantically motioned for him to pull over.

The man complied and Kathy kicked the dog in his ribs, making him fall back and she and Lance jumped to safety.

Lance shoved his hand into the air and flipped the man off, "Thanks a lot you creep. I hope your dog rips out your throat you sick bastard!"

The rancher laughed, spit out another stream of chaw and slowly drove off, waving in a friendly manner.

Lance and Kathy stood on the side of the dark highway and watched forlornly as the taillights of the Dodge disappeared around the next corner. Kathy clutched Lance's arm, "Are you okay? That really sucked."

"I hate dogs."

They heard a coyote howling, and then the chilling sound of a pack baying back. There was a full moon, and it was getting colder. Snow flakes begin falling, lightly at first, and then increasing in volume, quickly accumulating on the ground. They were still miles from Quincy. Lance and Kathy started trudging towards town.

They got lucky when their stoned neighbor, Greg, stopped to pick them up in his black Cadillac Hearse. He was friendly and had the heater blasting and passed them a lit joint. The inside of the Hearse was all red velour.

After a short ride, Lance had Greg drop them off a hundred feet from Howard's Grocery, which was located on the north end of town where it was pretty dead at night.

"Thanks, Greg," said Lance in a friendly voice before slamming the heavy door.

"Observe the deserted streets, Kathy. Nine o'clock, Saturday night, and its like they roll up the sidewalk. Notice you don't see anyone. They're either at home watching Lawrence Welk, drinking at one of the bars, or having unprotected sex with their livestock. I bet this store is getting ready to close."

"Yeah, so maybe we should walk faster."

"No, wait. We gotta have a plan. Here it is. I'm good at this sort of thing. I go in first and scout things out, see who's on duty and check out the vibes. You count to 60 and enter and go up to the cashier and ask for something odd. Ask if they have it in stock and distract her from the fact that I'm in the store, shoplifting. I'll shove a package of chicken inside my jacket and just walk out."

"Can't you get a couple of Mexican TV dinners? Chicken takes too long. Do you even know how to cook it? I don't. Truthfully, I usually eat cold Spaghetti O's."

"Yeah, that is a better idea. We can heat them up in 45 minutes, once we get back. Okay, you ready?"

"Yeah. I know my part."

Lance entered the grocery store and paused. momentarily blinded by the fluorescent lights. He nodded to an older lady sitting on a stool who didn't nod back.

"Nice to meet you too," he muttered, heading for the frozen food section that was against the far wall. He could hear the humming of multiple freezers.

Before he even had a chance to find the TV dinners he heard Kathy's frantic voice at the front of the store, "Excuse me maam. Do you have any books on witchcraft? Can you show me where they are? Nice store you got here."

An older man wearing a green apron came charging out of the back room just as Lance was shoving two Swanson Deluxe Mexican frozen dinners into his jacket. He had already lifted a can of corn and a box of crackers.

"Put that food back, you dammed stinking hippie! Wanda! Call the Sheriff!"

Lance held his arm across his jacket as he ran from the store with his long lanky strides that few could match. He had a determined grin on his face from the adrenalin rush of pulling off a crime.

Kathy was a few strides behind him. They both stopped and looked back. Wanda was out front with a broom, shaking it in their direction.

"Shit," said Lance, "We gotta get off the main road or we're gonna get busted."

They walked into the roadside bushes and crept along, hoping that they could jump out in time to hitchhike if it wasn't a cop. The idea of walking ten miles back to Quincy in the dark with melting TV dinners was not appealing. In addition, snow was falling harder, covering up the ground and making the walking even more difficult.

They heard movement in the woods, as though something was tracking them.

"Oh Lance," said Kathy, clutching at his arm, "I'm scared."

"So am I, but we'll be fine. Trust me babe."

"I don't have any other choice, do I?"

VETERANS

CHAPTER FOURTEEN

Two days after Maureen Hess was released
from the psych ward at Quincy General Hospital, Gary
Hess drove his Willys downtown. He was looking for
his step dad, Sheriff Big Dan McGrew. His cruiser was
distinctive, as it had an extra big star on the front doors,
indicating that he was numero uno in law enforcement
in town.

Gary cruised past the local VFW building and
there was Dan's car, backed into a parking spot that
said 'Police Only.'

Gary parked on the street, got out and pulled on
his heavy denim jacket that was getting a little tight.
Matter of fact, he couldn't even button it anymore. He
hunched forward and walked quickly past Roy's Barber
Shop, Peg's Diner, a beauty saloon, and the Elks Club
bar that had their door open and was full with wall to
wall drinkers.

Gary thought about the town elders who hung
out on this block virtually all day and night, starting at
Peg's for biscuits and gravy and coffee. They had
personalized mugs with their nickname stamped on it,
like Dick Bob, Jimmy Joe, Assbite, and Ralph. They
shared their views on current politics, the creeping
cancer of communism, and the damned hippies. They
all agreed that the U.S. Military should stop screwing

around and bomb the gooks in Vietnam back to the
stone age. They figured about ten nuclear bombs
dropped simultaneously would do the job.

Around noon they would either go home for a
nap or gravitate over to Roy's Barber Shop and chat
with his customers as Roy cut their hair. They also
knew where Roy kept his stash of dog-eared Playboys.

After some quality time at home with the little
woman and a meat and potatoes dinner, many of them
would return that night and drink at the Elks Club or
VFW.

The VFW had a supposedly serious business
meeting every Wednesday night at 6 P.M, and Big Dan
was on the board of directors. They went through the
motions of a structured meeting, someone reading
boring notes from last week, and somebody else asking
if there were any new proposals. After ten seconds of
silence, the gavel would bang down. Meeting over in
ten minutes. Then it was time to belly up to the bar and
get plastered.

Most of the active members were veterans of
World War Two or the Korean War. Some of them had
served in both. Only a few of the recently returned
Vietnam Vets bothered to join the VFW.

The elders were proud to have served honorably
in the last, great war. They, along with the Korean War
vets, rarely complained about the hardships they had
endured over seas. If no Vietnam Vets were present,
they were often ridiculed and mocked. It was a common
feeling that the kids coming back from the Vietnam
War were a lesser breed of men than themselves.

Gary huffed as he climbed the stone steps up to
the front door of the VFW. The last time he was here
was when they dedicated a plaque in honor of Jimbo.
His brother, James Raymond Hess, was the first local

boy to come home in a pine box. Everyone knew there would be more. Guys suddenly didn't want to be nineteen or twenty anymore and be subject to the draft. Many felt as though it were a potential death sentence. Now there were plaques for Steve Blocker and Ivan Glass too, all local, dead U.S. Marines.

Everyone swiveled around and gawked when Gary entered the hallowed halls. Normal citizens were not granted admittance without a member present to sponsor them.

Gary was okay because of dead Jimbo and Big Dan being his step father. That being said, Gary was not very popular there. No one greeted him. Veterans who had put their ass on the line, deeply resented the fact that Gary had maneuvered himself into 4F status. His excuse was that he had flat feet caused by his excess tonnage. Just for good measure, he also claimed to be color blind as well as an Asthmatic.

Gary got what he wanted and didn't care what any of the frigging VFW Vets thought of him. Why should he volunteer to be killed like Jimbo? What good would it do? Absolutely none. They should draft all the minorities first anyway. Didn't being a righteous and true white man count for anything anymore?

Big Dan held court at a large round table in the center of their meeting hall. Five of his cronies were with him, taking turns in telling their scariest combat experience. Dan, in uniform and on duty, drank coffee while the rest of them clutched beers or mixed drinks.

The only time Dan ever drank on the job was when it was snowing heavily and he was out in freezing weather for long shifts. He would spend the majority of his time orchestrating the rescue of dumb shits who tried to drive on frozen roads and were discovered upside down in a ditch. They should have stayed at home like all the local weather people were advising their listeners.

"Howdy, Gary," said Dan, raising his cup in greeting, "What brings you down town tonight.?"

"Hi, Dan. I need to talk to you about something important. I didn't want to bother you at the house."

Dan laughed for five seconds, "So you decided to bother me here, in front of my brothers?"

"It's about Maureen."

"Pull up a chair and tell me what's on your mind."

"It's kind of private. Family business."

Big Dan set his coffee cup on the table, "Fella's, can you excuse us for a few minutes?"

Without a word, the five veterans scooted back their chairs, grabbed their smokes and carried their drinks over to a table on the other side of the room.

Gary sat down.

"What's up?" asked Dan.

"What I came to tell you is that Maureen was just released from the hospital. She was in their psych ward for three days."

"How come no one called me? How is she? What happened?"

"She overdosed during an LSD trip and lost her mind for awhile. Sam is home with her now. She's still pretty loopy."

"You haven't told your mother any of this, have you?"

"No. That would make matters worse."

"Exactly. It might push her over edge and into the hospital herself. She's a very sick woman you know."

"Yes. I do know. Now Dan, a couple months ago, there were hardly any illegal drugs in town. The

263

Indians use Peyote for their religious ceremonies, and that's fine. The Mexicans, they smoke a little weed here and there. Not a huge deal. Some of the truckers coming through have speed, but it's for their own use, not for sale. Now, all that's changed. Since the college punks from the 'Gay Bay' moved in, both Quincy and Keddie have been saturated with drugs. Hard drugs, Dan. Someone's gonna overdose and die. Maureen came close."

"Tell me something I don't already know, Gary. Do you have any names for me? Guys that are openly dealing?"

Gary paused. A bald veteran at a nearby table was telling a loud, animated story about using a flame thrower on Japs on Iwo Jima, "We turned em into crispy critters I tell ya. That's why to this day, I can't eat at KFC. You know, crispy chicken."

Everyone at the table laughed heartedly.

"Yeah, I got some names for you, Dan."

Big Dan pulled out a pocket notebook and black pen.

"Lance Potter and Joe Bailey are the main dealers in Keddie. Potter looks the part. He's tall with long brown hair and gold rimmed glasses. He likes to wear this old leather jacket that has mold growing all over it. I hear he sells everything, from pot and LSD to heroin.

"What about Bailey?"

"I can't figure him out, unless he and Potter are queers. I don't get why they're together. He has short hair and has a current bumper sticker from the Coast Guard. Boy, is he in for a surprise when our heavy snow starts and his convertible top caves in."

"So you figure Bailey must be involved because he lives with Potter?"

"Yep. He must play some part in the operation. How could he not know?"

"Anyone else?"

"Yeah. There's something real fishy about this new cook at the lodge, Jesse Barnes. He just showed up one day, strutting around in a leather jacket. I hear he deals speed and cocaine."

"That a fact?" Big Dan raised an eyebrow, "We got a parole report on him from Sacramento. I guess I can let you in on this, since you gave me some good leads."

"Yeah, I won't tell no one."

Big Dan flipped to the middle of his notebook, "Jesse Ray Barnes. Age 34. Paroled from San Quentin in August after serving a ten year stretch. Check this out. Former President of The Skull Digger's motorcycle gang in Sacramento."

"Wow. Do tell. Does it say what he was in for? Dealing dope? Murder?"

Dan shut his notebook, "Naw Gary, it don't say. I'll contact Sacramento PD and see what kind of rap sheet they got on this guy. I've seen him around town in his leather jacket. Not a real big man, but tough looking for sure. Kind of reminds me of Steve McQueen a little bit. Just like you remind me of the wrestler, Haystack Calhoun."

Gary started to stand up. He knew Dan was lying about not knowing Jesse's crime. If he got a parole report, obviously it would be on that. Did Dan think he was dense? Plus, he had just insulted him by comparing him to a four hundred pound pro wrestler.

"Sit down for a minute more, Gary. I've got something different to talk to you about."

"Yeah, what?"

"You remember me telling you about that Elliott

Rosen kid?"

"Yep."

Dan looked behind him and turned back, "Seems as though his father is some big time lawyer in San Francisco, and he's starting to rattle some important cages. He wants some arrests. A few days ago, his dad chartered a helicopter for ten grand to transfer his son down to a hospital in San Francisco where they have spinal specialists. I guess the kid is still paralyzed from the waist down."

"What's this have to do with me?"

"I know you were there, Gary. Along with Randy-Bob Casey, David Krebs and Reno Converse. Why do you hang around with such half wits?"

Gary shrugged his shoulders.

"What I'm telling you is I'm getting a lot of heat from the flipping California State Attorney General. If I don't arrest someone soon, they've threatened to send a car load of FBI agents to Quincy to solve the case. This Rosen guy has a lot of juice. The fact is, this isn't the first time you idiots have done this sort of crap. Everyone knows about you beating up and robbing the Indians, plus some Mexicans too. All I'm telling you is that I'm not going to be able to hold them off much longer. This is the last thing your mother needs right now, especially with Maureen in trouble too."

"Are you done?"

"Yeah, I guess so, unless you got something you'd like to say."

"Why don't you do your job and arrest these assholes who are openly selling drugs? As far as the assaults, I don't know nothin. You got the wrong guy. When am I supposed to be doing all these terrible crimes? I'm working full time, going to school and studying. I don't have time to assault Jew hippies,

Mexicans and Indians, not that they don't deserve it."

"So you're claiming you weren't there when the Rosen kid was assaulted?"

"Damned right," said Gary, standing up and storming across the floor, bumping into a couple of members by accident and running down the stairs. His mind was a mass of jumbled thoughts. Screw his sobriety that had lasted three whole days. He needed some drinks.

It was eight in the evening when Joe strolled into the Keddie Restaurant. He knew they closed at nine and he had time for a meal. Jesse was behind the counter and gave Joe a barely perceptible head nod. When entering a place, Jesse had explained to Joe, you didn't want to necessarily run up and greet somebody you knew. Unless you had business with that person or they were otherwise expecting you, a slight head nod was appropriate.

Full acknowledgement could possibly blow that person's scene if they were about to rob the place or were cheating on their spouse with a hussy. Why get involved in a beef or crime that wasn't yours? It wasn't smart, explained Jesse.

Joe was surprised to see Carlene working as a uniformed waitress. She placed a glass of water with no ice in front of him.

"Do you know what you want?" she asked without greeting him.

"The usual."

"Which is?"

"The hot Roast Beef sandwich. Jesse knows how to fix it the way I like it."

Carlene concentrated on writing out Joe's order

in cursive. By the time she handed it in, Jesse
already had his sandwich ready. Carlene put it down in
front him, "Did you want some aw-jouie sauce to go
with that?"

Joe shook his head, trying not to burst out
laughing. *Aw'jouie sauce?*

As soon as Carlene wandered off to fill napkin
holders, Jesse brought him a large glass of milk and
joined him at the counter and smoked a Camel.

"How's it going, pal"

"Okay, I guess." Joe sprinkled some salt on the
Roast Beef.

"I had fun the other night shooting stick with
you at J.D.'s. We'll have to do it again soon."

"Yeah. It was a totally new experience for me.
Next time I'll be more relaxed. Heck," he said, chewing
a bite and turning towards Jesse, "I might even win a
pool game one of these times."

"You did all right, kid, especially for being a
rookie. Now, I've told you to not ask so many
questions, but I wanna ask you one and I hope it's not
too personal."

"What?"

"How come I never see you with any chicks?
Geez, man, they're all over the place. If I was you, I'd
have me a different broad every night"

"I'm not gay if that's what you're insinuating."

" Never crossed my mind. I don't even like
switch hitters either, friend."

Joe knew Jesse was referring to people who
swung both ways sexually, not baseball hitters who
could hit either left or right handed.

"I've decided to concentrate on my studies and
not waste my time in a temporary relationship. That
being said, my primary problem, the way I see it, is my

short hair. Chicks probably think I'm a square or a nark."

Jesse thought it over before offering a suggestion, "Why not get a short hair wig?"

Joe drained his milk, licked his lips and wiped his mouth with a napkin, "I can't afford a wig. Hell, I can barely pay for food. If it hadn't been for you, I'd have missed some meals, Jesse, and believe me when I tell you I'm grateful."

Carlene walked by with a blank expression. Joe and Jesse both stared at her ass when she bent over to fill the salt and pepper shakers.

Jesse whispered to Joe, "Bet you'd like some of that. Think you could handle it?"

"I don't know. Doesn't look as though I'm ever going to find out. I'm not sure she even knows my name."

"Tell you what pal," said Jesse, his voice getting harsher, "If you can give me a ride to Sacramento this Saturday, I might be able to fix you up with a wig. No promises. Things have changed a lot in the last decade, and I'm not sure the place I have in mind is even still there."

"Sounds okay with me. I got nothing else going on. Why do you need to go back to Sacramento?"

"I need to pick up the rest of my stuff from Stella's house. Make sure your trunk is empty because I'm probably going to fill it up. Then, maybe we'll stop by and have a beer with The Skull Diggers in their clubhouse."

"I don't know Jesse. I think I'd feel out of place. I'm not a biker. I'm just a student and a shitty one at that. Besides, you told me never to party with those guys."

Jesse pinched Joe's cheek, "You'll be safe with

me, kid. I don't like to brag, but I used to be President of the Sacramento chapter. I'm sure I'll still know a lot of the guys. One bit of advice though. Just drink your beer and mind your own business. Don't stare at anyone, especially the broads. If someone challenges you while I'm taking a leak or something, just say you're with Jesse Ray Barnes, and they should back off. Don't worry, Joe, you'll probably be fine."

"Probably?"

"Yeah, that's what I said. Probably."

"Okay, what time do you want me to pick you up."

"Meet me here at the restaurant at six A.M.. I'll cook us a big breakfast before they open at seven. We should be down and back by early evening."

Jesse got up to cook an order for a train worker who had just arrived.

Joe got that familiar uneasy feeling in his stomach. He wondered what he was doing hanging out with this convicted felon. So far, he hadn't steered him wrong, but partying with the Skull Digger maniacs? Well, too late now. He was committed.

THE PEOPLE'S COMMUNE

CHAPTER FIFTEEN

On Monday morning, a somber Gary Hess headed for Maureen and Sam's house to check on his sister. He pulled his green Jeep up in front of the small rental, got out, adjusted his stomach and pulled his cowboy hat down. Sam answered the door, loomed over Gary and stepped aside without saying a thing.

As Gary passed Sam he whispered, "Bite me."

Sam slammed the door and then stood behind Maureen with his arms crossed.. She was resting on their couch covered by an Indian blanket with a bedroom pillow under her head. A thick pocket book, 'Dune' lay folded across her lap.

Gary removed his hat and held it in front of his stomach, hoping that might make it appear smaller, "How's it going, sis?"

Maureen looked up at her older brother. Her mouth seemed crooked, her whole face a bit lopsided, her blue eyes cloudy, "I've been better."

Gary sat down in a nearby armchair. Maureen and Sam winced as they clearly heard wood cracking.

"Here, Gary," said Sam, rushing over and shoving Gary toward the couch where he landed with a thud, "Sit over there you fat fuck. Thanks for breaking our chair, bitch."

Maureen looked at Sam with new admiration. Oohh, she liked it when he got mad and fought for her. It was an intimidating side of him that she suspected existed, but had never seen before. What was next? Random mayhem?"

Gary managed to straighten himself out, even holding onto his precious black hat He eyeballed Sam,"Tough guy, huh? Try that again when I'm facing you, instead of attacking me from the side like a cowardly lap dog."

"Shut up you walking piece of shit. What do you want?" demanded Sam.

Gary ignored Sam.

"Maureen. How are you doing? I was real concerned about you the other day."

"Well, thank you for your help, Gary, but I think you overreacted a bit. I really didn't need a three hundred dollar ambulance ride to Quincy General. All I needed was some orange juice and someone calm who could talk me down. Have you ever had your stomach pumped, bro?"

"No. Does it make you lose weight? If it does, I might try it."

"You dumb shit."

"You know, this is exactly why I don't take drugs. Sorry, sis, I really thought your life was in danger. Your pulse was slow. What if it been something serious, like Bladder Cancer or the clap. What then, huh?"

"My whole experience, start to finish, sucked," said Maureen, sitting up. "The hospital was the last place I needed to be. They locked me up in their padded psych ward for three nights. I wasn't in danger, Gary, I was just a little too high. Remember, whatever goes up must eventually come down. Basic Physics, really.

Your aura is cloudy. And, why does everyone keep dogging me about getting and spreading VD?"

"Aura? What's that? A leafy green vegetable that tastes like shit but is supposed to add a month to your life? The kind of organic crap Doc Johnson keeps trying to shove down my throat all the time. Screw that. I require meat."

"What?" asked Maureen, a strange look on her face as she moved her fingers in and out of both of her ear canals simultaneously.

"That was supposed to be a joke, Maureen. You know, lighten up the mood here. Like ha ha."

"Yeah. Ha Ha. Real funny. Now I have a huge hospital bill for three nights lodging in Hotel Hell, as well as the ambulance ride, plus I can't work right now."

Maureen burst into tears.

Sam bent down, hugged her and handed her two Kleenex.

Gary stood up and put his hat back on. He hadn't expected both a physical and verbal assault. Maybe they were both high on something. He decided it would be a good time to leave.

Maureen shrieked at him, "You're just a drunken fat head, Gary. Right now, I hate you."

"Sorry you feel that way."

"I suppose the whole frigging family knows about this, right?"

"Big Dan knows. I didn't tell your mom or Roger if that's what you're asking. I mean, wouldn't you want to know if I was in the hospital?"

"Not really."

"I told Big Dan all about your doper connection, Lance Potter. I also turned in Joe Bailey and Jesse Barnes."

A bright red glow appeared on Maureen's cheeks. She sat up and pointed her finger at her brother, "You dim witted asshole. It's not like Lance is some big dealer. He mostly sells to friends to afford his own supply. And Joe Bailey being a dealer? What a joke. All he does is sit in the corner of that damned ugly couch, drink, smoke dope and write caustic prose and poems that don't rhyme.

"Why in the world did you give them Jesse's name? He's just a damned cook, trying to survive. Gary, you could get him sent back to San Quentin when he's done nothing wrong. He doesn't even like heavy drugs. What the hell is your problem? Are you seeking attention?"

"Well gang, it was real, but I've got to go. As far as you sis, if you ever get dragged to my house again, half dead, I'll just heave you up on a snow bank and watch as you get frostbite and hypothermia before you die. There. How's that for a dumb shit?"

Sam approached Gary with an empty long necked beer bottle dangling from his right hand. Gary felt vulnerable and backed towards the closed front door. He was basically defenseless if the big Dane should decide to swing on him. He knew Sam didn't fight much, but was quite experienced in no rules street fighting. He had grown up in some tough European ghetto in France or Nigeria, some place like that, over there.

"You need to leave now. You can see how much you've upset Maureen."

"Sorry," said Gary as he paused at the front door, "Goodbye sis. Just remember one thing, girl. We're blood. We're family. Always have been, always will be. You can't disown me. If you try, I'll come back on you like a tainted Mexican TV dinner and give you green enchilada food poisoning. Don't ever forget it. Goodbye."

They listened as Gary clomped down the stairs, entered his Jeep and drove off.

"Sam. Take my VW. Drive to Keddie to warn Lance, Joe or Jesse, whoever you find first. Then they can alert the others that a drug raid is sure to go down soon. Also, stop in at Greg's cabin at the top and warn them too. They all need to get their stashes out of their cabins, right now. I know my step dad. He's likely to pull a big raid any time. He'll probably call in the State Police and the Highway Patrol too."

"What about the National Guard? I don't think they're busy right now."

"This isn't funny, Sam. This is no time for jokes. Just go. I'll be fine by myself for an hour or so."

Sam bent down and kissed Maureen on her forehead, "I'll take care of it right now, babe. Need me to pick you up something while I'm out?"

"Yeah. Get me four bags of Frito's, a quart of cheap Scotch, six cans of Coke and some beef sticks. I feel like getting drunk."

"Are you sure, Maureen?"

"Yeah, Sam, I'm damned sure. Everyone else around here gets snookered. Why not me?"

"I just might have to join you then."

"Why? You don't have to."

"I know. I just don't want you ever going some place without me again."

They had all started out that night wearing white robes with different colored sashes. Lance asked if there was a significance to the color worn, and indeed there was. The color indicated the mood of the wearer, and also if they were seeking sex. Lance immediately asked what the sex color was, and was handed a red sash. Kathy selected the same thing. As they wrapped their red sashes around their middles, they both had time to reflect on what was happening and glanced sideways at each other.

Their evening progressed with a tab of brown organic mescaline. Malcom himself distributed a pill to each member. He stopped in front of each willing space cadet, looked deep into their eyes until he was satisfied with their inner glow. Then he would reveal his wise man's grin, and put the tab on the persons tongue, much like a Catholic Priest would do with the thin wafer.

Malcom would then bow his head, fold his hands together, and mutter a short, untelligble prayer. He wished them luck on their journey on their inner train, far into the depths of their own imagination. "Be at peace," were Malcom's last words before he moved onto the next person.

Ruth followed behind her prophet husband and offered a drink of water to wash the large tab down. "Drink as much as you wish, friend. We're going to be flushing out your toxins soon. Be as one." she would say in a dreamy voice.

The atmosphere was thick with excitement and anticipation, and Lance felt himself blasting off on a contact high, long before the mescaline was supposed to kick in.

"This should be an awesome trip," is the last thing he remembered saying.

With his task complete, Malcom sat cross legged in front of them on a colorful pillow. Ruth sat on her own pillow, slightly behind her man.. Lance and Kathy joined a semicircle of members, all facing Malcom, who sat in a full lotus position, his hands outstretched, palms facing upwards. His eyes were closed, meditating on his next, inspired words. Satisfied, he opened his eyes and scanned his beaming members.

"Welcome, beautiful brothers and sisters. I love you all. Ruth loves you all. What I have given you is one hit of organic, brown mescaline. It is supposed to produce a very mellow high. It will not be harsh, abrasive, or scary, like LSD. Ruth and I as well as a few others have not partaken. We will watch over you and keep you safe, much the same as a Sheepherder guards his flock. Our purpose tonight is for you to experience consciousness without ego. This should allow you to move up and discover your third eye."

Lance jumped and then smiled when Mary handed him a large water pipe and said, "Take a hit, brother. It is marijuana mixed with hashish. It will help smooth out any rough edges you might have brought in here with you tonight."

Mary flashed him a sexy grin, as she often did, and she squeezed into a spot on his right while Kathy sat on his left, taking her turn with the pipe. As they chatted, if Lance said something funny, Mary would tilt her head back as far as it would go and laughed from deep within her belly.

Mary frequently touched Lance's bare right arm with her warm hands, sending currents of electricity and desire throughout his body. He tried to hide his flirting and infatuation with Mary, but Kathy was sitting right there, observing, not saying a word. He knew that she knew, yet he couldn't help himself.

Lance and Kathy sat cross legged on brightly colored pillows on the floor of the tepee. along with the others. It was midmorning, and their all night mescaline adventure was drawing to a close. They were all nude and muddy.

Lance could only recall flashes of action and events that had transpired in the preceding twelve hours. He recalled a wild orgy and random acts of debauchery, and also having awesome sex with Mary while Kathy watched. Now, he sat there, dazed, hungry, and filthy. He wondered where they had left their robes, and why they were all covered with dried mud, from head to toe. He wasn't sure what had been real, and what been drug induced fantasy.

Kathy poked him hard in his ribs, "Did you have fun with *Mary?*"

"It was okay, I guess. I really don't remember much."

Kathy's voice got excited, "I've never had sex with a living prophet before. It was an experience like I've never had. Almost, well, heavenly. Plus, his beard tickles."

"Living prophet? You really believe that?"

"Yes. Malcom was sent here to organize this commune to prepare for the return of Jesus. They're still building up their numbers, but the restaurant in town is doing so well they've also opened a bakery where their they feature a local specialty bread….."

"No, Kathy. Don't say it. I swear to God I'll puke."

"Organic Brown Bread by Susan."

"I told you not to," said Lance, who stood up and heaved up his guts in front of everyone. Lance couldn't shut it off. It continued to spray out like a fire hose, splattering everyone around him. People screamed and ran outside, muddy, burned out and now splattered with foul smelling vomit.

Someone guided Lance out of the tepee, where Paul, the commune's Minister Of Trips stood there with a dripping garden hose, puffing on a pipe full of hashish.

"Okay," said Paul in clipped English tones, "Anyone who is ready to get clean fast and doesn't mind a little cold water, line up, and I'll hose you down."

Lance stood there, wobbly, with no one within ten feet of him. He looked up at Paul, and wondered why he was dressed like a Hopi Medicine Man. His outfit included a full Indian headdress, a loin-cloth that looked like a car chamois, and a brown leather vest. Several strings of colored beds hung around his neck. His face was wildly made up with streaks of day-glo paint.

Paul turned on the nozzle full blast and hosed down the twelve members as well as Lance and Kathy, who now stood as far away from Lance as possible. Paul moved slowly forward, grinning, methodical in his cleaning, as though he had done this many times before. Satisfied with their fronts, he gave further instructions, "Now, everyone turn around and I'll clean your arses. Ha Ha."

After they were hosed off, a small older woman handed out towels while another gave everyone fresh white robes with their choices of sashes, "Take black, Lance," whispered Mary into his ear. She was behind him and he could feel her warm breath on his ear, "It means you want sleep, and are not to be awakened until you are fully refreshed."

"Thanks," he muttered, moving forward like a robot with his dripping arms held out in front of him.

Upon drying off and dressing near Mary, he asked her a question, "Where's Malcom and Ruth?"

"In their home. It's nearby. Big and gorgeous. You ought to see it,. and you shall if you continue on with us and officially become a member and shave your head."

"Home? I though he lived on the bus with the common people."

"He and Ruth started out there. As our numbers have grown, and our income increases, we have been able to expand. There our other houses and cabins too, plus a ranch near Lake Tahoe."

"Where does all the money come from for these places? Surely you don't generate enough profit from your restaurant to support such an enterprise."

"The lord always provides for those who have faith. There's breakfast at the restaurant. That's where you'll find me. You and Kathy should join us."

"I'll be there sometime. I'm not sure about Kathy. I think she's jealous about you and me last night."

Mary laughed, "She'll get over it. We trade partners all the time."

As Mary sauntered off, Paul came up with Kathy, "Good morning Lance. I trust you had fun last night?"

"I think I did," answered Lance.

"He did," said Kathy bitterly.

"By the way, do either of you come from families with money?"

"No," answered Lance for both he and Kathy, "Do you have a place we can crash, Paul?"

"Yes, certainly. The good lord provides for those who help themselves. Follow me my children."

Lance whispered to Kathy, "Notice his answers don't match my questions?"

Kathy remained silent as he and Lance followed ten paces behind Paul who pulled out a flute and played and skipped down the path towards the restaurant and bus.

"As far as God," continued Lance, "He's also the vengeful God of pestilence and floods, as well as an eye for an eye and a tooth for a tooth."

"Why don't you just shut up for once," said Kathy in a scathing tone of voice. She increased her pace until she was directly behind Paul, leaving Lance to bring up the rear with no audience for his pontifications.

Paul paused in front of the wildly painted 1948 International school bus, "Would you two care for some breakfast before crashing? We have our organic wheat porridge."

Kathy shook her head and Lance managed a no thanks.

"Suit yourself, Follow me aboard."

A green propane camp stove sat on a wide shelf behind the drivers seat. A small refrigerator was below it, humming away. A long black cord hung out a partially open window. Next was a fold up table that could seat four.

Paul walked down the center of the bus, indicating with his right hand for them to follow. Beyond four rows of original seats was a catacomb of sleeping quarters that were partitioned off by tapestries from India and old sheets from Monkey Wards. Lance chuckled when he saw a pair of Scott's sheets that he had donated hanging in front of a sleeping cubicle.

The air inside the bus was musty and thick. It was a stale mixture of incense, old meals, dirty clothes and sex. Lance stopped in front of one closed off space that smelled heavily of Patchouli Oil.

"Sunshine sleeps in there. Smells nice, doesn't it. She's really a delightful, beautiful person. Up there," pointed Paul at a sleeping loft set in the very back of the bus. A rope ladder led up to the opening, "That's where you two can sleep for now. It's our guest accommodations. I trust you will find it suitable."

Paul turned and departed.

Lance looked at the flimsy ladder and then at Kathy, "You first."

"No, you bastard. You go first, and I hope the rope breaks."

"Are you sure we should still be sleeping together?' asked Lance, finally realizing the depth of the hatred towards him that was being spewed out by his former lover and best friend.

Joe sprawled on his bed inside the cabin, chewing sunflower seeds and reading a Jack Kerouac Novel, 'The Dharma Bums.' Joe especially enjoyed this book because of scenes that took place in Berkeley in cottages on familiar streets like Channing Way, Shattuck Avenue and Dwight Way.

Joe loved the nomadic lifestyle that was described in the Novel. He fantasized about replacing Neal Cassidy, the driver on Jack's frequent, manic cross country drives in in allegedly stolen cars.

He imagined having deep and profound conversations with Jack with the sun sinking in the west and them streaking across a seemingly endless New Mexico highway while the red and pink sky slowly turned to black. Then, the headlights would take over and cut through the night.

Of course, Jack would probably drink cheap screw top wine all the way there and back. Also, oddly, Jack, the wild and crazy life of the cosmic party, never learned to drive. No problem, thought Joe. They would have a band aid tin full of cross tops, sometimes keeping them awake for three days before finally collapsing in a heap on some vague acquaintance's couch and snoring for twenty four hours.

The trouble with the entire scenario was the fact that Jack Kerouac had died the year before. There would no cross country adventures. Nor would there ever be any trippy conversations with his writing idol. He would have to settle for pretending Jack was sitting there on his long drives by himself, riding shotgun and making sardonic observations in between swigs out of his latest bottle. A quick glance in the back seat would reveal dozens more empty quart bottles.

"Wanna stop and get a burger, Jack? I know a happening place just down the street."

"Naw, why bother," he would say with a sour look on his still handsome face, "Besides, I ate last week."

Yeah, that was the solution, thought Joe, leaning back on his pillow. He would bring along Jack and Neal in spirit. He would buy a bottle of Thunderbird wine and store it in the trunk so he was legal. No, two bottles. Also one of 'Mad Dog 20-20 for Neal.

He was hoping his natural wanderlust would lead to his own cross country adventures. He wanted to drive Route 66 in the hot sun with a car load of impulsive, certifiably insane riders. Plus, he could pick up cool looking hitchhikers and meet new, fun and slightly odd people. Heads were now popping up all over, like stoned weeds in the summer. Except for Ohio. He'd heard that state remained pure and unmolested.

Just this morning he had run into Debbie Glenn at the General Store and she told him that Lance and Kathy were staying with Malcom and Ruth at the People's Commune. Joe laughed out loud, imagining them eating that swill from the restaurant.

To be honest, Joe was glad they were gone. He had the bedroom to himself. He resented the fact that Lance had just moved Kathy in without at least running it by him first. After three days, Joe had set off Lance when he asked a perfectly legitimate question, namely how long Kathy was staying.

Lance was hostile, "Till the end of the quarter, and then we go our separate ways. You got a problem with that?"

"Even if I do, and I'm not saying that's the case, but nothing I can say will change anything. So why even talk about it? It's done, and I'm just gonna have to deal with it. Right?"

"Yeah. Basically that's where it's at."

Outside Joe's closed doors, his other roommates and their girlfriends were playing Twister while drinking white wine. Their laughter was getting louder and was beginning to annoy him. So much for him having the place to himself. Joe wondered if this would be a good time to break Scott's nose. He knew how to do it right. He would just calmly walk up to him with a demented smile and then nail him in the face with a heavy left hook. Naw, he thought. He'd get arrested and it would be a big mess. Once you were an adult, it just wasn't worth slugging people anymore.

Joe heard the front door open. Scott spoke to someone who answered in an authoritative voice. The next thing he knew his door was flung open and two Deputies charged in and pointed their pistols at his chest.

"Don't move, kid," said the bigger man, "Are you Joe Edgar Bailey?"

"Yes. Can you please stop aiming your guns at me? What's this all about?"

"I'm Mr. McGrew, the Sheriff of Quincy."

He holstered his piece and unfolded an official looking paper with a large gold seal on it.

"This here is what you call a search warrant for you and your cabin. Turn around and put your hands behind your back, son. I've gotta cuff you for our protection."

As Big Dan snapped on the cuffs he made them extra tight, "Search warrant," managed Joe, "For what? Underage prostitutes?"

Big Dan back handed Joe, "Don't be a smart ass, or I'll really hurt you."

Joe nodded, his face stinging. He felt his left cheek already swelling up.

"Rusty," said Dan, "Take the kid out to your car and put him in the back seat and then guard him. I don't want any local kids getting the idea they can spring their buddy."

Rusty guided Joe out of the bedroom and paraded him through the center of the cabin with his arms bent uncomfortably behind his back. He caught a sideways glance of Scott and wondered if he had also helped set them up because Lance and Joe had gone a little crazy and urinated on his bed. Maybe it was the rotten green hamburger they stashed in his lower dresser drawer so their room smelled real bad now.

Having cuffs on was a new, unpleasant experience for Joe. He wanted his arms and hands back. Plus, the cuffs were incredibly tight.

The closest he came to being arrested before was when he was clocked doing 110 miles an hour through fog just outside of Bakersfield in a borrowed, souped up 1965 Corvette. Initially, when Joe saw the police lights come on, he briefly considered trying to outrun the cop. He was confident of the fuel injected

365 HP 327 under the hood of a car made of fiberglass and figured he could reach 140MPH before the car would become airborne.

Then, he remembered that they would just get him down the road with roadblocks and a helicopter hovering over him. Remarkably, the cop liked him, and after a stern lecture, let Joe slide because it was his birthday.

Rusty opened the back door of his cruiser and helped Joe sit down without banging his head on the doorframe. Joe could see action at Greg's place too, more cop cars and additional beefy policemen.

A large crowd gathered outside the lodge, including drinkers from the Keddie Club, who murmured amongst themselves, repeating clichés like 'About damned time,' and 'It should have been done a month ago.'

Rusty got inside and read Joe his Miranda Rights. "You have the right to remain silent. Anything you say can and will be used against you in a court of law. If you can't afford….." Yeah, yeah ,yeah, thought Joe. How ironic. Occasionally it was him, holding a longshoreman at gunpoint while on Port Security duty. He would read him his rights while others handcuffed and searched the suspect. He knew his legal rights by heart, and he also recalled Jesse's advice to never admit anything.

Joe got a free ride downtown in Rusty's car. Snowflakes deflected off the windshield, with the wipers making slow swipes. Rusty didn't say a word to him. The handcuffs dug into Joe's wrists, and he was fearful that his hands would turn black from lack of blood flow and they would wind up being amputated at Quincy General where old Doc Johnson was on call.

If that scenario went down, he would request an

artificial hand for his left and a gnarly Pirates hook for his right that also came with a can opener attachment.

He knew Gary Hess, not Scott, had originally narked them out, but he also suspected that the Marlboro Men might have something to do with it. Why, though? He had no clue, nor could he come up with a possible motive other then they didn't like the local heads much, and heard about Lance being a drug dealer.

They left him in a holding cell by himself for two hours. The only place he could sit was a hard, cold, steel bench. They came for him and brought him into an interrogation room with two officers. One of them was the Sheriff, the other was some detective in a cheap tan suit named Hal, who had a receding hairline and bags under his eyes.

They accused him of selling dope to minors, a charge they said was a felony and would land him in State Prison. Joe didn't fall for any of their B.S. They had nothing on him, unless they searched his trunk and found his weed, which they obviously hadn't because they had never asked for his car keys. No, the only way they could nail him is if they planted something in his room, like packets of heroin or cocaine. Joe didn't think the hick cops were smart enough or desperate enough to pull that one off.

Joe asked for his one phone call, an attorney and a cup of water. He also requested that his handcuffs be removed. He turned around and held out his hands, and indeed, they were turning dark colors. Big Dan grunted, stood up and unlocked them. Joe immediately looked at his hands and the deep red grooves in his wrists. He rubbed at them furiously, trying to restore circulation.

When Joe repeated his previous requests, Big

Dan laughed at him, "It don't work like that up here with us dumb shit redneck cops. We make our own rules. As far as the phone, the last time it worked was....."

"The Eisenhower administration," said Hal, "Around 1955 I believe was the last time it functioned correctly. We're on the repair list, but it's taking a long time because we're so backwards up here, no one knows how to fix anything. "

Big Dan got a kick out of that one, slapping his knee. Joe was confused. After watching many episodes of Dragnet, it seemed like the cops always played the 'good cop' bad cop' routine. Here, they were both being assholes.

"And," continued Hal, "We're so isolated we don't even have a full time attorney in town. I hear one might be coming through on a stage coach next week, though."

Joe failed to find any of their malicious banter amusing, "Well, how about a cup of water. Come on, I'm dying of thirst."

"Sure thing, kid," said Hal, springing up and leaving the room with the door left open. Joe eyeballed it and Dan casually put his hand on his pistol, "Don't even think about running for it, junior. All the doors to the outside are locked."

Hal returned with a Dixie cup full of water. He handed it to a grateful Joe who took a look before he drank and saw a cigarette butt floating on top.

"Very funny," he said bitterly, placing the cup on Dan's desk.

Dan looked angry and swatted the cup at Joe, drenching him with cigarette water, "I don't recall giving you permission to put any of your trash on my desk, boy."

Joe felt as though he were back in boot camp, about ready to get his ass kicked again.

Hal chuckled, drank out of a cup of vending machine coffee and lighted a smoke, "Now, if your memory should suddenly come back, we need you to sign a statement agreeing to testify against Lance Potter. Then I'll get you whatever you want to drink, as long as its water or coffee. Ha"

"I'm not going to sign shit without consulting with an attorney."

"Why not?" said Hal, "Lance is in the next room, spilling his guts about how you are the mastermind of the whole drug dealing operation.."

"I don't believe you."

"Then," said Hal, "In our last interrogation room we have in custody Jesse Ray Barnes, who is also selling you out because he doesn't want to go back to San Quentin for five more years, and who could blame him for that."

"Screw you," said Joe. "I know my friends, and they're not going to rat me out, especially because I haven't done anything illegal."

Dan moved quickly and kicked Joe's chair over with him still on it.

Hal rose to block him off, "Don't start kicking him, Dan. You know how you lose control sometimes."

Joe spent the night, isolated in a small, uncomfortable cell. It came with a cot with a thin, stained mattress, an old blanket that smelled like it had never been washed, and no pillow.

Joe was released the next morning at eight, with no charges filed. Despite a thorough search of the cabin, the cops hadn't found a thing. They told him getting back to Keddie was his problem, since they weren't a taxi service. He was without a coat or hat, so he stood there shivering, his thumb out, praying for a ride. Heavy snow began falling, and just as he was about to surrender to despair, Greg pulled up in front of him with his Hearse and Joe gratefully jumped inside.

"What's happening?" asked Greg, "Did they keep you all night?"

"Yup," said Joe, angry, hungry and seething with resentment and making plans for revenge. Gary Hess had declared war on them, and Joe was ready to fight back. He needed to see Jesse right away.

THE SKULL DIGGERS

CHAPTER SIXTEEN

Jesse cooked them breakfast at six on Saturday morning. He didn't have much to say to Joe, who speculated that Jesse was nervous and hiding his emotions. Who wouldn't be a little leery about meeting up with the infamous mad dogs, The Skull Diggers motorcycle gang.

As Joe drove them down the familiar highway that would lead them past Oroville and Chico and eventually to Sacramento, he felt that same heavy sensation in his stomach. Creeping paranoia and it's frequent companion, morbid dread. Occasionally, they brought along demented Cousin Chaos, and then there would be real issues and problems. He couldn't take them anywhere without them misbehaving, taking over his body, brain and most importantly, his mouth.

He glanced sideways at Jesse, who was dressed from head to toe in black leather and wearing large black shades that hid his eyes. Jesse had his window rolled down and propped his right arm out, trailing cigarette smoke that joined the wind.

It struck Joe that he knew very little about Jesse, and even less about the Skull Diggers, except for their fearsome reputations as deadly street fighters who weren't afraid of getting hurt or dying. As far as the Diggers were concerned, they were divorced from the real world and often their families and old friends. They didn't care to play by society's stupid little rules of correct conduct.

"Where's the founding chapter of The Skull Diggers?" asked Joe, curious and hoping to lure Jesse out from his tormented inner cave, old memories apparently poisoning his mood.

Jesse slowly swiveled his head and gave Joe his frightening 'death stare,' "There you go again, Joe, asking me more questions."

"What's the big deal. Is it like some big secret or something? Is it California, Texas, Ohio….."

"Stop!" demanded Jesse in his raspy voice that was getting harsher.

"Okay, sorry. After we get past Chico, we should be able to get good radio reception from Sacramento."

"Yeah? So what?' sneered Jesse who turned back and stared out his side of the windshield. His mouth was moving like he was talking to someone, but no sounds were coming out. He got more agitated and gripped his arm rest and then folded down the visor and stared into the mirror, practicing his skull looks and death stare.

"So, Jesse. Besides your life in The Skull Diggers that you clearly don't want to share with me, and your ten years in prison that you won't talk about, what did you do in Sacramento before being sent away?"

"You just don't give up, do you kid? There's not much to tell. I came from a broken home and was basically on my own from twelve years on. The older kids took me along on burglaries and taught me which cars were easy to boost and take for joy rides. In addition, I was also learned what others were better off being taken to a warehouse and parted out. I also worked as a backup."

292

"What's a backup?"

"Let me finish my biography before you start with the endless questions. Tell you what, slick. You can ask me three more questions and then you gotta shut up until we get to our destination. I need to mentally prepare myself for walking back into the clubhouse after ten years. It could get heavy if the new prez doesn't appreciate my presence and thinks I'm back to reclaim my spot, which I'm not."

"Okay, that's fair."

"By the way, before we start playing three questions, do you know how to use a knife?"

"Just to eat with."

"Never stabbed or slashed someone, not even your brother or some punk in your neighborhood who needed to go down?"

"No, sorry. That's not a skill that was practiced much in Berkeley."

"Oh."

"Besides, finish your story. It's starting to sound like a Hollywood movie script."

"You think so?" asked Jesse, running a hand through his dirty blonde hair that was tucked back into his usual tiny pony tail. He looked back into the mirror, grimaced and then slapped the sun visor back into place.

"Okay, so I learn fast, and also find out I'm a good teacher too. I have my own gang by the time I'm sixteen. We called ourselves 'The Nasty Boys,' and I'm not jiving when I tell you I was clearing over five hundred a week back in the mid fifties.

"Well, the asshole cops planted a rat in my organization and he acted like he was my friend while all the time he was taping me and making a list of our crimes. After a few weeks, they busted my ass. I got a hanging judge who sent me to a juvenile boot camp ranch in Phoenix."

"That must have been a nice break, being on a ranch in Arizona."

"Are you freaking kidding me? You ever been to Arizona? Why do people live where it's a hundred and ten everyday? I hated the place and beat up as many losers as I could just to keep in practice. You gotta build up your elbows and feet you know."

"What about your fists?'

"Only stupid people hit with their closed fist. It ain't like the moves, kid. Most guys who do that break their hand or wrist. They call it 'Boxers Fracture,' but it's more like 'Fools Injury.'

"So, how old were when you got arrested as an adult?"

"Twenty four."

"Why didn't you return to Sacramento to live? You probably know a lot of people there. Maybe they could have helped you."

"Maybe. Too many bad memories. Like I told you, my wife, Stella, sold my chopper and then divorced me six months after I was locked up. Talk about being pissed and feeling helpless, that was it, Joe. Ten freaking years of my life, gone, and I come back to nothin and gotta start all over. Oh well, I suppose it's better than being dead."

"Cool, Jesse. Now see, that wasn't so hard, was it? You actually talked a little bit. Doesn't that make you feel better?'

"No."

"You never did answer my first question. What is a backup?"

Jesse smoked another Camel as Joe pushed the 64 past eighty. He'd never seen any Highway Patrol on

294

this road. They raced across a huge cement overpass that was hundreds of feet above the Feather River. The metal center divider made a roaring noise as they sped past.

Jesse spoke, "How can I word this without incriminating myself, because I usually plead the Fifth Amendment to everything. Okay, a backup goes along on an armed robbery, kidnapping or rub out, anything where violence is on the agenda. He usually hangs out by the door, and hides his piece so no one thinks he's with the robbers. Then, if someone stumbles into the middle of it or tries to play hero, then the backup steps in and deals with the situation in an appropriate manner."

"So he shoots innocent bystanders?"

"Make what you want of it, son. That's all I've got to say on the matter. Say, Joe, stop at the Shell station and I'll buy us some Cokes."

"At nine in the morning?"

"Sure, why not. It's not like we're drinking booze before noon or something."

"Okay."

"You say you can't use a knife. How about a tire iron? Ever hit a home run on some chump's face with one of those, huh?" Jesse's voice rose in excitement, "I just love it when blood splatters everywhere. The more the better. And if I really don't like the prick, or he's screwed my old lady when I'm out making money, I'll kneecap him too."

"Kneecap?"

"Yeah, kneecap, you dweeb. Don't you know nothin? Huh? I break their freaking kneecap with the tire iron. Maybe an elbow too, on the opposite side. That's funny, man, when a roid has two casts on."

"Yeah. Sounds hilarious," said Joe.

Ten minutes later they continued south, sipping on cold Cokes that Joe had to admit tasted good.

"So, Stella sold your Harley, huh? Was it in good condition?"

"Good condition? It was a show bike that I drove on the street. It took two years to build, and it looked awesome and was fast. The bitch sold it for five hundred bucks and a jar of speed. It was easily worth six grand. By the way, that's way past your third question, Joe, so now you gotta shut your mouth. Every time you say something between here and Sacto, I'm gonna slug you. If you understand, nod your head.:

Joe nodded his head and made a big show of closing his lips and then pretending to zip his mouth up.

"Funny guy, huh? I usually like funny guys. As long as they make me laugh. You don't tell parrot in the bar jokes, do you?"

Joe shook his head,

"Good, good. Now we're finally getting somewhere. Jesse leaned back in his seat and closed his eyes.

Joe reached over and shoved Jesse's shoulder. He abruptly sat up, "What?"

"Wake up. We're just a few miles out of Sacramento. I don't know where to go."

Jesse looked disappointed, as though he had expected to wake from his dreams and be someone else. Somebody with a normal life, a square job and a house with a wife. Maybe even a couple of kids. He was tired of starring in his own bad movie, living a harsh life, one of crime and fear and prison.

Jesse blinked rapidly, and his hands shook a bit as he reached for a smoke, "Take the next exit and hang a left."

Jesse squirmed around like a caged wild animal who was about to see freedom. He inhaled and exhaled his smoke in rapid fashion, quickly reducing it to a butt, which he flicked out the window into some dry roadside bushes, "Screw Sacramento."

Joe did as he was told, and headed north east on a four lane road that quickly dropped down to two. They passed generic strip malls, fast food joints like Burger King and gas stations run by surly Arabs.

A few miles later, the open businesses were replaced by boarded up storefronts, liquor stores with armed guards outside checking I.D's, and seedy looking massage parlors. Mean looking hookers milled around, eyeballing their competition, trying to lock eyes with potential Johns as they drove by. Ah yes, thought Joe. The perennial weakness of man for new flesh. The lure of strange and different women. Banging a stranger in exchange for pieces of green paper. Intimacy without commitment.

Something different. Something wild some-. thing probably diseased and hooked on hard drugs, like heroin or meth. If they were infected sick cows, they would be shot in the head. Instead, the whores were allowed to exist in the shadows, forever singing the tired siren song of the streetwalker. Tying to lure good men on a date, which could possibly lead to their infection with a contagious disease, all for a cheap thrill.

When they reached the grimiest part of town, where nearly everything was closed boarded up, or partially burned, Jesse spoke sharply, "Stop here."

Joe pulled over, swerving to avoid a scatter of broken glass on the street. He left the engine running and looked around, seeing potential death and dismemberment behind every street sign, every knocked down door, every shattered window.

Joe followed Jesse's gaze across the street to a shop with six black choppers lined up in a neat row. A big guy with wild hair and black leather pants and a dark muscle shirt under a bikers vest paced back and forth, a shotgun propped against his beefy shoulder. His entire upper torso, arms, chest and back were covered with colorful tattoos. Joe thought that only a complete frigging idiot with a recent frontal lobotomy would even think about messing with a Skull Diggers most prized position. His bike.

"Are you sure you need to go in there, Jesse?"

"Yeah, of course I do, I gottta find out where I stand with them. I gotta go over and check things out. You stay in the car for now. Leave the engine running, lock your doors and don't unlock them for anyone but me. If I think it's okay for you to come in and drink a beer with the boys, I'll step outside and give you two quick whistles. If I just whistle once, burn rubber and come over and rescue me. It means they don't like me anymore, and I'm about to get stomped."

Jesse got out of the convertible and then leaned back in, "If, on the other hand, you don't see me in ten minutes, take off and find a phone. Call the cops and tell em I'm being murdered. It'll probably be too late by then. Basically, Joe, I don't give a fuck We can share a beer or they can plunge a shank into my heart. It don't really matter to me."

"Right," answered Joe. Jesse slammed the door hard, looked both ways and then jogged across the street. Joe watched as he greeted the guard and they gave each other soul shakes and half hugs. Jesse said something and they both laughed and then he disappeared into the clubhouse of the satanic influenced Skull Diggers.

Joe grabbed the rear view mirror and stared into it and saw fear in his own eyes. He carefully put it back and tried to slow down his breathing, telling himself everything was fine. He also glanced at the side mirrors for potential trouble.

He half expected a horde of murderous crazed foaming at the mouth Skull Diggers to come pouring out of their clubhouse, whipping chains over their heads and screaming obscenities. They would break out his windows with a claw hammer and then someone would bury a shank in his throat. They would steal his wallet, take out what little money he had, and disdainfully fling the empty wallet back in his lap that would be drenched with blood.

Then again, he could be invited over for a beer and a friendly game of pool and The Skull Diggers would act like regular guys, just misunderstood. Yeah, right, he thought to himself, looking over his shoulder. Dream on.

Joe kept glancing at his watch, feeling more fearful as each minute ticked by. He looked behind him and put his hand on the gear selector. After nine minutes inside, Jesse reappeared on the sidewalk, shook hands with the guard, raised his right hand in departure and jogged back across the wide avenue. No one followed him. Joe unlocked the passenger door.

Jesse jumped inside, a smile on his face for the first time Joe could remember.

"Hit it, Joe! Go straight for a mile and then you'll be making a right."

Joe slammed the big Ford into drive and floored it, his tires spinning on the wet pavement, causing him to slide sideways in a controlled burnout. Then he straightened the steering wheel and roared down the street.

"Any cops around here?" asked Joe, watching the speedometer needle race past 65.

"Hell no. They're afraid to come down here. They might, uh, mysteriously disappear."

Great, thought Joe. Jesse was a cop killer too?

"So, how did it go in there? You got a smile on your face. You ought to do it more often, Jesse."

"What?" he turned towards Joe, "If I smile I might almost seem *normal?"*

"No."

"Liar. Anyway, it went great. I'm cool. I shook hands with the new President, Mongo, who I used to run with back as a kid. He was in my gang then. Funny how things turn out, huh?"

"Yeah. I guess."

"Because of my parole restrictions I'm not allowed to associate with know felons, or at least not in public. Mongo said I can wear my colors in Quincy, but he advised against it since he and my bros are so far away. Oh," said Jesse,"He told me to remove my Prez patch, because he respected my past but he was the boss now, and I'm fine with that. He also says he knows where my chopper is, and we're going to make a raid soon on the asshole who has it stored in his fancy three car garage, and get it back."

"Cool. If things went so well, how come you were in such a hurry to leave? I thought we were going to have a beer."

"Shoveler Sam is in there."

"Shoveler Sam?"

"Yeah, he's a full patch member who's solid in rumbles but he's a little, well, weird."

"How so?"

"He always likes digging graves when we, uh, have expired people to bury. Matter of fact, he loves it. Says it gives him a good workout, but mostly he just digs the smell of freshly dug up earth. I didn't think it would be a good idea to bring you in when he's there. He don't take to strangers much. Good news though. We're invited back this afternoon for a pig barbecue. There's a big pit in the back where they roast the damned thing, with an apple in it's mouth. One of our brothers, Samuel, is from Samoa and does a great job."

"What about Shoveler Sam?"

"Not an issue. Said he's heading for Dago in an hour. He's got a hot little Mexican babe waiting for him. They're heading to Tijuana for a vacation. I can think of safer places to go. Mongo warned him about wearing his colors when he's by himself in a foreign country. Better to go as a straight looking tourist, a mean looking one that no sane man wants to mess with. That's how you travel incognito."

"Are we going to be turning soon? asked Joe. This neighborhood seemed only marginally better than the one they had just left.

"Make a right turn two corners up. Her dump is halfway down the street. I want you to cruise by slowly, so I can see what we might be up against."

"Up against?"

"Yeah! Damn it, Joe! Stop repeating everything I say to you back to me as a fucking question!"

"Okay."

Jesse reached over and squeezed Joe's right bicep with a steel like grip, "Listen. You. keep yakking about all these famous writers and their big adventures, and how you want some excitement too. Well, here's your chance, kid. Don't blow it."

"Let me go so I can make the turn," said Joe.

Jesse peered out Joe's window as Joe drove slowly down the street. It was a decrepit neighborhood of run down cookie cutter ranch style houses. Dead lawns, drunk driving wrecks and abandoned appliances all littered the scene.

Dirty faced kids played baseball in the street using a board and some sort. of a road kill. A pack of a dozen dogs charged down the street after Joe, barking and snapping at the tires and trying to pee on the hubcaps while the car was moving.

"Circle around the block," instructed Jesse, "And then I'll show you where to park."

"What about that pack of dogs?"

"What about em?"

"Nothing." A blanket of gloom settled over Joe. He felt like maybe he had come here to die. He had assumed that he was supposed to drown. That was unlikely to happen here. What in the world had he gotten himself into?

"Here," barked Jesse in a strong voice, pointing to a spot where the asphalt was buckling upwards because of roots from an overgrown tree. Jesse pointed to a house across the street, "That's where the bitch lives with two of The Diggers."

The house had two overflowing garbage cans and wide oil slicks on the driveway. There was a broken down yellow Plymouth station wagon with a cracked windshield and four flat tires. A green tarp covered the roof near the fireplace.

Joe and Jesse got out and stood in front of the car. The engine was ticking as it cooled off. Jesse handed him a tire iron."Here. Stash this inside your coat. We might need it. Don't pull it out unless I yell your name. This is just in case," he said casually, pulling his jacket apart, revealing a large hunting knife.

"I got this too." He pulled a gloss black, snub nosed revolver out of the front of his pants.

"I know. Just in case."

"You got it, sport. Just follow my lead. I don't want no trouble. I just wanna get my shit out of here and go kick back with my old crew and drink some beer and rip off chunks of barbecued pig."

"Sounds like a plan, "said Joe, sweat breaking out on his brow. His heart thudded in his chest.

Jesse moved across the street with long strides, seemingly growing in stature the closer he got to the house. A gigantic, mean looking Doberman stood at the fence and barked at them. Jesse disdainfully spit a big luge on the dog, who yelped and moved back.

Joe looked up at the cracked front window held together with Duct Tape. He saw two eyes peering at them from behind a ripped curtain. The person disappeared and the curtain stopped moving.

"I just saw someone." whispered Joe. He clutched the tire iron, not wanting it to fall out and expose him for the rookie that he was.

"Forget about it. Follow my lead. Don't say nothin. You're a deaf mute. Got it?"

Jesse bounded up the stairs, and Joe slowly followed him.

They stood together in front of the door. Jesse was more alive than Joe had ever seen him before. He actually seemed to be looking forward to some violence and bloodshed. He was still on parole, thought Joe. It made no sense.

Jesse turned to Joe with his eyes dilated, "You ready?"

"Yeah. I guess so." Right now, Joe, wished he were back in the safety of his cabin, laying on his bed, reading a book and spitting sunflower seed shells into some of Scott's sissy boy underwear. No, instead, he was probably about to suffer a violent death in Sacramento, of all the embarrassing places to get killed. Too late now, he thought.

Jesse pounded on the front door. It was flung open. A mammoth biker towered over them. His large stomach fell over oil stained blue jeans, pushing against a black T-shirt and the standard black leather biker's vest.

"What?" he shouted.

"Stan the Man," replied Jesse in a friendly voice and a smile, "It's me, Jesse."

"Yo, Jesse. I didn't recognize you at first. It's been a long time. I thought you were down for fifteen."

"Yeah. I just did a dime at San Quentin. I'm still on parole."

"Oh." Joe noticed that Stan was missing several front teeth and his gums were black.

"Who's the punk?"

"New friend of mine. His name is Gary Hess and he's a deaf mute."

"So, waddya want Jesse?" Stan already appeared bored with the reunion conversation.

"I need to get whatever is left of my stuff. I know Stella sold some of it along with my chopper."

"Yeah, damned shame about that. You had one sweet bike."

"I'll be getting it back soon."

"Who is it, Stan?" came a shrill voice, "You're letting all the cold air in."

Stan shrugged his shoulders and stepped aside. Jesse entered first with Joe on his heels.

The house smelled real bad, like dog urine, dirty ashtrays and spoiled food. A skinny Platinum blonde with multiple tattoos grimaced when she saw who was standing in her front room.

"I thought you were still in the joint."

"I was, but I got out on good behavior."

"Well goody for you. Why are you here?"

"To get the rest of my stuff. Some old lady you turned out to be, Stella. You never answered any of my letters, you sold my custom chopper for next to nothing, you bitch. Then you divorced my ass."

"I needed money to live on, asshole. You think it's easy turning enough tricks to cover all the bills? Plus, now I have another mouth to feed."

"Stop dogging Stella," came a loud voice from the couch. A man with white hair and braided chin hair stood up. A sawed off shotgun dangled from his right hand.

"Spider. It's been a long time, brother. You guys both banging Stella now, is that how it is?"

"Yeah, Jesse," answered Spider, not smiling, "That's how it is."

A young girl appeared in the doorway. She had an innocent face and beautiful blonde hair, "Mommy. Who are these men? Did they come to see me?"

Stella looked at her daughter and then at Jesse, "They're nobody, Champagne darling. Go back to your room and play with your Barbies and mouse traps."

"Mommy," said the girl, looking at Jesse, "Is that man my daddy?"

"No, sweetie. You know I told you that your daddy went to heaven ten years ago after a motorcycle accident."

Joe couldn't but help notice the strong facial resemblance between Champagne and Jesse.

The little girl took a final look at Jesse and then turned and ran for her room.

Spider scoffed, "Nothing's changed has it,

bro. You still upset everyone you come in contact with. Nice visiting with you. Maybe it's time for you to leave now," said Spider, pointing to the front door with the barrel of his shotgun.

"Soon as I get what I came for we're outta here and we're not coming back."

Stella spoke sharply, "What's left of your crap is out in the garage. You and the puke kid go back out the same way you got in. We'll open the garage from the inside. One of them door springs is busted, so it may take a minute. By the way, mister ex prez, you're supposed to be paying me child support from the first month you got out."

"How much?"

"A hundred bucks a month."

"A hundred bucks a month! Geez Stella, I don't make that kind of money."

"Too bad, That's what the court granted me. If you don't pay up, I'll sic the law on you. Where did you say you're staying?"

"At the Holiday Court cabins on 10th street in downtown Sacto."

"Okay, write down your address and phone number and then wait outside."

Joe took in deep breaths as he and Jesse stood exposed to the cold. They could hear Stan and Spider grunting as they put their backs underneath the sideways garage door and opened it up. "Damn," remarked Stan, "That door gets harder to open every time."

Inside, the garage was a gigantic mess. Dominating the front were two beautiful Harley Davidson choppers with custom paint jobs, flames on the fuel tanks and extended handlebars. Parts and trash were strewn across the rest of the floor. Cardboard boxes leaned precariously in teetering piles. Joe thought that if someone were to sneeze, it might start a chain reaction and everything would come tumbling down.

"Now, where in the hell did we put Jesse's shit? asked Spider.

"Over here," announced Stan, who maneuvered his way to the back and then handed two cardboard boxes to Spider, who dropped them at his feet.

Stan the Man reappeared a moment later.

"That's it?" said Jesse, "Where's the rest of my stuff.? I had at least eight boxes."

"Had," said Stella, "I sold the rest of it at garage sales and donated a lot of it to the Salvation Army. It was mostly all crap anyway."

Jesse bent down and looked inside the boxes and shook his head, "Yeah, but it was my crap, Stella."

"Come on Gary," said Jesse, handing him one of the boxes, which was light, "Let's get out of here."

As they started across the street Spider yelled after them, "I thought you said the kid is a deaf mute."

"He was, Spider. He just made a remarkable recovery."

For Joe, the short walk back to his car seemed to take forever. His hands were shaking as he pulled out his car keys."

"Gimme those," demanded Jesse, opening the trunk. They both threw their boxes in."Hurry! Get in the passenger seat. I better drive."

Joe got in after Jesse unlocked his door. As Jesse fired up the 390. Joe looked back at Stella's house and saw Spider come charging through the garden gate with a huge African Lion on a thick leash. The lion was dragging Spider across the street and roaring.

"Jesus Christ Jesse!" shouted Joe,"Get us out of

here!"

Jesse rolled down his window, flipped off Spider, slammed the gear shift into drive and nailed it, spinning out and roaring down the street. Jesse sped through a stop sign, the manic don't give a fuck skull look and crazy grin etched on his face.

"What the hell was that?" asked Joe. He continued to look behind him, as though somehow the Lion could follow them at eighty miles an hour, dragging a protesting Spider behind him, his arm hopelessly entangled in the foot thick leather leash.

"You don't want to know!" shouted Jesse, sliding around the next corner with the tires screeching in protest. Jesse continued to scare Joe as he blasted through stop signs and red lights, several times narrowly avoiding a high speed collision.

"Slow down!" shouted Joe, "You're gonna kill us."

"No I'm not. I know what I'm doing."

Joe held on as Jesse sped until he found what he was looking for. It was a Red Onion burger stand, and Jesse hit the driveway doing better than 50 MPH. He stood on the brakes, furiously cranked the steering wheel to the left and skidded to a halt.

Joe sat there with his mouth hanging wide open. "Jesus Christ, thank you lord."

Jesse handed Joe his keys. "Car runs okay, but I think it could use a tune up. The engine starts missing when you approach a hundred miles an hour. I can do it for you at no charge, pal. I got lots of talents you don't know about."

Joe could only manage to nod his head. He opened his door and fell onto the pavement, dizzy. Jesse ran over, grabbed Joe's elbow and helped him up.

"You okay, man?"

"Yeah, sure."

Jesse bent down and picked up the tire iron. "Here, put this back in your coat while we're still in the shitty part of town. Let's go get some burgers. I'm buying."

Jesse and Joe sat at the counter of The Red Onion. Joe watched as the Mexican kid cooking worked right in front of them, grilling a dozen meat patties at a time. He moved in fluid motion, flipped buns onto the warm up side of the grill, then dumped out a heaping pile of fries inside an open warmer. He shook a lot of salt on them with his right hand while simultaneously flipping burgers with his left, just at the right time. Then he put down another batch of French fries and dealt out slices of cheese on top of the sizzling burgers.

Joe and Jesse sipped at their giant sized cokes.

"Those people back there are deranged," observed Joe.

Jesse laughed and watched the kid dish up their orders and place them in baskets and the waitress carried their lunches five feet, "Ketchup?" she asked. When they nodded she pulled a bottle out of her uniform, set it down and walked away.

"Tell me about it, kid," said Jesse, shoving some fries in and shaking more salt on them, "I used to be married to Stella. She once stabbed Handsome Steve, one of our patches, in the gut with a barbecue fork because she thought he had snorted her last two lines of meth. We knew enough not to pull the fork out. People can die that way."

"Did he snort it?"

"Naw, she did and forgot. Steve was just in the wrong place at the wrong time."

"Did she go to jail."

"Nope. Skull Diggers and their mama's don't file charges against each other. We worked things out with him on the side, and everyone walked away, not only alive but happy." Jesse picked up his dripping cheeseburger with both hands and took a large bite.

Joe took a chance, "Was that your little girl back there? She sure is cute. Looks like...."

Jesse punched Joe in his bicep, hard, "I thought I told you to stop asking me so many dammed personal questions."

Joe nodded his head. He looked down at the lead filled gloves Jesse was wearing. No wonder it hurt so much thought Joe.

"Okay, you gotta answer me this one without slugging me again. It has nothing to do with prying into your past."

"No guarantees, pal. Make it a good one," he said, shoving a handful of French fries into his mouth followed with a large gulp of Coke.

"Why did you call me Gay Hess back there?"

"Because I'm gonna start dropping his name with the Diggers as often as I can. Don't worry, I've got special plans for the prick, and you and Lance are gonna help me. It's either him or us, and I ain't going back to the joint to do another nickel because of some lard butt who wipes his ass and then sniffs the edge of his hand."

"Sounds promising."

"Yeah. I already told Shoveler Sam that Gary Hess is walking around Keddie bragging about how he kicked his ass in a bar fight recently. Sam was genuinely interested, so when he's back from Mexico, maybe Sam and a few of the boys will pay Gary a midnight visit. This should play out pretty funny."

Joe took his last bite of burger, "What about

Spider and the lion?"

Jesse laughed again. The excitement and danger had energized him, "Spider and Stan raise them in the backyard and sell them for big money."

"Who buys them? Zoos and circuses?'"

"Occasionally. Usually it's to neo Nazi's, gangsters, and Mexicans using them as drug runners. Mainly people with cash who want something a step up from attack dogs. You gotta admit, lions are intimidating. Can you imagine being a U.S. border patrolman and you're out at night in your vehicle and you see a pack of lions coming your way. Are you gonna jump out with your pistol and say, 'Halt! You're under arrest,' or are you going to pretend it was a hallucination and find somewhere else to patrol?"

"I see your point. What else can they be trained to do?"

"If properly trained, they're better then watch dogs. A whole lot scarier. Sometimes for fun and practice, they transport half a dozen hungry ones down to the hobo camps and set them loose. Nobody misses bums. They die all the time and no one cares. Heck, riding the rails can be mighty dangerous. They get robbed and stabbed all the time, sometimes over a buck or half a bottle of Ripple. Then, they're given the special train burial."

"What's that?" asked Joe, eating the last of his crispy, tasty French fries.

"They get their body heaved out of the side door of a freight car going 60 miles an hour. It's called 'bum tossing.' Whoever throws a body the furthest is the winner."

"Now, please tell me we're not going back to the Pig Roast at the clubhouse."

"Naw. The more I think about it the less I like it.

311

Mainly because of you. I think if you're there longer then an hour, they might want to mess you up just for fun."

Jesse became quiet, wiped his face with a napkin, wadded it up and threw it down, "Stella wants a hundred bucks a month. What a joke. I can afford maybe fifty."

"What are you going to do?"

"Send her what I can, until I can get a big score."

"Oh." Joe knew better than to ask any questions about that. He once again wondered if Jesse was cooking up a crime and wanted him to participate.

Jesse took a last slug of Coke and chewed on some ice,

"We do have one other stop. It used to be right down the street. We'll be there for about an hour and then split town while we're still able to. It's actually on the way to the freeway."

Jesse directed Joe to another strip mall, "Good," said Jesse, "It's still here."

He had Joe park in front of a corner storefront that had a large overhead sign that read, 'THE WILD HARE.' Joe thought it odd that the display windows were close to being blacked out. Large framed pictures of scantily dressed woman were displayed, along with smaller signs indicating that they sold women's wigs.

Jesse flicked a cigarette butt into the gutter, "Come on kid. Lets go inside. I'll introduce to the owner and we'll see if she's got a short haired wig for you. She owes me a favor or two, so now I'm here to collect."

Outside, Jesse put his arm over Joe's shoulder and walked in step with him down the sidewalk. He smelled heavily of nicotine, leather and sweat, "You can get anything you want here, Joe, if you know what I mean."

Joe nodded his head and pulled away, He didn't like being touched by another man. Besides, what did he mean. 'anything he wanted?' Joe was aware that he was still carrying the tire iron.

A overhead bell tinkled when they entered the dark shop. Inside it was cool, and what little illumination there was came from red lights that were scattered around in lamps. Joe's feet sunk into plush carpet. Along the wall closest to the street were racks of different colored wigs. He also observed a long couch, some easy chairs and a large TV that had the picture of a soap opera on but no sound. Joe sniffed the musky air.

A well dressed heavyset black woman with a jowly neck and fleshy arms stepped through a strand of beads. She stopped in her tracks, "Oh my lord," she said," Is that really you, Jesse?"

"Yep. Hello Mama Doris."

The woman reached out her arms, wrapped them around Jesse in a full body hug and then lifted him easily off the ground, set him down and gave him a peck on the lips. "Sweet thang, it is so good to see you. When did you get out, honey?"

"About a month ago. Mama Doris, I'd like you to meet my new friend, Joe."

"Well hello, Joe," said Mama Doris who gave him a friendly hug.

A buxom redhead in a frilly black lingerie slipped through the beads. Joe thought her to be pretty in a hard looking way. Why was she walking around half dressed?

"Nadine!" cried out Jesse. She smiled widely and met him in the middle and they too hugged.

"Jesse, baby," she cooed, putting her right hand under his chin, "So nice of you to drop in and see us." She turned towards Joe, who could now see how heavily her face was made up, "And who is this young man?"

"This here is my bro, Joe. He was nice enough to give me a ride here today."

263

"Where you staying, hon.?" asked Mama Doris."

"North of here. Can you see if you might have a short hair wig that Joe can wear so he can go to his Army Reserve meetings without getting a haircut?"

"Coast Guard," mumbled Joe.

"Whatever," said Jesse.

"Why sure, hon. You go on back and visit with Nadine. By the way, she's got an appointment in an hour."

Nadine grabbed Jesse's hand and led him through the beads, "Come on baby. Let Nadine help you release all that tension."

Yeah, baby," said Jesse, looking over at Jesse with that leering skull grin, the one that advertised that he didn't give a fuck. It also implied that he was aware of things that others weren't.

"Now," said Mama Doris to Joe, "Let's see what we can find for you."

ROOF TOP TALK

CHAPTER SEVENTEEN

It was already dark when Joe and Jesse arrived back at Keddie around six. Jesse asked to be left off at his sister's nearby house. He and Joe had been mostly silent on their ride back from Sacramento. Mama Doris had given Joe a long haired wig that he put in a paper sack stored in his trunk for safekeeping. He was excited about the prospect of going over a full month without a haircut.

Joe stopped and opened up the trunk and Jesse retrieved his two boxes, "If this wasn't so pathetic, Joe, it would be funny. After thirty four years of living, this is basically all I have. Two boxes full of bullshit and the clothes I have in my sister's house. Oh well," said Jesse, trudging up the wooden stairs. He paused at the top, "Thanks for the ride, kid. You done all right today."

Joe pulled into the slanting driveway next to their cabin. He shut off the headlights and clicked on the dome light as he gathered up his things. He opened the glove box to get his bag of weed and stopped with his hand halfway through the air. He was looking at Jesse's black .38 pistol.

He wasn't sure what to do. He didn't feel like driving back to Jesse's sister's house and taking the chance of being observed handing an ex con a pistol. Joe used a shop rag he kept underneath his seat to pull the gun out. He didn't want any of his fingerprints on it. It might have been used in a crime. Maybe even a murder. Being a revolver, Joe could see the pistol was loaded with five rounds. He let one fall into his hand and examined it.

It looked like a hollow point bullet to him. It appeared as though Jesse was a serious shooter. Hollow point bullets make a small hole going in and gigantic ones coming out. They were designed for maximum carnage. Supposedly, 1930's Chicago Gangster Al Capone, rubbed garlic on the tips of his bullets, believing if the shot didn't kill, the resulting infection would.

Joe decided to temporarily store the gun underneath the spare tire in the trunk and would return it to Jesse as soon as he could. Then again, Jesse might be concerned about not having it on him, so he was liable to come calling for it anytime.

He removed the spare tire, revealing a large grocery sack. It was almost full with baggies of different colored pills in various sizes. Great, thought Joe. He and Jesse had just been in Sacramento speeding around like maniacs, with Jesse running numerous stop signs and red lights.

If they'd been pulled over and searched, they would have been screwed. Anger surged in Joe's chest. The least his old friend Lance could have done is told him he'd decided to once again use his car as his warehouse. Joe didn't even want to think about Jesse carrying around a gun and hunting knife.

On impulse, Joe shoved the .38 into the middle of Lance's bag. He slammed the trunk shut and looked around. He felt quite fortunate that they hadn't been busted or gotten involved in a fight while in Sacramento. He didn't know how guys like Jesse lived that way every day. Never knowing when violence would erupt or someone would drive by and shoot at you or get behind you in line at Safeway and slam a shank in between your ribs.

"Hey, Joe!" It was Lance, and he was standing on the roof of their cabin. Joe looked up and saw the shadowy outlines of several others.

"Yeah? What are you doing up there?"

"We're star gazing. Grab a drink and join us. The view is spectacular."

"Okay," said Joe. He gathered up his odds and ends and entered the cabin by the back door and passed by Scott and Chris, who completely ignored him. Good, he thought. Who wants to waste time chatting with a hook nosed dweeb and his organ grinder monkey, rich white Chris with his styled black ghetto dreadlocks.

Joe threw all his crap on his bed and returned to the kitchen just as his roommates were leaving by the front door. Good timing, thought Joe, who mixed himself a gigantic drink in the biggest tumbler they had. Half a pint of Dark Bacardi Rum and half a can of Coke over the rocks. He took a tentative sip, "Aahh," he smiled. This was exactly what he needed. He headed around back to where they had propped a wooden ladder that led to the roof.

Lance and Kathy were sitting in lawn chairs dressed in white gowns with green sashes and newly shaven heads. Seated across from them were Malcom and Ruth.

"Joe Bailey, please allow me to introduce you to our living prophet, Malcom, and his saintly wife, Ruth."

"Hello." said Joe, almost choking on his drink. Lance's bald head was misshapen, almost oblong, like a football. Without her hair, Kathy's plainness was more pronounced.

"Most heavenly greetings, brother," said Malcom with his deep, hypnotizing voice, "I remember you from a recent community dinner we hosted."

Joe lighted a Marlboro and sat in the lotus position, as there weren't any more chairs, "I remember you too."

"Look at the stars, Joe" said Lance excitedly. Joe looked up. It was true. He had never seen it this clear before. He could make out the big dipper and Lance pointed out some of the other smaller, lesser known constellations. Joe was in awe of the black canvas above them filled with twinkling stars, worlds and planets that were thousands and millions of miles away. He felt small and insignificant. "Far out."

Lance spoke, "Well Joe, I can guess by looking at us that you can see that we've decided to join The People's Commune. We will be moving our stuff out as soon as there's room on the bus. People come and go. We are going to follow the teachings of Malcom and recognize him as a living prophet of God. This is the last night we will drink alcohol. We're just having a going away party and a celebration of the start of our new lives."

"I'm happy for you, man." The dark successfully hid Joe's smirk. They'd bloody well starve to death in a month, if the rest of their meals were anything like that dog shit like goop they had served him at their community dinner.

Lance continued on, sounding like a pre-programmed talking box at the zoo, "We are quite fortunate to be on earth at this time, to prepare for the second coming of Christ.

"We will also be maximizing our potential as individuals, raising our base level of consciousness to one of enlightenment. Then, we will join together, two dozen as one, and our collective power will be awesome."

Joe had to interrupt Lance's present train of thought, otherwise, he was liable to continue on spitting out the same religious psycho babble dogma for hours.

"What about school, Lance?"

"I think I'm failing all my classes except a couple. I've missed so many lectures that it's hopeless. Basically, I've decided that College is a bunch of bullshit. I've been in school my whole life. I honestly can't stand the thought of another four to six years of this crap. For what? So I can pursue the great American Dream? It's more like the great American Nightmare. I don't want to end up like my old man, stressed out over a huge mortgage and car payments and keeping up appearances.

"He's so messed up now he's had two heart attacks and has bleeding ulcers. He's fifty eight and looks seventy. He's an alcoholic, and so are you, Joe."

Joe's hackles went up. How dare Lance accuse him of being an alcoholic, when he himself was the heaviest drug and alcohol abuser Joe had ever known. Then again, he would have the room all to himself. He took another drink, making the ice cubes rattle on purpose, and let out a contented "Aaahhhh."

Joe felt as though he should respond to Lance's negativity, "I know how you feel bro, and I'm no better off than you. That being said, I intend to return to Berkeley in January and get serious about school. It's a big hassle now, but it should pay off in the long run. Maybe you just need a break."

"Yeah," laughed Lance, "A long break."

Malcom spoke in his commanding, enunciated baritone, "College Degrees aren't worth the Parchment Paper they're written on. The way to succeed in life is to develop yourself first. To grow from within, building a solid base of consciousness. Personal growth is how you set the stage for your future. I find it amusing that so many in our culture focus on their outsides when they really should be paying attention to what's going on inside. Then, and only then, wisdom and truth shall be revealed to you, and your face will reflect your secure inner peace and faith in our almighty God."

Joe felt like engaging with the prophet, "Where does your group get all the money to buy multiple properties around town and elsewhere? Surely you can't be making much of a profit selling that organic pig swill that you call food."

There was uncomfortable silence. Joe couldn't believe it. The Mighty Malcom was apparently afraid to engage with him. Instead, the creep refused to talk. This was the schmuck Lance and Kathy were going to follow? Joe laughed out loud.

"What do we live on, Joe? We live on faith, and hard work. The Lord helps those who believe in him and lead righteous lives. As far as the extent of our holdings and how we acquired them. I don't see where that's any of your business. Lance was right in his assessment of you."

"Which is?"

"That's for you two to discuss. Shall we dear?"

Malcom stood and extended his hand to Ruth, helping her up. They walked past Joe and Lance and Kathy and headed back down the ladder.

"Nice going, Joe, " said Lance accusingly.

"What did you tell him about me?"

"The truth,"

"Which is."

"You're a person of base level consciousness

and a big ego. You're also sarcastic, cynical and negative."

"Nice. Wait until he's around you for a few days. Thanks a lot, *friend.*"

"Sorry."

"Hey. I didn't know prophets were so sensitive. I think I was getting a little close to the truth for his comfort."

"I can tell you about other ways they make money. They have a bakery, and I'm not even going to tell you what their best seller is."

"No, Lance. Don't say it. You either, Kathy."

Joe realized that it was the first time he had ever spoken directly to her. How odd.

"Plus, they've got an organic fruit and vegetable stand."

"That ought to do real well in the snow," said Joe in his snarky voice.

Lance handed Joe a pipe and some matches, "Don't spill it."

"What is it? I can't afford to go on any weird trips right now."

"Opium. Don't worry. I saved it just for you. We'll watch over you, make sure you don't fall off the roof."

"Okay," said Joe, getting that funny feeling in his stomach as he lighted the pipe and took in the rich tendrils of thick opium smoke that quickly shot to his brain. Soon, pleasurable endorphins came spinning out of his ears like multiple sparklers that were electric purple. Everything was now in bright, clear techno color. Life was grand!

Joe glided across the billowy clouds. He turned his head towards the great yellow ball of fire they called the sun, and he knew it was the opposite of the moon. He smiled and felt balanced, a near perfect combination of ying and yang, good and bad, positive and negative, up and down, forwards and backwards. He was capable of going in all directions at once. Joe felt ten stories tall, like he could reach up and put his fist right through a cloud. He closed his eyes and felt himself traveling back in time.

Joe opened his eyes and he was sitting on a leaning wooden chair in Lance's third floor Walnut Street Apartment in Berkeley. Lance sat in his cracked red leather armchair that was reserved for his use only. Everyone else had their choice of a seat on a smelly, lumpy orange couch that some fool had put in a dumpster, or an assortment of dangerous, rickety wooden chairs.

Steve Whisenor was there, as he frequently was. He tied a roach clip to some string, bravely stood on one of the chairs and tacked the other end to the center of the ceiling. He stepped down, lit a bomber, took a hit, attached it to the roach clip and tossed it towards Lance who wasn't looking. It bounced off his forehead, "Ow! Damn it Steve. Warn me first that the frigging thing is coming. That smarts."

Joe felt as though he were in a dream inside of a dream. Everyone seemed slightly out of focus. He gazed around the room and saw Jimmy Joyce, a drunk, and Tim Blodget and his old lady, Tina, who were full blown junkies. With Lance and Steve, that made six of them. He felt that familiar scratchy feeling in the back of his throat, and the heaviness in his stomach that preceded the onset of the high from ingesting a psychedelic. He last recalled smoking opium, so why was he coming onto acid?

He remembered eating a few stale potato chips in Lance's empty kitchen. He had also taken a slug out of half a pitcher of red Kool Aid. Had it been dosed? What else could it be? Then his eyes fell on an empty plate on the living room floor. Tim was down there on all fours, looking like a dog, licking up crumbs.

Joe addressed him, "Tim. What was on the plate?"

"Why, chocolate chip cookies with lots of LSD sprinkled on top."

"How many did I eat?"

"How should I know? Stop talking. You're bothering me. Your a bummer."

Joe looked around, wondering who else had eaten the cookies. Obviously Lance had devoured some. It was hard to tell with him sometimes, because his normal demeanor was spacey. Yeah, one glance confirmed Joe's suspicion. Lance was gripping his armrests, like he was enduring heavy G forces coming from a personal tornado. What was strange was that Lance's long hair was pushed straight back, as though he were indeed enduring gale force winds or was sitting in a wind tunnel.

Steve rarely took anything stronger than mescaline. He claimed that tripping on LSD made him suicidal, so everyone told him the same thing. Stop taking it.

Again, fairly obviously, anything Tim took, the same thing Tina took, so that made four of them Joe suspected were tripping on acid. Jimmy Joyce was a little older, and liked to stick with booze and marijuana. He had never taken any other drugs and had no desire or intention of doing so. He was cautious never to eat or drink anything at Lance's except for tap water.

Joe started to panic as the room began tilting to his left. He jumped up and ran and braced himself under a doorway, terrified.

"What are doing, Bailey?" asked Jimmie.

Joe forgot how to talk. He sat down and held his hands up to his ears to drown out the blast of the rocket engines as his brain launched into inner space from Cape Walnut Street. Joe hung on, wondering how far out he would go this time. All the while, he continued to have the impression that he was merely in a drug induced dream, or real life stupor. It was way too complicated, and he clearly had more questions than answers.

Lance stood and picked up the Cal cheerleader's blue and gold megaphone that he had swiped last year, "Now hear this. All hands on deck. Prepare to move the party to the roof. That is all."

Joe reacted in horror. The roof? He was hiding under this doorframe, and Lance was ordering him to the roof? That meant climbing up the outside fire escape two more floors up, and getting over the edge without slipping or falling. That could lead to almost certain death, and probably quite a painful one at that. The worst part was getting higher and having to climb down in the dark. Oh no, he thought.

Joe heard his friends outside, talking and laughing, their voices echoing as they climbed up to the roof. Their talk soon faded away, and Joe moved back to a wooden chair, crossed his legs and tried to think.

He observed Steve striding across the room with his ever present vacuum cleaner, cleaning rags and disinfectants. He got down on his knees and began scrubbing the walls, a grim determined look on his face."Germs," he shouted, "Die germs die!"

Joe looked the other way. He was consumed

with doubts and worries, endless possibilities and multiple what ifs. What if a stranger should come lurching through the front door. Oh no, thought Joe, it was that asshole Frankenstein again, with his arms forever outstretched, drool hanging from his perfectly straight false teeth that he got a heck of a deal on at Walmart. He would spin in circles in the front room, like a gigantic sized wind up toy stuck in circle mode. Steve would look at Joe accusingly, as though this manmade monster had somehow been invited in by himself.

What if it were the Cops, or the Mattress Police?

Joe stood up, deciding to join his friends on the roof. Steve was blowing him out of the room with his high powered Kirby vacuum cleaner that sounded like jet exhaust. He was capable of rubbing it over the same piece of carpet for hours.

Joe climbed through the open third story window that led to a small area to stand, and then you had to swing around and grab onto the ladder with both hands simultaneously and take that scary first step.

He froze halfway up to the fourth floor. He wrapped his arms around the ladder, and made the mistake of looking down. Gawd that would be a long way to fall. He saw his Ford convertible sitting there, waiting for him. It might as well be a mile away. What would he do if he did manage to get out of this weird building? He was way too stoned to drive. He could sit on the front seat and endure crappy top 40 AM radio with the hyper, irritating announcers with funny names, like Duke, or Sebastian, or Jerry-Jerk off.

He'd probably run the car battery down and have to beg Frankenstein to give him a jump start He would have to approach Frank as he spun in circles in the middle of the street. If any drivers dared to try and pass by him, Frank would laugh and kick his leg out with his five hundred pound iron shoes and knock the car sideways to the curb, "Huh huh."

"Frank, over her for a minute. I need your help."

"Nope, *Joe,* here comes another fool. Huh huh."

"Hey Joe! Up here!" yelled Lance. Joe looked straight up and wondered why Lance had multiple heads, all of them mutated versions of himself. He clutched the ladder and closed his eyes, trying to stabilize his spinning vision.

He looked down, and there was Steve, staring at him, "Are you all right, Joe? You've been out there for half an hour, and you've only made it four steps."

Half an hour thought Joe. How could that be?

"Aw shit," said Steve, climbing up and joining him. "This is easy, dude. You've done it many times before. Just look straight ahead and take one slow step at a time, and you'll be on the roof in no time."

His legs feeling weak. Joe reached up for the next rung and managed to move up slowly, a step at a time. Steve was behind him, encouraging him and letting him know that everything was okay.

"Keep climbing, Joe. You're almost there."

As Joe crested the ladder, Lance and Tim reached over to help him up.

"Geeuz Joe," said Tim, scratching with bloody fingernails at another one of his multiple, puss oozing open sores, "You had us scared there for awhile. We wondered if we should call the fire department and then we realized that we didn't have a phone. Isn't that funny?'

Tim and Tina and Lance all laughed weirdly, just as Steve crested the ladder. Holy crap, thought Joe, Steve had forgotten to remove his Suzy Homemaker apron.

Steve fired up a bomber, took a big hit and handed it to Joe. By the time Joe passed it to Lance, Steve had lit up a second huge joint, and then another. He had a seemingly endless supply of high grade weed and hashish that he generously shared every time they were together.

Aahhh, thought Joe. The weed was exactly what he needed to mellow out his trip.

He turned towards the west and looked down on busy University Avenue. It was early evening, and the view was spectacular. Streetlights provided guideposts for the cars and trucks, whose headlights and taillights were colorful orbs that blended together in one surrealistic live action scene.

Joe wrapped his arms around himself and listened to the night noise. As usual, he was somehow able to listen in on people's conversations from hundreds of feet away. He knew most of them were talking amongst themselves about his chances of survival, once he began descending. Some of them were laying money down on the eventual outcome. They speculated on whether it would be life or death. Some even gave odds and bet money.

Joe drifted over to the center where everyone else was milling about. There was some air ventilation equipment and a small, aluminum tool shed that was kept locked. A few pathetic wooden planter boxes held some sickly looking vegetables.

Joe looked on as Tim Blodget urinated on some wilting tomato plants.

"What are you doing?" yelled Steve.

"Isn't it obvious, you tackling dummy. The plants are thirsty because no one is watering them. This will help revive them."

"Junkie piss won't help them," said Steve, "It'll kill them you fool. Do it again and I'll throw you off the roof."

"Down boy, down," slurred Tim, staggering towards Tina who handed her man a smoke. Tim and Tina were passengers on the death train called Heroin addiction.

Lance hopped down from his temporary perch on top of the shed. He took a slug out of a jug of a jug of cheap red wine called Spinyada that had appeared from somewhere.

"Ew," he said, "Tastes like shit. You know, my old man is threatening to cut off my support checks if I don't return to college soon. Fortunately, Joe and I have plans to attend Feather River College starting in September. I almost feel as though I should report my father to the authorities for causing me mental stress."

"How about the Mattress Police?" asked Joe.

"The what?"

"The Mattress Police. You know, the uniformed guys dressed and armed like cops who knock down your front door at night with a battering ram. Then a dozen of the slime balls charge through your house while holding you at gunpoint. They examine all your sheets, pillows, and mattresses to make sure they still have their tags on them."

"What tags?" asked Lance, looking increasingly confused. He had been set to launch one of his endless pontifications, and Joe had thrown his timing off.

"The ones that are required at all time, to make you sleep legal. They say, 'Do Not Remove Under Penalty Of The Law.'"

Jimmy addressed Lance bitterly, "Stop your incessant whining, Potter. The day I turned eighteen, my frigging birthday mind you, my old man told me to find a job, collect all my shit, and get out. He informed me that I was an adult and free, and he no longer had any legal obligation to support me. If I choose to remain at home, I would have to start paying room and board."

"That was quite insensitive of your father, Jimmy," replied Lance. "None of us asked to be born into this hostile, violent, preposterous planet. Our parents created us, so I feel they have an obligation to support us at least while we're in college."

"No age or time limit?" asked Jimmy.

Lance rubbed his face and then stared at his palms, as though they were some recently discovered appendage that he been completely unaware of just two hours ago.

"Do you put a time limit on your love for your parents? Does it expire when they pass sixty five, and is it then subject to renegotiation? I suppose thirty five might be an agreeable cutoff point. If one is engaged in humanitarian work or pursuing a PHD, support should continue indefinitely."

"That's absurd," laughed Jimmy, "It sounds like you plan on sponging off mommy and daddy forever. All because you refuse to get a job and help pay your own way."

"But I do have a job, Jimmy. I'm an entrepreneur." Lance pulled a half full baggie out of his jeans and held it up for all to see,"For just a pittance, I'll sell you some sweet dreams. Six for five bucks."

"You think that being a small time drug dealer is a job? What are you going to put on a job application for previous employment. Drug dealer with references?" sneered Jimmy.

Lance fought back, "You are so negative dude, I can't stand it anymore. Why do you even hang out with us? You don't seem to enjoy our company very much. Oh, I know. It's because you like smoking our weed and drinking our beer, but you never bring anything to share."

"I do so," said Jimmy indignantly, "I brought the Spinyada."

"Wow, a bottle of cheap screw-top wine. Gee thanks, Jimmy."

"Screw you, Lance." Jimmy walked over to the fire escape ladder and disappeared over the edge.

Steve, Tim and Tina followed, leaving just Joe and Lance.

"Man, Lance. You really unloaded on Jimmy."

"I've had it with his leech bullshit and lousy attitude. Wow Joe, even in the dark I can see how dilated your pupils are. How high are you, anyway?"

"I lack the vocabulary to attempt to explain my present condition. Well you help me get off the roof? I think I'd like to go
back down now."

"Sure, buddy. What time is it anyway? I hocked my watch for food money."

Joe lifted his watch close to his face and peered at it. He saw the two arms and numbers, but he couldn't interpret the information to form a coherent answer.

"Let me see," said Lance, "It's eight O'clock. Yeah, let's go back."

Lance held Joe's arm as they walked close to the edge of the roof.

"I'll go first," said Lance, "Just follow my lead. Don't look down. It's easy I tell ya."

Lance disappeared and Joe crouched down and put his sweaty hands on the iron rails, took a deep breath and swung his body over onto the ladder. On the street, someone honked their horn. Joe carefully lowered himself down to the third story landing. He climbed through the window into the hallway, and joined the others inside Lance's apartment.

Someone had plugged a small transistor radio into the wall, and they were listening to 'Louie Louie' on a shitty little speaker, making it sound like they were playing it from a hundred miles away.

"Wake up, Joe."

He opened his eyes. It was Lance.

"You've really been tripping on that opium. The others are in the cabin, ready to leave. I need to join them.

Joe nodded his head and lighted a Marlboro. He was still unable to speak.

"Well come on then, Joe. Let's climb down."

JOE BAILEY'S THIRD EYE

CHAPTER EIGHTEEN

Gary Hess tromped through the thick woods behind his A Frame. He carried his deer rifle, spare ammo, a canteen with water and a bag of breadcrumbs. He made no pretense of walking softly. Instead., he stepped like Big Foot, kicking plants out of his way, breaking small trees in half with his gloved hands and stepping on as many slugs as he could.

Everything had turned to shit. Big Dan McGrew stopped by the mill and bitched him out in front of everyone, blaming Gary for the failure of their big drug raid and apparently embarrassing Dan. They'd come up empty at Jesse's sisters house as well as Greg's cabin.

Elliott Rosen's dad filed a huge civil lawsuit against Gary and his friends, forcing the Plumas County Grand Jury to convene and examine the evidence against the local boys. Now, Gary needed to hire an attorney, but all he had in his bank account was a hundred and fifty six dollars.

College had gone from tedious to boring to unbearable. He hated all his classes, thought all his instructors were out to get him, and he despised his fellow students from the Bay Area. That cute chick he spotted, Carlene, was working at the restaurant, but she acted like he didn't exist, taking his orders like a robot and avoiding all eye contact. He was going to stop leaving her tips.

Maureen was still pissed at him and was now insisting that Gary pay half of her huge medical bills. Incredibly enough, his hours at the mill had been cut in half because business was slow, and he was warned that he might be laid off altogether.

Then to top it all off, there was his scary experience just that afternoon at the Keddie Club, where he had always felt safe. He had the day off from the mill and stopped in after school for a quick drink or two. He had been sitting there, minding his own business, when all of a sudden, Jesse Barnes was sitting next to him, not saying a word. He just stared at Gary with his skull like death glare and his eyes, thought Gary. He had never seen anything like it. Glittering orange and yellow hypnotizing orbs with pinpoint pupils.

Without a word, Jesse turned around so Gary could see his colors and bottom rocker on his worn, black leather vest. It read 'The Skull Diggers' at the top with a patch of a giant blue skull with a dagger thrust through it in the middle. On the bottom it read 'SACRAMENTO'.

Gary said "Hi" but Jesse's steely glare never changed. He didn't even seem to be breathing. Gary tried turning away, but he could see Jesse in the big mirror behind the bar, not blinking or swallowing, just glowering at him.

Finally, Jesse spoke in a barely audible horse rasp, "I don't like rats. You'll be seeing me again, punk, when you least expect it. Rat."

Gary had thrown a five on the counter and walked out, genuinely fearing for his life. Maybe it hadn't been such a good idea to throw Jesse under the

333

bus the same time he was narking out Lance and Joe.

Gary stopped when he spotted a squirrel perched on a nearby limb, chewing on a nut. Gary quickly brought his rifle up, glanced into the scope, saw crosshairs on the squirrel's face, and squeezed off two rounds just as the animal darted up the tree and disappeared behind some leaves.

"Damn!" said Gary. His luck was so bad he couldn't even kill a squirrel anymore. Maybe his sights were off. Naw. It was just more of his never ending streak of bad luck. His downward slide was easy to trace. It started when the commie kids had hit town, led by that skuzzy doper, Lance Potter, and his weird buddy, Joe Bailey. Things had tilted completely out of control when Jesse Ray Barnes had sauntered into the Keddie Club with his leather jacket and biker attitude.

He was positive that his information about Lance Potter was correct. That stoned dipshit back at his cabin, Ross, had confirmed it under duress. Gary had to admit that he'd used the shotgun approach when revealing the other names to Big Dan. If you shot in a wide enough arc, you were bound to hit somebody. In this case, his gun had apparently been loaded with blanks, and he didn't know who had tricked him or why.

That was it, he thought. Maureen. Of course. He had slipped up while at their place and bragged about singing like a Canary, and she had probably warned them, or had that big lummox Sam do it.

The day after the failed raid, Gary was summoned to the table of the Marlboro Men.

"What the hell went wrong?" demanded Clint Mapes.

"Damned if I know, Clint. Someone must have

tipped them off that a raid was coming, and they all got rid of their dope. I did my job. Other people evidently didn't do theirs."

"Well," remarked Slim, a thin guy who looked like he had skin cancer on his arms and nose, "I heard they're right back in business."

:"Outside help is on the way, Gary. This has obviously gotten bigger then you and Big Dan can handle," said Clint, folding his hands across his stomach.

"Hey," said Gary, feeling himself losing his temper, "I'm not a Deputy Sheriff. Don't blame me if they can't manage to arrest anyone while drugs are being openly smoked on the streets."

That is what directly preceded Gary's impulsive hunting trip. He needed to kill something, preferably big. An ironic grin crossed his face. The way his luck was going he would be shot by another hunter, or he himself would mistakenly kill Bambi. Then he would be a full fledged pariah, not that he wasn't at least already halfway there.

Gary stopped, sat on a mossy log, lighted a smoke, and thought about his encounter with Barnes. Who the hell did he think he was, trying to intimidate him with his vest? Sure, Gary respected and feared the Skull Diggers, but they were in Sacramento, not Keddie.

Gary wondered what it must be like to roar down a road with fifty other bikers, all wearing the colors and patches that they had earned with blood and prison sentences. There would be the nasty roar of fifty Harleys, driven by wild men with long hair, waving pliers for pulling teeth and claw hammers for bashing in skulls.

Their mamas sometimes rode along, tattooed arms wrapped around their man's vest. If their shirt were pulled up on their back, it would reveal their universal 'tramp stamp' tattoo that had the blue skull and in big black letters, 'Property of the Skull Diggers.'

Gary moved deeper into the woods and further away from his problems. He was quieter now. He never carried a compass anymore. He knew these woods well, having grown up around them.

Even his old friends and drinking buddies were annoying him, their drunken and violent antics growing tedious. Plus, that idiot Randy Bob had run over that kid. Now look at the load of shit that was being dumped on them all, even though he himself was half a mile away with Reno when the accident happened.

Gary tried talking to his friends, saying they needed to meet and agree on a story before they were arrested. They just laughed at him. Randy Bob signed over the title to his dune buggy to his brother, Nate Bob, "What can they take from us? We don't own nothin."

Gary tried to tell them about how they could attach their future wages, and they had laughed some more, "What future wages?" asked Dave, "We're all gonna lose our jobs anyway. You can't bleed turnips out of a rock."

Gary briefly thought about joining the French Foreign Legion. First though, he needed to lose some weight and learn to speak French, "Bon jower mon sewer," he said, practicing the language while he slowly swiveled his big bore gun back and forth, scanning the brush, "Parley view mon chapot. Je suite, French Bread mon bacon."

He finally reached his prime killing spot, a grassy meadow exactly two miles from their cabin. It was peaceful and calm. He was about to change all that. Gary carefully placed his rifle on the berm, and then went to a raised mound of dirt fifty feet away and spread out the breadcrumbs. He returned and laid out prone, his face resting up against his beloved wood stock, his finger resting lightly on the trigger.

He didn't have to wait long. Several black birds landed and pecked at the bread while the rest of their flock circled overhead, waiting to make sure it was safe to land. Gary carefully sighted in, took a deep breath and exhaled as he squeezed off four rounds. They all missed."Shit!" screamed Gary, standing up and lurching around, kicking at bushes, ripping up ferns, looking in vain for something to kill..

Joe finished his breakfast of half a box of Kellogg's Frosted Flakes, a piece of toast with butter and coffee. It tasted better since Claire tried a cup awhile back and spit it into the sink. Claire pulled the lid off the coffee pot, couldn't believe what she saw and smelled, and gave the boys a quick lesson on how to clean it.

He settled into his favorite corner of the couch and smoked his first joint of the day. He was halfway through Kerouac's 'Dharma Bums' and was struggling with the erratic plot. 'On The Road' was clearly a superior Novel, but the 'Bums' was still worth reading, because it had been written by his hero.

Lance came shuffling out of the bedroom, rubbing his face. It was hard for Joe to believe, but Lance and Kathy had only lasted two days and nights at The People's Commune. Lance was vague about what had gone wrong, but insulated that it was merely a temporary setback.

Joe wondered if Lance had looked in his drug

bag recently. If he had, he surely would have noticed the additional weight and found Jesse's pistol. It was odd that Jesse hadn't come asking for it yet.

"Can I have a cup of your coffee, Joe?"

"Of course you can. When did you start having to ask for my permission? There's also a new loaf of Wonder Bread for toast, plus we have a cube of butter."

"Thanks, man. Can Kathy have some too?"

"Of course. Why are you being so weird?"

"I guess I'm embarrassed. One day we get our heads shaved and move out, and two days later we're back. I wish I could explain it, but I can't. Not yet."

"So, you don't want to talk about it?'

"No."

"Lance, I hope I'm not prying, but are you and Kathy eating okay?"

"Not really. We ran out of cash a week ago. I don't want to turn yellow again."

"Aren't you still selling drugs? I saw that huge bag you stashed in my trunk that you forgot to tell me about. Tell you the truth, pal, that pissed me off. You put Jesse and me in jeopardy when we went to Sacramento."

"I didn't know you were going. Otherwise, I would have told you," said Lance.

"I guess that makes sense. So why aren't you selling if you're so broke?"

"Would you start up business again right after that raid? I wasn't here, so they tracked me down at the commune and searched me and where Kathy and I were sleeping. They found nothing, but now I'm scared. The other big issue is the bad acid I sold to Maureen and a few others, who also got sick. I think it was cut with strychnine, so now it has a bad rap. Kathy and I have been trying to use it up. We usually each take three hits a day."

"Don't you get sick too?"

"Naw, it's not too bad. I think we got immunity or something now."

Lance poured himself a cup of coffee. "I really don't know what Malcom's prime issue with us is. I know he was pissed when the Sheriff's showed up to hassle me. They don't believe in eating meat or using white sugar or processed flour. I'm hoping he'll change his mind and let us back on the bus. I feel stupid now with no hair. Today Kathy and I are going to hitchhike into Quincy and sell some blood to make some food money."

Joe shuddered when he speculated on the fate of someone who was given a transfusion of Lance's blood. Their life would never be the same. In fact, it was possible they would immediately nose dive into an unstoppable death spiral. They would be drawn to San Francisco. They would find themselves standing on the east side of The Golden Gate Bridge, contemplating suicide. Cars would roar by, drivers and passengers oblivious to their inner pain and hopeless despair. To show they were serious, they would be clutching a loaf of Susan's now world famous brown bread. If the fall didn't kill them right off, having the stone like bread strapped to their stomach would make them sink like a chunk of concrete.

Lance popped two pieces of Wonder bread into their filthy toaster that was full of crumbs at the bottom, with a frayed cord making it a fire hazard. He slammed the black lever down and sparks flew out of the wall and left a black mark on the outlet. "Shit, Joe. Nothings working out. Other then begging in front of Ralph's Groceries I don't know what else to do. We've been banned from nearly every store in town as suspected shoplifters."

Lance buttered his toast, clutched his coffee and sat in the front room chair, "Besides that, Kathy whines and complains too much. She's really starting to annoy me."

"I heard that, asshole." Kathy entered the front room wearing one of Lance's long shirts and nothing else. With her baldhead, she looked like a miniature female Mr. Clean clone. Her glasses now stood out as her most prominent facial feature. Tiny tufts of fuzzy brown hair were beginning to sprout. Joe wrinkled his nose. She smelled bad.

"Morning babe. Sit down," said Lance, "I'll get you some coffee and toast."

Lance returned and handed Kathy her breakfast, "By the way, Joe. I can't believe I forgot to tell you. In Quincy, three different people told me that pea brained local, Gary Hess, is allegedly packing a gun and looking for us."

Joe felt a lightening bolt travel down to his toes, "I better tell Jesse right away. He'll know what to do. He told me he has plans for Gary. Maybe he'll need to speed them up. I believe the jerk will shoot us if he can. Maybe a sniper shot from the woods while I'm driving us towards Quincy."

"Think so?" asked Lance.

"Yeah. If I was Gary Hess, and I knew that Jesse Barnes and possibly the whole Skull Diggers Sacramento chapter was out looking for me, I'd split to someplace like Ohio."

"Why Ohio? What exactly is your issue or problem with Ohio?"

"Why not Ohio? Why do they call you Lance? How come you're not *normal* like everyone else? I've never been to Cleveland, and have no plans to do so.

"Back to the subject of food and your potential starvation….." Joe stopped. He looked out their front window and saw a line of ten Marlboro Men, standing on the top edge of the parking lot, smoking in synchronization, and staring down at them. What exactly was their trip anyway, wondered Joe? That was it, he thought. Yes. The broken down cancer riddled old hacks had fed Gary Hess information on them and then pulled his strings like he was a marionette, probably getting him to squeal on them to Big Dan.

"Yes," said Lance, "You were starting to talk about food."

"Damn, Lance. That's it."

"What's it, Joe? Make up your mind on what you want to talk about." Lance ran his free hand across his head that now was showing signs of regeneration. It was like he expected that if he said ten Hail Mary's, along with twenty Gary Hess's, his long hair would suddenly reappear. It had taken him over a year to grow it out this last time.

Joe stood up and flipped the bird with both fingers at the long line of men all wearing bright white cowboy hats. He knew they couldn't see him, but it helped him unload some of the sudden rage he felt, "Those decrepit, despicable bastards. The freaking *Marlboro Men*, sitting around their stupid round table every morning, clearly monitoring our activities and trying to get us arrested. The bastards!"

Lance seemed to get it,"You mean like a conspiracy, man?"

"You're dammed right it is! I gotta find Jesse."

"Cool, man. Let's try this subject one more time. Food."

"Yeah," said Joe, "Have either of you thought about getting a part time job?"

Lance was silent.

"I had a job once," said Kathy, deliberately exposing herself to Joe who turned away and stuck out his tongue, "I worked the counter at the Albany Fosters Freeze for nearly a month."

"Why only a month?" asked Joe, glancing out the window. The creeps were gone, slithering back to their portal to Hell. It would be a dark cave hidden in the nearby mountains with a weathered skull and crossbones sign posted out front, warning potential trespassers to beware.

"I quit. My boss, or overseer, was a male chauvinist pig asshole who tried to feel me up in the cooler. I told him to quit after five minutes of his groping."

"Yeah?" asked Joe, wishing he had a tape recorder. No one would believe this conversation.

"For my own sense of self worth, I had to quit. He was black and claimed his name was Cho Mama. What a strange name. He was clearly a tool of the capitalist establishment. Workers labor lines the pockets of the corporate greed mongers. Joseph Stalin is my hero."

"Stalin?" spit out Joe. "He killed more of his own people then Hitler, Attila The Hun and President Nixon combined."

Kathy sat up straight, "I. am a Marxist Revolutionary," she proclaimed.

"Right," said Joe.

Joe was still tying his shoestrings when the squeaking of the bedsprings started. He dove out the front door, putting on his jacket, an apple clutched in his mouth. He had to find Jesse. This Gary Hess crap was getting scary.

Joe found Jesse sitting alone on the steps to his sisters house, smoking. Jesse didn't act at all surprised regarding Joe's theories about the Marlboro Men being involved. Jesse told Joe to stay indoors if he spotted Gary's Jeep. Jesse promised that he would fix Gary soon, and for him not to worry so much. Joe forgot to ask him about the gun.

Joe and Lance decided to go to school for a change. They needed to get out of the cabin. They left Kathy sitting on the couch, staring at the wall with her mouth open. Joe figured she was coming onto her daily three hits of acid.

"Did you drop this morning, Lance?"

"Of course. I told you Kathy and I are cleaning up our supply. Don't worry. I do it every day. I'll be fine."

It had snowed the night before, and Joe cleaned off his car windows and roof. Lance came out onto the porch, took one step and slipped on his ass and then slid down the stairs.

Joe laughed, "Hey. Space cadet. You okay?"

Lance got up gingerly, wiping snow off his butt. "Are you sure we can drive in this snow with no chains? It looks dangerous to me. Why haven't you purchased any?"

"Buy them with what?"

Joe and Lance got in and buckled their seat belts.

"Hey, Guy limped over here last night and told me that I got that job over at the restaurant."

"Yeah? Doing what? Picking up cigarette butts in the parking lot?"

"No, man. I'm gonna be a dishwasher. It's a buck fifty an

hour, and for every eight hours I work, I can order a free meal off the menu."

"Anything you want? Steak?"

"Yep."

"They got any more jobs?"

"Yeah. They're looking for someone to pump gas at the station. Why don't you apply? You've got experience."

"Okay. Thanks Lance. I'll put in an application when we return, assuming we get to Quincy and back in one piece."

Fresh snowflakes glided gently to the ground, landing on top of the piled up snow left over from the previous night.

"Shit," said Joe, "Here goes nothing. Hang on" He put the big Ford in gear and the rear tires spun and the car crept forward. They hit the parking lot and Joe gave it more throttle and the back end began sliding down the hill towards a wooden fence.

"Do something Joe!" yelled Lance, looking around in panic and bracing himself against his seat back.

Joe floored it, the rear tires squealed and then gripped the pavement and they shot forward heading for a line of vehicles parked alongside the restaurant. He jerked the steering wheel hard left and they blasted up the hill and sailed across the road, landing grill first in a snow bank.

"You okay?" Joe asked Lance, who nodded his head.

Joe got out and looked, "No problem. No damage. Ha, that was cool." Joe leaned into his side of the car and grinned, "Wanna try it again?"

"No. Go straight and don't do any more of that flying car shit. Your driving has gotten suddenly crazier. Why?"

Joe laughed, got back in, put it into reverse and headed down the Keddie road that was freshly plowed, "See," he said to Lance, "I told you we'd be fine. Maybe we should find a Safeway and borrow a basket and shove you down a big hill in a shopping cart." Joe was drenched in sweat.

Lance rolled down his window and took in large gulps of frigid air.

They reached the highway with no further challenges, even though the snowfall was increasing. Joe took a left onto the highway and started towards Quincy, driving cautiously. A couple of locals in four wheel drives roared past them, honking their horns, leering red necks flipping them off. One of them threw empty beer cans at them. "Fags!" he yelled.

Joe looked in his rear view mirror,"Oh shit, Lance. We've got company, and it's not good."

Lance looked back, "Oh crap."

Right on their bumper was Gary Hess, driving his 1953 Willys. Gary wore a manic grin. He honked his horn repeatedly and flashed his headlights.

"He wants you to pull over," advised Lance.

"No shit," answered Joe, giving the Ford more gas. If the pavement was dry, he could easily outrun Gary's Jeep. In the snowy conditions though, they were at a disadvantage, "If I stop he'll shoot us."

Gary honked his horn again and then rammed their rear bumper with his front, which was heavy duty because he had a winch mounted on it. Gary swerved out into the opposite lane, got just a bit ahead of them and cranked his steering wheel hard to the right.

"Shit!" said Joe, slamming on the brakes, fighting to control the Ford as it skidded back and forth across the road, barely avoiding sheer cliffs that plunged hundreds of feet straight down into the Feather River.

Gary threw a full bottle of beer at them and it smashed on Joe's door and splattered liquid all over the side..

"What a maniac, Joe! He's trying to kills us!"

Joe got it straightened out and Gary was barely in front of them when he slammed on his brakes. Joe swerved hard left, floored it and sped past the Willys. Gary's hand was hanging out the window, flipping them off.

"He's done now," said Joe, confidently increasing their speed, "There's no way he can catch up."

"Shouldn't we go to the Sheriff and file a complaint?"

"With a bag full of drugs and a gun in the trunk?"

"A gun? Whose gun? Is it yours? What's going on, Joe?"

"Oops. That was supposed to be a surprise."

"A surprise? You know I don't approve of firearms. I demand that you remove it at once."

"Chill, dude. When we get back we're gonna clean out my whole car of contraband."

Joe parked in a nearly deserted parking lot at The County Fair. There was no sign of Gary's distinctive vehicle.

"What class are we going to?" asked Joe as he and Lance walked onto the large lawn that was covered with fresh snow. "Archery?"

"Yeah, just follow my lead." The boys gathered with other cold students in a loose circle. The temperature was dropping, and some kids in light jackets and no gloves were shivering. A couple of guys they sort of knew laughed about them actually showing up for a class. Most of their classmates had never seen them before.

"Here he comes," said Lance, pointing to a thin man with a clipboard running towards them, "Mr. Benjamin. The instructor."

Two students were tacking targets to hay bales. Mr. Benjamin clapped his hands in excitement and spoke in a high pitched voice, "Okay people. Gather around. Listen up now.

"Today is your final. It will be the boys against the girls. Whoever has the highest grand total gets 20 points towards their final grade. The losers, well, they only get 10 points."

Mr. Benjamin placed his hands on his hips.

"Whoop-dee-do," said Joe in his duck voice.

Mr. Benjamin was right on it, "Did you have something to say, young man?"

Joe shook his head, holding his breath so he wouldn't burst out laughing at this flaming queen. How had he managed to survive so far in macho land?

Mr. Benjamin clapped his hands again, and jumped in the air in excitement, "All right then people, let us begin."

Joe used his duck voice again, speaking to Lance, "Say big boy, let me see your equipment. I swing both ways you know."

"You savage you," said Lance, who put an arrow in his bow, aimed it straight up into the air and let er fly. "Oh goody," he said, mocking Mr. Benjamin's voice and then dropping his bow and clapping his hands together and dancing in place. He stomped his cowboy boots down, splattering Joe and nearby classmates with snow and slush.

He and Joe watched as the arrow reached its peak altitude, and then headed back, arrowhead down, picking up speed. It plunged into the earth just a foot from Mr. Benjamin, who jumped back, "My goodness," he said angrily. "Who just shot this arrow?" he demanded, "You could have killed someone!"

Lance raised his hand, while planting his other on his hip, "Oh Mr. Benjamin. I'm afraid it was me, shooting my arrow, prematurely. You know how that is, don't you? Premature?"

Mr. Benjamin got in Lance's face, "Exactly who are you? I've never seen you in this class before."

"My name is Gary Hess. I'm going to go file a complaint at the office that you've been coming on to me because I'm a homosexual German Jew." Lance wandered off towards the administration building.

Joe was next.

"And just who are you supposed to be?"

"The real Gary Hess. That other guy is a liar. His actual name is Scott Scheinblum, and he lives in Keddie in Cabin twelve. Just ask for ass breath."

Mr. Benjamin frantically looked at his class roster, "I don't see either of your names on here."

"Tough shit, beanerd" said Joe, turning and following in Lance's footsteps.

"Come back here you hoodlums! The Dean of Students is going to hear about this! I AM NOT A BEANERD!"

Joe worked his first four shift at the gas station the following night. He'd only had three customers in three hours, and was bored out of his mind. He would have to bring his notebook and a couple of pens next time so he could write in his journal.

Guy had trained him in a few minutes, showing him how to use the ancient pumps and run the cash register. Guy was whistling the usual Disney ditty, 'Just Whistle While You Work.' Joe couldn't wait for the little troll to leave. He was way too happy for someone of his short stature.

The office had a wood burning stove, and Joe kept it stoked. It was freezing outside and icicles were forming. He had been unable to drive today. The pavement froze up, and his car just spun around in circles. He was lucky to get it into the driveway. He went out every few hours with a broom and pushed the accumulated snow off the now sagging convertible top and pushed it onto the ground.

Joe decided to explore the two bay shop. It was like walking into a huge freezer.

A white 1959 Chevy Apache pickup was parked over one of the hoists. The hood was off and the engine was covered with a shop blanket.

An overhead metal rack held a dozen used tires. A battery charger stood in the corner, next to a small stack of oil in cases and an open box of anti-freeze. He didn't see any tools.

"Some shop," said Joe, walking back into the warm office. He poured himself a cup of coffee from the blackened pot on top of the wood stove.

The hose outside dinged. It was a blue 1962 Plymouth Savoy. Joe came out the door and stopped cold. Jesse sat in the driver's seat, grinning at Joe. Carlene sat next to him in the middle, snuggled up to Jesse, who had his arm thrown casually over her shoulder. He was wearing his Skull Diggers vest again, along with a pirate like scarf over his head. Jesse said something and Carlene giggled.

"Oh hi, Joe. When did you start working here?"

asked Jesse.

"Tonight. What will it be?"

"Gimme two bucks of regular."

Jesse got out,"I gotta take a leak."

Joe was already pumping the gas, "The bathrooms are both broken. Do not go in there. Just piss in the phone booth. That's what Lance and I do."

"Sounds about right," replied Jesse, walking rapidly in that direction.

Joe ignored Carlene. He didn't feel a thing for her anymore. Only numbness. The fact that she was obviously with Jesse now meant nothing.

Jesse returned from the phone booth, tugging on his zipper,"Oh yeah Joe. Better check the oil and water. This is my sister's car, and I don't think her old man ever takes a look."

Joe opened the hood and pulled the dipstick out. The level showed full but the color was dark black, "You better tell her to get an oil change. This stuff is wasted."

Jesse sidled up to Joe with a smirk on his skull face, "I gotta tell ya, Joe. This Carlene babe is pretty hot in the sack."

Joe shut the hood, "Well, she should be. She's certainly had enough practice."

Jesse tilted his head sideways, "Jealous, huh kid?" He reached out and touched Joe's shoulder, and Joe felt a surge of electricity passing from Jesse to him.

"Two bucks. Sorry I can't give it to you free, this being my first shift and all," said Joe, holding out his hand.

Jesse handed him two dollars, "By the way, Joe. I forgot something important in your glove box. I need it back, preferably tonight."

"No problem. I get off in an hour. It's in my

trunk."

"You'll see me sometime by midnight."

"Okay, I guess."

Jesse gave him that condemned man wink. He knew he was supposed to die young, but for some reason was still around, waiting for the inevitable. That's why he claimed to not give a fuck anymore. He really didn't, thought Joe.

Jesse jumped back into the Savoy, gunned the motor and then fishtailed out and sped north at a high rate of speed. Joe thought he might be heading for J.D.'s, but how would Carlene get in? She was younger than Joe. Not his problem, he thought, returning to the office with a sick heaviness in his stomach. Jesse and Carlene. What a couple they made.

DREAM ON

CHAPTER NINETEEN

The cabin was dark when Joe returned a little after nine. He felt a little spooked as he stood on the lightless porch and realized the front door was un-locked. Was it just a simple case of forgetfulness, or was Gary Hess inside, waiting for him?

Joe flipped on every light he could, and no one was waiting, at least not in the front room or kitchen. Joe grabbed their dull steak knife and thoroughly searched the rest of the cabin. Satisfied that it was empty, he fixed himself a snack and grabbed a cold Coors and sat on the couch. Now, because of Jesse, he was supposed to wait up until at least midnight so his pal could retrieve his .38. Jesse had suddenly decided he needed it. Of course, thought Joe, it very well could have to do with the Gary Hess death threats, and a potential response from Jesse. That bastard Gary had tried to kill he and Lance earlier today, and the more Joe thought about it, the angrier he got.

Joe went outside, knocked the snow off his trunk and opened it. He lifted the spare tire and pulled out the grocery sack full of pills. Yeah, the bag was way heavier. Good, he thought, it's still in there. Once again using his shop rag, he carefully lifted the pistol out, looked around, and shoved it down the front of his pants. *Now, he thought, go ahead and come for me, Gary Hess. I've got five hollow points with your name on them, fat boy.*

Joe woke up, sprawled on the couch, his head dangling over the edge. He sat up. Black and white versions of Kathy and Lance stood in front of him, flickering in and out, like partial TV reception. Their hair was long again.

Spooky Halloween decorations hung from the walls and ceiling. Joe was wearing a red Satan costume, complete with a tall, three-pronged Devil's fork. Joe noticed that his exposed skin was also red.

"This is weird," observed Lance, his voice gurgling as though he were speaking from underwater. He stroked the flowing white beard that went with his Sorcerer's costume. His tall pointed hat. was covered with pictures of the sun, moon and stars. "Who am I supposed to be?"

"Yul Bryner?" replied Joe.

Kathy wore nothing, and her head was a carved pumpkin. Candles burned in the holes where her eyes should be. It looked strange, to Joe, to see that Kathy was still wearing glasses, the ends wrapped around large Mr. Potato Head plastic ears.

"What are you doing in my dream, Bailey?" demanded Lance. "It's Halloween night you know. We should be anticipating the imminent arrival of hordes of sugar starved children, dressed up as beggars, ghouls and apparitions. They're going to be pounding on our door soon., demanding treats or they will torch our cabin with us inside as their trick. Do something, Joe. You're the only one of us in color."

"Or," suggested Kathy, "We might see a green witch with a scary face scratching at our front window, trying to get in."

"Yeah," managed Joe. His lungs felt full of water. How could he drown in his own living room? Clearly, something was very wrong.

"Yes," said Lance, fading out altogether, "And we have nothing to offer the little extortionists."

Lance came flickering back, looking like a scene out of Star Trek, as his body particles flew back together and became whole again, though still colorless

"How about offering them me?" suggested Kathy. Her normal head with hair was back. She spread her arms out, exposing her small breasts and large, baby bearing hips.

Music started up from their record player all by itself. It was Led Zeppelin, singing their signature song, '*Good Times Bad Times.*'

Joe wondered why Lance was so sure that he was appearing in his dream. Why couldn't he and Kathy be in his? After all, they continued to be flickering x ray images of themselves, looking as though they were caught between two worlds.

Joe gurgled out more words in an unknown language that they all somehow understood, "I remember how your family dealt with Halloween, Lance. Your folks shut off all the lights and played cards at the kitchen table and refused to answer the knocks that still came, even though the porch light was off."

"Mundane and uninteresting, but essentially factual." replied Lance.

Kathy morphed into a colorful clown while Lance remained black and white. Her outfit became a collage of polka dots scattered across a flowery dress. She wore floppy pink two foot clown shoes, and her face was heavily made up.

Kathy began turning her head completely around in a circle, and then did it again and again, each time at a faster speed. Her eyes were wide open, and her tongue hung out two feet from her red clown mouth, lagging behind her high speed whirling face.

Lance put the lampshade on his head and stepped up on the coffee table. Kathy shuddered to a halt, her bony shoulders twitching, and then her head slumped forward and she stopped moving, as though her batteries had gone dead.

"Hello brothers and sisters. Kathy and I love you. I don't think Joe does. Thank you for coming out in this inclement weather. I an here tonight to explain life to the unrepentant If you're looking for the lecture on selling your soul to become a multilevel marketing icon with your own TV show, then go back to the elevators and push the button that says basement. It's four thousand feet down, and known in polite company as Hell.

"There are three distinct phases in everyone's life, which leads into my statement that life is a metaphor for Halloween.

"When you are but an innocent child, Halloween is the one night of the year that you are empowered. You travel from door to door in stupid costumes and extort candy from strangers."

"Extortion, huh?" said Joe, seawater spilling out of his mouth and all over his shoes. Where had all that come from, he wondered? A blue fish flopped around near his feet. He looked up and saw that Kathy now had a killer whale sharks head. Enormous mouth wide open, blood dripping from rows of ragged teeth and dripping onto the floor.

Lance continued, "Children first turn cynical when they realize they've been lied to repeatedly over the years, by people they thought they could trust. They make up Santa Claus, The Easter Bunny, The Tooth Fairy, and Ed Sullivan. All lies."

"What is the next phase?" inquired Joe, holding onto his chair, feeling weightless like he was a helium filled balloon about to be let go.

"Why adulthood, of course. We've just entered it, whether you like it or not."

"What's the final phase, Lance? Is it when we're incontinent, and confined to smelly rest homes where we race around in wheel chairs since we have no legs, dragging our full bed pans behind us?"

"No, my friend. The final phase is death. None of us can avoid it."

Joe felt himself blacking out, sinking deeper into his chair. His last conscious thought was that his strange and bizarre journey was not over.

He reappeared in 1962 on Halloween night. He was standing in front of his house with his eleven year old best friends, Lance Potter and Alex Chance, getting ready to start ringing doorbells and demanding candy.

Lance's long limbs stuck out of his Beatnik costume, which was a lumpy black sweater, a French beret and dark glasses. Alex wore a cool store bought Pirate outfit that came with a plastic Buccaneer's sword. Joe had on a claustrophobic Wolfman mask and a magician's long cape. He knew his costume looked stupid, but he didn't care. If any of the kids made fun of him, he'd slug them in the mouth.

The boys ran down Santa Fe Avenue, hitting both sides of the street and collecting a decent haul. They decided to go around the block and work Curtis Street, which had always been fruitful territory for them. They especially liked it when some unwitting adult held out a big bowl of candy. They would immediately plunge their hands down deep, greedily grabbing as big a handful as they could, shove it into their bags and run over to the next house.

Alex had once rationalized their borderline rude behavior, "Look, we're kids. Adults expect us to do stupid, dangerous things, so why disappoint them?

Halfway down the west side of Curtis Street, Lance rang the doorbell of a single story stucco house done in a typical California stucco with a red tile roof and a green awning over the front picture window. The three of them stood huddled together in the enclosed porch. Three Pumpkins sat on the porch wall, with a candle burning in each one.

The front door slowly creaked open. It was a tall adult male, expertly made up to look like Dracula. He smirked at the boys. In the house, there was the sound of a movie projector running, and they could see shadows dancing off the walls.

"Yes, boys?" he said in a heavily accented voice while rubbing his white gloved hands together, "Vhat can I do for you?"

"Trick or treat," they said without enthusiasm.

"Grand. I vant a trick. Vhat can you do to amuse me?"

The boys milled around, looking hopelessly at each other. No one, in the five years they had been trick or treating, had ever asked for a trick before.

The temperature suddenly dropped . A harsh wind sprang up from nowhere, blowing garbage cans and small dogs down the street.

"No treeks, huh boys? Zats okay. I give you a treat anyways."

Dracula held out his large hands folded into fists, "So, who vants ze treat?"

They all received something unknown and heavy. They yelled thanks and then followed Alex across the street, where they gathered under a buzzing streetlamp. The wild wind stopped as suddenly as it began.

Alex spoke first, "What did that creep give us?"

They rummaged through their bags until Alex pulled out a dripping ice cube.

"That jerk put ice cubs in our bags."

Alex was okay, because he was using a pillow case for his haul, but the bottom of Joe and Lance's bags ripped out at the bottom, spilling candy all over the sidewalk.

Joe was crestfallen, "Now what are we supposed to do?"

"Hold on fellers," said Alex. He ran up to a nearby door and came back a minute later with two fresh garbage sacks. He helped Lance and Joe scoop up their loads.

Alex looked serious, "Are we gonna let that schmuck do that to us? Are we men or boys?"

"We're men!" they shouted.

Using a simple plan designed by Alex, the boys returned to Dracula's house, dropped a cherry bomb inside each pumpkin, rang the bell and then ran back across the street and hid behind a station wagon. Dracula came out on the porch just as the explosives went off, splattering him and his porch with pumpkin guts, plus cracking the front window. Dracula put his hands over his ears, ran inside and called the cops.

The boys quickly ran down to Washington Street and started working their way south. They spent much of their time trading high fives and boasting about the success of their well planned commando raid.

When Joe returned to his family's Santa Fe house, all the lights were off. His friends were already gone. He walked through the back door cautiously, and crept through the kitchen. Still no one. Where was his family?

Just as he was entering his old room, he woke up to find himself in bed in his cabin at Keddie. He looked over and saw that Lance and Kathy were somewhere else. Man, he thought to himself. What wild dreams he'd just had. It had all seemed so real.

There was an urgent knock at the front door. Joe jumped up. Jesse, come to claim his piece? Joe answered the door and Jesse came in holding Carlene by her hand. Joe noticed her hair was disheveled, and her shoes untied.

Jesse stuck out his hand.

Joe pulled the .38 out of the front of his pants with his shop rag and held it out.

Jesse grabbed the gun, rolled the cylinder checked the load and shoved the pistol into his right front coat pocket.

"How long you been carrying my piece around like that?" asked Jesse.

"A few hours."

"Good day to blow your nuts off."

Carlene giggled.

Jesse turned to leave, "Don't worry, man. I've set the wheels in motion to take down your fat ugly friend. You're gonna have to play a part. Even Carlene's gonna participate. Aren't you, babe?'

Carlene puckered up and Jesse met her lips and they started making out. Joe opened the door so they could see their way out. All he wanted was a good nights sleep.

HOME ALONE

CHAPTER TWENTY

The next big storm took the boys by surprise. Snow was piled up everywhere, and no one was driving on it much, not even the four wheel drive fellas. Word spread quickly that college had been canceled for the day. The residents of nearby cabins and the dormitory poured outside, laughing.

Some girls built a huge snowman, with a carrot for a nose and rat turds for eyes. While the girls attention was diverted, a wise acre ran up and moved the carrot down to the snowman's crotch, which made many chuckle.

The girls started a snowball fight with the boys, some of who fired back rocks covered with snow. "OW!" yelled one girl, nailed in the forehead with a heavy one.

Joe, Kathy and Lance stood on the front porch of their cabin, sipping coffee and observing the high jinks and taking in the sheer beauty of the winter wonderland. Nearby evergreens had turned white and snowflakes continued to fall. Patches of deep blue sky were visible high above the clouds.

"Snow is far out," observed Kathy.

"Not when you have to drive in it," replied Joe.

"Especially with no tire chains, Joe," said Lance," Have you ever considered how it would be for

us if your car went into a ditch and flipped over,
being a convertible and all."

"No. Why worry about things that might
happen?"

"I wonder if your car will even start, Joe. It was
below freezing last night and that can crack your engine
block."

"Thank you, Mr. Sunshine."

They carefully descended the stairs and
maneuvered slowly to the driveway, holding their arms
out for balance. Joe slid into the car and gripped the
driver's door handle with his thin black gloves, but it
wouldn't budge. It was frozen. The door probably was
too, figured Joe. His feet slipped beneath him.

Lance tried the passenger door with similar
results, "Geez, Joe. I think the door handles are frozen."

"No shit, Sherlock. Obviously, I can't get in
either. If I could, then I would be inside the car, not
standing out here and having a moronic conversation
with you."

"Why are always so sarcastic, Joe? Can't you
see how it drives people away from you?"

"Who cares where I drive everybody? I'm sick
and tired of people continually pointing out the obvious
to me. Like'Hey Joe, it's been snowing.' Duh, okay."

A small solitary figure approached them from
the lodge. He struggled under the weight on an
oversized blue down jacket and had a noticeable limp.
As he got closer, his tiny eyes were visible through the
black ski-mask that covered the rest of his face. He
wore green rubber boots that came up to his knees.

"What's the problem, Guy?" asked Joe,
increasingly angry at everything, "Did the station come
up short a quarter last night?"

Guy ignored Joe and stopped in front of the

361

drivers door and sprayed some liquid into the lock,"Give me your keys," squeaked Guy.

Joe reluctantly handed them over. Guy sprayed more of the fluid on the key and then he inserted it into the door lock. It turned freely and the lock-rod popped up. Guy pulled on the door but it wouldn't budge.

Joe stepped forward, "Step aside, junior. Let a real man try." He pulled on the door handle to no avail. Guy and Lance joined him, and the three of them finally got the door to creak open. Snow that had piled on the roof dropped all over the front seat, "Shit," muttered Joe.

Joe put his key in the ignition and got a light buzzing noise. He tried it three more times with the same result.

"The battery is dead," announced Guy.

Joe got out and stomped around, shouting, "This is exactly what I'm complaining about! I know the battery is dead. I worked in a gas station for two years!"

"Sorry." muttered Guy, looking down.

Joe opened the hood, "Got anything you can jump my car with? Sorry about my temper tantrum. You didn't deserve that. It's just that everything has been turning bad on me lately."

"I know how that is. One time I went to make my baloney sandwich and I noticed that it was green."

"What did you do?"

"I made a special sandwich and gave it to Mr. Singh. He thanked me," said Guy, stuttering and then laughing.

"Great story," remarked Joe, "You got a truck handy or not?"

"Look," said Lance.

Clint Mapes was heading their way in his black Ford 4x4 that was chained up, moving slow but under control. Sitting next to him, bouncing up and down was Slim.

Joe lighted a cigarette, took one puff, decided it tasted like shit and threw it down in the snow where it sizzled and went out.

Kathy joined them at the front of the car, "Is something wrong?" she asked innocently.

"No Kathy. We enjoy standing around in freezing snowy weather with the hood open, bonding with the frozen engine."

"Stop insulting and mocking me, Joe."

"Shouldn't you be inside Kathy? Staring at the walls or entertaining the train engineers and Marlboro Men?"

Lance stepped between them. "And what the bloody hell is that supposed to mean?"

"Just what I said, Lance. She smells bad."

"Ever since I offered Kathy a place to stay while she got her act together, you've been acting like a complete jerk to both of us. We're sick of your boorish, rude behavior. Why do you think we were so eager to join The People's Commune? To get away from you and your corrosive personality, *friend.*"

Joe glowered at them, willing them to go away and get out of his life.

Lance put his arm around Kathy's shoulders and walked her back inside the cabin. Joe wondered how long before the bed springs would be tested again. He chuckled, thinking about how close they were to finally crashing the headboard through the wall.

Clint drove up next to Joe's open hood. He got out, "Howdy, son." He stuck out a large hand, "Clint Mapes. I've seen you around."

"Joe Bailey. Yeah, I see you guys up at your table all the time."

Joe felt someone tugging at his coat. He turned around and there was Slim, who wasn't looking so hot today. He coughed into his hand and then offered it to Joe, "Slim Perkins."

"So you need a jump, huh Joe?" asked Clint, bending over to look closer at the big block.

"Why you wanna do that, Joe?" asked Slim, darting next to Clint and standing behind the right front fender, "You ain't going nowhere, boy, even if we get yore engine running. Don't you know about tire chains, kid?"

"Yeah. Hey. I'm a poor starving college student. I can't afford them."

"No matter. We'll jump you. It's a good idea to fire it up and let it warm up a bit. Keeps the vital fluids in your motor circulated," revealed Clint.

Clint retrieved his heavy duty jumper cables from his truck bed. He put his black ground on first, then his red to the positive. Joe nodded, connected his red and then completed the circuit when he put on the ground. Slim was behind the wheel, and he gunned the big Ford truck motor for a minute until he nodded his head at Clint.

"Go ahead, son," said Clint, "Try it now."

The husky 390 turned slowly at first and then roared to life, white smoke belching out of the exhaust, dirty water blasting black holes in the snow.

Joe and Clint unhooked their cable ends, "Thanks a lot, guys," said Joe cautiously.

Clint put his flat hand up to his forehead and stared at the sky above the train yard. He turned back to Joe, "How's old Bud doing?"

"You mean my dad, Bud?"

"Yup."

"How do you know him?"

"I just do. Is he okay or not?"

"Yeah. He's great. Good old Bud." Joe knew he sounded sarcastic but he couldn't hide the bitterness that flowed out of him.

"See ya around, kiddo," said Clint, tipping his white cowboy hat and revealing that he was bald.

"Don't worry, Joe," yelled Clint like he could read his mind," Many guys are bald by thirty. Women dig it. Says it makes you look sexy, like Yul Bryner."

Joe waved goodbye, yelled thanks and couldn't wait for them to leave. So Clint knew his dad, huh? How was that possible? Did his father's influence really extend this far, hundreds of miles from the Bay Area, just like he'd boasted?"

After letting the Ford run for ten minutes just like Clint said, Joe shut it off. This time he left the doors unlocked. There was nothing inside worth stealing.

Joe slipped and over to the lodge and bought a S.F. Chronicle. He needed some connection to his home. He missed the Bay Area and his life that had been going okay before this disaster called Keddie. He went inside, sat at the counter and drank a cup of coffee and devoured a glazed donut. He loved pastries. Some new tall kid manned the grill. There was no sign of Jesse, Carlene or any of the Marlboro Men.

Joe sensed the change the moment he entered the cabin. Something felt wrong. He entered their bedroom and stopped. All of Lance and Kathy's possessions were gone. A piece of binder paper sat on his bed. He picked it up and read the few words written in ballpoint pen, "Have joined commune for good. Lance."

Joe crumpled up the piece of paper and threw it

against the far wall, "Good!" He realized that now he would finally have the room to himself. No more bedsprings squeaking, no more hiding out in the restaurant, no more of Kathy's repulsive odor.

Joe spent the next couple of days holed up in the cabin, writing a long story in his journal. He wondered where Jesse was. One morning when he went in for breakfast, he saw Carlene working and asked her where Jesse had gone. She revealed that he had borrowed his sister's car to go to Sacramento on some pressing 'business.' Joe hoped that the pressing business had to do with Gary Hess. Joe was still reluctant to travel to Quincy, knowing that maniac Hess was somewhere out there, gunning for him.

When Carlene walked around with her coffee pot and expressionless face, Joe didn't even bother checking out her ass anymore. He was finally over his infatuation with her, and felt as though it was perfectly fine for her to hook up with Jesse. He'd give it two weeks, maximum, before she was available again.

Joe decided to hit the road for the Bay Area and his reserve meeting before the next blizzard hit. He looked in the mirror at his longer hair and felt good about letting it grow out. He made sure his shorthair wig was still in the paper bag in the trunk. When he lifted up the spare tire, he saw Lance's drug bag was gone. Excellent, he thought. He was through with all the pills, and intended to stick with booze, weed and cigarettes from now on. Heading out of Keddie early on Friday morning, he felt a rare sense of peace and calm, unburdened by acidheads or ex felons at last.

Joe parked in front of the family home on Santa Fe Ave. at mid afternoon. His dad's black and white

Ford pickup sat in the driveway, loaded with front room furniture, boxes and miscellaneous items. Bud slung a rope over the load and tossed it to Joe's brother in law, Vern.

Joe approached them cautiously, not knowing what was going on, "What's happening?" he asked.

Vern looped the rope under a hook and tossed the remainder back over to Bud, who was working with a cigarette in his mouth. "What in the hell does it look like we're doing? Plowing up a field of cow shit?"

"Huh?"

"About goddamned time you got here, boy. Most of the hard work is already done. This is our last big load."

"Load?"

"Yeah genius. We're moving into our new house out in Pinole. Don't you remember?"

"What new house?"

Bud flicked his butt over the fence into their neighbor's yard, "The one we just had built, dumb shit. Didn't your mother write you a note when she sent you our last free ride food check?"

"No, of course not. Nobody tells me anything. What's new?"

Joe walked past his grumbling dad and Vern and up onto the cement porch and into the kitchen. Alice was cleaning out the refrigerator, stacking perishable food in their camp cooler.

"Hi mom."

"Thanks for showing up to help, now that all the work is mostly done. Vern has been here helping your dad all day, and he's not even a blood relative."

"Well excuse me. How was I supposed to know we were moving? Osmosis?"

"Don't use profanity on me, Joe. I'll tell your

father. Also, what's with this 'we' stuff. You moved out, remember? We don't have a room for you anymore. The third bedroom is small, so I'm going to make it my sewing room."

Marvin entered the kitchen making frog noises, his glasses askew. He greeted his brother with a belch voice, "Hello Joe. Waddya know, Joe?"

He walked near Joe clutching his prized Radio Shack short band radio, bumped into him on purpose and then headed out the back door.

"See what you've done to him, Joe. Now he's getting weird, just like you did, only years sooner."

"No ma. You got in all wrong. You and dad messed him up, not me."

Alice ignored her eldest son and packed Bud's buttermilk and tins of sardines.

Joe walked down the short hallway, probably for the last time, and entered his empty room. He felt sick to his stomach. He sat down on the tiled floor and leaned against the Knotty Pine paneling that went halfway up the wall. He slowly surveyed his childhood domain, snapping a mental picture of every wall, every window, and every corner.

Marvin joined him. He smelled bad like he always did. Worse even than Kathy. He continued to talk in his frog voice, "Dad wants to know if you're going to hide out in here all day or drive to the new house and help unload. Can I ride with you?"

"Only if you change your shorts and promise not to fart in my car."

"Yeah, sure, except all my clothes are packed. You'll just have to drive with the windows down."

"How far away is the new house?"

"Half an hour."

Joe stopped at the small turnout at the top of Yrbea Buena Island. He got out, retrieving his short hair wig. He hadn't bothered trying it on since his hair had grown out. The bag was wet. He pulled out his wig and it smelled like 30 weight Pennzoil and was dripping. He twisted it like a chamois, and oil oozed through his fingers. He turned it around and around, not sure what was supposed to be the front.

He carefully placed the wet wig over his own hair and tried to snug it down. It resisted and when he added his hat, the whole stack rocked back and forth precariously and made him appear to be a seven foot tall cone head. Dark liquid continued to leak from the soaked wig, leaving little trails of 30 weight oil down his face and neck.

Then he looked at his shoes that he had been putting Johnson's floor wax on for several months. Sometime during the preceding month, the finish on the shoes took over went bad and now there dozens of cracks. It was too late for him to go get his other pair of shoes, that were marginally better. Now he was royally screwed.

Joe got inside his car but couldn't get a full look at himself in the rear view mirror. He suspected that things were not going to go well for him at inspection.

Joe drove down the windy hill and stopped at the guard shack in front of the base. As usual, two U.S. Marines manned the station. He casually handed his altered I.D. to one of the guards, who looked at his picture, and then up at Joe. He burst out laughing, "Nice hair, swabbie."

At inspection, Captain Harvey stopped in front of Joe, who was trying to hide out in the back row, hoping that his line would be skipped as they sometimes did when short on time. The Captain looked him up and down, frowned and knocked Joe's hat and wig flying. It landed on the parade grown looking like an oil soaked road kill of unknown origin.

He screamed at Joe, told him he was a disgrace to his uniform, God and his country, adding in himself at the end. He ordered Joe to go get a haircut, and report back to his office no later than noon. He also screamed at him regarding his cracked shoes. He would most likely be given a 'Captains' Mast' and dealt some sort of punishment.

After a quick haircut at Vince's on Solano Avenue, Joe shoved the useless smelly wig into a Salvation Army donation box with a tag indicating that it had been donated by Gary Hess from Quincy, California.

On the way back, out of habit, Joe drove past Alex Chance's family home on Ventura Avenue. He was pleasantly surprised when he saw his old friend out front, playing Frisbee with his older brother, Horse.

Joe pulled over and had a quick reunion with his pal. When Joe found that Alex was staying for over two weeks, he impulsively invited him to return to Feather River for a couple of days of partying. Joe promised to bring him back on Wednesday, when he had to come back anyway for a dental appointment that had been made six months ago. Joe told Alex he would pick him up around five thirty on Sunday evening.

Upon returning to the base with a crew cut, Joe trudged up to Captain Harvey's office, ready to be dealt another ass chewing and a punishment. He hoped they weren't going to threaten to send him to Vietnam again. He wasn't sure if he would go if ordered.

When he entered the office, Captain Harvey's

assistant, Lt. Downs, told Joe that the Captain had been called away on emergency business. Lt Downs inspected Joe, told him to report for duty, and that a Captain's Mast for him would be scheduled for the next months meeting. Joe knew it was only a temporary reprieve, and now, just one more thing to worry about.

TRAGICAL MYSTERY TOUR

CHAPTER TWENTY-ONE

Joe enjoyed his ride back to Keddie with Alex, who entertained Joe with hairy stories of his ongoing Army training. Alex was also quite naturally apprehensive about flying helicopters in Vietnam, but overall was nonchalant about the possibility of him dying, "They say only the good die young. I'm not gonna get killed, Joe. Nothing bad ever happens to me. You know that."

Joe revealed that he and Lance once speculated on whether Alex would fly a combat mission on acid. Alex shook his head no. Then Joe got Alex laughing when he repeated the Safeway shopping cart race story that had nearly gotten he and Lance hurt or killed.

Alex laughed louder and then told more funny stories that he had shared before. It was okay, thought Joe. He pretended that it was the first time he'd been told the stories, just to make his friend feel good. He made sure to laugh in all the right places.

Joe summarized his touchy situation with the village idiot, Gary Hess, and instructed Alex to identify himself as Gary as much as possible during his short visit. He also told him a bit about his new ex con friend, Jesse Ray Barnes. He made sure that Alex knew Jesse was the ex president of The Skull Diggers and then alluded to how he and Jesse had gone to Sacramento to party with his bros. He never bothered telling Alex that he hadn't gotten out of the car at their scary looking clubhouse.

Their drive time went fast, and Joe pulled up to the cabin in a good mood. He and Alex dumped off their few things, and then Joe let Alex drive them into Quincy so he could get a break. The roads were clear and the sun was shining, but it was still chilly. Joe and Alex intended to buy a keg of beer just for themselves. Then, they would return to the cabin, drink, smoke cigarettes and weed and party. Joe would play records and they would visit with each other, shouting back and forth above the music. Neither one of them seemed concerned about not having any food or snacks.

Things in town went from casual to bad real quick. Joe told Alex to drop him off in front of Brady's Liquor Store and then to circle around the block since there were no close by parking spots.

It took Joe ten minutes to fill out the paperwork for the beer, to pay for it and leave a deposit of twenty dollars. One of the workers wheeled the huge keg of draft beer out onto the sidewalk on a hand truck and dumped it off near the curb.

"Thanks," said the man. walking back inside.

Joe stood there for ten minutes, wondering why Alex never appeared. He left the keg where it was and jogged down to the far end of the block.

Alex had rear ended a 1965 Pontiac Catalina. Joe saw Alex talking to the other driver, who was a well dressed man who appeared to be in his mid forties. Joe ran towards the wreck.

Joe recognized the man as Alan Morgan, who taught history in a converted horse stable at the college.

Alex observed Joe approaching, "There he is, sir. The legal owner of the car. I'm sure he has car insurance, being Bud's kid and all."

"What happened?" asked Joe. The front grill on his car was pushed in, and there was a large puddle of antifreeze forming underneath the radiator that was belching out white steam.

"It should be obvious, uh....."

"Joe. Joe Bailey, sir."

They shook hands, and Mr. Morgan continued, "Your Army buddy here, Gary Hess, was checking out a hippie chicks ass and plowed right into me. We're both fine, thank goodness. The only damage to my car is my left taillight lens. I'm afraid your car got the worst of it."

Mr. Morgan used a corner pay phone to call the Pontiac Dealer about the lens he needed. He returned shortly.

"They have the lens in stock and it's sixty five dollars. If you'll just pay me for the part, I can install it myself. It's probably only got three screws holding it on."

Alex handed over thirty eight dollars to Mr. Morgan and signed a hand written promissory note for the balance in the name of Gary Hess.

Joe took a chance, poured in a gallon of coolant that he kept in the trunk, and quickly drove two blocks to the Quincy Radiator Shop before all the coolant leaked out and he damaged the engine again. This time, if he called his dad asking for big money for another motor repair, he would probably be lucky to get sent a bus ticket home.

The mechanic on duty came out, checked the damage and quoted Joe $75 to pull the radiator out, repair it, and reinstall it. Plus, two gallons of anti-freeze. Joe had no choice but to okay the work, not knowing where he was going to come up with the money.

Joe and Alex walked back to Brady's Liquors. Remarkably, their keg was still sitting on the sidewalk, unmolested.

"Well," said Joe as they stood out in the street with their thumbs out, hoping a pickup truck would stop for them,"I've got twelve bucks left on me and another twenty back at the cabin. I get another twenty back when we return the keg, so that makes a total of $52, which means we're short at least thirty three dollars. Any ideas?"

"No. What about you?"

"Well, I've got my parent's Master Card, but I asked the dude at the radiator shop and they only take cash or checks."

"Shit," remarked Alex as traffic continued by them with no one stopping, "What about the money owed to Mr. Morgan by Gary Hess?"

"Gary's name is on the promissory note. Let him deal with it."

Alex laughed, "You really got it in for this Gary guy, don't you, Joe."

"What would you do? He's already tried to kill Lance and I once. I hope Jesse hurries up with this grand plan of his. I know it somehow involves me and Carlene, plus I think some of his Skull Digger buddies."

"Real live Skull Digger's here, in Quincy?" said Alex, "Look, Joe, we'll figure out something to get the money. In the meantime, we got a keg of beer that's gonna get warm and go flat if we don't get a ride soon."

After a fruitless hour with no one even slowing down, Joe ran over to the hardware store. He came back with a large piece of cardboard with a message.

"Free beer!" said Alex, reading Joe'shandiwork, "That ought to do it, bro."

Five minute later, Malcom's Commune bus creaked to a halt right in front of them.

"Check it out," said Alex, approaching the wildly painted International and running his hand across the right front fender, "Very cool," he pronounced.

The bus door swung open, and the driver, a bald young man wearing a white robe with a blue sash leaned out, "My name is Michael, and I love you."

"What?' said Alex, jumping back.

Malcom himself got off, greeted Joe like they were old buddies, met Alex, and then had some of his stronger men help them load the keg onto the rear porch of the bus. It had been added on to carry luggage when on a long road trip.

Upon boarding, Alex was instantly mesmerized by the odd bus and it's strange riders. The interior, as always, smelled heavily of Patchouli oil, weed, and assorted husky body and sexual smells.

"Geez," said Alex, "This bus is way cool, and you know these people?"

"Sort of. I call it The Tragical Mystery Tour. You know, Lance and Kathy might be onboard in the back somewhere."

"Lance? Man, I'd love to see him. I don't know Kathy."

"You don't want to know her."

"Sit down, boys," said Malcom, pointing to two empty seats right behind the driver.

Michael moved a lever, the door folded inward and shut. He spent a minute grinding gears to get it into first before finally succeeding and the old bus lurched forward.

"Where to?" asked Malcom. "To share your beer?"

"I thought you people didn't drink."

"Some of us don't. I'm okay with the younger members letting off a bit off steam now and then. I recognize that they are young, and if I forbid them to drink. they'll sneak around behind my back and do it anyway. It is daily, or even weekly use that must be avoided."

"Let's go back to my cabin in Keddie," suggested Joe, "There's plenty of room to park the bus, and we can party right there. I've got a stereo and quite a few records."

"Okay, sounds good. Michael, please drive us to Keddie.."

Michael raised his right arm signaling okay, and then continued to experience difficulty shifting gears.

"Ruth," said Malcom to his wife who sat next to him in the right front seat, "You remember Joe I'm sure. And this is…..?"

"Gary Hess. I'm on leave from the Army, then I'm going to flight school so I can fly choppers in Vietnam."

Ruth turned towards Alex, "May God have mercy on your soul, Gary Hess. We will add your name to our prayer list, and you shall feel God's warmth and safety, and you shall return unharmed."

"I sure hope so," said Alex.

Michael managed to get the bus up to forty five miles an hour when they were going down a steep incline. The front wheels wobbled, and it felt to Joe like one of the rear tires was near flat. The engine screamed, obviously over revving, but Michael was unable to up shift into third gear, "Hang on everyone," he shouted. Joe watched as Michael frantically pumped the brakes, with the peddle going to the floor.

Malcom and Ruth didn't seem too concerned.

Joe turned around and saw only languorous smiles on the faces of the Commune Members who were visible. Their essence was one of unconditional love for all living things, and full acceptance of all events.

Joe spoke to Malcom, having to raise his voice to be heard over the racket of the engine and transmission, "Are Lance and Kathy onboard?"

"No," shouted back Malcom, who left his seat and bent forward in front of Joe and Alex and spoke in a softer voice, "I'm afraid I have some bad news regarding your friend, Lance."

"What's that?" asked Joe. Malcom was acting as though Lance were dead or something.

"Lance suffered a complete mental breakdown. Too much school pressure we think. We sent him to our Zen Ranch at Lake Tahoe to recover. He should be fine, but these sort of matters take time. Don't worry. He will receive the best of care."

"What about Kathy?"

"We have no idea where she is. She disappeared the day after we sent poor Brother Lance away to a well deserved rest."

"No big loss," laughed Joe.

Michael parked the bus in front of Joe's cabin, effectively blocking off three driveways. Two dozen members filed solemnly off, maintaining their advanced mystical auras. Joe and Alex left next, followed closely by Malcom and Ruth. Michael was busy putting wooden blocks in front of the tires, since the parking brake was not working.

"My brothers and sisters," said Malcom in his best, hypnotizing voice, "Gather around please. I have a pleasant announcement."

Malcom put his arm over over Joe's shoulder,

"Our good friend, Joe Bailey, has graciously agreed to allow us to have a celebration of life here at his cabin. There is free beer on the back of the bus.

"And," said Malcom, moving over to where he could put his arm around Alex's shoulders, "This is his good friend, Gary Hess, who is going to Vietnam soon. We will pray for his safe return. We love you Joe and Gary. That is all. Please enjoy yourselves everyone, as we have to leave in two hours. We have some meditation and chanting lessons set for six at an independent church in Quincy."

Malcom clapped his hands three times, which seemed to awaken the members from their collective stupor. They started talking and laughing. Joe and Alex were escorted to the front of the beer line by Malcom. He directed Michael, who was manning the beer dispenser, to fix the boys up. They were both given large paper cups full of cold, frothy, draft beer.

He and Alex took long drinks, and then Joe handed his cup to Alex, "Here. Hold this for me while I put on some tunes."

Joe dashed into the cabin, slid the front window wide open, put on *Jumping Jack Flash* live, and cranked it up to maximum volume.

Couples and single members began dancing in the front yard. Joe came out and sat in a sea shell chair. Alex joined him. Joe had already decided that if Malcom offered him mescaline, or anything else for that matter, he would politely decline. He would advise Alex to do the same. Joe had grown weary of being out of it and non functional.

Joe looked up at the top of the road, and once again, ten Marlboro Men stood in a row, smoking their cigarettes in perfect synchronization. A growing crowd of spectators stood near them, all staring down at the wild hippie party. Who was going to show up next, wondered Joe? Jack Kerouac, Neal Cassidy, William Burroughs, Big Dan Mcgrew, the real Gary Hess?

Alex observed the crowd, "Don't they have TV around here to amused themselves?"

"Not really."

"Just ignore them. They want to join the party too, but they're afraid," observed Alex.

"Well, we do have a lot of beer to share," said Joe.

"Plus," said Alex,"We were lucky to get a ride back here."

A slim waif of a girl wandered out of the cabin. Joe speculated that she might have been using the bathroom.

Alex greeted her like he was in a raunchy pickup bar in Cleveland, "Say gorgeous. I love your eyes. What color are they? Green?"

She stopped and looked right through Alex, "Are you in the Army?"

"Yep," he said proudly, thrusting out his chest. "I'm already a Sergeant, and I'm going to Vietnam to fight soon."

"So, you're going to be a mother raper and baby killer."

"What?" exclaimed Alex.

The girl put her hands on her hips and screwed up her face in a show of utter and complete disdain, "You're going to Asia to murder. You're going to have blood on your hands. You poor fool."

Alex stood up, dropped his cigarette at his feet and ground it out,"Who the hell brainwashed you, little missy? The liberal commies who have infiltrated our public school system, the same bastards who insist on fluoridating our drinking water? I bet you eat nothing but rabbit food and screw a different draft dodger coward every night."

The girl smiled weakly, "I realize with your base level of consciousness, my revelation to you is coming as quite a shock. Don't you get it? You're being used by the capitalist greed mongers who are also raping our planet, mother earth. Don't go. Don't be a dupe and a pawn and possibly wind up dead or paralyzed."

Alex turned his back on her, "I don't need shit like this, Joe. I'm going over to the restaurant. You can join me, or I'll come back when I see the bus leave."

The Marlboro Men observed Alex stalking out of the yard and up towards them.

"That shore is a right funny looking paint job on that bus," remarked Slim, who had shrunk more overnight, "Looks to me like a bunch of retards painted it."

He launched into a severe coughing fit.

"Or a collection of misfits on drugs," added Clint, "Led by that pied piper like dude, Malcom. I bet in the old west he would have been hawking snake oil cures at the state fair.

"I heard The Retrievers successfully picked up Lance Potter at the ranch he was being held hostage at," confided Clint to the others, who gathered in a circle similar to a football huddle, their right arm resting on their brother's shoulders, "They're headed this way to finish their job."

"About dammed time," said Charley Bowen, spitting chaw on the pavement.

"Let's go back into restaurant and talk to that new blonde friend of Joe's,." suggested Clint.

Joe went back inside to change records. He was thinking about playing Ten Years After. Everyone liked their music.

Joe came face to face with Malcom, "Joe. Do you remember Sunshine, from our dinner?"

"Yeah."

Joe hadn't even thought about Sunshine. Was she here he wondered?

"She's in her personal space on the bus. She'd like to see you."

"Cool," said Joe, surprised and pleased.

"Dinner will be served in an hour, Joe, then we must be on our way," said Malcom,"What happened to your Army friend, Gary?"

"He got tired and went over to the lodge to drink some coffee. He feels like being by himself right now."

"I understand completely," said Malcom, "Go now. Sunshine is waiting."

Alex sat by himself at the restaurant counter. He was eating a bowl of chili and reading a two day old newspaper. He still had a little money left. He wasn't about to walk around destitute. It wasn't his fault that asshole Mr. Morgan had suddenly slammed on his brakes when his attention was temporarily diverted. He'd been checking out a cute chicks buns as she strode up the street.

Clint Mapes joined him, straddling the stool to his right, smoking a Marlboro.

"Pretty good chili, huh?" asked Clint, smiling, smoke escaping from his mouth and nose at the same time.

Alex looked up, "Yeah. Better then store bought, that's for sure." He looked back down at his paper.

"So. You're in the Army, right? I mean, you're wearing a uniform."

"Yep."

Clint offered Alex his gigantic hand, "Clint Mapes. Pleased to meet you."

Alex shook his hand, "Gary Hess."

"What?" responded Clint. "How can there be two of you?"

"Huh? I'm nothing special, mister. Just one guy. Me."

"Forgive me, Gary. It's just that it's not a common name, and we have a local here who goes by the same name."

"That so," replied Alex, crumbling some crackers on top of the chili. He had already eaten all the shredded cheese that gave the chili its special flavor.

"I'm not trying to crowd you," continued Clint, "But me and my buddies are veterans."

Alex looked towards the window and saw two full tables of older men in various stages of decay, all wearing white fluorescent Cowboy hats. A few of them gave him head nods.

"That's cool," said Alex.

"Would you like to come over to our table and visit some? Me and the boys would be mighty pleased to talk to a patriotic young man like yourself. So many young people today are way off course, taking drugs and looking for an easy way out."

"Okay, sure," said Alex, picking up his chili and coffee and following Clint over to the tables where he was introduced to nine more men. There was no way he was going to remember their names except for Slim, who continued hacking into his handkerchief, occasionally lowering it to take another puff or drink another gulp.

Gary Hess sat behind the wheel of his Willys at the bottom of the hill. He was watching the wild hippie party. They couldn't see him. He caressed his rifle stock and held it up, looking through the scope at a tall, gyrating dancer. Gary loved tracking big game, lining up his shot, focusing on the crosshairs. Satisfied that he had a solid shot, Gary squeezed the trigger and his gun made a snapping noise. He knew it was bad for the firing pin to dry fire his rifle, so he didn't do it often. Sometimes, like right now, he dreamed about putting a real bullet into the chest of some hippie loser that no one would miss.

Gary was primarily there to track Joe Bailey's movements while he considered whether it would be a good idea to plug him. Obviously, he would be one of the prime suspects, and he was in enough trouble already, so he carefully put his deer rifle back on the rear window gun rack. Besides, he thought, Joe had entered the bus over half an hour ago and he had not yet come out.

Joe was currently Gary's number one target. That dorky Lance character had vanished, and Gary didn't think it would be such a hot idea to assassinate Jesse. The Skull Diggers probably wouldn't appreciate it.

Oh well, thought Gary. Something was going to happen soon. He could feel it in his bones.

THE HEIST

CHAPTER TWENTY-TWO

An hour later, Joe joined Alex at the counter of the now empty restaurant.

"That was a trip, Joe."

"What?"

"Those freaking Marlboro Men. You should be leery of them. I'm certain that a few of them, especially that big guy, Clint Mapes, have mental problems. It's like they saw too much combat."

"You actually visited with them?'

"Yeah. It was okay, I guess. The last of them just left. How about the bus?"

"It's gone. It was awesome, Alex."

"What? Partying with weirdoes?"

"No. Sex."

"Sex? With who?'

Joe sighed, "A chick on the bus named Sunshine. I met her once before."

Alex smiled widely and slapped Joe on the back, "Good job. Now you're a real man."

Carlene shuffled over with her coffee pot and filled both of their cups. She had nothing to say, as usual thought Joe. He noticed her eyes were puffy and red, like she had been crying recently.

As soon as she headed back into the kitchen, Joe spoke,"What's wrong with her?" Did Bobby Carbo suddenly show up?"

"I think she and Jesse just had a fight."

"I didn't know he was even back in town."

"I've never met the guy, but I'm pretty sure from your description that he was not among the ten Marlboro Men I met."

"I bet the fight was Carlene's fault," said Joe.

Back at the cabin, Joe and Alex started in on the hard stuff. Segrams Seven with Coke over the rocks. Joe put on Steppenwolf, music they could rock out to.

Suddenly, Jesse was standing in the front room, giving them hard looks.

"Jesse," said a surprised Joe, "How did you get in?"

"The back door."

"Jesse, this is my good friend, Alex Chance. We grew up together."

"Yeah," said Jesse, checking the front door lock, "You might die together too."

"What do you mean?" asked Joe. Alex walked over and pulled the needle off the record. Talk was getting serious.

"What I mean is, Gary Hess is stalking you with a deer rifle, slick. If he had come through the back door instead of me, you'd both be full of holes by now."

"What should we do?" asked Joe. Alex sat down on the couch.

"The asshole needs to go down. Now I think we have enough pieces to make my plan work."

"What is it?" asked Joe. Alex looked up hopefully.

"Shut up and listen. You can't ever learn nothin Joe, not while you're always yakking."

"Sorry."

"Carlene," said Jesse, "Come on in."

She appeared from the kitchen, dabbing at her eyes with a Kleenex, "What do you want me to do, Jesse?"

Joe Edgar Bailey reported for his evening shift at the Flying A station. He had Alex with him. Joe relieved some local freak named Max. As per procedure, they counted the till together and agreed that it totaled a hundred twenty eight dollars and 66 cents.

After writing the figures in the ledger and them both initialing it, Max volunteered that he was headed over to visit Maureen, who he'd heard still wasn't back to normal and was really struggling with depression.

Joe turned to the pot belly stove and peered inside the coffee pot. His hands shook slightly as he poured himself a cup.

"Nervous, Joe?" questioned Alex.

"Well yeah. Aren't you? We're taking a gigantic risk here."

"Geez, Joe. Jesse had us practice our parts and stories like what, ten times? And then he separated us and grilled us apart, just like he predicts the cops will do to us. What could possibly go wrong?" Alex was wearing that Mad Magazine 'What, me worry?' smile.

"A lot of things. We've got a lot to remember."

"What choice do we have? According to Jesse, who should know, being an ex con and biker and all, we need to strike first. If not, Gary is going to take a shot at us. Hell, he could be across the street hiding in a tree, drawing a bead on you right now."

Joe moved to the entrance of the shop that wasn't visible from the street, "Okay," he said, "Let's do this thing."

"All right then," said Alex. He exchanged high

fives with Joe. Alex's eyes narrowed and he spoke seriously, "Remember, Joe. Answer the cop's questions, but don't volunteer any additional information. A single slip up could get us arrested."

"Right," said Joe, adjusting his Coast Guard watch cap that always made his head itch. He paused and looked back at his old friend who had one more thing to say, "When they accuse us, which they will, act pissed off. After all, we've just been robbed at gun point and they got a lot of nerve accusing us. After all, we're highly trained Military personnel, and we don't scare easy. "

Joe burst out of the gas station office, ran across the empty highway and started jogging to Keddie. He blew out great gasps of frigid air as he sweated, his lungs almost frozen. He kept telling himself to maintain a steady pace during the mile long run. He listened to his own shoes slamming down on the snowy pavement. There were no other sounds, just an icy stillness, the calm before the storm.

Every running step brought Joe closer to the point of no return. He would soon cross the line, and there would be no chance of turning back. He grew pensive as he struggled up the big hill right before Keddie. He was heavy hearted with the inevitably of it all. Whatever happened was already predetermined. He was just following Jesse's script.

It was up to Joe to light the fuse that would set off the huge shit bomb that would blow up Gary Hesse's life. He just hoped that he and Alex wouldn't become causalities when the crap hit the fan in just a few minutes.

He slowed to a fast walk for his last hundred feet to the lodge. His breath came in ragged gasps. This was his last chance to turn back and call the whole thing off.

The lights of the restaurant blazed in the dark. He caught a glimpse of Cheryl heading to a table with a tray holding waters.

Too late now, thought Joe as he trudged up the lodge steps. He knew the Singh's worked late, and someone would be in the office. He met Debbie Glenn in the entranceway, "What's wrong, Joe. You're all white, like you've just seen a ghost."

"We just got robbed at the gas station!" shouted Joe.

Joe's stomach dumped upside down, and he bent over and clutched his knees and tried to catch his breath and look traumatized at the same time. He had started the live play, with all the actors in place. He stood back up straight, determined.

He exploded into the office, "We just got robbed!"

Joe's sudden panicked appearance startled Mr. Singh and Guy.

"What is going on Joe Bailey?" asked Mr. Singh in the sing song voice of his native India.

"It just happened. I didn't have a car, so I had to run all the way!"

"I said what happened, young man? Calm down and give me the facts."

Joe collapsed onto one of the overstuffed chairs, "I was working and had my friend Alex with me. Some short fat guy wearing a full ski mask burst into the station office with a gun and took all the money."

"Guy!" shouted Mr. Singh, "Call the Sheriff's office at once. Tell them the gas station just suffered an armed robbery."

As Guy dialed the Sheriff's office, Mr. Singh

looked at Joe with concern, "Were either of you harmed?"

"No. Just scared the shit out of us. The lard ass demanded that we lay on the floor or he said he would shoot us."

Joe remembered Jesse and Alex's instructions not to add details, but he felt like he had to throw that in. He and Alex had already agreed that this would be part of both of their descriptions as to how events had gone down.

He pulled off his watch cap and twisted it in his hands and looked scared, all minor touches that Jesse suggested to make his angst appear real. Actually, thought Joe, he was scared. Not from the alleged robbery, but from his looming encounter with law enforcement and interrogation he knew was coming shortly.

Mr. Singh spoke again, "How much did they get, Joe Bailey?"

"A hundred and twenty eight bucks and some change."

"Well, that is a lot of cash. The most important thing is that no one was hurt. Money is not worth dying over. You were wise, young man."

Guy held the phone out to Joe, "Sheriff McGrew wants to talk to you."

"Hello," said Joe in a tentative voice. He still had bad memories of this bastard, the Sheriff, and his asshole detective buddy Hal, and how they had mistreated him recently.

"This is Sheriff Mcgrew. Is this Joe Bailey?"

"Yes, sir."

"How may robbers?"

"Only one short fat guy came inside. I don't know if there

was an accomplice or driver."

Damn, though Joe. He had just done it again, providing more information then asked for. Then again, maybe it would make his story more realistic, like he was sincerely interested in helping law enforcement find the scoundrel. Armed robberies in Plumas County were rare.

Joe could hear background noise coming from the other end. He listened as glasses tinkled and people shouted. He figured Dan was probably calling from the V.A.

"Did you see what sort of vehicle the assailant was driving, or what direction he headed?"

"No. He had us lay on the floor and said to wait five minutes before getting up. He implied that there was a shooter in the woods nearby, ready to plug us if we got up right away."

"You say he was armed with a pistol. Any description of the weapon?"

"Yeah. It was a gloss black snub-nosed .38 Special."

"How do you know all that?" asked Big Dan, sounding dubious.

"I'm trained with firearms. So is my buddy, who's in the Army. He said the same thing. A .38. Not a real scary looking piece, but it can kill you all the same."

"Okay. I'm getting road blocks set up thirty miles away in either direction. There should be a squad car at the station by now. I'm heading there myself. I'll want to see you at the gas station, Joe."

Joe looked scared and handed the receiver back to Guy who was sympathetic.

"I know how you feel, Joe," squeeked Guy, "I was in Reno one night with my mother and we were robbed at gunpoint by a scary looking Negro. I can still recall looking down the barrel of the gun and wondering how bad it would hurt when we got shot."

Joe nodded his head and saw Mr. Singh looking at him in an odd way. He knew, thought, Joe. They all did, except for Guy, who probably still believed in the tooth fairy.

"Guy," said Mr. Singh harshly, "Get our truck. We must go to the filling station and meet Sheriff McGrew. Joe, you ride along with us. There is room for three of us up front."

"Because I'm small," said Guy, who selected a set of keys off a nail on the wall and limped out.

"I can't believe this happened here in Keddie, Joe," said Mr. Singh, donning his heavy down jacket, ear muffs and gloves, "If we were in Reno or Cleveland, I could understand it. But up here, in the mountains? Only a crazy man would do such a thing."

Guy pulled up in front of the snow covered steps with a mid 1950's Dodge Power Wagon. It was bright yellow, the headlights blazed and the big V8 sounded powerful.

Joe got in first, scooting up next to Guy, his left leg near the floor mounted gear shift that rose over two feet into the air. Mr. Singh climbed in and slammed the door. Joe was stuck in the middle and was sweating like a pig. He could smell fear on himself.

Guy put the big Dodge in four wheel low and crept forward as the snowfall increased dramatically. He had the heater on full blast, and Joe could hardly breathe.

The truck was chained up, but they started sliding sideways as they came down the far side of the big hill towards the bridge and the swollen river and a 500 foot drop down nearly sheer cliffs.

Guy fought the wheel for control. Joe looked down and saw that he had foot long extenders on his rubber boots so he could reach the peddles. They slowly came to a stop at the bottom, and Guy turned the wheel and they crept across the bridge. Even inside the cab with the windows rolled up and the engine noise, Joe could still hear the roar of the Feather River.

"Guy," said Mr. Singh, "What time do you normally pick up the days cash at the station?"

Guy struggled to see, as heavy snowfall piled up on the windshield faster than the one speed wipers could keep it clean, "Around seven O'clock. Why?"

"Because whoever did it must have known this would be the most fortuitous time to rob the station, before the cash was reduced back to fifty bucks."

The atmosphere inside the station was tense. Multiple overhead fluorescent lights cast a harsh glow over Alex and three cops. The local law enforcement men wore bulky brown leather jackets with their logo on each shoulder. Their brown watch caps also had the Sheriff Departments patch. A lone California Highway patrolman with a dark blue coat also stood there, and he was even bigger then Dan McGrew, who was asking questions.

Everything stopped when Joe and Mr. Singh squeezed into the office. Guy, knowing there was no room for him, ducked into the shop that had icicles hanging from the ceiling and work benches. He stood there and shivered.

"Aah," said Dan, "The infamous Joe Bailey. Our paths seem to be crossing lately. Hello Mr. Singh. Sorry about what's happened here."

Joe desperately wanted this whole scene to be over. He wished he were snuggled into his bed, thinking of Sunshine, and how blissful their sex had been for him, and hopefully her too.

"I have confidence in our truck and Guy is an experienced winter driver."

Dan continued, "I've been talking to Alex here, getting his version of what happened."

"I thought it was a holdup?"

Dan clamped his hand down on Joe's shoulder and squeezed until it hurt.

"Rusty, take Mr. Bailey here out to your car and ask him the same questions I've just asked Mr. Chance."

"Okay boss. Come on Joe," said Rusty, leading him out with one hand on his elbow.

"Are the roadblocks in place?" asked Mr. Singh.

"Yeah, but we need more to go on. A short fat guy with a .38 isn't much. We need to know what he's driving. Is he alone or with friends? We don't even know if he went north or south. If he's a local and knows the back roads, we'll never find him. He could be anywhere."

Joe sat in the back seat of Rusty's cruiser. The door stayed open despite the heavy snowfall. Joe was glad of that, because the stench on the back seat was close to unbearable. It was nasty mix of vomit, blood and body odor.

Rusty sat in the front. closed his own door, leaned around and spoke to Joe through the metal screen that separated the two seats,

"Okay, Joe. Tell me what happened from the beginning, and don't leave anything out. You never know when a seemingly inconsequential detail can be important enough to lead to an arrest."

Joe hesitated for a minute while troubling

images cascaded through his mind. He wondered what it would feel like to get handcuffed again and get another ride to the downtown Sheriff's office. He imagined being charged with a crime, and using his one phone call to contact Bud. Joe wondered what his dad's reaction would be. Would he bail him out or leave him in to teach Joe a valuable life lesson?

Joe took a deep breath and repeated the story Jesse had made him practice repeatedly until it became automatic. Joe was glad for that now.

Rusty wrote down a few things and told Joe it was time to go back inside and see Big Dan. However, Dan came out first, looking for fresh tire tracks in the snow, "Crap," he said to Rusty, "It's snowed so much that its no use. Everything is covered up already."

Dan turned to Joe, "You know anything about cars, kid?"

"Like what?"

"Like maybe you heard the getaway car start up, and the starter noise or engine sounded familiar, like a Chrysler or a Ford."

"Well, I do have some gas station experience, Sheriff McGrew, and I can't swear to this, but it almost sounded like a Jeep. What do you think, Alex.?"

"Don't answer that, Chance. Joe, I'm in charge here and I ask the questions."

Dan's eyes betrayed his interest, "A Jeep, maybe. What do you think, Alex?"

"Yeah. It could have been."

Joe caught Alex's eye, and his friend gave him a confident wink, just like they were eleven years old again and chose to teach an adult a lesson.

They returned to the office and crowded in with the others. Big Dan McGrew warmed his hands over the stove, "Let me see your wallets, boys."

Jesse had also anticipated this. Alex had no money on him on purpose. Joe's wallet held a five and two ones. Big Dan grunted and handed them their billfolds back.

Alex shoved his wallet into his back pocket and appeared angry, "Are you satisfied now, Sheriff? Joe and I just survived a traumatic event where some asshole threatened to fill us full of lead, and you're practically accusing us of doing it."

"No one is accusing you of anything. Yet."

"What do mean by that, Sheriff?" asked Alex. Joe held his breath, wondering if his friend was overplaying the pissed off victim card.

Big Dan removed his hat, "Let's cut the bullshit, huh fellas? Why don't you just admit that your entire robbery story is a fabrication. Just give Mr. Singh his hundred and twenty eight bucks back and then we'll just forget the whole thing ever happened. My dinner at the club is getting cold."

Neither Joe nor Alex said anything. They clearly remembered Jesse's warning to never admit anything.

Big Dan searched their faces and sighed, "Why don't you boys wait outside while I discuss some issues with my men and Mr. Singh."

They stood in the snow, one hand thrust into a pocket, the other holding a smoke. Neither of them spoke.

A few minutes later, the cops all filed out followed by Guy, and then the lights for the whole station went out. Mr. Singh emerged, closed and locked the door and dropped the keys in his coat pocket, "Come on Guy. Take me back. Something stinks around here."

Big Dan McGrew stood in front of Joe and Alex

with his arms crossed, "You boys are free to go, for now. Don't leave town. I'll need to follow up with you tomorrow."

All the cops drove off, and Joe and Alex stood alone in the dark parking lot. Snow covered up the road, "Come on," said Joe, "Let's get some dinner at the lodge. I don't think we've eaten all day."

Alex nodded his head and they walked across the highway, holding onto their caps as a harsh wind blew through them.

Gary Hess was naked, tied to a lawn chair that was just a few feet from a roaring bonfire. He was deep in the woods, and could see his Willys parked next to six black choppers with chrome extended handlebars. His Jeep and the motorcycles were covered with a fresh dusting of white power.

Spider stood near Gary holding up a white piece of paper. Stan the Man stood behind Spider with his gigantic tattooed arms folded in front of him. They were both wearing shades, even though it was dark. The Shoveler stoked the fire, throwing on more branches and logs and using a pool cue as his poker. A fourth Skull Digger, Handsome Steve, knelt, holding a large branding iron over the flames, slowly rotating it until the entire stamping surface was glowing red.

Gary looked back and forth at his tormentors. They had swooped in and kidnapped him from the A Frame at four O'clock when he'd been taking a well deserved nap. They had hog tied and gagged him and heaved him into the back of an unmarked van driven by some creep named 'Pounder.' He had driven Gary somewhere a half hour away. Gary listened as the choppers followed behind. He was terrified, wondering what they intended to do to him. He held his breath after they stopped. Were they planning on shooting him, or maybe setting the van on fire with him trapped in the back?

Pounder had opened the back door, picked Gary up like he was a roll of carpet and heaved him out the back door, "Out of my van, rat."

So far, no one had said another word to him as they went quietly about their business.

"Hi Gary," said Spider, "I'd introduce ourselves, but we don't like rats."

"A rat?" said Gary, acting outraged, "I never ratted you guys out. I've never even seen any of you before. I'm telling you that you got the wrong guy."

Spider elevated his voice just as Shoveler Sam threw a gigantic log onto the blaze, "You calling me a liar, huh? Are you, punk?"

Sam came over, holding his shovel. He rocked back and nailed Gary in his face with his right elbow.

"Ow! Goddamit!" yelled Gary, "Why'd you do that?"

Shoveler leaned on his shovel, "I hear you been going around town claiming you beat me up."

Gary's eyes bugged out of his head. Blood flowed from his nose, "Who said that? I don't even know your name."

"Shoveler Sam," he said, spitting in Gary's face.

"This is messed up!" shouted Gary, "What's your beef with me anyway? Are you aware that my stepfather, Big Dan McGrew, is the Sheriff in Quincy?"

"Who gives a shit," snarled Spider, "We don't. Here's how it's going down, fat boy. We got information from a reliable source that you been going around your town claiming to be an associate of The Skull Diggers. Now, Gary. You know that's not true. I bet you don't even own a bike, do you?"

Gary shook his head and watched as his blood leaked down over his protruding bare stomach and onto the ground. It was beginning to get mighty hot where he was sitting. "As far as your stepfather, he should be watching out for us, not the other way around. We drove a long ways today on slick roads just to have this special time with you, Gary."

"What do you want from me?"

"I want you to shut up or I'm going to have Sam smash you in the face with his shovel."

There was near silence, just the popping of the bonfire.

"Good," said Spider, "That's more like it. I'm going to give you three options, rat."

"Like what. Choices?"

"Yeah. Exactly."

Spider put on his reading glasses and held the paper close to his eyes. He almost looked scholarly.

"Option number one is we don't give you any more options and shoot your fat head off. We'll be doing the world a favor,. and we take these things into consideration."

Ajax, a tall rangy Digger with a wicked scar running down the right side of his face pulled the slide back on a .45 pistol. Gary knew the sound well. Ajax stood behind Gary and placed the barrel of the .45 against the base of Gary's skull.

Gary Hess burst into tears, "Sweet mother of God. Don't do it. I'll do anything you say, just don't kill me."

Sweat mixed with tears on Gary's face The fire was getting incredibly hot. He remembered watching the scary guy named Shoveler digging a grave when they first arrived. The big biker had worked like a maniac and finished it in record time. That was it,

399

thought Gary. The grave was dug for him. No one would ever find his body way out here.

Spider continued in a mater of fact voice, "Option number two is quite painful and will last forever. See the branding iron?"

Gary looked over and observed Steve, smiling and holding the hug branding iron up so Gary could get a good look.

"We brand you on your lower back, right above your fat ass. It's a male 'tramp stamp,' made specially for swine like you who are headed for prison. Beefy dudes like you with man boobs and a big ass are popular, so we'll just whore you out until you get aids and die."

"What's number three?" asked Gary.

"Option number three is fairly new but has become quite a popular choice. We have a lot of biker brothers who for one reason or another need a Kidney transplant, and lord, you have no idea how long the waiting list for organs is. So, we move to the head of the line with your help."

"What do you mean?"

Spider put his glasses back on, held up the paper and a pen,"Just sign here."

"What am I signing?"

"A legal paper drawn up by our club attorney where you agree to donate one of your Kidney's out of your own free will, and you also gotta pay all your own medical expenses. I think it cost the last guy somewhere around forty thousand dollars."

Gary tried to talk, but only blubbering came out.

"And," said Spider, "You get exactly one minute to decide." He held up one hand and then dropped it, "Staring now!"

Gary gulped in a breath and looked frantically

from side to side. These guys were nuts.

"Ajax," asked Spider, "You ready?"

Ajax smirked and nodded.

"Handsome Steve?"

"Oh yeah, bro. I've got it really hot this time."

"Shoveler?"

" *Gary.* Choose option number one, and I'll have you in that grave, buried, pushing up ferns in half an hour. How's that sound?"

"Time!" yelled Spider.

"Number three!" blurted out Gary.

"Aw shit," said Shoveler. Ajax stepped back and Steve threw his iron down.

"Good solid decision making, Gary," said Spider. "We're gonna be leaving you now. We'll need your blood type from a doctor. You can figure on being operated on shortly after you go to prison. Look on the bright side. You'll lose a little weight, you obese rat.

"By the way, don't get any bright ideas about splitting town or welching on our deal. If you do, we'll find you, and we'll let Steve brand you before Ajax shoots you in your knees and elbows and then Shoveler gets to bury you alive. Plus, if you squeal us out again to the cops, we'll shoot your nuts off first before we do the rest of the stuff."

"Got it."

"Good," said Spider, pulling out a buck knife and cutting Gary's ropes, "Your keys are in the ignition. Sorry, we forgot to bring your clothes. Take care, buddy."

"No, we didn't forget," said Ajax, throwing Gary's jeans, shoes and shirt on top of the bonfire."

Gary felt something hard hit him in his right temple, and then his world went black.

Joe was chewing a bite of his succulent New York Steak when he swiveled on his stool and observed Sheriff Big Dan McGrew peering at them from outside the big window.

"Oh, shit," he said.

"What?" asked Alex.

"The Sheriff is outside, staring at us."

"So? We got a right to eat just like everyone else."

"Don't you think it looks odd, us supposedly being broke and now sitting here eating steak dinners?"

Alex took a bite of baked potato, turned, and looked, "I don't see anyone. You must be getting paranoid."

Big Dan came striding through the restaurant door, "Howdy boys. Enjoying your dinners?"

He stopped directly behind them and put a heavy gloved hand on each of their shoulders.

The boys stopped eating.

"Well guys. Sorry to interrupt your meal. It seems kind of funny though, watching you two shovel it in like you don't have a care in the world. Most robbery victims that are threatened with death don't have much appetite, and some even get the dry heaves."

"Yeah, well we're both Military," said Alex.

"Actually, the real reason I'm here is to find Jesse. You know where he is?"

"No," said Joe, "Why don't you ask someone who works here?"

Dan laughed, "I'll be in touch tomorrow, boys. You can count on it."

PURPLE SUNSETS

CHAPTER TWENTY THREE

Jesse, Joe and Alex hid behind thick foliage, a hundred feet from the local landmark, 'The Mystical Pond.' The sun peaked over the eastern horizon, warming the cool morning shadows along the Forrest floor.

Jesse sat comfortably on his haunches, chewing on a stem of grass, unable to smoke because they were in full surveillance mode. He moved his eyes slowly back and forth, from side to side. Their target could emerge from anywhere, at anytime now, except from behind them. Spider and the other Skull Diggers were camping out there with an armed sentry.

Alex stood, bent over, weary of squatting. He wore his combat fatigues that he brought long as his change of clothes. He had on a floppy bush hat and had smeared black grease paint underneath his eyes.

Joe flat out couldn't find a comfortable position. He shifted his body once again, and Jesse shot him a withering look.

Jesse aimed his binoculars to the left and spotted a contingent of Marlboro Men, about fifty klicks away. He counted four of them. They lounged in green lawn chairs, not smoking either, but downing cups of MJB coffee from a twelve gallon pot that was standing up in the back of Clint Mapes truck.

They had Military issue camaflogue netting covering the rest of the vehicle.

Jesse slowly scanned to the right and stopped, "There he is," he whispered. Joe and Alex followed his gaze. They could see him too. A short squat figure walking through the center of the tree line, cautiously glancing around him. A flock of black birds shrieked overhead, screaming as one in with their horrid bird cries, thousands of them appearing out of nowhere and disappearing just as quickly.

Gary stopped in his tracks. He wore his hunting clothes and carried a long rifle. He also had a holstered pistol hanging from a thick brown belt that had extra ammunition pouches. Gary was carrying a shovel in his other hand. He looked directly at them, as though he could see their hiding spot.

"SSShhh," whispered Jesse, "Don't move an inch. There's no way he can see us, unless one of you shifts, and then we're gonna get shot at."

Seemingly satisfied that he was unobserved, Gary headed directly for the muddy shoreline of the Mystical Pond. It looked cool, with green reeds sticking up out of the water near the edges. There were patches of algae floating on the calm and tranquil small pond. The water in the middle was clear, and it was large enough to make it worthwhile to launch a rowboat or canoe. Rowing around in the early morning sun was cathartic and good exercise. Plus, if you were an angler, you might be lucky enough to catch a wide mouthed Bass that you could fry for breakfast.

"Carlene?' said Gary in a loud voice.

There was no answer. Joe saw the glint of something bright coming from near the curved wooden bridge that spanned the pond. He wondered if it was a mirror signal of some sort.

"Carlene?" said Gary in a louder voice, bringing his hands up to his mouth to form a crude megaphone.

Gary looked around again, shook his head and then walked towards a red bandana tied to a straight branch that was sticking out of the mud. Gary ripped the branch out and heaved it behind him into some ferns. He began digging where the stick had been, quickly piling up mounds of mud. He threw the shovel down and retrieved a dirty blue bowling ball bag.

Gary unzipped the bag and looked inside. He pulled out a black revolver and a large bag of change.

There was a sudden flurry of movement as Sheriff Big Dan Mcgrew, Deputy Rusty and a third officer with a snarling German Sheppard police dog rushed forward.

Big Dan and Rusty had their pistols out, "Drop the guns, Gary!" ordered Big Dan.

Gary dropped the pistol but held onto the bag of coins.

"The rifle and your belt with the other pistol too! Now!"

Gary did as he was told, a resigned look on his face.

McGrew sprung forward, kicked the pistols towards Rusty, "Turn around," he told Gary, who complied. "Give me your arms." Big Dan snapped on chrome handcuffs. Rusty came over and gathered up the rifle and two pistols.

"Dan," said Gary, "What the hell are you doing here, and why am I being handcuffed?"

"Arresting you for armed robbery, stupid. I can't believe you would stoop to such a thing. If you needed to borrow some money, all you would have had to do was ask."

"And what would you have said?"

"No, of course."

Big Dan grabbed the change bag from Gary and

held it up, "You're going to go to jail over a lousy hundred and twenty-eight bucks? Plus, you dumb shit, your sentence will probably double because you used a pistol in the commission of your crime. Where's the rest of the cash?"

"What cash?"

Rusty held the .38 by it's short barrel and dropped it into an evidence bag.

"You gotta be shitting me! That's not my pistol. Why would I own a piece of shit like that? A woman's gun is what that is." Gary spit on the ground and struggled with his cuffed arms, "And I didn't pull off any dammed armed robbery!"

"Of yeah, sure. If that's so, why are you out here digging up the evidence? "

Rusty bent down and rubbed some mud off two gold letters on the bowling bag, "Says G. H. That's your initials, right?"

"Where were you last night between six and seven?" demanded Dan.

Gary looked up at the sky and twisted his head, "Out driving around. Late last night, I got a call from a chick I sort of know, and she said she needed my help. Asked me to come here this morning with a shovel and dig a grave for her puppy." Gary leveled his gaze on the Sheriff, "I'm telling you, Dan, straight up. This shit is not mine. Someone stole my bowling ball bag to set me up. What is it I'm supposed to have robbed anyway?"

"The Keddie Gas Station."

"What!" raged Gary, "If I was gonna rob a place, it sure wouldn't be there. I'd go where there was some real cash, like a bar or liquor store, or maybe a bank. "

"We got you, son. Now just own up to it and I'll do everything I can to help you."

"I want a lawyer," said Gary in a barely audible voice. His head hung down.

"What's the name of the girl who called you?"

Sweat ran down Gary's face and he kicked at some mud, "Her name is Carlene Romo, and she works at the lodge."

"Yeah. I've seen her." replied Dan.

"I've tried to get to know her before, but she just blew me off. Last night, when she called, she told me that she needed a real man like me in her life. Said she'd been checking me out for some time. It was gonna be like our first date."

"So, she suggested you meet her here right after dawn and to bring along a shovel on your first date?"

"It wasn't like that at all, Dan. Listen to me, please. She told me her ex boyfriend, Jesse Barnes, got pissed at her and stomped her new puppy to death. Carlene was crying, saying she wanted to bury little Joe here at The Mystical Pond, where she used to walk him. She told me to dig a small dog's grave where the red bandana was. That's all I was doing, Dan. Then I pull out my own bowling ball bag. Why would I do that? I'm telling you, this whole deal is a setup."

Dan looked at his watch and laughed, "What a dumb ass story, Gary. One Carlene Romo came in last night to the station and filed a complaint against you for rape."

"What! I've haven't even seen her for days! I've never even touched her, the bitch!"

Dan pulled out his notebook and flipped to the front, "Says here that you, Gary Hess, kidnaped her from the side of the highway, drove deep into the woods and raped her. Several times. Ms. Romo stated that her face was bruised because you slapped her around for fun. Therefore, using simple logic, it would seem highly unlikely that the same Ms. Romo would then call you up and ask for your help. How did she get your number?"

"I gave it to her at the restaurant once. She must have saved it or got it from one of the guys from the bar. Hell, even Clint and his pals have it. That don't prove nothin."

Gary looked up hopefully, as though Dan would suddenly realize that this was all one big setup. He'd been framed, and it was own fault, being dumb enough to fall for it.

"Well then Gary, let me really take a dump on your birthday cake. The Plumas County Grand Jury just handed down an indictment against you and your retarded buddies for assault, kidnapping and attempted murder. You know, between all four of you idiots, there might be half a brain somewhere. You're so stupid you don't even make a good redneck, Gary."

Gary fired back with a final salvo, "Nice theory on the holdup, *Dan*. If, I had done it, why wouldn't I just heave the gun into the river, shove the cash in my wallet and go on a drinking binge?"

"Come on, asshole," said Dan, grabbing Gary by his elbow and then moving him towards his cruiser that was hidden a quarter mile away, "Don't ask me to try and figure out why your bullshit story is full of holes and makes zero sense. Why was it in your bowling bag, huh genius? Plus, you match the physical description of the robber, not to mention you were holding the exact gun that was described to us."

On the other side of the Forrest, the Marlboro Men were packing up. They'd used high-powered military issue binoculars to watch the whole thing go down.

"Serves that asshole Gary Hess right," commented Clint, "Going to the draft board and groveling, telling them about all the stuff that's supposed to be wrong with him. He should be embarrassed, getting 4F status when his country needs him."

"Made my day," said Slim, climbing onto the passenger seat. Charlie and Earl crawled into the bed of the truck and leaned against the back of the cab. Clint started up the Ford, backed up and put it into drive. "We got one more stop to make," he said to Slim.

Joe, Alex and Jesse jogged back to the highway where the convertible was parked under an evergreen.

"That was a great idea, Jesse," said Joe, breathing easily.

"What?" asked Jesse without turning his head. He was running with a lit Camel in his mouth. He looked like a hard guy with an exhaust pipe.

"Stealing Gary's bowling ball bag out of his garage."

Jesse laughed, "Like I told ya, kid. Red neck garages usually don't have doors. That way, they can be like Gypsies, and steal shit from each other. After awhile they forget who originally owned it, especially if it's something popular, like a chainsaw."

Alex chuckled as he too jogged easily, even in his combat boots, "This Keddie and Quincy place is bizarre man. It's like a whole other world."

"Yep," agreed Joe, "They play by another set of rules around here, and no one tells you what they are."

They reached the Ford and flopped against the trunk and rear fenders. Carlene had the convertible top down, her sandaled feet propped up on the dash. She was listening to a transistor radio that was playing The

Doors *'Break On Through To The Other Side.'*

Her puppy, Joe, had his leash tied to the rear bumper. He yipped excitedly, seeking attention.

Suddenly, a caravan of three vehicles roared up and slid to a stop behind Joe's car, pinning them in. An enormous cloud of red dust covered everyone.

"Eww," yelled Carlene, holding her hands in front of her eyes, "Don't hit my dog you fools," she yelled.

"My God!" exclaimed Joe, as he watched his dad, Bud, exit his work truck, slamming his door like always.

Behind his truck was a World War two era green Army ambulance with a driver and a passenger, both of whom also got out.

Bringing up the rear were the Marlboro Men in Clint's black Ford 4x4 that was now covered with dust, "Howdy boys," said Clint as he got out holding a baseball bat. Slim hopped down from the cab brandishing a golf club. Charlie and Earl jumped to the ground also, both with tire irons.

"Shit," managed Joe, "This don't look so good, Jesse."

"Don't panic, kid. Nothin bad has happened. Yet."

Bud approached his son with a claw hammer in his hands.

"Dad," exclaimed Joe, "What are you doing here?"

"Hi Mr. Bailey," chimed in Alex, as though Bud Bailey were merely on a social call.

Bud stopped two feet from Joe, "Well, son. I'm here hopefully to save your life."

Joe watched as the Marlboro Men lined up behind his dad, slapping their weapons into their hands.

The two men from the ambulance stood back with folded arms. They were dressed head to toe in white and were both wearing sunglasses.

"What do you mean? What's with the armada here?"

"These are my friends, son. Listen, Joe. I know you're hooked on hard drugs and need to be hospitalized to get you off of them. We've already got your strange buddy Lance inside the ambulance. He's heavily sedated and heading for treatment also. His parents have been in on this from the beginning. You didn't really think I was going to let you move so far away without some supervision did you?"

"I guess not."

"Those guys in white are known as 'The Retrievers'. They work for my Carpenters Union, picking up family members who need mental health care. That's how I know these other guys too." Bud paused and pointed to the Marlboro Men, "We're all union members in good standing.. They know all about you and your queer buddy Lance, and all your drugs and banana peels and secret messages from Tom Jones in '*What's Up Pussycat.*"

"That sort of makes sense," replied Joe. It was just like Lance had tried to warn him. It was one big conspiracy.

"Well, let me make it easy for you then." Bud turned back around and yelled at the ambulance attendants, "Show him the straight jacket, Johnny."

Johnny, the taller of the two, smiled and held up a stiff white jacket with multiple straps.

"That one's for you, Joe. So you don't attempt to harm yourself. Lance is already in one, and he's so zonked out he doesn't even know it."

Jesse stepped forward until his chest was an

inch from Bud's "Look, pops. You ain't taking Joe nowhere. Him and me got traveling plans, today, and they don't include you and your dumb ass buddies. So, before you get hurt old man, why don't you split!"

Bud raised his claw hammer into the air, "Boys? You ready?"

They answered as one in the affirmative.

Just then, a deafening roar came towards them from the north. Six, big black custom Harley's driven by massive men squealed around the corner, entered the turn out and slid sideways to a stop next to Bud's caravan.

The Skull Diggers swung their legs over their choppers and produced weapons. A whipping steel chain, pool cues, a tire iron and a nice touch, a chain saw manned by Ajax who ripped the cord down and fired up the nasty looking saw. Shoveler Sam wielded a gigantic crossbow that was loaded with an arrow. He grinned, sensing the blood letting was about to begin.

Sam spoke up, "No way I'm digging graves for all these fools, Spider. I'm gonna need some help for once.

"No problem," said Spider, his chain making a whooshing noise as he whipped it close to Bud's head.

Bud looked back and forth. The Marlboro Men mumbled 'sorry' and retreated to Clint's truck and threw their weapons in the back. The ambulance attendants got back in their vehicle and locked the doors. Bud stood alone.

"I like these odds better," said Alex.

Spider spoke "You got some kind of problem here, Jesse?"

"Not anymore we don't, bro. Good timing."

Bud slid his hammer back into his tool belt.

"It's up to you, Joe," said his dad in a soft voice.

His eyes no longer smoldered. "You're of legal age. I can't force you to do anything. All I'm doing is offering you help before it's too late. If you say yes, I can have you at Napa State Mental Hospital in five hours. If you say no, that's your choice. But be aware, if you choose to continue on with these beasts, then I'll disown you. You'll no longer be my son."

Joe hugged his dad and stepped back.

"I love you dad, but I'm staying with my friends. My life with you, mom and Marvin is over. If you choose to disown me because I'm taking my own path, it'll make me sad, but it won't change my mind on how I want to spend my life. I'll send you a postcard as soon as I get a new address."

"Don't waste your stamp, kid." Bud turned his back on his first born son and returned to his truck.

Jesse followed him and looked into the bed of his truck. "Hey pops?"

"Yeah?" replied Bud, stopping at his open door and looking back.

Jesse held up a package of Susan's Brown Bread. The whole truck bed was loaded with the bricks, "What's with all this?"

"I use it for weight when I'm driving in the snow. I got a deal on them at Monkey Wards on a close out."

"Fine," said Jesse, tossing the heavy brick of bread back where it landed with an audible thud, "Have a nice day."

"What about Lance, Joe? Aren't we going to rescue him?" asked Alex.

"No."

And then, Bud's caravan was gone.

Jesse gave his Skull brothers soul shakes and half hugs, "Thanks a lot, guys. You really saved our asses."

"Don't mention it," said Spider, "Although I
was looking forward to messing some people up."

"Not my dad, I hope," said Joe.

Spider ignored him and looked Jesse in the eye,
"You know, pal. Mongo said you're cool to join back
up, as soon as you're done with your parole that is.
We'll get your bike back, and it'll be like old times."

"Thanks, brother. That means a lot to me. But,"
he said, putting his arm around Joe's waist, "Me and
my buddy here got other plans. We're gonns move to
San Francisco, and I'll hook up with local Diggers."

"Cool" said Spider. The Skull Diggers
remounted their choppers. Spider stood up and romped
on his starter, and his Harley roared to life. The others
followed suit. Six loud Harleys idled as one, the riders
resting their boots on red dirt. Spider raised his right
hand and the pack peeled out, manic grins on their
faces, roaring back the way they came.

Joe and his friends listened until the motorcycle
noise faded into the distance, leaving only the lonely
whistle of the wind, caressing the Pine Trees and
flowing past the ferns.

"Joe," said Carlene, "Can I talk to you for a
moment in private?'

It took Joe by surprise, and he looked at Jesse,
who nodded his head.

Carlene led Joe by the hand towards the river,
where she stopped and looked into his eyes, "I gotta tell
you something, Joe."

"What?" he managed.

"I know you like me, and I've ignored you on
purpose, even though I like you too."

"Why then?"

"Because you deserve better. I'd be no good for

414

you. Find yourself a nice girl who you have
something in common with. The reason I'm telling you
this is. I'm coming with you and Jesse to San Francisco
to start new lives. I don't want any hard feelings
between us,.okay?"

Joe nodded his head.

Carlene reached up and gave Joe a peck on his
lips, "Come on then, the rest are waiting."

Joe got behind the wheel of his car. Jesse and
Carlene cuddled up in the back seat. Alex was riding
shotgun. Joe was going to return his buddy home.

As Joe pulled out onto the highway, Carlene
held her dog's head out the back window and let him
experience the wind, so he too could know what it like
to feel free.

.

WHERE ARE THEY NOW 1998

JOE BAILEY : Joe moved to San Francisco, and he and Jesse and Carlene tried living together for awhile, but after a few months. Joe struck out on his own. His story will continue in another Novel, 'Bohemian Jesters.'

JESSE BARNNES : Jesse did all right for a time, then was returned to prison for a parole violation. Upon getting out and off probation, Jesse moved to Florida to become a traveling preacher. He too joins the cast of the next book in this series.

LANCE POTTER : He spent two years at Napa State, trying to regain his mind. Once straight, he enrolled at Cal Berkeley and received an advanced degree and joined the Mormon Church. He currently lives in Provo, Utah, and is a marriage counselor.

GARY HESS : Gary spent five years in prison for the Elliott Rosen assault and armed robbery. All the other charges were dropped due to lack of evidence, or in Carlene's case, splitting town and leaving the D.A. no choice as he no longer had a witness. Gary moved to Boise Idaho and makes a decent living selling used trucks. He was forced to quit drinking after donating one of his Kidneys in prison.

CARLENE ROMO : Married and divorced four times. Carlene is currently living in the desert in a tent in

Santa Fe, New Mexico. She is a massage therapist..

BIG DAN McGREW : Dan passed away in 1979 from liver cancer brought on by his chronic alcoholism. None of the Hess children attended his funeral.

ALEX CHANCE : On his one month anniversary in Vietnam, Alex was arrested for using his Army helicopter to attempt to smuggle heroin. He was dishonorably discharged. He became a homeless drunk. The last time he was seen alive was 1976 when he was reported seen hitchhiking into Death Valley with no water.

MALCOM AND RUTH : Malcom disbanded his commune in 1974. He and Ruth made a fortune in multilevel marketing with Amway. He then became a real estate investor and is now said to be worth tens of millions. He no longer wears a white robe, proffering tailored suits.

MAUREEN HESS : Maureen quit drugs and alcohol all together. She married Sam and has three cute children and leads a happy, contented life.

ROGER HESS : Roger never went to college. Instead, he joined the computer revolution and became quite wealthy by buying early stock in Apple and inventing several money making products. He remained single, and has a personal zoo in his backyard in Silicon Valley

ABOUT THE AUTHOR

Thomas J. Turner is a full time Novelist and short story author. He grew up in the east bay in the San Francisco area. He moved his family of five to Vancouver Washington in 1988.

He currently still resides there, just a bridge ride away from Portland

Tom is currently readying another Novel, 'To Die In Your Dreams' to be published in 2014.

He is also a 'gear head.' He drives around the Portland area in a souped up 2007 Mustang GT. It was a hood scoop with decals identifying the car as 'The Beast.'

Made in the USA
Charleston, SC
24 September 2013